BEAUTY

LOUISE MENSCH

headline
review

First published in Great Britain in 2014
by HEADLINE REVIEW
An imprint of HEADLINE PUBLISHING GROUP

1

Cataloguing in Publication Data is available from the British Library

ISBN 978 0 7553 5896 0 (Hardback)
ISBN 978 0 7553 5897 7 (Trade paperback)

Typeset in Meridien by Avon DataSet Ltd, Bidford-on-Avon,
Warwickshire

Printed and bound in Great Britain by Clays Ltd, St Ives plc

Headline's policy is to use papers that are natural, renewable and
recyclable products and made from wood grown in sustainable forests.
The logging and manufacturing processes are expected to conform to
the environmental regulations of the country of origin.

HEADLINE PUBLISHING GROUP
An Hachette UK Company
338 Euston Road
London NW1 3BH

www.headline.co.uk
www.hachette.co.uk

BEAUTY

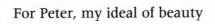

For Peter, my ideal of beauty

Chapter One

The maternity ward was having a bad day.

And so was little Dina Kane.

The newborn lay in her plastic cot, coughing and mewling; she was wrapped in a cotton blanket, and the little beanie on her head had slipped to cover one eye. Her mother lay on a bed a few feet away, passed out from the pain. Nurses rushed around, thankful that the mother was unconscious, the father at work on a building site somewhere in the Bronx. No question of a day off for him; this family needed the money.

In another room they had a woman bleeding after a botched C-section, and two breech deliveries were going on at the same time. Dina's mother, Ellen Kane, had screamed all the way through, like she was being tortured. This was her second child, and it arrived fast. By the time Ellen Kane got checked in to a bed, she was already seven centimetres dilated – too late for an epidural.

Too bad for Ellen.

It seemed every poverty-struck woman in Westchester County, New York, wanted to pop out a kid at the same time.

The midwives ignored Ellen's screeching. They were too busy trying to staunch the horrible flow of blood from the mother who was dying because of their obstetrician's mistake. Others were massaging and wrestling the breech deliveries round. Nobody cared about the regular birth – agonising or not.

1

No health insurance? No goddamned sympathy.

'Hell,' one of them hissed at Ellen, as she moaned and tossed on her sweat-soaked sheets, 'just push – push. Women have been doing this forever.'

'Please,' Ellen shrieked, but she was casting her voice into space.

Nobody feared a lawsuit. This was a Medicare family, too poor to sue. And so Dina Kane entered the world to the sound of her mother's horrible screams. As she slithered from the womb, a harassed nurse cut the cord, hung her upside down and slapped her tiny bottom.

Baby Dina screamed too – a thin little wail.

But it was the only sound left around the bed.

Her mother had fainted. The baby was roughly – incompetently – swaddled, dropped in her plastic cot and left alone.

Faintly, Dina cried, ignored. Making her first bid for attention. Trying to force the world to notice. Her tiny fingers, with their translucent nails, curled into her soft, wet palms.

Dina Kane was already making a fist.

The journey home was better. Dina slept in her carrycot in the back of the car, as Paul Kane tried to think of a few nice things to say to his wife.

'She's real pretty,' he lied. 'You did good.'

What the hell? His daughter looked like a hairless gnome, all wet and wrinkled – like all babies.

'Thanks, honey,' Ellen said, wearily.

She didn't look back at her daughter. Ellen excused herself with trauma and exhaustion. Before the birth, big as a house, she hadn't slept for days. Now, here Dina was, the fruit of all that effort.

Not like when Johnny was born: her firstborn, her son and the apple of her eye. Of course, Ellen had been younger then – four years younger – and the birth was OK and, besides, they'd both *wanted* a kid – and he was a boy, which everybody said was easier.

Turned out kids were expensive.

Ellen prided herself on running a tight ship. Paulie made good money on the construction site, and she had big dreams. They rented an apartment in Mount Vernon, but she wanted to own her own house one day. Maybe even something in Tuckahoe, a village a few miles away – but a world of difference. Ellen wanted the family to drive a better car, maybe go on a vacation to Florida once a year. She even had dreams of Catholic school for Johnny. Ellen could see herself, still trim and pretty, going to meetings of the PTA with those rich suburban moms, putting Christmas decorations on her own lawn, hosting her parents for Thanksgiving.

She wanted to stay pretty and young, not beat down like those other wives of the construction guys, the ones who got slobby and spent all day in sweat pants, or went to answer the door with their curlers in. Ellen Kane spent a bit of money on keeping herself groomed, as cheap as she could manage, and she had a gift for style. She could pick out the one pair of well-cut slacks donated to the charity store, she found the best cheap place to have her eyebrows plucked, and she dyed her own hair. Paulie was happy – he loved that his wife looked good, loved all the jokes the guys on the construction site made about it – and Ellen worked on her dream.

Johnny was a good boy. They loved him; they spoiled him. He took the breast, and didn't complain when Ellen switched him to the bottle aged three months.

'I want to keep myself nice,' she said, coyly, to Paulie, as the baby slept in his bassinet, out in their closet.

'Yeah.' Paulie nuzzled his face against her tits; they still felt full, bouncy. He was so relieved. He didn't want Ellen getting floppy and loose like all those women he saw around their way. 'Real nice, baby; real nice.'

He had a good marriage, mostly. Ellen wasn't the best cook, but she looked sexy. He valued that a lot more than a pot roast. Paulie earned the wage, his house looked neat, he had a wife that was a step above, and a boy. He was happy.

The trouble came as Johnny started to grow. Baby clothes – new ones every couple of weeks. Formula was expensive. The kid needed toys, bibs, diapers, a play mat . . . Paulie felt like every day he was being asked to shell out more cash.

They cut back. His night at the bowling alley became a once a fortnight thing. That truly sucked, and he wasn't happy. Paulie found himself working extra shifts, longer hours.

'Jesus! Borrow the fucking clothes,' he hissed at Ellen.

She pouted. 'I can't, Paulie. I don't want Susan DiAngelo's castoffs. She'll tell all the girls. They'll laugh at us.'

He nodded, grimly. Saving face was very important around the neighbourhood.

Then the teething started.

'Fuck!' Paulie tossed in his bed, staring at the ceiling, their bedside alarm clock saying 2:15 a.m. 'Won't that goddamned kid ever shut up? I have to *work*.'

Ellen dragged herself out from under the covers, teary-eyed from lack of sleep, and walked to the closet to pick the baby up. He was bigger now, and his cot filled almost all the small space.

'We need a bigger apartment,' she said, weakly. 'Like, with a second bedroom.'

Paulie couldn't disagree. He worked still more hours, took on a second job at weekends and went to his local *capo* for help. Paulie Kane was exactly the kind of guy the mob took care of, wanting little in return: he worked their sites, didn't bitch about joining any unions, took on overtime and kept his mouth shut about the things he saw there.

And he had *no* ambition. Guys like that, the fodder, prospered.

They gave him a rise. Then another. Within three months,

they were renting a bigger apartment, a place with a tiny second bedroom of its own.

Sex resumed, and Paulie liked it when Ellen was happier. He took on another job on Sundays, when most of the guys were resting. Six months moonlighting at the bowling alley added a little pot to their savings, and soon they had a deposit down on the longed-for three-bedroom colonial on the Tuckahoe borders. It was more Eastchester, the lousy end of town, but Ellen didn't care. She had a tiny scrap of garden and they could see a church spire from their bedroom window. The fence in the back was chain link, not picket, but this was their dream and everything was going so well. Ellen had plans to train as a hairdresser when Johnny went to nursery next year; she could make good pocket money doing a shampoo and set for the old ladies that wandered into the village's only salon during the daytime.

And then the disaster happened.

Just when they were on top of it. Just when he was getting straight. The baby was sleeping nights and Paulie was back to bowling in the alley, not cleaning up behind the bar.

Ellen got pregnant.

'Jesus! You're kidding?'

She whimpered, looking grey. 'The doctor ran the tests, Paulie.'

He was stunned. 'What the fuck happened?'

Ellen shrugged. 'The pills didn't work, I guess.'

No use saying Paulie should have used a condom. Ellen thought she'd been OK, taken most of her pills through the cycle, but she did forget things sometimes, got busy, got distracted by another diaper or the pasta on the stove . . .

'You forgot.' Her husband's voice was tight with accusation.

'No way, Paulie. I took them every day.' Ellen was so definite, she'd almost convinced herself.

'We can't. We don't need more.' Screw what his mother said; Paulie Kane had no intention of being a big Irish family. His small, neat family suited him down to the ground. With horror, he glanced at his wife – still slim, with those perky tits. Would they survive another go round? He liked Ellen's body, liked how she kept herself pretty, kept herself lithe and sweet in his bed. Soon that handspan waist would soften, grow, she would pack on the pounds, her tits would be milky, motherly, far from anything he wanted to know about.

A surge of fury bubbled deep within his belly.

'Get it seen to.'

Ellen's eyes widened. 'Paulie, no. No.'

'What are you, some kind of God-botherer?'

They were Catholics – sort of. Not that they went to Mass outside of Christmas and Easter, but that was the tribe – St Patrick's day and going to your friends' kids' Holy Communions. Paulie didn't know if he believed in God and he'd certainly not discussed it with Ellen. Their church wedding was fun, but so what?

Paulie believed in Paulie. And perky tits. And weekends off.

'We can't afford another kid. *Get it done.*'

And, although Ellen ran into the next room crying like a baby, he was unmoved. He went to the bar and got drunk, then spent the night crashed on his friend Mikey's couch, just so as to ram the message home.

Paulie thought that would do it. But, when he came back from work the next night, Ellen was waiting for him.

'I can't.'

She sat at the kitchen table, her hands twisted in her lap. Ellen had never defied Paulie before, but he could see instantly that she was about to now.

'I went down there,' she said, 'to the clinic. And they put me on the table and poked around and I said, "I need some time to think," and I got up and ran back here. I can't do it.'

Ellen Kane looked sick.

'You got pregnant on purpose,' Paulie accused.

'The hell I did! I don't want another baby, either.' Ellen turned her big green eyes towards her husband. 'But, Paulie, you know how it is. People know I'm pregnant.'

His heart sank. 'What people? How do they know?'

'Mona Ruffalo. And Agnes Monticello knows. They were in the doctor's when I got tested – congratulating me and such.'

Paulie was never going to graduate the Ivy League, but he had a good amount of native cunning. He saw immediately where this was going.

Mona and Agnes were both soldiers' wives, part of the Italian ruling clique that controlled all the sites locally. They were fat and greasy and wore too much make-up, not like his Ellen, but their husbands were mafiosi – made men – and they gave Paulie his orders.

Crime round here ran strictly on its own morals. Steal from the poor, but never show disrespect; fuck all the whores you want, but out of sight of the family; kill husbands, brothers, sons – but don't abort a baby.

He wasn't Italian. He would never rise, not really. But Paulie could be one of the best-paid worker bees, somebody the boys liked to drink with, trusted and rewarded. The *famiglia* didn't like abortion. Might give their own wives ideas.

'We have to do it,' Ellen said, and burst into tears.

Paulie kicked the garbage can, but made the best of it. He went to the *capo* again, explained the predicament, got a little more money and a stern shake of the head.

At least the house had three bedrooms.

'*No more mistakes,*' he hissed to Ellen.

The little mistake, Dina, grew unwanted and unconscious in her mother's belly. She didn't hear her father's sighs of disappointment when the scans reported back that it was a girl. She didn't hear her mother privately curse and rage at the gods because they had given her another baby.

There would be plenty of time for that once Dina kicked

painfully out of the womb and tried to make herself heard in a world that wanted to ignore her.

Paul Kane stopped at a red light and glanced back at the baby. She was sleeping – that was good. He related to babies best when they were sleeping.

'Hey, it's not so bad,' he said to his wife. 'We can make the best of it, right?'

'Right,' Ellen said, wearily.

The first thing she'd done when she came round was ask for her purse. Inside were her birth-control pills, the ones she'd lumbered to the pharmacy to purchase last month. They said breast-feeding protects you, but Ellen wasn't taking any chances – ever again.

She looked over at the sleeping baby and felt nothing but resentment. This one *was* going to ruin her figure, empty their bank account and keep her away from her little Johnny. Plus, the Italians always said girls were the difficult ones.

'A girl steals her mother's looks,' cackled Mary Kane, her mother-in-law. The old witch.

Ellen hoped to feel something for the baby, like she had when Johnny was born, but there was nothing. The most she could say for Dina was that labour was finally over.

'It's not so bad,' she lied. 'And the baby's beautiful.'

That was what you were supposed to say about girl babies, even when they looked like bald pink rats, like this one.

'She is, right?' Paul agreed, with equal enthusiasm.

Duty done, the new parents drove home, determined to forget about Dina as much as was humanly possible.

But she *was* beautiful.

The pink rat opened her big eyes and, after a little while, a soft thatch of dark hair appeared on the bald head. Even in her Baby-gro, Dina was something special: pale skin, raven dark hair and those wide blue eyes that started to deepen to green. Ellen had green eyes too, but not like this. Dina's were as bright as a clover field, richly coloured, striking in her soft little face. Her tiny nose was delicate and her lips were full; she was a gorgeous little baby.

Ellen enjoyed the compliments at first. Even if she didn't have those maternal feelings, nobody needed to know. She cuddled and kissed Dina and pushed her in her chair alongside little toddler Johnny, and everybody congratulated her on her 'beautiful family'. Johnny was the only one to truly love Dina, not that she understood it yet. He would stand for hours over her bouncer, trying to interest his sister in a threadbare stuffed dog or his old set of plastic keys. Dina loved Johnny back, and smiled and laughed whenever he was around – a little chortling baby laugh that even Ellen thought was cute. Dina kept Johnny quiet, so that was another plus for her. *Best toy ever*, Ellen thought to herself.

Dina was given her brother's stuff, even a navy blue romper suit with an anchor print. She looked good in everything.

Paulie went back to being ignorant. He couldn't worry about the home fires. The mortgage was a struggle, and the building trade wasn't going so well. There were extra jobs, moonlighting. He didn't want to hear his wife's complaints.

As Dina grew, her beauty just increased. There were angelic brown curls when she was three, and Ellen had to put her in little dresses. Dina loved to draw, to paint, to pick out clothes – just like Momma.

Maybe it would make them closer.

But Ellen was getting older. The sparkle was draining from her eyes. She was still stylish, but fewer of Paulie's friends ogled her when she visited the building site. He was irritable, snapping at her when he got home. More interested in dinner than sex.

And Dina grew bigger. So carefree. So pretty.

Ellen looked at her daughter resentfully.

She caused all this.

One stupid mistake, and they were back slaving for every cent.

'Oh, your little girl's so pretty.'

'What a cutie!'

'She's adorable. She's a real *beauty*. Where did she get those eyes?'

Ellen would force a smile. 'My eyes are green.'

'But not like that,' Tony Verzano said, admiring Dina as she romped around in her little pink dress. 'She's so stunning. You must be proud.'

Ellen wanted to be proud of *Ellen*. She wanted the attention, was used to it.

Why is Dina even here?

Nobody could see at night when Dina held out her little arms to her mother to be snuggled.

'I'm busy with supper.'

'Go get in your bath.'

'I have to practise Johnny's reading.'

The little girl would screw up her face and cry.

'Stop making that racket.' Her mother held up Rabby, Dina's favourite stuffed rabbit. 'If you don't behave, I'm throwing him in the trash.'

Dina's round mouth opened wider with horror. She lowered her arms from her mother and stumbled closer to save Rabby.

Ellen threw the toy at her. 'Behave, Dina. Go and be quiet.'

Clutching the rabbit to herself, little Dina Kane went to her tiny room to look at picture books and be quiet. She had dollies there – Daddy liked to buy her dollies; it assuaged some of his guilt.

She would dress the dollies up so they looked cute and stylish, like Mommy. If she was more like Mommy, perhaps Mommy and Daddy would like her.

And, meanwhile, she waited for Johnny to come back from pre-kindergarten. He always gave her a hug.

In the kitchen, Ellen Kane was cooking, whistling to herself to drown out the sounds of Dina's stifled sobs. But that girl was always there, hanging around like a ghost. Dina Kane was always a problem.

Chapter Two

'This is an excellent piece of work.'

Peter MacAllister handed the term paper back to Dina Kane. His eyes met those startling green ones, fringed with the thick black lashes.

'Thank you, Mr MacAllister.'

She smiled, and it was like the whole classroom lit up.

At sixteen, Dina had legs that went on for days. She had pale skin that never seemed to catch the sun, but that just played up the raven hair and bright green eyes. Her face was almost pre-Raphaelite with an even nose and full lips.

Peter MacAllister realised he was staring.

'You have an excellent grasp of algebra,' he blurted out. 'Have you thought about pursuing math later? At college?'

The green eyes clouded.

'I'm not sure about college, Mr MacAllister. We can't afford it.'

'Really? Surely your mother has money?'

'She needs all she's got,' Dina said, defensively. 'My mom works so hard.'

Her teacher hesitated. Perhaps he should drop it. But Dina Kane *deserved* to go to college. She was the one really motivated, driven student he had in his entire class.

Eastchester public schools didn't send many to the Ivy League.

They were underfunded and overcrowded. Dina was different. From her first days, the teachers had marked her out. Eager to please, to be liked, she sought more from them. She worked incredibly hard, always looking for approval, and she was bright – intensely so. She had a particular gift for creative writing, math and chemistry. Dina loved mixing up potions and experimenting; her enthusiasm was a bright spot in a room full of sullen, resentful pupils.

It didn't make her popular.

'Teacher's pet.'

'Suck-up.'

'Such a nerd.'

MacAllister felt bad for her. School was a struggle for Dina, as far as the kids went. First it was her great grades, next it was her beauty. The other girls got jealous and banded together. There was a lot of spite. Dina mostly sat on her own at lunch, and the girls that would eat with her were the losers. Boys would ask Dina out, but then succumb to peer pressure and slouch away from her in the playground.

Dina Kane didn't care. She was relentlessly focused. Her average grade was an A. And she stayed for every afterschool programme she could.

'Don't you have a home to go to?' asked Ms Segal in chess club.

'Oh, yes. My mom really misses me,' Dina said, brightly. 'She just wants me to do well in school.'

'Your brother's at St Joseph's, right?'

'Yes.' A tiny cloud, but she smiled it away. 'There was only enough money for one of us.'

The Catholic school in Bronxville had a great reputation; it charged a small fee; class sizes were much smaller; the kids wore a uniform. They mostly headed to college and became professionals.

You couldn't say the same for Dina's school.

'That doesn't seem fair,' said Ms Segal.

'Better one of us than neither of us,' Dina replied. 'I'm doing fine here.'

And she was.

Dina dreaded going home each night.

'Hey, Mom! How was your day?'

She would smile and give her mother a hug, hoping against hope that one day things would be different. One day the hug would be returned. One day Ellen would be interested in Dina.

'What do you care? I just stay here and look after the house, cleaning and shopping and cooking –' Ellen made it sound like hard labour in a penal camp – 'while you just swan about at school.'

'I got a five hundred in my PSATs.'

'What the hell does that mean?'

'You know, Mom. Next year I take the SATs? For college? I got a really good grade in my practice tests.'

Ellen looked at her blankly. 'What the hell for? You ain't going to college. Not unless you win the lottery. I can't afford two of you.'

Dina felt the tears prickle. Mostly she tried so hard to ignore her mother's cruelty – the detachment, the coldness – but sometimes it was tough.

College was her dream, her ticket out of a hellish childhood, her chance to make something of herself, something special, something real.

But Ellen Kane was standing in her way, like a demon on a bridge.

It was Johnny first – always Johnny.

Her father's death had started the spiral.

'Paulie! Look out on the goddamned crane!' His supervisor's

yell came floating up from the ground, but Paulie Kane didn't hear him.

He was balancing on the heavy iron bar, trying to swing it into place. It was night and he was cold, but he had that good antifreeze, right in his pocket. Saturday frigging night and here he was, working overtime.

Johnny had started school and it all cost: tuition, books, uniform, everything. At least Ellen was happy again for a little while. He loved how she lit up when she saw her son, so cute in his blue uniform with the white piping. She was the mom of a private-school kid. And she got to take him there every day.

But Paulie was paying the bills. Ellen was obsessed with their status. When he'd said maybe Johnny could head to the elementary school across the block, for free, Ellen had sulked and refused to have sex with him.

Everything *seemed* OK in their house. That was what all the neighbours thought.

But it wasn't. It wasn't.

Paulie barely saw the kids. On Sundays, he slept. He was packing on the pounds. When he was there, they clambered over him, not giving him any rest. And if he gave little Dina any compliments, Ellen scowled at him.

'She's demanding. She's spoiled. You're encouraging her.'

'Come on, now.' Paulie wasn't so fatherly himself, but his wife's barely-concealed hostility perplexed him. 'She's just a little kid.'

'If you give in to her, she'll always be whining for attention,' Ellen said. 'Don't you see how she plays up to it?'

'She's real pretty, that's all it is.'

Exactly the wrong thing to say. 'She's vain, Paulie – vain – already, at four. Don't make it any worse.'

So he would disengage the little hands from his neck, and then, when Dina cried and Ellen yelled, he'd feel even more guilty.

The bar seemed like a good place to go.

A real good place – where you could get your stress relief cheap and fast, at a few bucks for a glass of rye whiskey, his favourite.

Paulie started to spend a lot of time there. He came late to the building site, dropped bricks, made mistakes. A warning came back through the channels: *Cut it out.*

He was smart. From that day on, Paulie never went back to the bar. Instead, he worked Saturday nights, and he brought a hip flask.

Drinks tasted good when you were bored. Booze ran like antifreeze through your veins when you were cold. He had to work while the boys were out bowling or watching football, so at least there was a little bit of relief in his pocket. That made work more fun. And he didn't have to think about the kids. Or his wife. Or his bills . . .

Paulie unscrewed the top again and tilted the metal bottle towards his mouth. Sweet relief . . .

Drip. Drip. He swallowed nothing. *Fuck!* It couldn't be gone already?

He had four more hours in this dump.

His body was wedged against the corner of the bar as it swung over the street below.

'Paulie! Jesus Christ!' Marco DiCapello was calling.

Jesus? That's funny: they think I'm Jesus. Paulie swayed and giggled to himself, then stood up on one leg, bracing his arm against the crane, to shake the bottle and tip out the last drops . . .

He didn't see the ice, or even feel it. There was a split second when he realised his arm wasn't bracing. Was reaching into air. Like the rest of him.

Eighty foot was too short a fall to scream.

* * *

'So sorry for your loss.'

Sal Rispelli was the local *capo*. He was used to this scene and did it well. Ellen Kane was playing her part too – the grieving widow with two little children – wearing a fitted black dress. She had fixed her hair and put it up in a ladylike bun, and she had done her make-up carefully. Despite her age and cares, she looked good today. Maybe it was the adrenaline.

'He was everything to me.' Ellen looked truly distressed, even frightened. Of course, Paulie was working off the books. 'I don't know how our family will survive.'

'Don't worry.' Sal placed a hand over hers.

'But I have to worry. There's our mortgage . . . and Johnny's school. And what will we live on? I can't go out to work. My darling Dina needs me.'

Ellen missed Paulie some. But she missed her security a hell of a lot more. The mascara-thickened lashes batted themselves at the *capo*.

'Anything you can do for our family, Signor Rispelli,' she said, humbly.

There was something very sexy about a pleading woman, humble and submissive. The way they should be.

'Paulie was family.' *That stupid drunk*. 'We take care of our own. Don Angelo has already paid off your mortgage. And you are receiving a lump sum of two hundred thousand dollars.'

Ellen nearly fainted. She swayed in her chair.

'What?' she whispered.

'Two hundred grand,' he repeated. Hell, they hadn't put the workers in safety harnesses. It was a lot cheaper than workman's comp. He'd chewed out that jerk-off, DiCapello, at the site this morning, and *now* the worker grunts had harnesses. But they were grumbling over Paulie. Watching a man die will do that to you.

The *famiglia* didn't like deaths they hadn't ordered. It was in their interest now to take real good care of Ellen Kane.

'And, for yourself, a pension wage. You come down to the salon for an hour every lunch and style the ladies' hair. You'll get very well paid.' A pretend job made things easier than a stipend to her little schmuck bank account.

'I can't believe it!' Ellen gasped. For once, she wasn't faking her emotion. She grabbed Rispelli's hand and kissed the back of it, just like she'd seen them do in the movies. Softly, again and again.

He was starting to get uncomfortably aroused. Time to get out of here and over to a strip joint. One of their hookers could finish what Ellen had started.

'You and the kids won't miss a beat. Remember, you're under our protection. So act respectable,' he said, with a thin smile.

Ellen heard the warning: *No drinking. No screwing. A grateful client household.*

'Yes, Signor Rispelli. Thank you so much.'

Joy was rushing through her, joy she had to lower her eyes to contain. No more worry. No more fear. This was the best thing Paulie ever did for her.

'Better get back to your daughter, then,' Rispelli grunted, waving his hand to dismiss her. 'Like you said – she needs you.'

'I have to make this money last,' Ellen said. 'It's all I have.'

Dina looked round their house. There was all new furniture and a fancy TV and videotape machine. The garden was now planted with roses. Her mother wore a soft, pretty dress made of pink wool and her hair was piled up neatly on her head. She went out to the beauty salon each Thursday.

'We live pretty well, Momma,' she said, pleadingly.

'I know.' Ellen turned to study her reflection in a gilt-edged mirror. She didn't believe in making investments, hadn't tried to sell the house and move up the property ladder. But she did love stuff that made her life easier: pretty dresses, hairdressing appointments, manicures, expensive mirrors.

'I take you on holiday twice a year,' she said, proudly. 'Disneyland! How many other kids get to go to Disneyland around here?'

Dina sighed. At Disneyland, Mom had a great time. She and Johnny were bored out of their brains. But, no matter how much they asked to go someplace else, it was always Ellen's choice.

'Yes, Momma, thank you. But, you know, school's more important.'

'Johnny is at Catholic school.'

'I meant me.' Dina brushed her dark hair back behind her ears, nervously. 'You know they get much better results at St Joseph's. I want to go there too.'

'Honey, you know there isn't money for the both of you. You wouldn't want to deny Johnny his chance?'

Dina flushed. 'I love Johnny.'

'Well, I can't afford to pay twice. We all have to make sacrifices.'

'Maybe . . . Maybe you could get another job.'

Ellen's hour or two at the salon was hardly backbreaking.

Dina's green eyes begged. 'Momma, lots of parents work, you know? And maybe we could skip the vacations? Save our money for the fee for St Joseph's?'

'Dina, please stop *whining*. It's all about you. I work so hard raising you two kids without Daddy. All on my own, with nobody to help me.' Ellen's voice cracked with self-pity. 'Now you want me to slave till I drop for private school.'

'It's not fair.'

'What?'

'It's not fair,' Dina repeated, louder. She could hardly believe she had actually spoken the words. They had been swimming around her little head for so long. 'You treat Johnny better than me. You love him more than me.'

You love him would probably have been enough.

All her young life, Dina Kane had been wriggling away from

this moment, from admitting it: her mother didn't love her. Didn't really even like her.

And now, aged ten, it was staring her in the face.

'You're such a spoiled little madam. You think you're so special,' Ellen hissed. 'Asking a *widow* to work extra hours?'

'Don't you want me to get a good education?'

'The local public school is perfectly fine. Besides, Johnny needs it more. He's a man; he has to make his own way.'

'What does that mean?'

'You know well enough.' Ellen tossed her head. 'You're a girl. And you're not ugly.' It was as close as she would come to paying Dina a compliment. 'You can marry some poor schlub. Maybe he'll have more patience for your nonsense than I do.'

'Momma,' Dina's eyes filled with tears, 'I went to see the principal at St Joseph's and asked about aid. You know, for the poor kids. But she said we have money, so they can't pay it. The money we got when Daddy died?'

'You want me to give you my pension? Public school is good enough for you, Dina. Life's what you make it.'

Life's what you make it.

The taunt was seared into Dina Kane's mind.

Her mother had given her life, food to eat and shelter. Not too much else – cheap Christmas gifts and holidays that she didn't want.

But she had also been given the gift of determination – hard and cold as a diamond, deep inside her.

Johnny was the light of her life.

'Hey, sis! Looking beautiful.'

'Hi, Dinasaur! Have a great day at school?'

'How's my little princess? Still smarter than all her teachers, right?'

Johnny would hug Dina, kiss her, sweep her up. She'd clung to him ever since her tiny arms could snake around his neck.

Johnny made her childhood bearable. Dina knew she was loved, loved by someone, loved by family.

Often she wished that they were like all those orphan brothers and sisters in the fairy stories: no parents. Just two children out on their own.

A dead mommy could be mourned.

Dina constructed a fantasy world. Her mommy loved her. Her daddy watched over her from heaven. She was at PS 935 because it was the *best* school and Mommy wanted the *best*.

And so Dina worked to make it the best.

She occasionally got a few friends – at least for a while – but it never lasted. Girls would invite Dina to play. Then, as Ellen never reciprocated, the playdates dried up.

'But why can't we have Susan over?'

'I don't need my neat house wrecked by a gaggle of screaming kids. I have enough on my plate.'

Dina didn't argue. She suspected Ellen was as embarrassed as she was – any strangers might see how much her mother disliked her.

As she grew and blossomed, her friends drifted away. There was jealousy, cattiness – rumours about her mother.

'Did you see Ellen Kane in that short skirt yesterday?'

'God, I know. It's so ridiculous. She's, like, *thirty*.'

'Older than thirty.'

Priscilla Contratto turned on Dina as she walked past, carrying her books. 'Your mom looks like a tramp. Can't you do something about it?'

'Shut up, Prissy. My mom looks great.'

Truth was, Ellen feared the loss of her looks and had decided to do something about it. The skirts got shorter. The hair got blonder. She started wearing a red slash of lipstick to go grocery shopping.

Dina tried to speak to her about it.

'Mom, I think the grey skirt looks really chic on you.'

'The grey?' Ellen held it up. 'No fun.'

She was moving into a black leather mini. Dina gulped.

'You know, maybe that's more . . .'

The green eyes, duller than Dina's own, narrowed to chips of ice. 'More what?'

'More, like, for teenagers?'

Ellen flushed. 'Don't be stupid. And, anyway, my boyfriend likes it.'

Dina squirmed. 'Who is your boyfriend?'

'I keep my business private. I'll let you know if I decide to get serious.'

It wasn't long before Dina was doing her homework alone at night. Johnny would be at after-school programmes, or in his room, studying for SATs. Ellen would not be there.

A succession of black Lincoln town cars would pull up at the front of their place.

Different cars. Different licence plates.

Ellen avoided talking about it. She wore expensive jewellery and smiled a lot, except in the mornings when she was hung-over. Sometimes she talked about 'the boys' and snapped if Dina tried to ask her anything.

Her eyes got redder. Her skin developed a pallid tinge. Ellen was drinking and partying like she could make her tiny life go away.

'We have to do something,' Dina said to Johnny.

He was in his room, playing with his video games. 'Like what? She doesn't listen.'

'Maybe she'll listen to you. She likes you.'

Johnny shrugged. He was well-meaning, but saw no reason to get involved with lost causes – like his mother's relationship with Dina, or his mother's need for help. Johnny Kane wanted an easy life, and that mostly involved turning a blind eye. He gave little Dina affection and, in return, she didn't push him. On anything. It was their unspoken bargain.

'Hey, Mom's not talking. Let's leave her to her own life.'

'Johnny—'

'Drop it, Dina.'

But if Ellen wasn't talking, everybody else was.

Tramp. Bike. Plaything.

There was Sal Rispello – he was first, putting aside his earlier scruples. After all, she was offering it on a plate. Then there was Paolo Cottini, Giorgio Amalfi . . .

'Why's Dina's mom like table salt?' Lorna Fay shouted out in recess.

Dina scuffed her shoes in a corner of the playground, pretending to read her copy of *The Catcher in the Rye*.

'Because she gets passed around!' Lorna shrieked.

Dina heard the cackles of laughter, the hoots. Tears stung her eyes, but she didn't move. She wouldn't give them the satisfaction.

The next day, she skipped school for the first time in her life.

Angelo Tallarico sat by the pool, drinking coffee.

It was a serene scene. Angelo sat in his custom-designed chair, next to a side table made of marble. The lawns of the estate were so closely trimmed, the green grass looked like satin. Angelo wore a white summer suit, tailored in Savile Row, London. His Rolex was heavy, solid platinum, and his fingers were covered with enough diamond rings to make them look like a knuckle-duster. They sparkled as he lifted his crystal glass of ice tea to his mouth.

The infinity pool was perfectly blue; it lapped gently with its artificial current. The house behind him was white, Edwardian and huge. Angelo liked the English look. He'd had the place fitted out with rose gardens and topiary hedges. They had colour all four seasons.

You could barely see the bodyguards stationed around the place. All of them wearing back. All of them strapped to the nines.

Angelo loved to hire ex-military. The boys of the family were great, but, in a crisis, you wanted an accurate shot. Just one more way he was modernising his role.

They used the old terms: *Don Angelo*. But not in public. That was catnip to the FBI. Angelo despised the old guard who liked to court publicity. All they did was bring trouble on everyone's head.

He was training his new recruits in different techniques: arms trading, union corruption, public-sector payoffs.

Nobody does gangster like the politicians.

But Angelo didn't want to go too fast. He needed to carry the soldiers, the captains with him. The construction sites and gambling houses stayed open; the drug deals were still run on the corners – he was peeling back from them, but only slowly.

All in good time. Even if he hated that petty shit.

Angelo told himself he was patient. That was why he was now the Don. Two cousins shot, another doing twenty-five in maximum security. His uncle Claudio had been poisoned, so they thought. So Angelo avoided stupid mistakes, like trampling on the old ways, at least until he was ready.

He shifted in his chair, enjoying the sun. August was tremendous in New York. In retirement, he wanted to leave the bitter winters, head to Florida, maybe even further afield. Get a hacienda in Mexico, where they understood security.

There were two young girls waiting in the bedroom. A soldier had talent-spotted them at one of the family's strip joints. Legal age – he'd checked. Big tits, curvy asses and mouths that knew how to do stuff other than talk.

The soldier got a tip. The girls got a new assignment.

Angelo would keep them for a month, then send them packing.

He liked fresh meat, no involvement. There was no wife, nor did he want one. When he married, years from now, it would be a classy girl, not some painted screecher from round here.

'Signore?' This was a new take on *Don*. Angelo liked both. 'There is a girl here to see you.'

Angelo stretched. 'I didn't order another one yet. I like how that redhead grinds.'

'Yes, sir.' A grin. Sometimes the boss would order his girls down to the security barracks, with instructions to please every man in the room. It kept the men loyal, taught the females their place. 'It's not a whore, this one. A schoolgirl.'

Angelo looked up. 'What?'

'The daughter of one of your workers.' He shrugged. 'He died a few years ago.'

'Boohoo,' Angelo said. 'What the fuck does she want?'

'To see you. She said she won't leave till she does.'

'Jesus! Get rid of her.'

'Yes, sir.' The man straightened up, putting his hand on his gun. 'We'll escort her to the road.'

Angelo sipped his tea. 'Wait.'

His spider-sense was tingling, as if this could be a mistake, this could be trouble.

'How old is she?'

'Sixteen, seventeen . . . I think.'

'And whose kid?'

'His name was Paul Kane.'

A bell was ringing, but he couldn't place it. 'Pretty?'

The guy laughed and kissed his fingertips. 'Ass like a peach. Better than those two you got upstairs, signore.'

'I'll see her.' What the hell? He could give her five minutes, just to make sure this wasn't some problem. But better, older men than him had been assassinated by kids. 'Frisk her; frisk her thoroughly.'

'And if she refuses?' He licked his lips.

'She's somebody's daughter. But, if she refuses, throw her out.'

'Yes, sir.' The bodyguard walked off.

'Spread your legs, baby.' The guard ran his hands down her ribcage, pausing to cup her breasts under the bra. She tensed, and he jiggled them, then laughed. 'Full search. We don't know what you've got under there.'

Dina bit her tongue. She was facing a brick wall. There were bloodstains on it. Reluctantly, she widened her legs.

'Great ass,' his colleague said. 'Spread 'em a little wider.'

'Why?'

'Because I said so.'

He came behind her, ran his hands over her legs, starting at her ankles, squeezing tight. Then he felt her ass, briskly, and then, with more leisure, fondled it, cupped her pussy.

Dina gasped.

'You a virgin?' he said, idly.

'Joe, cut it out. She's not for us.'

The hands were removed and Dina was allowed to step back. She raised her head, scarlet with embarrassment.

Both guards laughed.

'She's clean.'

'Not for long,' his friend said. 'I'd give a week's pay to pop that cherry.'

The first guard smirked, then beckoned her. 'Follow me. Don't say shit. Understand?'

Angelo looked over the girl standing before him, with her curvy figure and come-hither eyes.

Marek was right. She was better than the hookers he had inside. Fresher. Prettier. Those cheap jeans and the white T-shirt did absolutely nothing to hide her assets. She was gorgeous looking, with a soft, aristocratic face.

'What was your father's name? Kane?'

'Paul Kane, Don Angelo. He was killed in a construction accident out in the Bronx.'

'Sorry to hear that.'

'You took care of our family, sent my mother money. My brother goes to Catholic school. We live in Eastchester.'

He nodded. 'You are here to ask for more money?'

The girl shook her dark head. 'No, sir. It's . . . It's my mother.'

Despite himself, Angelo Tallarico was starting to get interested. It was the courage of this little slip of a girl, standing before him. The guards would have had their fun, but she was still here.

'What about her?'

'She sees men.'

'That happens when you're a grown-up, kid.'

'No. She sees *your* men. A few of them. At night, in fancy cars. They give her presents. People talk.' A slow flush was making its way up Dina's neck, but she ploughed on. 'My mom is drinking more. These men don't care for her.'

Angelo hesitated. Why was this his problem? He should tell the feisty little piece of cooze to get back to whichever small-town hell she came from.

'Mr Rispello; Mr Cottini; Mr Amalfi.' Recklessly Dina named them. 'Mr Casini, I think.'

All captains. All married.

'Then maybe have a talk with your mother.'

'She doesn't listen. But you could tell the men, Don Angelo. Warn them off.'

'Honey –' he sipped his tea – 'interfering in people's private lives . . . is not what I do. Bad for business.'

Dina shook her dark head. 'See, Don Angelo, my daddy worked for you. And he died. You took care of us. All the other workers know it. But now people are talking bad. Like, your bosses will use a guy's widow. All the kids in school –' the blush got deeper – 'they all know. And some of them have fathers who used to work alongside Dad. Still work for you now. They won't like the thought of that happening to *their* wives.'

Angelo considered this. Then he turned away and rifled through the papers in front of him, on his white marble coffee table. He didn't trust computers. They could be hacked, traced, run through by the FBI. Reports were typed out and sent to him; he read the papers and burned them each night.

Construction site delays in Brooklyn, Bronx.
Workers quitting. Sickness. Retired. Morale low.
Experienced hands replaced. Younger guys making mistakes.
Costing money.
Project budget may need revision.

Angelo saw through the dry lines of old-fashioned ink. There were problems. The old guys were dropping out.

The girl is right.

'OK. I'll speak to the boys.' *And your mother*, but he didn't tell her that. It was time for Father Confessor Angelo Tallarico to pay a visit to Ellen Kane, and he would have a stern penance to deliver for her sins.

'You were right to come to me,' he said. She had stopped the rot. 'What's your name again, baby?'

'Dina.'

'You can leave school next year, right? Want to work for me? As a secretary?'

He could station her out of sight of her father's old gang, working the head offices in Jersey City. She was smart, and she had that look about her – that she'd fuck like a freight train once the right guy had warmed her up.

Dina's green eyes opened wide. 'Oh, no,' she said, like it was a stupid question.

Angelo was amused. Working right for the Don was an opportunity girls round here would kill to have. 'Why not?'

'Because I'm going to make something of myself,' Dina said, artlessly.

Angelo Tallarico laughed aloud. 'You know what, kid? I don't doubt it.'

The next night, in her room, Dina was hunched over her desk, working, waiting for the limousines.

They didn't come.

She heard her mom making calls. They were short; there was shouting. And after that, nothing.

Ellen sloped round the house, getting drunker, missing her days at work, lashing out. She stopped cooking, cleaning. Dina quietly did it all herself. She poured out the vodka bottles she found hidden under the sink, but her mother bought more.

Still, the kids at the school stopped talking. Dina went back to her schoolwork. Johnny looked a little less hunched, less defeated.

Ellen Kane was drunk.

She didn't know why. Just a little hair of the dog from last night. That was bad; she had the shakes. She needed it.

And then she felt so much better. One more wouldn't hurt. Anyway, she was quitting after this bottle. It cost money, it would be a waste to pour it away.

She deserved it. They were all bastards, all of them – using bastards. Something had happened, something bad. It worried her nights. She had anxiety – that was it, anxiety. And if a little martini made you feel better, so what? It was better than them shrink pills. They would kill you.

The doorbell rang.

'Comin'!' she yelled. Her words were slurry. *Shit!* Maybe it was Paolo, come back. He was her favourite. The way he caressed her ass . . . made her feel good, sexy, young again.

But she was already, well, a little bit nice.

Ellen stumbled to her bathroom and swilled the Listerine around her mouth. Yeah – great. Now she was set.

She opened the door, steadying herself on the handle.

It wasn't Paolo. It wasn't any of them.

But it was a younger man, handsome in a kind of fierce way, with a scar on his cheek. And a fancy suit and a *reeeal* nice watch. He was Italian, for sure.

Ellen glanced behind him. He didn't have a town car. He had a limo you could take a bath in.

Maybe one of the boys had recommended her. *Recommended her*. That was kind of humiliating, but sexy, too. Ellen tossed back her blond hair. She liked to party; she was a pretty girl who liked to party. Not a goddamned crime, right?

'Hey, baby,' she said, carefully enunciating. 'Come on in.'

Angelo Tallarico sat on the couch and stared at Ellen. She was a sloppy, drunken mess. Now she was sobbing, her small shoulders heaving, eyes and nose streaming.

He glanced around; the little house was neat. Dina had probably taken care of that.

Tallarico was a murderer and a drug dealer – with very particular ideas about how things should be done.

And Ellen Kane didn't fit the template.

'Stop crying,' he said, coldly. 'I'm not your shrink. You understand me?'

She mopped at her face.

'The boys aren't coming round. None of them. Ever. Don't call. Don't email. You're an embarrassment to the family.'

Ellen trembled. She thought she'd get more compassion from a snake.

'We support you. But one more incident and that money is cut off. One more embarrassment, so are you.'

She moaned.

31

'Do you understand?'

'Yes.'

'You've had your last drink. If I ever see you drinking again, ever hear reports of you drinking, you will wind up in an accident.'

Ellen's whole body shuddered. Never had she wanted booze as much as she did in that second.

'Don Angelo—'

'Don't call me that.'

'I can't stop drinking . . . not right away. Give me a week, a month . . .'

'You have the weekend to clean up. Lock yourself in your bedroom and order a pizza. Monday morning, you're back at work. Sober. For good. If not . . .' he shrugged.

'I . . . I . . .'

'Call it the fast-track twelve-step programme, lady –' a thin smile at his own joke – 'one step: you stop. Or you die.'

'And men?'

'Nobody from the family. If you can find a nice single, divorced guy, date him like a civilised broad; you can get married. Good luck with that.' He laughed cruelly. 'I wouldn't fuck you with my gardener's dick.'

'Oh, God,' Ellen said.

'Spend our money. Live clean. Live quiet. Then you live. Shit, you could consider looking after that pretty little daughter of yours.'

Ellen collapsed into sobs. When she looked up, Tallarico had gone.

She fled to the kitchen and picked up the vodka bottle.

Outside, in the street, the limousine flashed and dipped its headlights.

Fear gripped her. Fear worse than the craving. Ellen lifted the bottle, so he could see, and poured all that lovely, calming liquid right down the sink.

Then she collapsed on to the floor and crawled upstairs to her bedroom on her hands and knees.

That pretty little daughter of yours . . . Pretty little daughter . . .

Dina!

It was Dina. She was here to curse the mother that slaved for her. Here to ruin Ellen's life.

Ellen bit her lip. She dared not say anything to Dina. The man – the bastard, Tallarico – would not like it. And, like a threatened animal, Ellen scented danger.

He was angry. If she did anything to worsen that, she was dead. And not in a metaphorical sense.

Lying on her bedroom rug, watching the ceiling spin and dance as she gasped and sweated and longed for a drink, Ellen Kane held tight to one thing:

She would have her revenge.

Chapter Three

Dina Kane graduated from school a major success – that is, if you were looking at grades. She was top of the class.

Despite her mom, Dina had applied to the Ivy League – and got in. There were acceptances from Columbia, Vassar, even Stanford.

But Dina could not afford the fees. She was considered too well-off for financial aid – her mother had almost three hundred grand in the bank.

None of her pleading meant a goddamned thing.

'No, Dina.' Ellen was colder these days in her dismissal. Unable to compete as an aging sexpot, she had taken refuge in the clothing of the upright. Hair twisted into a severe bun, Ellen Kane favoured long, stout skirts, membership of community organisations and a disapproving frown at all times.

For some time now, she hadn't touched a drink. Or any drug stronger than caffeine.

Ellen joined the PTA at Johnny's Catholic school. She volunteered in the St Patrick's Society. She was on the town-beautification committee. Their house grew cleaner and neater and Ellen gave gifts to local organisations so she could be thanked at dinners.

At first, Dina was thrilled. That horrible trip to Tallarico had had its effects. Her mother had said she was sick and barely came out of her room all week, but when she did, she was changed. Older. Sober. No mascara. Plain, sensible pants. She looked like a mom.

Unfortunately, she still didn't act like one. Dina got a square meal at supper and new clothes when she'd worn out the last set. And that was it.

They were strangers. No people came to the house; no men visited at night. Dina Kane started to live for the moments her brother came home from school.

'There's no money for you to go to college. I need it for my pension. I won't be marrying again and there's no security in welfare. Besides, this place has property taxes . . .'

The list went on and on.

'But, Mom, you've got plenty – really.' Dina didn't want to cry, but she couldn't help it. 'I need you to help me out, Momma.'

Ellen looked blank. 'Johnny's at college. I'm paying for that.'

Johnny was at a pretty nondescript, local private university – the best he could get into with his so-so grades. But at least it was college.

'You can't just favour one of us over the other, Mom!'

Ellen smiled, very quickly, very slightly, then swallowed it. She turned to Dina, her face set once more. 'It's clear from your school success that I picked the right place for you. Johnny might have needed more help. Putting one kid in college is all that I can manage. You should respect that, Dina. You can always get a job, work your way through.'

'I can't work through Columbia's fees . . .'

'I'm sorry. There's nothing to discuss.'

'Mom –' Dina tried one last, desperate tactic – 'if you *lend* me the money for college, I'll graduate, I'll have a career and I can pay you back . . . I'll do well in life, Momma; I'm going to work hard.'

Her mother laughed. 'Really, honey, don't get ideas above

your station. You should go out with one of the local boys. Get married, have some children. Life's all about a happy home!'

'So what will you do?' The principal, Mr Rogers, looked at Ellen Kane's departing figure with withering contempt.

She'd turned up at graduation, sat there for the ceremony and clapped politely as Dina received her cap and gown, and the meaningless little scroll that made her a high-school graduate. Then, as soon as she'd posed for a photo with her desperately smiling daughter and the slothful elder brother lolling around next to her, Ellen had turned around and walked off.

Mr Rogers had no doubt that the photo would be framed. It would go on her mantelpiece. Ellen Kane: pillar of the community, single mom of the year. But she had no few minutes to spend with her daughter – the one whose incredible potential she was just throwing down the drain.

'There's always community college.'

'My mom's too poor to afford college,' Dina said again.

He smiled sympathetically. Now wasn't the time for the truth. 'Sure, Dina.'

'I think I want to move to the city. Get a job and save some money. Then maybe I can reapply next year.'

He wanted to tell her she was crazy, but he had no answers. 'What kind of job?'

'I'll figure something out,' she said.

'OK.' Mr Rogers hesitated. 'Is your momma setting you up in an apartment?'

'Of course.' Dina smiled. 'Momma does everything for me.'

She walked home, thinking about it. Letting the warmth of the sun on her back calm her. New York was great when it was baking hot. It could distract you from pain.

Johnny had left home now . . . He couldn't bear to be around Ellen and Dina, to see the cruelty, the tension. Johnny wasn't built for confrontation – or, really, effort of any kind. He wanted to hug his sister, have a good time. And he avoided acknowledging how he hadn't protected her, skipping out whenever a bad scene came up, which was more and more often these days.

Dina never quite believed it – that the mom who raised her would dump her like this. In a few months she'd be eighteen, a legal adult.

Ellen was finally shot of her.

And it showed. Her mother could barely contain her jubilation.

'I hope you've worked at finding a job,' she'd said. 'And can you make sure your things are packed? I need a real guest bedroom.'

'But where will I sleep?'

'Sleep?' Ellen arched a brow. 'Dina, adults have their own lives. It's healthy for you to get on with yours.'

'I don't know anyone in the city.'

'You know Johnny.' Her brother had a tiny apartment near his college. Ellen gave him an allowance, part of his college arrangements, so she told Dina. As a working woman, Dina could afford her own rent.

When she turned the corner into her street, Dina Kane had made up her mind.

She looked up at the house in which she'd been raised. It was neat, well kept and pretty – exactly the same as it always was. Her mother's big break meant nothing. She spent all that money on herself, and spent it just to stand still.

If Dina got a hundred grand, she would do something with it.

Momma was right. It was time to move on. But Dina would do it on her own terms.

'Hey, Momma.' Dina walked into the kitchen and set her graduation cap down on the counter. She carefully hung up her cape on the hook on the kitchen door.

Underneath, she wore a pair of jeans from Gap and a plain

white T-shirt. On her, this was an absolutely knock-out look. Her naturally tanned skin popped against the white, and her breasts, medium sized and sweetly shaped, were outlined perfectly. Dina had a narrow waist and was naturally slim. Even in flats, she was absolutely stunning.

'Well, I'm glad *that's* over,' said Ellen, brutally.

Dina breathed in. The casual cruelty, so normal, so painful, gave her strength to come out with what she had to say.

'So, I'm not eighteen for two months. But I'd like to move out now.'

A slight flicker of a smile; it hurt Dina like a punch to the gut.

Why do I still care?

I love her. I hate her.

'You found somewhere?'

'I'm going to. I have places to visit today.'

'Places to visit? Aren't you staying with a friend?'

Dina shook her head. 'Rentals. I found them in the *Village Voice*.'

Ellen paused. 'But you don't have a job. And rentals need a deposit.'

'Yes – two months' rent, and security. It's more for me, though, because I don't have a job yet, you're right. I plan to move to the city and job hunt from there.'

Her mother saw where this was going.

'Dina, we've spoken about money. You can't ask me for any.'

Dina took a deep breath. 'Not asking you, Momma – telling you. I need fifteen thousand dollars.'

Ellen laughed. 'I can't lend you fifteen grand.'

'It won't be a loan. It will be a gift. And you're going to give me fifteen thousand right now.'

Her mother looked up from the stove, startled. There was a fire in her daughter's green eyes that she had never seen before.

'Write me the cheque and I will be out of your hair – permanently. Don't write it, and I will go and see Don Tallarico.'

Ellen gasped. Adrenaline prickled across her skin like she'd been doused with water. 'My God. It *was* you.'

'Yes, it was. And it will be again. Give me the money now, Momma. There's a pen on the countertop. Write me that cheque.'

And Dina Kane held out her hand.

The apartment was vile. It was tiny, cramped and filthy. The bathroom had a stand-up shower in it with a dead bug resting against the drain. The paint was peeling and the kitchen alcove was barely big enough for a refrigerator and a hot plate. A rickety double bed took up most of the rest of the space. There was a chair wedged right up against a large TV, one closet and stains on the green rug. Plus, you had to walk up eight flights of stairs to get there.

'Are all the apartments in the building like this?'

The realtor sniffed. 'Honey, you couldn't afford any of the others. This used to belong to the super. He was from Mexico.'

'So, for him, it was a palace?'

She shrugged. 'Don't give me any of that equality crap. You want it?'

The building itself was in a backwater, but it was secure and it was Manhattan. And Dina wouldn't have to share.

'Not at this price,' she said.

Ten minutes and a five-hundred-dollar discount later, Dina Kane had a deal. As she folded up her copy of the lease papers, she took note of the landlord's address.

As soon as she got the keys, Dina moved in. She called a handyman to remove everything in the flat and dump it into storage. Next, she got on the subway to a cheap furniture store in Midtown.

She looked around, thinking carefully about what to buy. After two hours, she was satisfied with her purchases.

'We deliver,' the saleswoman said. 'Twenty-four hours' notice.'

'See you tomorrow.'

'You getting everything delivered?'

'All except this.' Dina held up a sleeping bag.

Next, she headed to the local grocery store. She bought bleach, roach traps, dust cloths, mops and several pairs of bright yellow rubber gloves.

Long into the night, Dina was on her knees, cleaning. The stench was so bad, she had to stop twice to throw up. Heaving, she managed to open a window; warm air floated up from the alley below, but at least there was some oxygen in it. The stale odour of booze and sweat and sex dissipated under her assault – washing, scrubbing, mopping, till the place smelled like a hospital.

She showered in her clean stall, clambered into her sleeping bag and lay down on the floor.

The filthy net curtain on the single window had already gone into the trash. The bright lights of Manhattan streamed into her apartment. But Dina was content.

She was in the big city now.

In the morning, Dina woke early. She had no choice – her curtainless window got her up with the sun.

She showered, dressed from her suitcase and raced to the nearest hardware store. A few more dollars for brushes and paint. White – that was all she needed.

Dina painted with rollers and brushes. She wasn't her dad, and she had no practice, but the colour was basic, and forgiving enough that she did a reasonable job.

Besides, she was motivated. This was home. In a way, it was her first.

She was finished by eleven. Starving, she headed out to eat – anywhere, as long as it was cheap.

Dina had about two thousand dollars left in the account, and it had to last her. There was a Greek place across the street, the Olympia Café. She picked it because it was the closest, and she was so tired her legs could hardly hold her up.

She ordered a pork gyro. It would be hot, and she needed the iron. She waited and waited, but it didn't come, so she meekly flagged down a waiter.

'Jeez, baby, I'm sorry.' His shirt was open and he looked stressed. 'Girl's off sick again. I'll bring it right now.'

Dina ate the pita; it was nothing remarkable, but she was so hungry, and it tasted good. As she chewed, she thought hard.

'Check, please.'

'Nothing else? No coffee?'

Coffee was a dollar fifty. Dina shook her head. The tap water came free.

'You got it.'

'Your waitress often sick?' she ventured.

'Sick? No, honey; it's a Sunday. Saturday night on the town.' He looked fed up. 'Rolls around every weekend.'

'I can waitress. I don't drink.'

He laughed.

'I'm serious,' Dina said.

'Are you? Then turn up here at eight tonight. We're an all-night operation. Minimum wage; no benefits. You keep the tips.'

'Aren't you a waiter too?'

'I own the place. We don't spend money we don't have. Rents are high.' He smiled. 'I'll try you out. Sandwich is on the house.'

Her furniture was delivered just after three. Dina got out a hammer, some nails and twenty whole dollars to tip the delivery guys, who cursed her as they set the heavy stuff down.

'Eight goddamned flights. What a dump!'

'Have a nice day,' said Dina.

'Whatever.' He snatched the money.

Dina loved it – Manhattan attitude. She rolled out her new rug: chocolate brown, to hide any stains. The old bed and chair were gone; in their place was a neat, compact couch that unfolded to a queen-sized bed. She hung a plain cream blind over the window and a large mirror on the opposite wall, to catch the tiny amount of light and reflect it – that gave an illusion of space. Add a new fridge and a toaster oven to the cleaned-up hot plate, and the tiny studio was chic and respectable.

Dina added wire baskets to the single closet; she couldn't magic up more room, but she could make it work. There wasn't space for a lot of clothes. Good – that would mean she couldn't make any mistakes.

When she was finished, it was six p.m. She napped for an hour, then got up, showered and put on flats and a simple black dress.

'You're back.'

'Yes, sir.'

He grinned. 'I can't believe it.'

'It's ten to eight,' Dina pointed out.

'What's she doing here?' A heavy-set girl, twenty-two or so, with thick black eyeliner and greasy hair swept back in a ponytail, had marched up to the man.

'Working. What you should be doing.'

'We don't need you.'

'Not your call, Aella. Get back in the kitchen.'

Dina hovered.

'You done this before?'

'No, sir. But I'm a quick learner.'

'You don't have to call me sir. My name's Gil Barberis. I own the restaurant with my brother Dimitri. You'll see him in the kitchen. He cooks.'

'OK.'

'There's a changing room behind there with an apron you

can put on. Dimitri will tell you what to do. If he's busy, ask Aella.'

'Got it.'

'Any questions?' Gil asked, but she had already disappeared, walking into the back.

He realised he didn't even know her name.

Dina set her back to it. Dimitri, the brother, was fat, made good food and cooked it fast. He shouted out orders and she tried to get the hang of it. Aella cursed her and jostled her and tried to make her spill platters, but Dina was quick and focused. She dropped two plates and served three customers the wrong orders.

'I guess it didn't work out,' she said, at the end of the shift.

'Are you kidding? You were great. Can you work tomorrow?'

By the end of the first week, Gil was really pleased. This girl was something else. She showed up on time and learned quick. Plus, she actually smiled at the customers, passed the time of day.

And, goddamn, she was pretty.

Women gave her tips. Men gave her even bigger tips. Plus, they started showing up on off-times, just to catch a glimpse of her.

Dina Kane was a real gorgeous girl. More than that, she had a certain way about her. She wore form-fitting, minimal black clothes under the diner apron, just a little make-up, so that she always looked smooth, but not a drop more. She wore her hair high, in a clean bun. It made her look out of place. It made her look expensive.

He knew she needed money. She was grateful for every tip – thanked the customers personally. Gil was afraid to lose her. He offered her more work, the pick of the sessions. Aella and Katrina bitched, but bad waitresses were a dime a dozen.

'I can't. I have to look for a job,' Dina said.

'You have one.'

'I mean a real job. I need to make rent. So I have to take time out for that.'

Gil sighed, but he couldn't push things. He didn't want Dina Kane to leave completely.

Dina worked her shifts diligently, collected her money, went home and slept. In her off hours, she tied on her trainers and her cheap running clothes and worked out every day, following the streets down to the Hudson River and racing alongside the water. Men whistled at her, stared; she ignored them all.

She was running – from her mother, from her heartbreak, from a tiny life.

The waitress job paid enough to feed her, buy her make-up and clothes. It couldn't touch the rent, and Dina was scared. She had assumed the money from her mother would buy space and time, and that she'd get a real career, a foot on the ladder.

School had been easy; work – not so much.

'I'm sorry; you need experience to be a paralegal.'

'Our internships are unpaid.'

'Assistants at our company all have college degrees.'

'When did you graduate college, Miss Kane?'

'Nanny? Do you have referrals? A child-related qualification of some kind?'

'Babysitter? Our agency only takes girls currently at university. Which is yours?'

Great jobs all had something in common – Dina wasn't qualified to do any of them.

Some men at the diner had advice for her.

'Get a boyfriend – he'll look after you.'

'Baby, if you're nice to me, I can do you favours.'

'Lots of girls who can't afford college go dance in the clubs. I know a guy—'

'I'm not a stripper,' Dina said. She smiled at the customer, but her eyes were ice.

'Who's talking stripper? This is exotic dancing – like, artistic shit. They make the real money over there.'

I hate you, Momma, Dina thought.

Desperately, she tried to make something more of the job she had.

'Dimitri, maybe you could experiment. Cook some more authentic dishes.'

'What?' Her boss stared at her blankly. 'People come for diner food.'

'There are lots of diners. Lots of delis. Not too many Greek restaurants, not proper ones. I reckon, if you made some real stuff, people would come. You could try adding a few items to the menu. And a promotion.'

Dimitri looked at Gil. They'd already learned to listen to Dina Kane. Her simple suggestion of photocopying colouring pages and bringing in a stack of crayons in plastic cups had led to a real surge in moms with kids. Now the dead times between lunch and dinner covers had a healthy number of tables occupied with spaghetti and meatballs, coffees and cookie plates. Even better, Dina had sectioned off a corner of the diner, and they sat all the happy families there. Working men went the other side, away from the coffee klatches, where they could ogle the waitresses.

'What kind of promotion?'

'Get it grandma tested. Do a one-day promotion. Seniors eat free if they bring one younger paying adult.'

'That will cost.'

Dina wasn't listening. 'See, you print a flyer – but you only print it *in Greek*. Put it up in the Orthodox churches, the community clubs. You want to get the community in to talk up your place. Like – it's a small market, but not much competition. What do you think?'

They tried it. It worked like a dream.

'I want a rise,' Dina said.

Gil sucked it up and gave her another fifty per cent. It still wasn't enough.

One evening, about a month later, when Dina was looking at another three weeks before she defaulted on her rent, an older man came into the restaurant. His suit was beautifully cut, and it was clear he didn't want to be there.

Dina ran over to seat his party. She knew the lady he was with – Olga Markos, one of their first senior customers. Olga loved Dimitri's *gavros marintos*, small, spiky fish fried with spices and served with ouzo.

'Wonderful to see you again. Your usual table?'

The man snorted, and Dina returned his contempt with a smile.

'Oh, sir, this lady prefers to sit right by the window.'

'I do.' Olga nodded emphatically. 'So I can see the world, Alexander. Young Dina remembers.'

'First name terms,' the man said, dryly.

'Oh, it's Dina – everybody knows Dina round here.'

'Do they indeed?' he said.

Dina showed them to their table. It was clean, with a fresh white rosebud in a jar on the table. Those got changed twice a week. Another Dina innovation. The restaurant stood out.

As she worked her covers, Dina noticed the man watching her. She was used to that. All the men liked to stare, but she couldn't let it get in her way. Saturday night was their busiest, the ouzo and retsina flowed, and the tips were fantastic.

At the end of the meal, she brought them their check. Olga tipped her normal ten per cent. Dina smiled brightly, to hide her disappointment. The man seemed rich; she'd hoped for a couple of extra bucks from him.

But he caught her glance at the dollars on the change tray.

'You wanted a tip?' he said.

She flushed, embarrassed to be caught out.

'Oh, no, sir. The lady already gave me a tip, thank you, ma'am.' Dina scooped it up. 'You have a great day.'

'Here's your tip.' He took a business card out of his wallet and handed it to Dina. 'Call me tomorrow.'

'I certainly will. Thank you.' She slipped it into her apron pocket, without looking at it. She got a hundred of those come-ons a night.

'I mean it,' he said shortly. Then he stood up, ignoring her, and helped Olga from the restaurant.

That night, just as she was about to clear the paper waste into the recycling, Dina paused. She fished the small card out of the recycling bag and read it again.

Alexander Markos, it said. *Mount Java.*

She started. Mount Java was the newest, hottest chain of coffee shops to hit Manhattan. They sold their coffee like Baskin-Robbins sold ice cream – forty-five flavours, all lined up in urns, freshly brewed every two hours. And tiny pastries, from every country in Europe: French macaroons, Italian biscotti, Greek baklava, German strudel, jam tarts from England.

The company was founded and run by an American – Alex Markos.

New York was lapping it up. A coffee there cost eight dollars – not one – and New Yorkers couldn't get enough of it. The city was rich, and it paid for quality.

Dina clutched the card to her chest. Her heart was pounding.

'New boyfriend?' Gil said, hopefully, although he knew what the answer would be.

'New job,' Dina said, tears in her eyes, like any other girl would have when she announced her marriage. Gil didn't understand the kid at times. She worked like a machine; she just wasn't normal. Jesus! The boys died for her – so did the men. She could have had her pick.

She passed the card over. Gil studied it for a second, then made the connection. He whistled. 'Goddamn. Guess he wants you for more than a waitress.'

'I hope you don't mind.'

Gil knew when he was beaten.

'Go with God.'

Chapter Four

The office was located on the thirty-fourth floor, and Dina had to pass through four sets of security guards just to reach the executive elevator.

The lobby had marble floors and high ceilings. The guards wore designer suits. The reception desk appeared to be carved from solid ebony. Dina's heartbeat quickened as she walked. The scent of money was in the air.

The elevator was brass, with velvet carpet, a mirror and a padded bench – bigger than her little bathroom at home – and it went straight to Alex Markos's office.

She breathed raggedly. This was her big chance to get exactly where she wanted to be.

The doors hissed open and Dina found herself in a dazzling palace of glass walls and sweeping views. Behind the soundproofed window, the city went about its business. Dina walked up to the kidney-shaped desk of Mr Markos's secretary, an elegant fifty-something wearing what was unmistakably a Chanel suit.

I want to be like that, Dina thought, *only sitting in the inner office. Working for a big company. Chief Executive.* Visions of success danced in her head.

'Can I help you?'

'Dina Kane for Mr Markos.'

'He's expecting you. You can go right in.'

Dina walked up to the main door. The sound of her footfalls was muffled by carpet an inch thick, but the sound of her heartbeat crashed again and again in her ears.

She pulled the door open and walked in, trying to look more confident than she felt.

Markos was looking at a computer screen, his oak desk a small island in the vast room. Behind and below him, she saw the New York traffic crawling through the city's concrete canyons, flashes of sunlight glittering on the windscreens. This was money; this was power. Dina Kane felt it as a sexual thrill.

'Have a seat.'

There was a large chair right in front of him. Obediently, Dina sat, smoothing her dress on her lap. *Steady. Don't look nervous.*

'Thank you.'

'You impressed me yesterday. I asked my aunt about you. She told me some of the things you've done at that restaurant. How old are you?'

'Eighteen,' Dina lied.

'Why aren't you at college?'

She winced. 'It's a long story.'

'I see a lot of young people work tables. I make it my business to notice quality. It's pretty rare.'

'Thank you, Mr Markos.'

'What are your goals for yourself, Dina?'

'To make the rent next month. And then to go to college, when I have enough money.'

'And then?'

She grinned. 'I like your office, Mr Markos.'

He laughed. 'This job is taken. Found your own goddamned company. I have an opening for a junior manager in my new restaurant uptown. It pays thirty-five thousand a year, with a Christmas bonus.'

Dina quickly did the sums. That was almost three thousand

a month. But, of course, there were taxes. She would need the bonus.

'Do I get to keep the tips?'

He raised a brow. 'The words you're looking for are "thank you".'

'Thank you. Sir.'

Markos waited till she'd shut the door behind her. Maybe this was a mistake. They'd never hired a manager that young. Oh, and there was the question of her looks. Eighteen and all kinds of sexy, with a face that could stop traffic. As a waitress, she was an attraction. As a manager? Would they take her seriously?

He almost felt a stirring. Ludicrous. She was practically jailbait. And he'd taken a fatherly interest because the kid reminded him of himself.

Guiltily, he tilted the black-framed picture of his wife, Athena, towards himself on the desk. She was the love of his life. He'd lost all interest in women when she died. All interest in everything, except the game of business: the thing that kept him sane.

His wife's forty-year-old face – so lovely, so classic – stared back at him, frozen in time, in that blessed year before she got sick.

Gently, he calmed himself. He would never take advantage of Dina Kane, teen beauty alone in the big city.

Other guys will do that, said the voice in his head.

'Susan –' he punched his intercom – 'get me the manager of the store at a hundred and twelfth. He's got a new colleague.'

Edward Johnson was a golden boy.

He was in his second year at Columbia – Ivy League – studying pre-med. His plan was to become a plastic surgeon, one of the most upmarket in the city. He wanted offices on Park Avenue and a string of starlets and news anchors begging him to perfect their faces and tits.

Not that he needed money. Edward, smoothly handsome with his dark hair and even features, was an only child. He was close to his mother, Penelope, and stood to inherit everything from his daddy one day – Shelby Johnson was president of the hugely successful Coldharbor Bank. They had a townhouse on Eighty-First Street and Amsterdam, close to Central Park, Zabar's and the best delis in town. Edward had already succeeded to a portion of his trust fund. There would be more when he turned twenty-one.

Edward Johnson liked pretty women. He was clever – the Columbia place proved it – but he was easily bored, too. Finding cute girls to fuck was his hobby. When everybody you knew was rich, how else could a fellow keep score?

Edward's family voted Democrat, like all middle-class New Yorkers, but he was strongly conservative. He believed in social strata. Edward Johnson had been to the right prep school. He worshipped on Sundays at a smart, Presbyterian church. He relished his parents' social acceptability and their place in the world.

After all, wouldn't it be his place too?

Edward dated occasionally – girls with parents like his, girls he treated with respect, took to dinner, to the private dining clubs in town. But he didn't want to get married yet; marriage was for a few years down the line. So dating was nothing special. And if those girls slept with him, neither of them talked about it. Edward was respected. The future was looking good.

No, when he wanted something, he was careful.

Edward Johnson liked downtown girls – girls he picked up in late-night clubs; girls he could hit on, working checkout at the supermarket; girls from the bridge-and-tunnel crowd; young Jersey chicks with big hair and big tits and too much make-up; girls he could wine, dine and bang once or twice and then drop without a trace.

'Hell, man, you're a stud.'

'Ed, you are such a player.'

'Jesus! Look at that piece of ass. How does he do it?'

'Watch and learn, boys,' Edward crowed. 'Watch and learn.'

He loved it – the notoriety. They called him a pussy-hound, a babe magnet, a player, the king of clubs.

And if the girls called him, crying, after he dumped them, so what? Edward cut them off. What the fuck? They gave it up; that was their problem.

'Jesus, honey, give it a rest. I'm not interested.'

'What are you bothering me for, Camilla? We're done.'

'Mercedes, you were a one-nighter. OK?'

'No, it's not OK! You bastard! I thought you were different!'

'I don't see no ring on your finger,' he said, with an accent, mocking her. Then he'd laugh and hang up.

Edward felt no guilt. Why should he? The girls were easy – not his problem. They sold themselves for the price of a meal or two in a nice restaurant, some flowers or a bottle of champagne. He was sowing his wild oats, like they used to say, working it out before he got serious. Edward Johnson believed that girls like that – low class, gullible girls – were the natural toys of men like him. They wanted to ride in the fast car with the rich guy, eat at places they could never afford, go to the best clubs in town. And he wanted a lay he could show off to his friends.

'It's the four Fs,' Edward told the admiring guys who hung around him in the coffee shops as they nursed their hangovers. 'Find 'em, feel 'em, fuck 'em, forget 'em.'

And they all laughed their heads off.

Dina settled into the new job. It was steady pay, and she waitressed on the side.

'But you're a junior manager,' her boss, Mike, told her. 'You don't have to be out front.'

'I need the tips.' Dina smiled. 'And besides, that way I can hear what the customers are saying.'

She did everything she could. Showed up on time, worked hard, smiled, tried to remember the regulars. On the plus side, she was finally making her rent. There were no more night shifts and every couple of weeks, she could afford to take the subway out to Westchester to visit her brother at college. But she was no closer to her dream. With rent and food, she was still tapped out. College seemed a world – galaxies – away.

And Dina was frustrated. Helping run a coffee house like this was about half of a white-collar job. She did some accountancy, double-checked the takings, wrote up careful reports on what pastries did and didn't sell. But after she'd supervised staff – getting them to show up on time, be polite, follow procedures – there wasn't too much left to do.

Dimitri and Gil had *listened* to her. She'd made things happen at the Greek diner; she'd been innovative. But Mount Java was already a major company. It was expanding nationwide and Alex Markos didn't need much from her. There was only room to execute his ideas well – not bring in her own.

Dina knew she wanted more. Was she ungrateful? She hoped not. She was learning, soaking it up like a sponge. The simple importance of quality was what Markos's store taught her. They imported the best beans, ground them finer than most, used all-natural flavourings and changed the water often. That was the secret – sound expensive; be fresher than the other guy.

But what the customers didn't seem to get was that they were paying for flavoured water. And water was cheap.

It cost two dollars extra to go from regular to large, and less than a hundredth of a cent to pay for the extra coffee in the cup. The recycled cardboard cost more. But the range of flavours gave their shop an edge . . . Customers wanted to try walnut coffee, or Irish cream, or cinnamon. And through the seasons, Java brought in special-edition flavours: spiced apple in the fall, ginger nut in winter, Easter chocolate in the spring, raspberry in summer. The customers came back to the store, just for the special editions. They loved the idea, the brand.

Dina made sure her store was meticulously clean, that there were no scuffs on the burgundy leather seats. People bought luxury and, even if you couldn't afford a cashmere sweater or an Aston Martin, you could afford a warm cup of Java Mountain coffee, brewed fresh with Madagascar vanilla, served in a chic, recycled, green cup with the red mountain logo.

Dina learned. But she was stuck.

She applied to join the higher-management programme. Maybe the way to get on here was in the central company. But her application came back, struck through.

Employee employed for only four months. More experience required.

She didn't hear again from Alexander Markos. And, after three months of pouring and smiling and serving little pastries, Dina was starting to feel trapped.

One thing made it worse. Much worse.

At Mount Java, Dina served a good cross-section of New York: alpha males in their business suits, who stopped by at seven for a latte to take in the cab; mothers, who congregated after drop-off and before pick-up; lunchtime dieters, who didn't do lunch but stimulated their system with caffeine, not calories. But the crowd that hurt her feelings came in after the others had left, or in the dead hours – eleven o'clock in the morning, half-ten. Breakfast, for them.

College kids, either nursing hangovers, or recovering from pulling an all-nighter.

They liked the drinks large and sweet, full of punch. Dina would bring the cups to the table, smiling and chatting, and all the time dying inside. Those privileged girls were her age and just a little older. They had long glossy hair and Columbia scarves and sweatshirts. Carrying piles of books, dark folders and yellow legal pads, they laughed and talked to each other, placing their orders without eye contact, as if Dina was invisible.

Dina *felt* invisible, because they were going somewhere and she was not. They were on their way to the courthouse, the surgery theatre, the museum, the investment bank.

And she was serving them coffee.

Every day it beat up in her head an endless rhythm of shame and failure.

I've got to get on, Dina thought. *Got to get out.*

The college boys didn't see her as invisible. Goddamn, they were obnoxious.

'Hey baby. Get that cute ass over here.'

'What time do you get off, sweetie? I can get *you* off.'

'Honey, you want to earn the biggest tip of your life? Give me your phone number . . .'

Sometimes she had to swallow back tears. It was so hard, but she needed the job. Needed to make rent. Had no place else to go.

Dina didn't think about love. Not yet. Maybe one day she would meet somebody, settle down, get married. But the boys and men that catcalled and whistled didn't want a date. They wanted a lay.

The memory of her mom burned fiercely in Dina's heart: the cars, the laughter, the aging playgirl, drunk and drugged – available for rich, powerful men.

That wasn't going to be her. Dina hoped that one day a man would come, a guy who would blow her away, reduce her to rubble.

Trouble was, she didn't find men that impressive. Nobody had stepped up in her mother's life. Her darling brother was a flake. And the boys at school had been scared of being unpopular.

At seventeen, Dina Kane had learned the hard way.

Only rely on yourself.

'You want to hang out with me, sweetcakes?'

His name was George Linden, and he was one of the most persistent college boys. With a daddy in the oil business in Texas, bright blond hair and a footballer's physique, he could pick up almost any girl he wanted.

'Your coffee's coming right up,' Dina said, brightly. She hated him and his group of hangers-on, the boys that would crowd around the golden god and cackle at everything he said. She pivoted on one heel, back to the kitchen.

'Goddamn, that's a beautiful view,' Linden said loudly. 'I could watch that ass all day.'

'Mike –' Dina spat it out to the manager as he handed her the pitcher and the stoneware mugs – 'aren't you going to throw them out?'

'Come on, Dina. College is a big part of the store.' Mike shrugged; he hadn't liked having a teenage junior manager forced on him. As far as he was concerned, she wanted tips, so she was still just a glorified waitress. *He* didn't serve up coffees. 'You don't have to wait tables, you know. It's a choice.'

A choice she needed for rent. 'Sure. Right.' Dina gritted her teeth. She moved back to the table with the coffee, set it down, careful not to bend over too much at the waist. The dark pencil skirt of her uniform set her ass off nicely, and she hated the way the frat boys ogled and stared.

'Here's your coffee. Pastries?'

'No, baby. You've got all the sweetness I want right here,' Linden cackled. 'Do you serve private parties? Me and the boys are having one on Saturday.'

'Jesus, George! Cut it out.'

Dina lifted her head, blinking back tears, to see one of their number remonstrating loudly with his friend. He was slim and dark, with an intense look about him. 'You're such a giant douche bag,' he said, before turning to Dina. 'I apologise for our friend over here. He's a loser. When confronted with an actual live woman, as opposed to a computer screen, he falls apart.'

More laughter, but now the group had turned on George. Dina flushed with relief as they looked away from her, jostling the blond kid.

'Hey, fuck you, Edward.' Linden jumped up and pushed his way out of the group, storming out of the store.

'I apologise again. He was raised in a barn. Evidently.'

'Thank you, sir,' Dina replied, quietly, and moved away.

When the gang of students left, Dina found a twenty-dollar tip on their table, and a note.

I'm so sorry about that incident. I'm embarrassed. Yours ever, Edward Fielding.

There was a business card attached, with a cellphone number.

Dina took the twenty bucks. She didn't call the number.

At the end of her shift the next lunchtime, her dark-haired saviour from the other day was waiting for her.

'Miss Kane?'

Dina jumped out of her skin. What was his name? Edward . . . *Fielding*, that was it.

'Yes?' she said.

She felt a little safer dressed in her dark coat, her black trousers, blouse and sweater – a better New York winter uniform than that tight skirt and pumps.

'I'm sorry, I didn't mean to startle you. I was wondering if I could see you for a second.'

'How did you know my name?'

'I asked the store manager. I hope that's OK.'

Dina looked at him warily. He was handsome, and wearing a thick brushed-wool coat over what looked like a bespoke suit. His shirt had gold cufflinks, and the shoes and watch were expensive. But he was looking at her humbly.

'I got your apology, Mr Fielding. Thanks for saying what you said. It's all right now.'

'I'd like to take you out to dinner.'

Another come-on. Her eyes clouded. 'No, thanks.'

Gently, he put his hand on her arm. 'Not as an apology. I'm asking you for a date. Really. After your hours. I've seen you work and deal with all the bullshit. I'd like to have a meal with you tonight. Or see a movie. Anything, really.'

Dina hesitated.

'Not if you don't want to,' he said, falling back. 'I don't mean to harass you any further.'

She thought about it. He was smoothly good-looking, slim, confident. Not her normal style, but . . . who was she kidding? She worked so hard she didn't even *have* a normal style. There hadn't been more than a handful of dates at school – all disastrous. Dina had always thought she'd meet someone at college. Only, she wasn't going to college. Edward Fielding was, though. And he liked her . . .

'Maybe a dinner wouldn't hurt. Sure, I guess.'

'Do you live round here?'

'Downtown.' She gave him the address.

'I'll pick you up at eight.'

He was there punctually, knocking on her door. He didn't bring flowers, which Dina appreciated. That would have been cheesy.

'Wow!' Edward glanced around the inside of her apartment. 'Stylish.'

'You can come in for a second.' Dina was wearing a simple red dress, one of her favourites: DKNY and bought at Saks in the sale. She loved the way it clung to her curves, sat at the knee. This was the first chance she'd had to show off her style since she left her mom's house.

Dina Kane had no jewels, and needed none. Her dark hair was piled on top of her head, swept up in a regal up-do. She wore heels with a platform and a rounded toe, mid-height, and carried a small hand-held purse in dark green mock crocodile.

He looked her up and down. 'Nice.'

Her elegance was one thing – almost incongruous on that young body – but her face was something else. Edward was used to the pretty girl at the café, rushed off her feet, her face almost make-up free, like a weapon against the catcalls. Tonight she had paid attention to her beauty – a wash of tinted moisturiser, sheer against that teenage skin; a slick of bronzer, high on her cheekbones; glittering golden shadow with bronze liner and unusual navy mascara that made her huge eyes stand out. On her lips, there was a pale golden-brown gloss. She looked almost Egyptian, like a supermodel, like somebody else.

Edward Johnson – a.k.a. Fielding – was taking an inventory of the night so far. His dumb-ass friends were like a bull in a china shop. You couldn't get a chick like this just by calling her out. She would need *work*, more than the average bridge-and-tunnel skirt.

Right now, he was totally sure she was worth it.

Dina Kane was full of surprises. She did some management work at the coffee shop – so she was not just a waitress. This apartment, well, it was the size of a postage stamp, but the interior looked like it had been designed by a pro. There was space to stretch; it was clean, bright, popped with colour. The dress looked great on those curves. The up-do was classy. The make-up . . . Well, she was transformed; she was a supermodel.

Edward had a brief moment of doubt. Wasn't this a different girl? One he could take home to Momma?

Then he put it aside. Mixed relationships didn't do well. Dina Kane was a glorified waitress. She had attitude in that shop. There was a bet on as to who would bang her first. He was about to win that bet.

The fellows had been throwing themselves right at her for *months*. Pulling this chick would seal his college legend. Nobody had even got to first base with Dina.

Watch and learn, boys. Watch and learn.

'The apartment is beautiful – but not nearly as beautiful as you.'

She smiled slightly. It annoyed him how she lifted that chin, took his compliments for granted. She wasn't *grateful*. She, a waitress, was treating Edward Johnson as her equal. Not for long.

'Shall we go?' he asked.

The first night he kept it low-key: dinner in a semi-nice Italian restaurant; a chaste kiss at the door to thank her for a lovely evening.

The next day, he sent over flowers: a small bunch of yellow roses – nothing spectacular.

Wednesday, he asked her out again. They watched a movie, laughed about it on the way home. He asked her about herself, and drifted into his own thoughts when she answered.

On Saturday, another dinner – French, this time. Edward could be patient. One false move and the game was up.

Dina was incredibly beautiful. Each night, she made herself up so differently, yet always the same pretty face; it was like dating a thousand girls.

He almost regretted that the game was nearly over.

'You seem happy,' Mike said, suspiciously.

This wasn't the Dina Kane he knew. She was less of a robot, moving around with a smile on her face. She'd started to take her lunchbreaks, sitting with a cup of cinnamon coffee and reading those crumpled little notes her boyfriend sent her.

Even in the daytime, she had begun to wear cosmetics. His male clientele was slowly enlarging. Moms liked to be around her, too. Now their restaurant wasn't just super-efficient, it was cheerful.

'I am happy.'

'The new man? Who *is* this lucky guy?' Mike asked.

'It's a mystery. I could tell you, but I'd have to kill you.' And Dina laughed.

After three weeks, Edward made his move. They had been kissing; first on the cheek, then the lips, then a little tongue. She was nervous, ungainly. He liked that; it made him laugh. What if she was a virgin? Dina Kane was the trophy of the year in his set. If he popped her cherry too . . . Christ, they would have to set up a statue for him.

He did it right: dinner at a local restaurant downtown; lots of talk about family. He said he might like to meet her brother, her mom. Yeah, right – the Johnsons didn't socialise with those kinds of people. Daddy was going to run for Congress next year; he had all the donors lining up. Momma was a socialite and only mixed with exactly the right group. She threw benefit dinners to help people like the Kanes. The thought made him laugh.

Edward Johnson was never going to mix with the Kanes.

Dina should be flattered that she was getting any attention at all from him. She was the finest piece of ass out there on the scene for months, a trophy lay, and so he was doing something unfamiliar: he was actually putting *work* into her.

He asked around among the other waiters, offering a few twenties here and there, and he'd soon found out a lot of what he needed to know. Dina came from Tuckahoe, Westchester. She had been a good student, no boyfriends, the daughter of a dead, drunk workman. Her mother had fucked around with some Italian boys for a while. He liked that idea; it made him kind of hard, knowing her weakness. Hey, she had that prissy attitude, but the apple doesn't fall far from the tree. Edward fantasised about fucking Dina, breaking her in and getting the credit, then maybe passing her around his friends. Girls like her and her mom were just hookers by another name. You dressed up the tips with dinners and flowers, but in the end they were leisure activities for powerful men. Edward Johnson considered himself just that – a powerful man, in training. Hunting the stuck-up waitress was just too much fun.

He thought about her slutty mother, and smiled.

'I'd like you to meet my family.' Dina was acting shy; it was sexy. 'And you can take me to meet yours . . . I'd like to say hello to the Fieldings.'

She still hadn't twigged to the false name. That was the beauty of it. He paid restaurant bills in cash, always plenty of cash, and he'd bought a cheap phone he would throw away after tonight, so no harassing calls on his mobile. Once he'd banged Dina, the boys would stop showing up at the coffee shop. There was no Edward Fielding lodged at Columbia, so she couldn't find him there. She would never see him again. No harm done.

'I told Mom about you last night. She's looking forward to cooking for you.' Edward chuckled to himself. His mom hadn't picked up a frying pan since her wedding night. She just gave the menus to the cook.

Dina smiled, relaxed. 'It's so good that you respect me like this, Edward.'

'Why wouldn't I?' Respect her? Funniest thing ever. He couldn't wait to slip into that tight little pussy. Now he just needed to close the deal. He flashed her that bright smile. 'Let's celebrate. Waiter? Can I get a bottle of champagne for the table? Veuve Cliquot – perfect.'

Dina hoped she didn't look drunk.

She rarely took in alcohol. So three glasses of champagne and she was weaving.

Edward was being so nice . . . so sweet. He paid for everything; he told her all about his worries in class. Now he wanted to bring her to his parents.

They were going back to her apartment. She felt light, happy.

The wine ran round her bloodstream, warming her, taking away the fear.

Dina glanced over at Edward. He was tall, aristocratic, slim. But she didn't feel any desire for him . . . That undeveloped body. Was that normal? Was she normal?

She was eighteen. Most of the girls at school had sex long ago. Maybe it was time. She trusted Edward, and they'd been dating almost a month, a few times each week. Wasn't that how you were supposed to do it?

Perhaps it was always this way. Virgins probably didn't feel any desire, didn't actually ever want the guy. The way the TV showed it, it was always the husbands trying to get the wives into bed. Like sex was not something women wanted. Perhaps this was normal, the price you paid.

Dina wanted to be like other girls – to have a nice boyfriend.

Edward stopped at her door and slipped his arm around her. Dina tried not to shrink back when he thrust his tongue into her mouth.

'Can I come in?' he asked, softly. 'Be with you tonight?'

She shuddered, and he took it as lust.

'OK,' Dina said. 'Sure. Sure, Edward.'

Yes. He was her boyfriend, and this was the price.

Dina lay in her bed, looking at the ceiling. Wanting to cry.

She hated this sex – hated the pain when he penetrated her, hated how unaroused she felt, hated his weird smile as he moved on top of her. There was blood on her thighs and all she could think about was getting into the shower.

'Oh, this is great. You're so hot,' Edward said, gasping. 'You're so sexy . . .'

'Mmm,' Dina managed. She just wanted him to get it over with.

'You like this, baby. You like it, don't you?'

Dina could hardly say, *No*.

He was thrusting on top of her with a strange, triumphal smile. 'A virgin . . . God . . . you're a virgin . . . That's a shock.'

Dina gasped, looking at him.

'Popped your cherry!' he grunted, his face contorted in a weird laugh. He wasn't even looking at her, just staring at the wall. 'Popped your fucking cherry! Bet you can't wait to get banged again. Jesus! You're so fucking tight.' He gasped, grinned. 'Don't worry, baby; I'll give you a great review . . .'

She twisted, moaning in pain. 'What the hell are you talking about? What do you mean?'

'It's what all you bridge-and-tunnel girls like. Just like your momma, aren't you? She fucked around. Yeah, spread those legs for me, baby.'

Dina shrieked, tried to force him off her. But he was a dead weight. She couldn't move him. She was pushing against concrete.

'My momma? Edward, what the hell—?'

'Fucking around with the Italians. After your pops died. That's a great reputation, right there. Town slut. She lives nice, right?' He thrust. 'You treat me and my friends right, and we'll take care of you, too. No more attitude; your pussy's opened up now . . . Oh, oh, *God* . . .' He gasped. 'Dina! So fucking hot.' Then he grunted, went limp and collapsed on her.

Dina moaned in distress, tears springing to her eyes.

'Yeah, you loved it,' Edward said. He rolled off her before she could push him again.

'Edward . . .' she said, sobbing. 'What was that? What do you know about my mom? Why are you talking about me that way?'

She was hot, dehydrated, her head spinning from the wine. Did that happen? Did he turn into that grinning, taunting monkey, grinding away on top of her? She wanted to be sick.

He rolled his eyes. 'Let's not *talk*. Why do girls always want to talk? I'm going to sleep, OK?'

In seconds, he had fallen asleep, mouth open, like a large wet fish. Dina crawled out of bed and showered in her tiny stall. Then she dried off and crept back under the covers.

Maybe she was frigid. It felt horrible, felt so wrong. What the hell was he doing? Was that just dirty talk? It was like he'd turned into someone else – someone new and evil.

Dina's head pounded. Hell, had she imagined it? Was she just drunk?

At least . . . at least she had a boyfriend, a relationship. She would get to know Edward's family – hadn't he said that? Maybe she'd misheard him. Maybe it would get better . . .

After a while, feeling ashamed, nasty, dirty and exhausted, the alcohol lulled her into a fitful sleep.

Dina woke before the sun was up. She rolled over in her bed. Then she realised she'd rolled over.

Edward was gone.

All morning, his words rattled in her head: *Popped your cherry . . . Just like your momma . . . Town slut.* Dina wanted to tell herself that it was the hangover, that he never said it. But she knew it had happened. And her body, already tense and bruised, had writhed in rejection, while he laughed and kept pumping.

She made excuses: it was some twisted fantasy – erotic talk; he would never be that way; he'd call, explain, take her to lunch with his mother. Everything would be OK.

Dina waited for her phone to ring. It didn't. That was weird, but she had work to do . . . Maybe he was ill. She went to the coffee shop, but none of the boys came in, none of Edward's friends.

By lunchtime, she was worried. She called his mobile.

This number is not in service. Please check the number, and try again.

'Hey, Dina.' Mike was looking at her. 'What are you doing? The books need checking from last night.'

'Oh. Nothing. Sorry, Mike.'

Dina scurried into the back office, feeling sick. She tried the number again; got the same result.

By five o'clock, she knew something was wrong. She called the college and asked to be put through to Edward Fielding.

'We have no students here of that name.'

Hands shaking, Dina pulled out Edward's card, the original one he'd given her. She typed up a quick email: *Edward – where are you? D.*

In seconds, it bounced back to her: *Mailer Daemon. Address not valid.*

Numbly, she worked through her shift. Edward . . . whoever he was had had sex with her and disappeared.

It was as old as time, and she was just that stupid.

Dumb waitress. Plaything. Just like Mom.

Dina ran into the bathroom, sank to her knees and threw up. Somewhere, he was laughing at her.

'Dude, you're so full of it.' George Linden saw a way to get his own back. 'There is no way she gave it up to you.'

The boys laughed. Edward looked at them – Ralph and Charlie, Gideon and Homer – he despised them, really. They were minions, who backed up the winner of the moment in the battles for supremacy between him and George. 'Sure she did. Right on her back, legs splayed.' He smirked. 'Sweet little cherry, too.'

'Bullshit, man. Nobody was getting shit from that chick.'

Edward was annoyed. This was the first time anybody had called his prowess into question. He'd given up the idea of passing her round as soon as he'd come inside her; the irritating wriggles of protest and teary eyes told him she wouldn't be hooking herself out like he wanted. But, no matter, he'd fucked her, and that was what counted. And now he was supposed to be getting his props, dammit, not taking shit from George Linden.

'I banged her.'

George lifted his eyebrows, annoyingly. 'Show us the photos, then.'

'Jesus, man! She was lying right next to me.'

'And you didn't snap a quick shot of that sweet ass? Come on, Ed. Give it up.'

He coloured. 'I'll show you, you prick. Let's go have a coffee.'

Ralph lifted a brow. 'I thought we couldn't go in there again.'

'Just once. Apparently Georgie here needs proof. What are they going to do? Ban me because the waitress opened her legs?'

'Fine.' Linden was a little red now, too. 'I *don't* believe you. Let's see how she reacts.'

'I'm not drinking the coffee, though.' Edward was light now, giddy at the thought of showing off. 'Bet she spits in it.'

'Hey, Dina.' Mike was on her case again, but she didn't mind. For two days, Dina had been working numbly, trying to get through it.

She felt so dumb – so used, so humiliated. Edward Fielding – whatever his real name was – had just fucked her and vanished. After all the catcalls she'd brushed off, all the hooting men, this rich kid was patient for a couple of weeks, and she fell for it . . .

She didn't even like him. Didn't want him. And this would be the story of her virginity for the rest of her life . . .

Just like your momma. Town slut.

'Yes, Mike?' She was mopping down the counter in the back. Her rage and shame needed channelling. Dina had called the landlord of her building yesterday and made him an offer, a low offer, for her apartment. He'd accepted . . . Last time he saw the place, it was a grubby little dive.

She had a mortgage lined up. Credit was easy, and Dina had a plan. No income verification, a couple of points extra on the interest rate, but it didn't matter. The landlord wanted to close this month and Dina was more than willing. Her tiny savings would be the deposit, and she would flip it as soon as the ink was dry.

She didn't want to live where Edward had been. She didn't want him to be able to find her. The shame was so intense, she didn't even want this job.

One day, he might come back . . .

She polished the countertop aggressively. And, just as she was thinking about it . . .

'Your boyfriend,' Mike said, with a smile.

Dina froze. She put the cloth down, carefully. 'What?'

'Over there. With his friends. Ready to make up, I expect . . . ?'

She didn't rise to the question. Screw him; what business was it of his?

'Thanks.' Dina moved to look, her heart thumping. Maybe she had Edward all wrong. Maybe he'd been injured, in an accident, got sick and was here now to make it right . . .

He was there in the corner, sitting at his usual table with that group of goons all around him – including the one that had barracked her, the guy Edward apologised for. What was his name . . . ? George Linden.

George was born in a barn . . .

Only now they were sitting together and laughing.

Like nothing happened.

Rage surged up in her, so intense, so white hot, she had to steady herself against the counter for a minute. She was dizzy.

'You going to take their order?'

'Sure. Just a second.' Dina picked up a pot of coffee.

'That's old. Get a fresh one.'

'It's fine,' she said. She marched away from Mike, towards the table. Edward was sitting there, looking nasty, laughing and leering at her.

'Hey, Dina,' he said, and the other boys nudged him and cackled under their breath. 'How you been?'

'Can I get you something?' she said, coldly.

'Now, don't get an attitude. Just because I didn't call after sex . . .' He shrugged, laughed. 'You were up for it. How was I to know you were still a virgin?'

The eyes of his companions opened with shock. One of them laughed aloud, then comically clapped a hand in front of his mouth. They were all staring at her, the pack of them, raking their eyes over her like she was naked.

The anger crystallised to a white-hot point in her.

'Hey, somebody had to pop that cherry. Be thankful it was a nice guy like me.'

'Jesus, you fucking dog,' George Linden said, with reluctant admiration.

And then they all laughed – all the college boys, the Ivy Leaguers, laughing at the coffee-shop girl with her high-school diploma and the face of a sucker.

Dina forced herself to wait till the cackling died down.

'Don't worry, Edward; I know why you didn't call. You shouldn't be *that* embarrassed. I hear it happens to a lot of guys. Especially drunks.'

'Wait, what?' George Linden asked.

'He is Edward, right? That fake card . . . Classy touch, though. What's your real name?'

'Edward Johnson,' one of the other frat boys blurted out.

'Shut the fuck up, Ralph,' said Edward.

'Johnson by name; Johnson by nature,' Ralph said. 'But you'd know all about that, wouldn't you, miss?' And they all laughed again.

'Actually, not so much – Ralph. See, Edward here couldn't actually get it up. I really felt bad for him, at least at first.' Dina smiled brightly. 'He was crying in the bathroom, but then, he was pretty out of it.'

'You lying bitch! We fucked,' Edward snarled.

'Honey, you weren't fucking *anything*. I've seen stiffer plates of Jell-O.'

More laughter. They were really amused now, looking at Edward, enjoying the tennis match.

'I took your virginity. You were a slut, like all the others,' Edward spat. 'Like your mom.'

Dina swallowed her hatred and forced a sympathetic-looking smile, instead.

'Maybe next time lay off the vodka. Or get some Viagra.'

'Hey, sugar, give me a try,' George Linden leered. 'I won't let you down like Edward.'

'Any problems here?' Mike arrived. He looked critically at Dina. These customers spent money in his store – lots of it.

'No problems. Just a bunch of rich, arrogant bastards with dicks the size of maggots,' Dina said.

The laughter stopped cold.

'Jesus! You can't speak to them like that,' Mike said.

'I just did. Step back a second, Mike.' Her voice was so fierce, he actually backed away. 'These boys just need to cool down,' Dina said, and she lifted the coffee pot high and started to pour it all over them. Black, warm, scented coffee flowed over Edward, over George, over Ralph, ruining their clothes, staining their hair.

'Fuck!'

'Bitch!'

'Fucking psycho!'

'I'll sue you,' Edward Johnson hissed. 'This is fucking *assault*!'

'You're fired!' Mike shrieked at Dina's departing back. She had already untied the strings of her apron and let it slither to the floor.

'No,' she said, without turning round. 'I already quit.'

Edward Johnson, dripping, jumped to his feet. His friends were laughing at him. He was soaked. The suit was ruined. Instead of celebrating his triumph, they were all pissed off. And worse – he looked *foolish*.

Edward hated to be thought a fool. It was his biggest fear –
being mocked, ridiculed. He'd come in, just for a minute, for a
light-hearted poke at the stupid waitress, and now this.

She was in the back room, changing. Her boss was at the
table, trying to calm the fellows down, offering to pay for their
dry-cleaning. Bad publicity, lawsuits, a small item in the *Post*
– he didn't want any of it.

Edward waited until Dina emerged, minus her uniform,
wearing her plain back pants and the tight sweater. She looked
great, like he remembered. He hated her.

'Bitch!' He reached out and gripped her arm. 'You'll pay for
that. I know where you live.'

Dina shook herself free.

Edward glared at her, bitterly. 'I'm coming to get you,' he
threatened. 'Believe it.'

She smiled – and, for the first time that night, it reached her
eyes. 'Oh, no, Mr Johnson, you don't understand. I'm coming
to get *you*.'

Chapter Five

Shelby Johnson was having a wonderful evening.

His lecture series was going down so well. The students and young people were lapping it up. He loved to talk about his foundation, his charity work and his vision for the state. What they weren't doing up in Albany. How all New York's vast wealth never reached the poorest . . .

Of course, Shelby knew all about vast wealth. His charities were tax-efficient write-offs. Coldharbor Bank, where he was president, was doing so well; it was a private haven for the society rich, who all knew him socially. He had a marvellous wife who threw the most wonderful parties, and he arrived at all these events in his personal limousine, complete with vanity plates.

He hadn't announced for Congress yet; that was coming next week.

Frankly, the party machine didn't know what had hit it. He was just smarter than them – smarter than the lot of them, the striving State Senators and pushy little judges and district attorneys who thought they had a shot at the big time.

Shelby was self-financed. He didn't have to raise money – he could just write a cheque.

He had business success – a real track record.

And he'd donated to others long enough to have built up that reservoir of good will. People owed him favours, and Shelby was coming to collect.

This tour was the warm-up act. Nothing stirred voters' hearts like education, not here in New York. And Shelby loved receiving the adulation of the students and the educators. When he jumped on the platform at these community colleges or youth centres, they applauded like he was some kind of rock star. He especially loved it when the kids asked him for advice.

And if they were pretty girls . . .

His eyes slid across to the co-ed, perched on the back seat of his car. Goddamn. The way she looked at him with such hero-worship . . .

Her name was Laura . . . what was it? Oh, yes. Laura Fielding. She was a student at NYU, and she'd really taken to his politics – so to speak.

First he'd seen her in the front row at the Ninety-Second Street Y community centre. She'd asked a question, and smiled and clapped at his response, bouncing up and down in her seat, those firm little titties bouncing along with her.

Next, it was at the Lincoln Center, a free event, and she hung out afterwards.

'Mr Johnson . . . my name's Laura. Laura Fielding. I so admire your politics. Are you going to run? I'd love to volunteer.'

'Thank you . . .' He nearly said, 'honey,' but stopped himself in time. 'What are your contact details?'

She handed over a number on a piece of paper. That low-cut dress, modest below the knees, but – goddamn – what a pair!

He called that night – nothing special, just sounding her out. She was breathy, full of admiration. He was a great man. She wanted him to run. She wanted to help.

'How can I serve?' she said.

Shelby had invited her to the next event. She helped lay out programmes. She was diligent, and very discreet. She was also totally sexually available.

'I want an older man,' she said. 'Somebody who knows what he's doing.'

'I'm married,' he said, weakly.

She pouted and stuck out those fantastic breasts. 'Come on, Shelby, I can't be the first. Anyway, I want to come along for the *ride*. All the way to Washington.'

He couldn't resist. He didn't want to. And now, here she was, in his limo. His *aide* – in a fantastic short skirt, with old-fashioned stockings high up her thighs, and he could see a glimpse of milky-white flesh like a glimpse of heaven.

'We'll head to the hotel,' he told the driver.

'Oh my God.' He stared at the ceiling, panting. 'That was incredible . . . Unbelievable.'

None of the momentary distractions he'd been with before – and there had been one or two . . . hookers, strip-club hostesses – had given him anything like this amount of pleasure. Her firm, tight young body, the beautiful face . . . Echoes of lust were still throbbing in his groin.

'We have to do it again.' His mind was already on to the next time, the next campaign stop, the next hotel. Shelby indulged his fantasies. After he was elected a hero, she'd be given a nice safe job in his office. Nothing too big, of course, but something to keep her always available. Every powerful man should have a sexy mistress. He flashed on Laura Fielding in a silk blouse, tight pencil skirt, seamed stockings. Sucking on a pencil. Sucking on him. 'Maybe I'll see you next week? At Albany?'

'Oh, I can't come up to Albany.' She was across the room, already getting dressed, briskly pulling on some new clothes – a pair of jeans and a sweater. Not the clinging red number she'd been wearing earlier. Laura Fielding was the perfect lay – you banged her, and then she got right up and got *herself* out of the door. 'I'm busy.'

'When will I see you?' Shelby propped himself up on his elbows, looking after her.

'Don't worry.' Laura wasn't looking at him. 'You'll hear from me soon enough.'

The Johnson townhouse was a sedate fantasy of old money.

Walnut panelling lined the Victorian elevator. There was imported Italian marble in the bathrooms, a maid's apartment in the attic, a private garden and a library.

It was the perfect backdrop for the moneyed politician. Or for a bright young buck, launching himself into society – into the same glorious future his mother and father had enjoyed.

Edward Johnson loved his home. He especially loved how it smelled of his mother – the one perfect woman in the world. As her only child, Penelope Johnson had pampered and spoiled Edward since the day he was born. He loved wandering into her boudoir, drinking in the scent of her powder and rosewater. He loved seeing her dressed in evening gowns, tucking him into bed. He loved watching her give orders to the cook, kiss his father on the cheek and generally behave like the perfect wife. Edward loved perfection and his house and mother were the apex of it.

One day, Mrs Edward Johnson would be a replica of his sainted mother. He adored her and, when his friends called him Mommy's Boy, Edward replied, 'Absolutely!'

He was sitting on the covered terrace at the back of his bedroom, eating stuffed olives and sipping an iced tea. Edward regularly went back home for Sunday lunch; that was the great advantage of Columbia – he didn't need to stay in his student apartment any more than he wanted to.

'Darling! Lunch!' his mother called.

'Coming!' he shouted.

The housekeeper had set up their table al fresco, because his mother preferred to dine in the garden in spring. She was immensely proud of this ritual. Father was back from his travels, electioneering, and the three of them would sit around and chitchat over a glass or two of chilled Chablis, a Waldorf salad and some carved ham.

Shelby Johnson was already sitting down, the *New York Times* sports section laid out in front of him, when Edward arrived. His wife was hovering, wearing a light yellow silk dress and a smug expression. Shelby's ascent in the polling was smooth, her social dominance almost complete.

'Some wine, sir?' A butler hovered as Edward threw himself into his seat.

'Yes. Of course.'

'Oh, you're here, Mr Edward. There's a package for you.' The old housekeeper, Selina, came forward and handed him a manila envelope.

'What's this?' he asked.

'It was hand-delivered earlier, sir. There's one for you, too, Mrs Johnson.'

'Thank you, Selina. That's all for now,' his mother said.

'Wait.' Edward felt the first stirrings of unease. 'Hand-delivered? By whom?'

'A young lady.' The older woman turned to leave.

'Wait!' Edward said, sweating. 'Mom! Don't open that—'

Too late. Penny had already neatly ripped the paper and, as he stared in horror, the large, colourful, glossy pictures poured out – nearly twenty of them. They scattered over the table, across it, spilling everywhere, polluting his eyes.

Shelby Johnson – Edward's father.

Shelby Johnson – Penny's husband.

Shelby Johnson – for Congress.

There he was, in all his elderly glory, ridiculously naked, pink-faced, erect. A young woman was straddling him. Her face was blocked out, cut off, but there was no denying it. Shelby Johnson, handcuffed; Shelby Johnson, gagged; Shelby Johnson, licking a pair of stilettos.

Penny Johnson went ashen.

One of the butlers moved forward, to pick up the shots.

'Get back!' Edward barked. 'Leave it! Leave us!'

'Sir . . . ?'

'Now!'

There was a clatter as all the staff withdrew. Penny Johnson started to wail, a keen, high-pitched shriek.

'I . . . I don't know . . . These are faked . . .'

Shelby was puce, muttering. He felt sick. He was dizzy. He gripped the table, hoping not to faint.

'I need to lie down,' he whimpered.

A small, neatly folded piece of letter paper fluttered out of the dreadful envelope to the paving stones of their terrace. Mechanically, Edward picked it up. His mother snatched it from him, held it in trembling hands. Then she read it aloud – the worst words Edward had ever heard in his life:

'*Since your son fucked me for his amusement, I fucked your husband for mine.*'

There was no signature.

Penny Johnson screamed and ripped up the note. She rounded on Shelby. 'You goddamned bastard!'

'It was a mistake . . .'

But Penny was rifling through the pictures. 'A mistake? A mistake? These will wind up in the press. I'll be a laughing stock!'

Shelby looked, moaned in horror. It was worse than being caught cheating. He was ridiculous – totally ridiculous.

He thought of all his friends, laughing. The nudges at the club. The sly looks in the boardroom.

'I can find her, Mother . . .' Edward said. 'I can get her—'

'Get her? You *got* her already, whoever she is . . . You found the lowest whore in the world.'

'Mother!' His mother was swaying. He rushed to steady her. 'I won't . . . let her do anything . . .'

'Find the bitch. Her name is Laura Fielding,' his father said.

Edward moaned in his throat. *Fielding*. The name he'd used. 'That's not her real name.'

'Just find her. What will it take to buy her off?'

'I don't know,' Edward said.

'Find her.'

He looked. He looked for two days. But she was gone, vanished from his sight. The apartment was locked up – sold, so the super told him, twice in a month.

'She lived here.' A hundred-dollar bill loosened his throat. 'Sure, she bought the apartment from the landlord. Sold it three weeks later. She made a nice profit on it, real nice.' He was admiring. 'I couldn't believe . . . Used to be a dump, before her. That kid is going places.'

Yeah – going to jail. For blackmail.

He rang the coffee shop, but she hadn't gone back since she was fired. There was nothing registered in the phone book. And then, on day four, Edward had a bright idea.

He reconnected his old cellphone – the cheap one he'd bought to woo Dina Kane.

Almost instantly, the text came through. It had been waiting for him:

Missing me? You can call.

He rang the number and left a message. In an hour, she rang him back.

'You fucking bitch!'

'How are you, Edward? Don't tell me you've stopped laughing about our little tryst. I thought you and your friends were so amused by it?'

'What do you want? Money? Isn't that what whores want?' He was vicious in his contempt, his hatred. 'How much will it take?'

Edward's family was already shattered. His mother had demanded a divorce and locked herself in her room, throwing things and drinking. His dad had slunk off to the Pierre hotel. He wanted the nightmare to be over, but the pictures were burned into his brain. He blamed his father, and Shelby blamed him, and Penny was diving into the vodka.

'You think I'd ask for money?'

'We don't want those photos in the press.'

'And?' she replied, coolly.

'How much?' *Name a figure. I'll come after you till the end of time. Whatever it takes.*

'I'm not a blackmailer, Edward. That's a felony.'

He bit his lip; he had been hoping to go to the police. Edward's father had contacts there, lots of them.

'If I send those photos to the press, that's my right – first amendment, and all that stuff.'

'What do you *want*?'

'Nothing. But I'm happy to offer you some advice. If I were your father, I wouldn't run for office, and if I were you, I'd drop out of college. You don't deserve to study when girls like me can't.'

'Drop out of college?' He'd be nothing – a trust-fund brat who couldn't hack it.

'It's your choice, of course, but doesn't your mother need you?'

I hate you, he thought. 'You *are* blackmailing me.'

'Hey, you can ignore the advice if you want, Edward Johnson. Nothing you do will affect how I use the photos – or don't use them. What I want is for you to stay the hell out of my life. Got it?'

She was too clever to fall into his trap. He hated her.

'You used my father like a toy.'

'A toy? Like you used me? And how many other girls?' Dina's voice was ice. 'Was my mother a toy when you went hunting for information about my background, just so you could humiliate me in bed? You said my mom was the town slut. Well, what about your dad? Seems we have something in common, no?' She laughed, and he flinched, hearing the loathing in that sound. 'Get over it, Edward. Volunteer at a homeless shelter. You know – do something useful. Goodbye.'

And she hung up.

Edward Johnson looked at the phone for a long time.

Then he made two calls. By the end of the day, Shelby Johnson was no longer a candidate for office, and Edward Johnson had dropped out of college. He didn't ring Dina Kane to tell her.

He knew she would be checking up.

'You little prick,' Shelby Johnson said.

He stared down at his son, sitting there on the couch in his sterile hotel suite. Behind him, the television news channel had his face on it. His goddamned face – not in triumph, the way it was meant to be when he was elected, but grim, like a mug shot.

Shelby Johnson pulling out of Congressional Race. Shock exit by Shelby Johnson. Johnson leaves family home . . .

The headlines scrolled across the screen like a horrible ribbon of smut beneath the pretty, bland faces of the newsreaders, who were talking about him, talking about his family. His marriage. His disgrace.

'We don't know exactly what happened, Joanne, but we have to speculate that some kind of affair is possible. After all, Mr Johnson left the family home last night.'

'His wife briefly left the house this morning and was seen without her wedding ring.'

'The thought of a Shelby Johnson affair will go down very badly with the Democrats, and his employers, Coldharbor Bank, are known to be extremely cautious with their image in the community . . .'

He wanted to switch it off, but he couldn't. They were talking about him, and he was rubbernecking at his own car crash.

'Don't blame me, Pop. I'm not married.'

Shelby grimaced. Penelope was out of control, screeching at him. She wouldn't let him home and he didn't even want to go back. Facing the world seemed impossible. The Democrats wanted him to give a press conference. A press conference!

The thought of those pictures – him, tied down on the bed, legs spread, humbled, into bondage . . . Oh, God. He thought he would kill himself, except he was too cowardly for that.

'But you provoked her, didn't you?'

'I couldn't tell that she was a bunny boiler.' Edward loosened his collar. 'It's your fault; you gave her something to work with; you gave her the photos. The first piece of skirt to throw herself at you and you're off . . . You've humiliated Momma . . .'

'Please don't try to play the moralist with me.' Anger suffused him – at the girl, Edward, his screaming, drunken wife, himself. What the hell? Other men did it, even powerful men – *especially* powerful men, so they said – letting hookers tie them up. But they were *careful*. He hadn't been. It was all over. 'I've lost all the work I put in.' He mopped a tissue over his brow, sweating. The photos loomed in his mind again, as though they were already splashed over page one of the *Post*. 'You're such a self-righteous little jerk, Edward. You've never done a stroke of work in your life. It's my fault; I gave you too much. You should have been working a job this summer, not chasing pussy at some fucking coffee shop. Your grades were dire before this, anyway.'

Shelby thought of the awful phone call, worse by far than his wife's demented crying, from Conrad Peterson, Chairman of Coldharbor. 'We don't think you should resign. Just retire, Shelby. It's better this way, wouldn't you say? So many clients want discretion these days, not scandal, nothing flashy in the bank . . . What did you tell me? Others want publicity; Coldharbor runs from it.'

He hadn't said too much. A call to the lawyers first, perhaps. They couldn't fire him for having an affair. There was no morals clause in his contract.

But, whatever he thought, the ghastly image of the photos . . . being released in the press, passed round at work . . . sniggers, maybe a *bringing the bank into disrepute* line.

Jesus. He didn't know what to do. Shelby hated everybody in the world right now, and his feckless, entitled son most of all. *Edward brought this on him.*

'What are you going to do?' Edward asked.

'Do? What the hell can I do?' Shelby paced. 'Take retirement from the bank, I suppose. Work out a divorce settlement with your mother.'

'Divorce! You have to fight to get her back!'

Shelby rounded on his son. 'Do I? She hasn't exactly stood by me, after one goddamned mistake, has she? She threw me out! No. You know what, Edward? I don't think I owe either of you anything.' He imagined Dina Kane, as he now knew she was called: that firm young body, the ripeness of it. Compared to his wife's ultra-thin, waspish, menopausal flesh . . . Christ, why *should* he try to get her back? The loss of money, of status, of his political dreams – it was all bad enough. He couldn't tolerate months of apologies to Penny as well, just to be allowed back to that sterile bed.

'It'll blow over, Dad.'

'Not soon enough. When is she releasing the damned pictures?'

Edward ran his hands through his hair. 'I don't know. Maybe tomorrow, maybe never, if we give her what she wants: me leaving school; you leaving the race for Congress.'

'I wish she'd just get it over with. And she wouldn't take money?'

He shook his head. 'I offered.'

Shelby thought about it. Leaving, leaving . . . He still had some cards to play. Give Penny the house; take most of the cash. There was an irrevocable trust – she could live off that. He could offer Coldharbor a deal, too – a quiet exit in exchange for an extra couple of million on top of his retirement fund.

It was possible to disappear without resorting to suicide. Florida – it had year-round sun, very few bankers – he was always advising middle-class clients to buy mansions there. The Homestead laws meant your principal residence couldn't be touched, even if you went bankrupt and it was a six-acre palace with a pool.

Plus, nobody there knew him. In his current world, Florida was déclassé. The social registry preferred California for a winter haven – something chic in Malibu. He saw himself living large on half the money – living better, really – a pool, properly divorced, some good therapy, a few nubile girlfriends. And no fucking photos. It was an escape route, a fresh start at almost sixty.

Why the hell not? Let Edward make his own way. No family firm. No handouts. Penny would get the house and plenty for her needs.

He made his decision. Let them all rant and rave, he was going to drop out – in a very moneyed, sun-filled manner.

'The photos are of me. The marriage is over, Edward. You need to stand on your own feet. I'm going to call your mother tonight – or at least her lawyers – and offer a quick settlement.'

'But where will you go?' Edward yelped. 'What will happen to *me*?'

'You're an adult. Make your own decisions,' he said. God, how had he raised this snivelling wimp that wanted his hand held, even now? 'You should have thought about it before dumping on the mad girl. I'm going to leave the state. Nobody really knows me outside of New York. I will retire and go to Florida. And find myself, in peace.'

Damn, if it didn't sound noble, put like that . . . For a moment his mood lightened a little. Perhaps that vicious little tramp had done him a favour, after all.

Dina Kane smiled to herself. The photos were already erased from the memory card, the camera dumped from a car somewhere off the New Jersey turnpike. She'd bought a prepaid phone and called Edward from that – it was in a dumpster two minutes after their conversation.

Now, maybe, it was all over. Now, at last, she could have some peace.

Sleeping with Shelby had been disgusting. But, every second, she'd kept in mind the grinning, mocking face of his son, the way he'd threatened to pass her around his friends, like a piece of meat, called her mom the 'town slut', turned sex into rape, shoving himself deeper, even as she struggled to push him off her. Edward Johnson: a privileged yob who stood for every man who'd ever leered at, drooled over or assaulted her – the guards who'd felt her up in Don Angelo's gatehouse, the boss who'd let her be abused, as long as it kept the customers happy.

Dina no longer believed in love. Revenge was a much more achievable goal. She wasn't going to send those pictures any-where. Just let them sweat; let them all sweat – cheating, lying Shelby; Penny, who raised that pig of a son; and, most of all, Edward, who treated her like a joke.

I just want to level the field.

Shelby would be divorced – his political dreams over. She didn't want a rich, arrogant bastard like him anywhere near the halls of power.

Penny Johnson . . . Dina shrugged to herself. A woman who associated with these assholes was not her problem. There were lots of good divorce lawyers out there . . . And she was better off out of that fake marriage, anyway.

And Edward, the arrogant college boy who'd used her while she slaved just to make the rent. If there was no college for Dina, there would be none for him, either.

Edward Johnson screwed her. Now she'd screwed him back. It was time to move on, to put this behind her.

And Dina truly believed it would be that easy.

Chapter Six

Dina wanted a new start. With the profit from the sale of her studio, she had enough for a small nest egg and a deposit on a cute one-bedroom apartment. It was east of Fifth, but that was OK. Dina liked the neighbourhood, still home to artists, singers, poverty-stricken film-makers and their grim documentaries. The West Village was way too expensive; bankers and movie stars lived there now. But the East Village had its vintage clothing dens, its middle-eastern restaurants and its comic-book stores.

The fashionista in Dina loved it. It was up and coming – like she wanted to be.

The one-bedroom was another fixer-upper. She would insert a mezzanine platform – the ceilings were high – and sell it in six months as 'split level'. If she kept flipping like this, Dina thought, she could have money, real money, by the time she was twenty-one.

But, of course, a job would help.

No more coffee – she was through with waiting tables.

She thought about fashion, but starving new designers couldn't pay her anything and the glossy magazines were full of unpaid interns whose fathers came from the same social scene as Shelby Johnson. Dina experimented with photography, but she had no talent for it.

She hit the New York Public Library. It was no good trying to work her way up; she needed a qualification – some kind of badge. She knew she was good at investing in property and there were night classes to become a realtor, so Dina enrolled.

As ever, the nest egg wouldn't last. She would have to work to support her studying, but she wanted something better than waitressing. Maybe something secretarial . . . At least she could type . . .

The Green Apothecary was a certain type of store: one that did well in the East Village. It was small enough to keep the bills down, and it catered to freaks.

Dina Kane fitted right in.

'Do you like this brand?'

Dina glanced up. It was Hector Green, the old man with a German accent, who owned the store.

'I love it,' she said, honestly, turning over the small pot of cold cream in her hands. It was shipped direct from the Dead Sea, Jordan.

The tiny store had attracted her when she was out walking. Dina was tempted and had taken a break from looking for work. This was no ordinary pharmacist's. They didn't fill prescriptions here or sell Maybelline cosmetics. The higgledy-piggledy shelves were crammed with imported goods: perfume from Paris in dusty glass bottles, English hand-milled soaps, attar of roses from Egypt. Hipsters and old ladies in lace wandered in and out, buying mostly on the packaging, just to be cool. But Dina tried everything.

It was paradise, standing before the ancient, gold-framed mirrors, applying the creams, the buttery eye shadows, the bronze lipsticks. Aladdin's cave. Mostly, she couldn't afford it, but sometimes Dina would treat herself. And Hector would give her tips.

'Try this one.' He offered up a plain-looking ceramic jar. 'Solid perfume from Iran. White musk – thickly scented.'

Dina dipped a finger, and was transported.

'Don't touch that cream.' He warned her off a beautifully

engraved compact from Paris. 'It's anti-aging; the acids will irritate you. All you need is this.'

She picked up the latest, examining it doubtfully. It was a cheap-looking plastic tube from Austria. 'What is it?'

'Primer. Once you apply a few drops, the foundation stays on for days.'

And he was always right.

Dina hung out in the store, spending a lot more time there than money, but Hector never seemed to mind. Hers was the perfect face, and the cosmetics looked wonderful on her – even strange, non-standard colours; she was a young beauty, experimenting.

'I need some concealer. Like, stat,' a girl bellowed.

She was lovely, under it all – Dina registered that at once. She had jet-black hair, run slightly wild, expensively artless clothes and a strong Roman nose that gave character to her face. But her pupils were tight, her skin was haggard, she had spots and her teeth were yellowed. Reddened eyes made her look a mess. She had money, but, boy, was she messed up.

Dina pegged her immediately: the unhappy daughter of one of those rich guys in the West Village; likely saw a therapist a few times a week; heir to a fortune; miserable; self-medicating with alcohol and pot. Pretty, young, up all night . . .

'You don't need concealer.' Hector looked at her like she was mad. 'You need to sleep.'

'Yeah, thanks, Grandpa,' she snapped.

'Actually, you might want to try this – very exclusive – from Milan.' Dina moved forward; she just couldn't bear Hector's hurt look. 'It's a combination: tighteners and brighteners. Use about a quarter's worth on your cheeks and neck and you'll look like you live on carrot juice and sleep in, daily.'

The girl laughed. 'Get out of here!'

'Seriously. Sleep in a bottle.' Dina held it out towards her. It was a marvellous cream; Hector had pointed her to it after she was up all night studying and needed to look fresh for a job interview in the morning.

It cost twenty-three dollars.

'It's expensive though. I don't know if you can afford it.'

Hector opened his mouth, but Dina's green eyes warned him to silence.

'How much?' the girl said, greedily. She was staring at the tube.

'It's a hundred and twenty-three dollars,' Dina said, coolly.

'*How* much? That's bullshit.'

'Hey –' Dina shrugged – 'this isn't a corner pharmacy. I understand; you might want to walk over to Avenue A. They have a store on the corner that sells Revlon. Best drugstore stick for under the eyes.'

She turned to put the tube back on the shelf.

'No. Wait. I can afford it.' The girl hesitated, Dina could see it. Even for the privileged, more than a hundred dollars was a big chunk out of her allowance. 'Can I try a sample?'

'We don't have sample tubes. Up to you, but this will work great on you. I use it myself. We have similar skin.'

The girl cast an expert, assessing eye over Dina. She was slightly older, but her skin was still amazing and it glowed with the perfection of youth and clean living. And Dina Kane epitomised beauty. She was what everybody wanted to be.

'Goddamn. I'll take it.'

Without asking, Dina moved behind the counter. 'A hundred and fifty dollars, please.'

'I thought you said a hundred and twenty-three!'

'Plus tax,' Dina replied. 'And handling.'

The girl meekly fished the bills out of her bag, and Dina handed over the precious cream.

'This stuff really is amazing. Not like the promises you see in the magazines. It works.'

'For how long?' the girl said, suspiciously. Now she'd parted with her cash, she was hovering, like she might ask for a refund.

'For two, maybe three hours. It tightens; it brightens – gets you through your hangover.' Dina smiled. 'Nothing lasts longer, you know. The skin is the biggest organ in your body; it can't be changed by external creams. Temporary tightening effects are just that. This one has light-reflecting pigments and a sunscreen. You will *love* it.' She was congratulating the girl like she'd just won the lottery.

'OK! Great. *Thank* you.'

'Come back; tell us how it worked out. Nobody else stocks it,' Dina said, brightly.

The girl waved; she was already out of the door.

'My God.' Hector breathed out. 'Dina, what the hell were you doing?'

'Selling it,' Dina said, grinning. 'She was so rude. Besides, I think it's underpriced. And it will look awesome on her. She'll be a happy bunny. You don't mind, do you, Hector?'

She laughed and offered him the little sheath of banknotes. Seven twenty-dollar bills and a ten, right there in her hands.

'No. I don't mind.' Numbly he took the money. 'Thank you.'

'I should get going. I have another interview at a secretarial agency. Midtown.' Dina looked hopeful. 'Of course, if you want to give me any free samples . . .'

'No. I don't want to give you free samples,' Hector Green said. 'I want to give you a job.'

She wasn't interested in shelf stacking; she made that clear. And he was equally clear. He wanted her.

'*Liebchen*, I know what works.' Hector sat her down in the back, in his little office. It was narrow, the desk piled high with papers and books. 'I am a research chemist. In my youth, I studied dermatology.'

'Then . . . no disrespect, but how come you're running a beauty store?'

'My wife loved cosmetics. It was our game. I would be horrified at the stuff she put on her skin; I looked at the bottles. Sometimes I mixed lotions just for her.' He sighed. 'Maybe this is a way to stay close.'

'To stay close?'

'She died – in a car crash with our baby daughter.' He looked directly at Dina. 'You know, sometimes they say you will die of a broken heart, but that is a lie. It keeps pumping. And the bills don't care. I wanted to die.'

'And you didn't . . .'

'Kill myself?' His smile never reached his eyes. 'I wanted to do that, too. But my mother was alive. I couldn't leave her with the same loss: a dead child. And by the time she died, I was too much of a coward.'

'It isn't brave to kill yourself, Hector.' Dina felt sick.

'Isn't it? Sometimes I wonder.' His old, thin frame shuddered a little, as though he was shaking something off. 'At any rate, the bills were still coming. I just wanted to live peaceably. So, I don't mix creams anymore, but I sell them. Not well, but I still sell them.'

Dina looked back into the shop, to the cluttered chaos on the shelves. 'You make a profit?'

'Every year.' He lifted his palms. 'Because I buy things that are effective. This is the big secret. I didn't want to work hard. Just to live.'

She chewed her lip. 'You make money despite everything. Because your stuff works.'

'I look at the ingredients.' He leaned in again, as though she had missed the point. 'I'm a chemist.'

'Then what has changed?'

'Dina Kane . . . *Liebchen*,' he said again, affectionately. 'I am sixty-nine. I would like, now, to make a little money so perhaps I can stop working, and still live quietly. Until God sends me to join my Helga.' He lifted a brow. 'This is too morbid for you?'

She shook her head. 'I have longer to live, Hector. You do have great stuff. You realise the store is a disaster?'

He shrugged. 'You can fix that, yes?'

'Yes.' Dina nodded. 'I want you to give me forty per cent of whatever extra we make, on top of your take last year. Fair deal?'

'Fine.' He chuckled. 'You remind me of her, with more fire.'

'I'm not your daughter, Hector. I'm your partner. Your junior partner, but your partner.'

'You want a contract?'

She grabbed a piece of paper, a receipt from a Swiss factory, and wrote on the back of it. 'There. Sign your name, and date it.'

He did so.

'Wonderful,' Dina said, and she felt a shiver of joy run down her spine. Something amazing had just happened. Better than getting a job as a secretary; better than being a paralegal. This – this dusty shop, these unglamorous tubes – this was what she was born to do.

Dina left the office with a key. And when Hector arrived at eight thirty the next morning, the place was transformed.

'I . . . I don't understand.' He gazed around. 'Where is every-thing?'

Dina smiled. 'I've been here since five. Don't worry.'

The cluttered shelves were no more. Half his products were removed, in the back office, stacked in boxes. The rest were laid out, cleanly, on the shelves. Dina had tacked up square, cardboard signs, handwritten in crayon: EYES – DAY CREAMS – NIGHT CREAMS – HANDS – BRONZER – BLUSH, and on and on. Under specific products, like a high-class vintner, she'd written up a little pitch:

Egyptian – smells sexy for days.

From Finland – best European sunscreen for perpetual summer days.

This is mascara that never flakes – with plastic proteins to separate lashes.

95

Try this when you're sick – better than a facial.

Dina had rigged up lamps, little spotlights from Ikea that beamed on to the shelves. There was wood, but no dust – the floor was swept, the office vacuumed, even the shelves had been gone over with a feather duster. The counter was bare of junk: nothing there but the register and a small black machine.

'What is this?' asked Hector.

Dina smiled. 'Now we take credit cards. Welcome to the modern world, partner.'

Hector Green couldn't believe his luck.

At first, it was disconcerting – the way he was pushed out, moved over, swept aside. The girl ripped through his store like a mini-tornado, as though he had hired six of her. The first day was just the start. As customers came back in, and marvelled, Dina was on them like a wasp at a picnic. She read people – that was her brilliance – standing back when a woman just wanted to browse; right there when she looked like she might buy something. And it was never a simple, 'Can I help you?'

Dina Kane didn't ask women what they wanted. She told them.

'Your skin tone is a perfect match for this lipstick.'

'That's a great bronzer. Have you considered a hand cream? This one has the most natural self-tanner on the market. So light you can hardly see it.'

'You want something for your neck as well? This will tighten the skin and protect the décolletage.'

'Don't use that moisturiser under the eyes – different skin. Try this cream.'

'This Swiss shampoo deposits silver tones in your hair – it will kill the brassiness.'

And they listened – they all listened. Within a week, word was spreading. Ladies came back with their friends. He had less on the shelves, and was selling twice as much.

For the first time in years, Hector Green sensed an unfamiliar feeling – excitement. He could not help it. There was an audible crackle inside his tiny store. Shoppers who browsed were picking up items, buying them, returning for more. He started to see money, real money, in the till. The rent was paid off earlier in the month. He was released from standing around, could go back to his office to take control of his books, do a little stocktaking. Reluctantly at first, then more confidently, he was able to leave the store by seven p.m. Then six. He started to sleep better, to wake sooner.

Dina made things easy. Dina made things interesting.

'We've sold out.' She marched into the back room. 'Give me some stock.'

'I . . . I haven't ordered the new pieces yet.' Hector was flummoxed; it normally took months for his little orders to sell through. Now five pale-pink lipsticks would go in days. He wasn't ready for this level of traffic.

'Don't panic. Here's a list.' Dina handed him a piece of paper, with order numbers neatly typed. 'We just put the other stuff on the shelves. You'll need more quantity next time.'

'OK.'

The next week, she came into the office. 'I'm going to spend some money. About four thousand dollars.'

Hector had never spent that much in his life. 'On what?'

'A computer, a printer, some professional stock-taking software.'

Dina looked so certain, he never thought of arguing. 'OK.'

'We're opening new files,' Dina said, 'on our best customers. I've already done most of it. Can I walk you through it?' She sounded confident, and she was. Three years in the city and already she felt like Tuckahoe was another world.

There was no college for Dina, only slavish hard work. She

might have suffered abuse and humiliation at the hands of Edward Johnson, but she had paid him back. His father, too. And the work she was doing now, at the Green Apothecary – it was far closer to her dreams. Dina Kane was putting herself through an MBA – not in a classroom, but right out in the field, taking this old, creaking business and letting the light in. Automating it. Making it work.

Hector looked at the young girl. He was sixty-three; she was twenty – and sometimes he wondered who was the adult, and who the juvenile in the relationship.

'You need to know how it works, in case you have to do it. If I'm not here.'

He felt a rush of panic. 'What do you mean, if you're not here? Why wouldn't you be here?'

'You know,' Dina said. 'In case I take a day off.'

'A day off?' he repeated, slowly.

She smiled. 'People sometimes have vacations.'

People, he felt like saying. *Not you.*

Dina Kane was a machine. She worked six days a week; maybe she slept all day Sunday. He never heard her talk men, never saw her with a friend. It was one of the reasons he liked the girl. She was just like him.

'So, let me show you,' she explained. 'Here are the names – with notes. It's linked to the credit cards. When they swipe it, this will pop up on your screen. Abigail Adams: she's first on the list. Spends about three hundred a month. Age: early forties. Best products for her: moisturisers, tighteners, Dead Sea hand cream. Colours: she likes to buy pinks; steer her to pink golds – they look better on her skin and will get her more compliments. Open to perfume – think naturals. Last thing she bought: natural-fibre brushes from Japan.'

'Wow.' He didn't know what else to say.

'Look.' Dina jumped from her seat and did a little pantomime. 'Abi! How nice to see you. Did you like the brushes? They hold powders much better than the artificial stuff, don't they? Oh, Dina said that, if you came in, I should point out the new lip glosses from Portugal. A little company in Lisbon hand-makes them. Great rose-gold colours she thinks would suit your look. We only have a few in stock, though.'

He laughed. 'I'm almost ready for rose-gold lip gloss myself.'

'It's about getting to know them, so they feel it's personal.' Dina smiled, proudly, and her mentor felt the happiness, the glow of achievement, bouncing off her. Goddamn it, if he could bottle *that* look, he'd make his fortune.

'You told me once your shop worked because the products worked?' she said.

He nodded. 'Of course.'

'This takes it one step further: which products work best for which women. Beauty is personal; beauty is unique. So, when they feel you know them, they come back.'

My God, Hector thought. *She really is a little genius.*

'Little Sis!' Johnny exclaimed. 'It's so good to see you!'

'You too, Johnny.' She threw her arms around him. 'And Brad. How are you doing?'

'I'm good.' Brad came over and shook her hand, shyly. Johnny threw his arm around Brad, kissing him on the lips.

'I'm sorry. He gets all worked up about meeting family.'

Dina smiled at her brother's boyfriend. 'You tell Mom yet?'

A slight chill descended across the table. Johnny shook his head.

They were eating Sunday lunch together: dim sum at the Nom Wah Tea Parlour in Chinatown, tucked away in a little back street and with one of the best menus in the city.

'Are you sure you can afford it?' Johnny whined, when Dina offered to pay for his cab into the city. 'Taxi fares are horrendous.'

'Just get a car. I want to meet the new man.'

Johnny was her family, her life outside work. It was easier, these days, for Dina to hear about his time at college. It wasn't *his* fault that Mom played favourites; Dina hoped for Johnny to succeed. As weak and passive as he'd been, he at least liked her, loved her. She would head out to see him most Sundays, and they'd get a beer, or sit in a coffee house or the dorm and talk. Six months ago, he told her he was gay, and now he'd met someone serious.

'I guess it's a big shock,' Johnny had said, his voice trembling.

She was surprised at how obvious it suddenly seemed. 'Not at all. Good for you, Johnny. I just want you to be happy.'

He was scraping through his studies. He'd switched majors – and his GPA looked like alphabet soup: a B here, a C there. Now he was in Peace and Justice Studies, and had no idea what he was going to do when he graduated.

'Maybe go to business school,' Johnny said, vaguely.

'Mom doesn't have any more money.'

'Oh. Right. Well, I'll get a job in social work, I guess.'

'OK,' Dina said, anxiously. 'Have you thought about where?'

Johnny sighed. 'Don't bug me about it. I'm a student. Are you always so type A?'

Dina was happy to see Johnny, and at least she was getting to meet the boyfriend. Maybe Brad could save her brother – he was studying pre-law – maybe they would settle down, he could whip Johnny into shape . . .

She hoped so. Johnny was her only family. The only small piece of love in her life.

'So, Brad, you like dim sum?'

He rolled his eyes. 'Dina, please; I'm Jewish. I was *born* for dim sum.'

She laughed. She liked this guy already.

It was a pleasant meal; Dina found it hard to relax, but she was trying. Having Sundays with her brother said something important: that she was a person, not a machine; that she could feel, she could switch off.

Sometimes she asked herself why doing well mattered so much. But, mostly, she just didn't have time. Work consumed her; the Green Apothecary was everything. She wasn't going to be her layabout mom, depending on wise-guy money, or her dad, who worked and died on a building site.

She wanted more. Much more.

Sometimes, at night, when she was exhausted, Dina thought about a boyfriend. But Edward Johnson hung in her mind, as did the men that had swarmed round her drunken, wasted mom.

It all seemed pointless. She could only rely on herself.

Her big brother reminded her she was human. She had someone. It might be imperfect, but it was family.

'So, the store's doing well,' she said, brightly.

'That's good,' Johnny offered. 'Can I get some more pork buns?'

Brad passed them over. 'How long have you been there now?'

'Coming up for six months. We're making real money.' She already had her one-bedroom apartment fixed up and under offer; she was shopping for a new place. 'My guess is that, this year, I might make about fifty-five thousand.'

Johnny finally sat up. 'Who? You?'

Dina nodded with pride. God, it was *so good* to be able to tell somebody, to share this with her brother – someone who wasn't Hector.

'Goddamn. That's real money.' He nudged Brad. 'That's my sister!'

'I know, dude. That's awesome. Congratulations.'

'I'm getting a new apartment. There's a two-bedroom in Murray Hill I want.'

'Renting?' Johnny asked.

'Buying.' She blushed slightly. 'I've got a small nest egg, you see, from my other two places . . . Sold them both for a profit . . .'

'Two places?' Johnny's mouth was open. 'I don't get it. You only just got here.'

'It's been nearly two years, Johnny. I bought as soon as I could.'

Her brother reached over, pinched her. 'Are we really related?'

I wonder that sometimes myself, Dina thought. But she smiled indulgently.

'Hector.' Dina's voice was calling him from the back office.

He put down the tube of eye cream he was showing the young tourist from Tokyo. 'Excuse me.'

When his young partner called, he came. It didn't even occur to him to tell her to wait. Dina Kane never waited.

'It's crazy out there. It's just insane,' Dina said. 'Look at them.'

'*Ja*. I know.' The older man glanced back; his store was full. Women, and a few men, were crowding the place. For the last three weeks, it had been like this – after work, at lunch hour. People would flood in. The small store had no space.

'They're panic buying. Everybody wants in.'

'Isn't that a good thing?'

'Not really.' Dina scowled. 'We have a reputation, Hector. We're selling things that make women look good. *On them.*'

'Of course. Then they tell their friends.'

'Now women are just buying anything. I can't get out there to give advice. We're too busy.'

'So, we hire somebody. Just to stand behind the till.' He had thought about this for at least two weeks. 'You are more valuable than ringing up prices, Dina.'

She laughed. 'It's bigger than that. We need to expand. We need a new store.'

He blinked. 'What? I live here.'

'A second store. A system. Staff.'

The old man had a sinking feeling. 'Dina . . . this . . . this is not for me. I just want a quiet life.'

She gestured at the shoving, angry crowd; the moneyed women, all scared they were missing something.

'And how quiet is that?'

No matter how hard she worked, Dina could not persuade him. Hector didn't want the risk; his vision had been for a successful shop, nothing beyond that.

'We could run an online business. Sell from a website,' Dina suggested.

'I'm a chemist,' Hector muttered. 'I don't trust these things. And it's too complicated . . . how I pick my stuff . . .'

'But Hector—'

'No, Dina. Enough. I'm not you.'

'We think you'll love it here. Excellent access to First Avenue . . . and a view of the river.'

'Yes, thank you. I can see.'

'Would you like a little time to yourself?'

The realtor's smile froze on her face. *Bitch*, she thought. This young girl was so stuck-up, with her insistence that Laurel be exactly on time, and her sheaf of financials. She was probably some rich kid playing at living alone, anyway. This apartment was over a half million dollars. How would a girl like this even come close to the deposit?

'How big is the maintenance?'

'Oh, hardly anything. The building has a doorman, but rates are very low. Less than five hundred a month.'

'Offer four eighty-five.'

Laurel smirked. *Yeah, right.* She was hardly going to waste her seller's time. 'I'll need to see your financials.'

The girl looked her dead in the eyes. 'I have a mortgage commitment from Washington Mutual. I brought the pre-approval letter with me.'

She passed it over. Laurel Sloane scanned it quickly.

'This is a no income verification loan. You'd need a twenty per cent deposit for that, I'm afraid.'

'I have a twenty per cent deposit. And I'm liquid, ready to close in thirty days. Ms Sloane, I'm going to buy *something*, and you're obliged to pass my offer on. I'm sure your seller would want me to get this one.'

Laurel wavered. She disliked the girl, but there was some sort of certainty about her. Very disconcerting but, like the boss said, you never know who has the money . . .

'There are other places I could show you. More expensive, more space. There's one on Forty-Third with a balcony—'

'No. This is perfect.' Dina looked around the apartment again: one reasonable bedroom, a small second one, a bathroom with a shower, unremarkable small kitchen and a living room cramped with a couch and a TV. The windows were large, though, and the place was a block away from the UN. The East River was clearly visible, and the full west aspect would let light sink in there all day.

It was small – maybe a thousand square foot – and the décor was dark and overstuffed.

'Well – we all have our passions. If you've found your home . . .'

Dina wanted to laugh. Home? On Forty-First and First? She wouldn't be here above eight months. No, she looked around and she was already stripping the apartment, gutting it, adding light, space, and nearly a million dollars to its value.

'. . . Just buy it,' she said.

Dina didn't argue.

'I have the answer,' Dina told Hector a week later, 'if you really don't want to expand.'

She was stuck. She liked Hector Green; he was her friend – her mentor, in a way. He'd hired her and, in all this time, he never hit on her, never made an advance, never 'accidentally' groped her butt. With Hector, she'd found stability, success. She put Edward and Shelby Johnson behind her.

But Hector was doing something impossible for her to stomach. He was trying to stand between her and her goals. The old man wanted modest success, and then he wanted to pack up and go home. Already, Dina realised, her dreams were so much bigger than that. She didn't want to leave him, and she couldn't. Who knew of their success? Only Hector . . . and a few of their customers.

But his name was on the store. His name was on the bank accounts. She credited him for sourcing the products; she just sold them. Young Dina Kane wanted to be a businesswoman, but mostly now she was a talented shopgirl.

Hector was digging his heels in. The customers scared him. The pace . . . the ordering . . . even the money. Dina knew she was a great judge of beauty, of style, but she also believed in the fundamentals. What worked? She would not know that . . . not without a chemistry degree. Even if she walked out today, it wasn't as easy as quitting.

'Please, Dina. Not again.' Hector sat down heavily, rubbing his forehead. 'I am a scientist. This is *wunderbar*, *fantastisch*, really great. But you are going fast . . . very fast for me. I don't want to move. Not another shop . . .'

'Let's think differently. You're working hard . . .'

He nodded. So many things to order, calls to make. It had never been this quick. He was starting to feel overwhelmed.

'But you should concentrate on what you do best. You're a chemist; you analyse the ingredients.'

'Yes. That's what I do.'

'What if we didn't have three hundred products, and all these orders? What if we just had one product?'

Hector blinked. 'That's crazy. The women want skin, make-up, scent. Everything, everything.'

'Right now, yes. But, Hector, what if you, yourself, made up a cream? A day cream. Something revolutionary. Your own brand. And we got the packaging, we sold it.'

'*I* make a cream?'

'Yes. Later on, maybe, you could do more in the range – if you wanted. But for the start, just one cream.'

'We can't make profit by selling one product here,' Hector said, slowly. But his eyes were flickering; he was already thinking about it. For years it had frustrated him, picking the best creams of a bad bunch, the inconsistency in batches, everything.

'We wouldn't have to. If you make a great product, we can sell it other places, too. I can do that for you,' Dina said, confidently. 'I know I can.'

'Well, there is a place I can work. I have friends – chemists. I know a small laboratory in White Plains.' Hector's anxiety was already dissipating. He was thinking about the cream. 'There are ingredients most do not use, as they are too costly for the mass market, but they work. Topical peptides. Salicylic acid. Vitamin E . . . and I like the compounds found in the Dead Sea mud . . . with sunscreen, a light sunscreen . . .'

'What will it do?'

'Very mild exfoliation, hydration and sun. You see –' Hector began to get worked up – 'the commercial creams mostly over-exfoliate. You cannot use that every day. It will strip the skin of oils. They get dry . . . If you go gently, very gently, the skin will become cleaner, softer. And a strong sunscreen . . .'

'You see? You want to do it,' Dina said.

'Yes.' He looked back into the shop. 'But I will have to go away. It will take some time to formulate. To be perfect.'

'Work there three days a week,' Dina said. 'I can handle this.'

In the end, it took five months. Hector didn't spend three days a week there – he disappeared. Dina was on her own, and it was a liberation. Without asking, she took control of the books, the marketing, the merchandise. She hired a couple of beautiful, smart students from NYU to help on the till, and made them up so they looked like models.

Every day, Hector would call, or email.

'The mixing is smooth.'

'Acid balance not right yet.'

'I have a manufacturer . . . Test batches tomorrow.'

She wired him money from the store, money they could barely afford. The profit was dipping. Dina took decisions, only spending where she thought it best: staff wages; sanding the floors and painting them a light, pale green. She decorated the walls in eggshell and hung mirrors everywhere to reflect light; it also allowed customers to see themselves clearly. Dina chose real sunlight bulbs, and those were expensive. But she was committed to quality. *No-regret buying*, Dina thought; her customers would see the cosmetics in true light, not flattering store bulbs.

She sunk money into their accountant, into their computers. Finally, she began to get a grip on the stock, the income, the taxes. The Green Apothecary was ready. But the cash was gone.

Dina tried not to panic. It was her decision; Hector was absorbed in his batches and testing. They were ready now, ready for bigger things. But they had no money.

She reserved just a tiny amount. Not for petty cash – for packaging. And every Sunday she went back out to see Johnny, using Metro North, to eat in a Mount Vernon diner. No more dim sum. Neither she nor Johnny could afford it. For once, she had barely touched her new apartment. The refurb would take cash – and every red cent was sunk into the Green Apothecary.

Dina didn't tell Hector she was using her personal money. The cash-flow problem was hers to deal with; she wanted Hector as a chemist, with nothing on his mind but the cream.

'I'm coming home,' Hector informed her on the phone one Monday. 'I will be there tomorrow.'

'Fantastic,' Dina replied.

She couldn't eat much that evening, couldn't sleep. Both of their futures depended on this working.

Dina looked down at the jar.

It wasn't much – maybe an ounce. Plain, hard and grey. She tapped it with her elegant nail, painted in Chanel's *Rouge Argent*, a silvery pink she loved. It chimed, lightly.

'Vitreous glass,' Hector said. 'Porcelain will crack. Anyway, it needs to be dark, to stabilise the minerals.'

'Let me try it,' she said. Delicately, she dipped her finger in the jar. It was thick – really thick. Smooth. Cool. There was a faint scent, maybe violets, something watery and light.

'You must rub it in your palm.'

'Why?' Her heart sped up a little. People were not patient; they wanted immediate gratification.

'To loosen the oils and vitamins. Warm it in the palm, then rub it on your skin.'

She hesitated. 'Won't that put customers off, Hector?'

'Only if they are fools.'

'Right,' she said. 'Excellent.'

He shrugged. 'The best ingredients cannot be worked together into a simple paste. The binding agent will smother some of the effects. I use algae here – Dead Sea compounds.'

She did as she was told and the cream released more scent. Slowly, Dina rubbed it into her face. It felt wonderful: soft and perfect. She hadn't slept much, and immediately her skin was tautening, brightening. The ingredients were sinking in, different somehow from other creams.

'Wait. It is important to wait.' Hector instructed.

She took a little more, warmed it in her palm and spread it across her face, her neck. 'Eyes?'

Hector nodded. 'It is protective. It can work there too.'

Next she took a foundation, a liquid number from Berne, and applied it.

'Beautiful. See?' She turned her face to Hector. 'It goes on so matte. It's like a wonderful primer.'

'For you it will tighten. For older women, it temporarily softens wrinkles. The stuff is easily absorbed to the dermis. It gives a rosy look because it promotes blood flow to the skin. This will have knock-on effects: it will slow aging, environmental damage. The sunscreen is full.'

'Blood flow to the skin?'

'It has collagen.' He was almost not listening to her questions. 'It will add what city life takes out, like a day in the country.'

Dina looked at herself; her foundation was still airbrush perfect.

'Hector, you're a genius. That's what we call it: *Meadow*. Because it brings the countryside to you.'

'Meadow. I like that,' he said, and nodded. 'I tested it on people with severe acne – it helps; and on victims with scars and burns – it assists healing.'

She clenched her fist, trying not to get excited. 'How much does it cost to make?'

The old man looked shifty. 'Uh . . . That depends . . .'

'Hector. *How much*?'

'About sixty-five dollars a jar.' He looked defensive. 'There are costs . . . It will need chemists . . .'

Dina was quiet for a moment.

'Then this is a two-hundred-dollar cream. Top of the line. And we have to test it commercially, here, first.'

'We can borrow some money . . .'

'There is no money,' Dina said. 'Our customers will have to do the testing.'

She was cautious. At first, there were just whispers to their best, most respected customers: the older ones – the ones who spent all the money.

'Anti-age. Proprietary. Would you like a sample jar?'

'Oh, Mrs Cohen, it's really very expensive. Far more than La Prarie. Will you try it for us?'

When they loved it, Dina expanded just a touch. She gave small jars to students – the ones with the worst pimples; to a pretty girl with blotchy skin; to a rosacea sufferer; to a soccer mom in her thirties with a great look, nice skin, whom she asked to use it as a primer.

Everybody raved. They wanted more. Their friends dropped by, asked for samples of their own.

'Make up a batch,' Dina instructed. 'Five hundred jars.'

Hector was horrified. 'We don't have that kind of money. You wiped us out. We're barely making the bills . . .'

'Next month will be more. Hector, we have to have a real batch. Get me five hundred jars. I will take charge of the boxes.' She had the design already: pretty little stars and flowers scattered across recycled green cardboard, with the word MEADOW emblazoned in gold. *Bring fresh to your face*, was the slogan. *Meadow is different.*

'Dina.' Now Hector's nerves were returning. He loved going back to the lab, loved making the cream, adored the thankful women as they raved about what it did for their faces . . . But money . . .

He brought Dina in to fix that. For a while, she had. Now there was a black hole again. And she wanted him to borrow, to risk everything he had . . .

'Go to the bank. We need to sell this cream.'

'I can't.' As soon as he said the words, he knew. 'It's my home. I can't risk that.'

Dina put her head in her hands. 'Jesus! Then *I'll* do it. I'll go to the bank. There's money in my apartment.'

'But it's all you own.'

'Not for long.' Dina put her small hand over his large, wrinkled one. 'It's mine, though – if I get the cash. You need to give me the formula, let me control the marketing. I take half the profits for that; you take the other half, for inventing it. I'm going to get a lawyer to draw up the papers, and you need one, too. OK, Hector?'

Who could argue with her? He wasn't going to try. 'OK.'

By the time Dina came back to her apartment that evening, she was exhausted.

She'd visited five different banks, before she found one that'd lend her the money. Two different attorneys. A horrible meeting in a stuffy West Village office, as Hector passed over the paper, and they both signed in triplicate. Dina Kane was now down most of her life's savings and, in return, she had a piece of paper, the number of a small factory in New Jersey and half a pot of face cream.

She'd never felt happier. And, as she showered in her unpainted bathroom and scrubbed her body with plain carbolic soap, Dina Kane whistled to herself. She stepped out, towelled off and threw on her white waffle dressing gown. It was dark but, even on the edge of the city, electricity pulsed through her windows: the traffic driving up First Avenue, the lights of the barges on the East River, the looming towers of the UN.

This would be the last year she would see this view, Dina vowed. Next year – Fifth Avenue.

Nothing was going to stop her.

Chapter Seven

'Pass me that,' Edward said. He pointed.

The waiter bowed slightly. 'Yes, sir. Certainly.'

'No, man. Not the cigars. The paper.'

'Of course, sir.'

The older man handed over the *Times* with an inscrutable expression on his face. He had learned the hard way never to show any emotion, especially contempt. Johnson was just the latest in a long line of moneyed losers. He showed up to the club at eleven and was drunk by half past; cocktails before lunch, wine with his steak, a digestif with coffee, and an afternoon sherry to pass the time.

It ran in the family, so they said. After the big society divorce, Shelby Johnson had run out of town – left the state altogether. No more Congress. No more Coldharbor Bank. He stepped down with a modest payout and, rumour had it, he was living quietly in Florida. They had sun there, and a law that said they couldn't take your house. The gossips were having a field day.

Penelope Johnson had really fallen apart. During the divorce – and the huge settlement – ladies around town whispered that she had Shelby over a barrel. How else to explain the giant cash settlement, millions for the maintenance, the way she kept the house?

But Penny paid the price. Women, slowly but surely, stopped coming to her parties. Invitations dried up. After all, it was so much safer to invite couples. Penny was touched by some hint of scandal . . . Nobody knew exactly what yet. Why had Shelby left? Was it her? Was he gay? Besides, a single woman of fortune might tempt their menfolk . . .

She was drinking . . . even more. And now the doctor had given her pills, too: anti-stress; anti-anxiety; pills to sleep.

Penny showed up at town charity events wearing tight dresses, her hair suddenly dyed blond. She looked desperate. Her eyes shone with a chemical glow.

'Jesus, Mom.' Edward watched in horror as she clutched a champagne flute at the Metropolitan benefit. 'Seriously. You just *can't*. Stop.'

'And why shouldn't I have a little fun? You're such a party pooper.'

'Mom, you're forty-eight. Come on . . .'

'I'm still attractive. Surgeons can do incredible things these days.'

Edward called her doctor. 'My mother is sick. If you so much as touch her face, I'll file a malpractice suit that will knock you off your ass . . .'

It worked. Beaten, bowed, humiliated, Penelope just gave up. She retired to her bedroom and barely came out for weeks.

Edward was almost glad he was out of college. He couldn't take the snickering. Even now, his phone rang and he heard giggling at the end of it. He changed his mobile number. So they thought it was funny, did they? Fuckers . . .

He let his mother sit there, in the house, rotting with her booze and her pills. He couldn't take the actual work to get her 'better': the AA meetings, the humiliations of rehab. The perfect woman was ruined. He detested her now, like he detested the embarrassment, the weakness of his father.

And most of all, he detested Dina Kane.

The best you could say was that she was some poor little nothing, a shopgirl, a nobody. For weeks, he'd waited for those pictures to appear, waking every morning in a cold sweat, waiting for his phone to ring, for the emails to come in.

Nothing. Every time he picked up a copy of the *Post*, page six was empty. There was nothing.

So that was it. He dropped out; his father vanished. And so had that bitch of a waitress. *Forget it.*

Edward tried to. But his golden world had turned to tin.

He had no idea what to do. His so-called friends were gone; invitations were drying up. Edward was no longer a favoured heir. Instead, he was just the remnant of a family in a social death spiral. The only kids that wanted to know him now were the hangers-on, the poor ones, the middle-class thrusters who liked to be with the rich.

He had dreams, fantasies of revenge, of restoring his family name, acting the way his cowardly father refused to.

'No, Edward,' Shelby said on the phone. 'I'm not coming back up there.'

'Mom needs you.'

'She wanted the divorce. She got what she asked for.' His father's voice was distant, detached. 'Maybe it's all for the best. I'm enjoying my life down here now; I'm finding myself; the sun shines; you know . . .'

'Jesus! No, I don't know. I know you ran away.'

'Edward, my life up there is over. I don't want to see those people anymore.'

'Dad . . .'

'You're a young man. You have to make your own way.'

'At what?' Edward shrieked. 'I had to drop out of college! Because of you! I was supposed to work at the firm, but you quit! Now what am I to do?'

'It's not my problem. You're twenty-one now, Edward. When I was your age, I was working in Wall Street . . .'

'I didn't get to graduate,' Edward whined. 'I don't even have a liberal arts degree . . .'

'Then find a job. It's what most men do.'

Edward swallowed hard. 'I'm not most men, Daddy; that's not how you raised me.'

A long sigh. '"Daddy"! Listen to yourself. Come on, Edward, you need to discover your own purpose, not mooch off your mother and me.'

'With what? How?'

'I can't hold your hand. If you can't think of anything else to do, join the army. It's been the making of several young men.'

'The army!' Edward's shriek rose into hysterical, high-pitched giggles. 'The army! Right – that's good. Look, just wire me some fucking money.'

'I need what I have. Your mother has all the money.'

'I'm your son!'

'My grown son.' Another sigh. 'Obviously I failed you, Edward. You were meant to stand on your own two feet.'

'Spare me the fucking lecture, old man!' Edward screeched. But Shelby had already hung up.

There was the trust fund – but that was a pittance.

'Just advance me some cash,' Edward said, confidently. He was dressed in one of his best suits – Armani – with a crisp silk shirt. Rutger Helmand was his father's private banker; he had dined at the Johnson house many times over the years.

'From which account do you want it?' Rutger smiled sympathetically. They were meeting on Park Avenue, in his office, which resembled an English country drawing room. This was how the upper classes did their banking, with Persian rugs on the floor, oil paintings of pheasants on the walls; nothing so vulgar as a rack of terminals. He was glancing at the discreet computer monitor placed on his mahogany desk.

'The family trust.'

'Of course. I'm authorised to make disbursals. How much would you like, Edward?'

He shrugged. 'Not much. Just half a million dollars?'

Rutger's eyes widened. 'Oh, no. I can only allow you to have five thousand, every six months.'

Edward's eyes narrowed. 'I have a trust fund, don't I? Three million?'

'It matures when you're thirty-five.'

Thirty-five? He may as well be dead.

'And your father's sign-off will still be required.'

He buried his head in his hands. That only left his allowance. Ten thousand a month: it was a pittance.

'Goddamn it, Rutger.'

'You must talk to your parents. By the way, you do know your allowance has been stopped?'

The head shot up. 'Huh?'

'Your father wired me this morning. I'm afraid it's all in order. He says you will be earning your own money from now on.'

'That's . . . that's not right.' Edward started to panic. 'Call him!'

'I did.' Rutger began to squirm slightly, and Edward had that sinking feeling, that all too common feeling. He was in the middle of a scene. Only this time, he was causing it. 'Really, Edward, I can't interfere. Have you spoken to your mother?'

She was at home, no doubt, wearing a silk dressing down and downing her third vodka gimlet of the morning.

'No. But, of course, I will.' Edward pulled himself together, forced himself to stand up. 'How much is left in my own account?'

'Almost two hundred thousand,' Rutger replied, reassuringly.

Peanuts. That wouldn't get him to first base.

'Terrific,' Edward forced himself to say. 'I think I'll head out to the club.'

* * *

The waiter handed over the copy of the *Times*, and Edward snatched it closer.

His heart thumped. Now, even his sanctuary was about to be invaded. The club . . . He was listed on his father's membership. The Farmers' Club was one of the oldest in the city, with burgundy leather armchairs, fine wines, a smoking terrace for cigars and a reassuringly white, male and exclusive membership. Edward enjoyed the calm, the obsequiousness. His mother was nowhere about. He moved in the pleasant hush of old money, the hush he'd been born into. And nobody objected to his drinking.

If he wanted coke, he went elsewhere, stumbled out on to the street, fished the tiny glass vial and miniature spoon from a hidden inner pocket. Not in the Farmers' Club . . . Edward had no wish to get banned, not from his last, best home.

And now, there was that flash of recognition. His heart thumped. He snatched the paper off the silver tray, greedily holding the newsprint to him, reading it.

Dina Kane is a newcomer to the world of beauty. The twenty-year-old has impressed with early sales of the 'Meadow' facial cream, reported to deliver superior skin toning, priming and moisture benefits. Now stocked at Saks, Bergdorf's, Glamour and other high-end stores, 'Meadow' is already racking up healthy sales, with a local New Jersey factory struggling to keep pace.

'We're different. We're chemist-designed. This is beauty for all skins,' Ms Kane said.

Challenged on the soaring $300 price, she replied, 'Meadow isn't for everyone. With no compromise on ingredients, it means no compromise on price.'

Ms Kane reportedly has a fifty-per-cent interest in the new company. 'Meadow' cream is now obtainable at all fine stores, or direct via the company website. But, be warned: there's a waiting list.

Edward read the item twice, three times. His head was pounding. The dry text swam before his eyes.

Oh, it was her, all right. The grainy black-and-white photo showed that. The pretty, cruel young face next to the delicate jar of product. *Beauty*. Somehow it did not surprise him. Beauty was the one thing she had in abundance. Style on a shoestring. And, now, maybe not such a shoestring.

He hated the words 'Kane' and 'company'. That slut was nothing. She was a gold-digger like the rest of them, only more vicious. She was meant to be serving coffee – and more – to him and his friends.

Dina Kane had not gone away. Edward was here, drunk, lonely, almost broke. His mother was a slave to her addiction, his father a dropout. And she was attempting – actually managing – to move up in the world.

He hated her. He remembered her body. Underneath the drunkenness, it stirred him.

Edward pushed himself to his feet. He wanted women; he wanted pussy. There were drugs that could make the booze go away.

'I'll put it on your tab, sir, shall I?' asked the waiter.

But Edward Johnson was already gone.

'It's selling extremely well.'

Dina was standing in the executive offices of the Glamour store on Fifth Avenue. She nodded as Jane Bowes, the buying director, scrolled through her slides.

'As you can see, another seventy-five per cent volume in the first month. But our customers are complaining about wait times. It's bad for the store if we have to tell them to hold on.'

Dina nudged Hector, standing beside her, awkward in his new three-piece suit.

'We understand,' she said. 'We are shifting production. There's another factory lined up, in Canada. And one in Milan that will service Europe.'

'Glamour wants to be first in line.'

'You are a premium customer. We're going just as fast as we can.'

'Maybe you'd consider developing a new product, just for Glamour. Say, a night cream. We hold, as a chain, to ethical production methods . . .'

'We know that,' Dina said. 'No exclusives.'

The girl ignored her, addressing Hector directly. 'A million-dollar advance before you sell a single pot, Dr Green. And all your sales on top of that.'

Dina stood up. 'This meeting is over.'

'I understand you have an interest in Meadow cream, Ms Kane, and we respect that, but Dr Green is a free agent, isn't he? You don't own all his future work.'

Dina glared at Hector. 'We are leaving. Are you coming?'

He looked wildly from one woman to the other. Christ! *A million dollars.* He'd never have to work again. And before he sold a single pot . . .

And yet there was the girl, his young partner, glaring at him, like she was eighty years old and his mother . . .

'Yes. Coming.' He felt resentful. He had mentored this girl, offered her help, assistance. And she was ordering him around – had done from the start. Now his cream was working and Dina was taking half. Sure, he was grateful . . . and she was energetic . . . but if they wanted to give him a million . . .

She was in her twenties; he wanted to retire.

We are leaving. So easy for her to say.

But he got to his feet, and regretfully followed her out.

'We need to talk, Dina. I am not happy.'

She passed a hand over her forehead. 'Christ, Hector. It's all happening. Do you realise how much money you're making?'

'You don't understand. I just want to have enough – to stop – not to do this again.'

'And we will. It's going to be more than that; it's going to be millions . . . if you stay with me.'

He bristled. 'You treat me like a child. It's my cream.'

Dina saw red. 'Which you wouldn't market, Hector; you wouldn't borrow a dime. You'd have been happy to sell it in our cramped little store.'

He flushed. 'That shop is my home. You were happy enough when I hired you.'

She paused. 'This is stupid. We have to work as a team.'

But Hector was brooding. 'It was wrong of you to take half the rights. And now you want the rest of my work?'

'You have to be kidding. I put everything I have on the line for this cream.'

'I'm calling that woman back,' the older man said. 'I want a million dollars. It's my research; nothing to do with you.'

Dina blinked back tears. 'Hector—'

'Really,' he said. 'You are the one who brought in lawyers. Just let me be, now, Dina, OK? I have a life without you.'

'I'm worried about you,' Brad said.

Johnny's little sis, the model of control, of command, the workaholic – she looked a mess.

They had read about the beauty cream. Nice – Dina looked to be set up for life.

But here she was at his apartment, late at night and shaken. Her skin was grey and she was crying.

'It doesn't matter,' Dina lied. 'Just a business thing, breaking up. That's all. Hector's right: he can do what he wants.'

Brad, Johnny's boyfriend, came over. He was in awe of Dina Kane – so strong; so ferocious. Old beyond her years and, from what Johnny had told him, he could guess why. But today she looked just like a twenty-year-old: upset and lost, stiffed by the older guy.

'He can't, actually, Dina,' Brad said. 'I don't know what's gone wrong, but you have half of the Meadow product. Why don't you get yourself your own lawyer? I'm guessing he can't use the name, or anything in connection with the first cream, without you.'

She bit her lip. 'Yeah. Maybe.'

'You're not thinking straight.'

'I don't know. It hurts. Hector meant a lot to me.'

Because you never knew your father, Brad thought. But he wasn't a shrink. Johnny, his love, was a messed up, insecure, lazy, sexy delight, and that was OK – Brad was grounded enough for the both of them. But Dina was more like him, full of duty and responsibility and the need to get on. Besides, she was going places; you could tell that the second she walked in the room.

'I would just get a lawyer – not the local guy you had run up the contract – a good one.'

'I spent everything I had on this cream. The packaging, the manufacture, everything. My apartment is hocked up to the eyeballs. It's selling, but the money takes a while to flow in, and all the lab bills have to be paid first and—'

'I'm sorry.' Brad patted her on the shoulder. 'Just my two cents.'

He had his own worries. He looked over at her brother. Two weeks ago, he was planning to drive Johnny to Vermont, ask him to marry him. Gay marriage was legal there. They could get a little place. He had his first job lined up: tax law at a small firm in Manhattan. It was a good gig for an Iona graduate, and he figured he could do well, get a promotion, get more money. He wasn't going to wind up on the Supreme Court, but they could have a nice place together. Maybe Johnny would do social work; maybe he'd just be a hippy peace activist. Brad didn't really care when he had those smooth limbs wound around him and that handsome face purring in his ear. It was white-picket-fence time, and he couldn't wait. If he was boring, Johnny brought the fireworks.

But . . . maybe a few too many fireworks. Johnny was

drinking; that was nothing new – he'd been drinking since he arrived at college. It started out of relief about getting away from home, or maybe guilt over the little sister without any college tuition. Then, as Dina pulled herself up from the pit, it was just drinking to party. Brad told him off; Brad worried. For a while, he switched to weed. The grades were plummeting, so he got a prescription to treat ADHD and crushed his Adderall. Next it was cocaine, just a little, here and there, when they were offered it at parties . . .

'I'm OK,' Johnny said. 'I'm holding it together.'

But his grades were bumping along the bottom. Brad was anxious. Maybe he'd get chucked out. Maybe he'd get addicted . . .

Now here Dina was, and Brad didn't know if he had anything left in reserve.

'Poor little sis.' Johnny stumbled over and gave her a bear hug.

'Johnny, you stink of whiskey.'

'Jack Daniel's don't stink.' Johnny pouted. 'What's the problem? We don't all want to be a party pooper, like you . . .'

'Here, baby.' Brad came over with a big glass of ice water and two Alka-Seltzers. 'Take these.'

Dina looked up slowly, shaken out of her self-reflection. Suddenly, Meadow cream seemed miles away. Johnny was in trouble. Johnny – the only family she had. It was obvious from the look on Brad's face. She didn't want him to get sick, but maybe he was already.

'No way,' Johnny slurred. 'I'm getting some ecstasy; Stacey has some down the block. She works porn, did you know that? She always has the best fucking shit. We're here; we should party . . . You think too much, Dina. You worry too much . . .'

'Johnny –' her voice was sharp and commanding – 'take the glass from Brad.'

He tossed his head, but he took it.

'Now swallow the pills. And the water. *All* of it.'

He did.

'Thanks.' Brad passed a hand over his face. 'I'll take him to the bathroom, get him to bed. Can you stay a minute?'

He was back out in five, with Johnny moaning in their tiny bedroom like a stuck elephant.

'He needs help.'

Dina nodded. 'How long has this been going on?'

'Maybe a month, maybe two. But we have to stop it before it gets any worse. I don't know how.'

Neither did Dina. For once, her self-possession deserted her. 'I'll . . . I'll go and see Mom. She loves him.' *Even if she doesn't love me.* 'She can decide what to do.'

'Does she know yet . . . ?'

'Don't worry,' Dina said, with more confidence than she felt. 'I'll tell her.'

The train out to Tuckahoe was a long thirty minutes for Dina. Every stop was redolent with memories. Bad memories.

Her golden dream was going wrong all around her. Hector was drifting away from her, corrupted. There would be lawyers . . . lawsuits. Her job was gone, with all she'd ploughed into it. It might have been only a year, but to Dina it was an age – it was her life.

And now her darling Johnny needed help. Something was rotten in his soul, something from childhood. They dealt with it in different ways, he and she. He wanted to get along, quietly, and hope it went away. Booze made pain go away. So did drugs.

'Woodlawn,' said the conductor. 'Wakefield next . . .'

She shivered in her seat. It was January – icy cold in New York. Dina was dressed for it, though; the ticket inspectors did a double take; the louche teenage boys sprawling across the banquettes were openly leering. She didn't notice any of them.

Everybody else riding to the suburbs was bundled up in so many layers they looked like the Stay-Puft marshmallow man. Not this girl. Dina Kane was dressed with effortless style. Her silk T-shirt was copper, with a bronze cashmere sweater draped lightly over the top. The blinking ticket inspector didn't notice the thermal vest under that shirt, keeping her warm without thick layers; she was just stunning, her hair long and loose, her legs chic in chestnut leather trousers.

But the thing the ticket inspector noticed most was the determined look on that beautiful, minimally made-up face. He shot a warning look at the boys: *Leave the lady alone.* And then he walked on down the carriage. No catcalls on his train, no trouble, no thanks.

Dina was oblivious.

Even on bad days, she lived for beauty. She wasn't trying to attract attention – this was something she did for herself. Looking her best was her comfort, her armour. She felt stronger when she looked better. Today she wore Meadow cream – a perfect bulwark against the cold – and a light, airbrushed foundation from the store, a little number imported from Germany. Her eyes were playful: dark green shadow at the lashline, copper mascara, golds and browns up to the brow. And her lips were plain – nothing but a tangerine gloss. To her, this was as simple as putting on moisturiser. Why wouldn't everybody do it? Five minutes, and you could almost be someone else . . .

Today she wished she was someone else – someone with a normal family, a normal life. One of these kids, heading into the suburbs.

Oh, no, you don't, chided the small voice in her head. *Not at any price.*

'Tuckahoe.'

She grabbed her Mulberry purse and stepped out of the train. Good clothes, good cosmetics: these were luxuries for some, necessities for her. Dina invested, every time she stepped up the ladder. She bought key pieces, classics that worked, and let her face be her canvas.

It was her business. Had been, anyway.

She walked carefully up the stone steps by the platform and found herself at the centre of the village – the post office to her left, a diner to her right – just a few minutes' walk from Ellen's house. They hadn't spoken in a year, other than a snatched phone call on her mom's birthday and at Christmas. Dina hadn't gone back. What was the point in pretending things were great?

The house was there, much as she remembered it: tall, neat, well painted. Maybe there was some relief in that. Dina noticed that the curtains were open. She could see her old room; it had been repainted, and was now a garish pink.

She rang the bell.

'Yes?'

Her mom looked her up and down. There was a slight start of recognition, then shock.

'My God, look at you!' She couldn't keep the admiration out of her voice. Then it coloured with jealousy. 'What are you, some kind of model?'

'I work in beauty, Mom. In a store.'

'Right. You could never be a model. You're not tall enough. Not skinny, either.'

Ellen was wearing black slacks and a matching polo-neck, with ballet slippers. Her hair was a darker blond, cut straight; she wore a little powder, some blusher and mascara. Nothing on her lips, and Dina knew right away she was too proud to show the fine lines she had there, to let anything bleed. She was stylish, still, but nothing to match her daughter.

'Can I come in, Mom?'

'I guess.' She opened the door.

'Wow. Things are different.' Dina glanced around. Every trace of teenagers had vanished. There were pictures in frames, though, portraits of Ellen and Paul, the family together, lots of frames of Johnny. No pictures of Dina, unless she was with her brother.

'Yeah. This is the house my way.'

'You want to give me the grand tour?'

Ellen shrugged. 'You can go round if you want.'

Curious, Dina mounted the stairs. Johnny's room was there; the posters had been taken down, but his bed was the same, his rug, his framed artwork. In Dina's room, the pink walls were just the start; her bed, her carpet, her toys, everything had been removed. It was a Home Shopping Network fantasy, with a double bed made up in pink and gold, and matching drapes over the windows, a shagpile rug and silk roses in a glass vase.

'You got your guest room,' she said, lightly, once she'd returned downstairs. It only stung a little bit; she was hardened to her mother's hurtfulness at this point.

'Yes. Sometimes my friends stay – from church, or the Friends' Club.'

'That's great, Mom. Look, I didn't come to socialise . . .'

'Of course not; why would you want to see your mother?'

'You've never called me once—' Dina stopped herself, swallowed her anger. 'Whatever. This is about Johnny. Mom, he's sick.'

'Sick? What kind of sick?' Actual concern spread across her mother's face. 'Is it cancer?'

'No. No. He's OK; it's not that.'

'Jesus. You scared me, Dina. Always so overdramatic.'

'Mom, he's having a rough time at college. Like, maybe it's too hard for him . . . Anyway, he's getting into alcohol. And drugs.'

'A little pot and booze never hurt anybody.' There was anger in Ellen's eyes. 'You always were the goody two-shoes over that. You ruined my life, back then. You know that?'

'I saved your life. You were being passed round like popcorn, Mom.'

Ellen pursed her lips. 'Now I don't even dare to take a drink at New Year's Eve.'

'You're better off.' Dina couldn't stand the self-pity. 'You have an addictive personality. Johnny inherited it. He's drinking out of control and he's popping pills. Coke, ecstasy. Prescription pills.'

'Maybe he needs a good romance. I got one, you know,' Ellen said, triumphantly. 'I'm dating again. Oliver Guyden.'

'Of Guyden's Funeral Home?'

'It's a good business,' Ellen said, defensively. 'And his wife died. She was in the church group with us. Oliver and I have been going out for a while, since the summer. I think maybe he's going to pop the question.'

'That's great, Mom. Really.' Dina smiled at her mother. Despite it all, she still wanted her to be happy; maybe it would soften her a little.

'No thanks to you,' Ellen said.

'Let's sit down.'

'Why? Are you staying?'

'Jesus,' Dina said, softly. 'I'm your own daughter. Why can't you be nice to me?'

Ellen shrugged. 'I would if you ever showed any respect. But it was always all about Little Miss Perfect. Come on, Dina, I have work to do here. What do you expect me to do about Johnny?'

'Talk to him. Reason with him. He still loves you.' Dina took a deep breath. 'Mom, you need to give Johnny acceptance.'

'I've always accepted my son.'

'He's gay. He has a boyfriend – Brad Evans. He's steady, going to be a lawyer. He's just what Johnny needs.'

Ellen's face drained white. She stumbled and gripped the top of a chair.

'Bullshit,' she hissed. 'You're lying, lying just to hurt me. Johnny's not *gay*.'

'He is. He's with Brad.'

The whiteness drained and came back red. Ellen looked flushed, as if she'd just downed a fifth of Jack Daniel's. 'He's on drugs. You said so yourself. He's just confused. There's no way he's homosexual. His dad was always chasing strippers . . .'

'Mom!' Dina shouted. 'I don't have time for this. Johnny is gay; Johnny is almost addicted. He needs your compassion and your love. For once in your horrible life, think about somebody else. He was born gay and he's going to die gay. Put aside the nineteen seventies, focus on *your son*.'

Ellen sat heavily on her couch. 'What will Oliver say?'

'Nothing, if he loves you. And if he has a problem with Johnny, you should cut him loose.'

Ellen sat quietly for a few minutes, chewing on her bottom lip. Dina could see her mother thinking, see the hamster wheels turning as she chewed it over. 'I'll see my son; I'll see the boy-friend too. He's mine. I don't care. Whatever it is, that's what happens these days, right? Things are different.'

Dina breathed out with relief. *Thank God.* 'Yes, Mom, things are different. The ladies at church would judge you a lot worse if you abandoned your boy. You know that.'

Ellen was rocking to and fro, hugging herself. 'Why did he tell you? Why not me?'

'You never go to see him, Mom.'

'I pay for his college.'

'It's more than writing a cheque. I've been by most Sundays since I landed in the city. He was even nervous of telling me, at first. Then he met Brad and it kind of just happened.'

Ellen stared at Dina. 'You've been over there every Sunday. Trying to get in with him. Talking to him about me.'

'Mom, don't be crazy.'

'Crazy? I'm not crazy. Why is he talking to *you*? You're just trying to take him away from me. Encouraging him in all this drug-taking and gay stuff.'

'He can't be *encouraged*; he's just gay.'

'You'll do anything to be first – anything to make him drop me. Me – who raised you both from children, on my own.'

Dina breathed in, raggedly; her mother's cruelty was toxic to her. She found herself shaking; the lack of love was making her anxious, panicky.

'Do you want me to bring him to you?'

'No. He can come on his own. He doesn't need you, Dina. Johnny needs his mother.'

'You accepting Brad will be good. After that, you probably need to pay to put him in rehab.'

Ellen looked up again. 'Pay? I pay for college.'

'Rehab is expensive, Mom. Don't you have anything left?'

'I need my savings. Oliver and I are going to sell this place, buy something nice. It's all been discussed. We're going to move to Bronxville.'

Bronxville: the fancier village next door. Her mother had been talking about Bronxville for years before Dina left. It was her goal, her Shangri-la.

'But Johnny needs it.'

'Right. And he needed college, only he's blowing that. And so did you, but you have a job, correct?'

'I used to have a job. I'm kind of self-employed . . .'

Ellen wasn't listening. 'And what if I sink my savings into rehab and he comes right out and just starts up again? What's to stop him?'

'We just have to hope. There are no guarantees—'

'Well, I can *guarantee* that, if I don't spend my money on junk, I'll still have it.'

'Thanks, Mom.' Dina had had enough. 'I'll get Johnny to see you, at least. Maybe that'll do something.'

'I'll meet his boyfriend,' her mother said, grandly. 'I'll give them my blessing.'

But no money.

'That's great.' Dina stood up. Her mother didn't rise, not even for a peck on the cheek.

'I'm feeling faint,' she said. 'You can see yourself out.'

Brad took Johnny down the next day. Dina waited in her apartment; she had to think. She'd tried calling Hector, but he wouldn't pick up the phone. When she went round to the store and pressed the buzzer on his apartment, there was no reply; she'd seen his curtains twitching shut.

She moved to her windows, looking out over the street. This place was functional now, a little more her; even though there was no money to renovate as she wanted, Dina had decorated cheaply, had painted, hung a few mirrors. Already it looked more spacious. But she would have to do better if she wanted to sell.

She felt tired – so tired. She thought about Johnny, her mom, Hector, Meadow. Desperately, she wanted independence, to cut loose. There could not be any waiting, could not be any more limbo. Dina wanted a life, wanted power. She had come close, but something was standing in her way.

Hector Green looked about him. These were unfamiliar surroundings: the long, walnut panelled conference room; the green leather armchairs. Four lawyers sat opposite him with yellow legal pads, writing furiously, even though he hadn't said much. A young man with pallid skin and a foppish haircut sat next to them, wearing an expensive suit.

'And you are sure of this?' The chief lawyer was a white-haired man of Hector's own age, perhaps a touch younger. He was heavy around the middle and spoke with supreme confidence.

'I'm afraid so,' the young man said. 'Miss Kane is a fraudster. She was involved in an unfortunate blackmail attempt on my family.' Edward Johnson spread his hands. 'Mr Green, you were successful on your own terms before she came along.'

'She did bankroll the launch of Meadow.'

'After your sweat equity,' the lawyer said. 'You designed the product; you worked around the clock. She was back at the shop selling things you ordered. In essence, it wasn't bad for Ms Kane to ask to be paid. Our quarrel is with the ludicrous contract she had you sign.'

'She could have asked for recoupment of her loan – even ten times over,' Edward said, sadly. 'Instead, she took fifty per cent. It took you a lifetime of learning to devise Meadow.'

'She took advantage of an old man without proper represent-ation. It's eminently challengeable.'

Hector shook his head. He had no idea what to think. If only they would stop talking!

He blamed Dina for this. Why was she trying to stop him making money?

'I would like to do the night cream, and retire.' He shrugged. 'It is very simple. I wish to go somewhere warm. I am old, I cannot work any longer.'

'The problem is, it would be a Meadow night cream. And she co-owns the name – unless we fight in court.'

'I can make it a different name . . .'

'The Glamour store wants your branding: Meadow.'

Hector snapped 'Then why are we here? She owns half. She has a contract.'

'We can fight—'

'I am not interested in work; I am not interested in fight.'

'Mr Green, if you'll allow me,' Edward Johnson said, 'Ms Kane does not have the money to hire lawyers for a protracted period. She has a cash crisis. My suggestion would be that you merely threaten her. The firm here can serve her the notifications, file the actions. We can bury her in paperwork. She'll soon admit that you are the real owner of Meadow.' He laughed. 'You will be generous if you refrain from suing her for fraud – attempted theft.'

Hector gnawed on his knuckles, an old habit. 'I want this all to be over.'

'Do you think a twenty-year-old girl should steal a life's work?'
He shook his head.

'Then you have to do this. Are you willing? Mr Johnson is paying our fees.'

Dina was jogging down the street when the pretty student ran up to her.

'Are you Dina Kane?' she asked. 'You know, who makes the Meadow cream?'

'I'm Dina,' she answered, startled out of her thoughts of Johnny. Brad had found him in Chinatown that morning, badly beaten up and dumped on the side of the street. He was in a hospital, and sweating and puking through withdrawal.

They said it was narcotics.

Johnny Kane was going downhill like a teen on a helter-skelter, faster than anyone suspected. The visit to Ellen had not gone well. Brad told Dina everything over a plate of spaghetti: the tight lips, the wooden hugs. Ellen's new boyfriend was there, he said, and kept coughing every time Brad touched Johnny, or talked about their relationship. And Johnny asked for a drink, and left twenty minutes after realising there was nothing in the house.

'I don't know if she loves him. I don't know if she really loves anything.'

'She hates that he's gay. My mom cares how things look, always has.'

'Well, she's going to have a dead son, if she's not careful.'

Dina called up after that and begged one more time for money. She found a rehab centre up in the Catskills, a remote place with great therapists and a good reputation. Johnny should stay a month, maybe six weeks; that might cost sixty thousand bucks.

'You must be kidding, Dina. Oliver and I are starting our own lives. Let Brad take care of Johnny.'

'He's still a student, Mom.'

'Maybe his parents are richer than me. Anyway, Johnny needs to want this,' Ellen said, piously. 'I don't feel he's ready.'

Dina shivered. The gossamer thread she thought was there – Ellen's love for Johnny – was tearing, weakening. She wondered which was worse, the revelation he was gay, or the news that he spent time with his sister.

Dina didn't want to face that. She'd clung to the idea that at least Momma loved *one* of them. Today, she wasn't so sure. The jealousy . . . the pathology in Ellen Kane . . . But at least Mom was making her own decision easy. If Ellen wouldn't help – wouldn't support Johnny – Dina would.

'Well, I'm glad I found you, then,' the student said, jerking her back to the street and her jogging. She slowed up, looking at the girl. 'These are for you.'

She reached in a backpack and handed Dina some envelopes.

'Excuse me?' Dina gasped.

'You've been served. I'm sorry. Have a pleasant run.' And the girl took out a camera and, before Dina could move, snapped her holding the crisp white envelopes.

Dina looked up First Avenue, towards her apartment building, and her heart started to pound – with more than the exercise.

Shaman and Kebler, the envelopes were stamped. *Attorneys-At-Law.*

They were stiff, thick bond paper. She stopped and ripped one open.

Our client . . . fraudulent coercion . . . Intellectual property, rights and trademark . . . Advantage of the vulnerable . . . Suing for release of contract, costs and damages in the amount of ten million dollars . . .

Dina almost laughed. Ten million dollars? It felt like she barely had ten dollars. And, if she did, she'd need nine of them for Johnny.

Chapter Eight

'I'm sorry,' Eliza Sherman said.

She looked her young client over. Dina Kane was an interesting girl, one of the most unusual people ever to walk through her doors. She wanted to help her, but the kid had no money. Not enough to fight.

'It's just that they are such a big firm – corporate law experts. You have a great case, in my opinion, but they can file motion after motion. Without money, no firm is going to represent you. No-win, no-fee is a risk here, because they have so many lawyers.' She squirmed a little; here was a twenty-year-old who'd pulled herself up from nothing, got fifty per cent of a hot beauty product and was about to get skewered. 'Look, I can recommend some suburban firms, maybe. You'd need to try and get a bank loan. Or maybe you have a lawyer in your family . . . ?'

'So, what would you do, if you were me?'

'It's a tough break.' Sherman's small, cramped office on Third Street was full of law books, with a small window that looked out on to another building. She did bread-and-butter stuff, lawsuits at work, slips and falls, corporate liability. 'I think I'd hire a lawyer to write a couple of letters saying you'll fight it all the way, and then I'd settle.'

'Settle?'

'Give back your half of the Meadow line. For whatever price they offer.'

Dina leafed through the letters again. 'They don't sound like they want to settle. Unless I sign it back, they're going to sue.'

'And you can't persuade Dr Green?'

'Hector won't talk to me. The money stuff really changed him.'

'Yes,' said the lawyer. 'It can do that.'

Dina sighed. 'So, if I hire you to write the letters, how much could I get?'

Eliza shrugged. 'I'd try for something small – you're right, they don't want to settle – like, maybe, fifty thousand dollars, just to make the headache go away.'

Dina almost choked on the water she was sipping from a white plastic cup. 'Fifty thousand? That's it?'

'They're a serious firm.'

'Thank you,' Dina said. The older woman could see her thinking. 'Just one more question,' Dina continued. 'If I had the money to hire a firm like them, and I could fight it, would I get to keep my share?'

'Oh, sure. I really think so. The contract is tight, you persuaded him to develop the cream, you took over at the store – your fingerprints are on everything. And the fact that you re-mortgaged your apartment . . . it's all there.'

'I appreciate your time.' Dina rose to her feet. 'What do I owe you for the consultation?'

Eliza Sherman felt a pang of pity for the kid. 'Absolutely nothing,' she said. 'Good luck, Ms Kane.'

Dina sat at her kitchen table, an uneaten bowl of oatmeal by her side. She was lost in the *Wall Street Journal* and her laptop. Next to her was a simple white pad, with a list of names on it.

It was a short list.

So few men had the power to help her. And the name on the top of the list? Well, it was like approaching a legend.

Joel Gaines was one of Wall Street's major mavericks. He was forty-one years old and a venture capitalist of the old school – not a dot com in sight. Gaines bought companies, broke them up and sold them off. He founded his first hedge fund aged just twenty-five and, by the age of thirty, owned a Detroit automaker, a travel agency in New York and several citrus farms in California. He had a bad reputation as a brutal player, with a ruthless eye on the bottom line. Gaines cut jobs and made companies profitable. He also started with senior management first. He had married early, at twenty-three, to a society beauty, Susan, who threw legendary parties in the Hamptons and sat on several charity boards. There were two sons, seventeen and fifteen. His partner, Bob Goldstein, was older and very respected. He provided the prestige, and Gaines did the rest.

Dina loved the story. She wanted to be like him. One day – maybe.

Her fingers reached for her cellphone, then hesitated. It was such a long shot. Why on earth would a man like Gaines agree to see her?

But one thing she knew: in her place, at her age, Joel Gaines would have made this call. He would have made all the calls.

The letters from the law firm were piled up in front of her, their threats written clearly on the stiff cream paper. She wanted out, she had no choice.

'What's on the list today?' Gaines asked.

His assistant, Marian, placed a neatly typed list on his desk. Gaines always wanted a hard copy. He found screens distracting. Other bankers ran the numbers, did the algorithms; Gaines went out to the factories, talked to the workers, used the products. It was part of what made him the best.

'You have the Japanese team here for the breakfast meeting.'

'Very good.' He glanced out of his huge floor-to-ceiling windows. 'Bring them in shortly.'

'The *New Yorker* is here to profile you at ten.'

'We agreed to that?'

'Yes, sir.'

'Very well. Twenty minutes, max.'

'Yes, sir. Then you are talking to the union leaders from the plant in Milwaukee.'

'They can have an hour.'

'Lunch with Mr Goldstein.'

'OK. We'll go to Jean-Georges today.'

'Very good, sir. You have forty minutes after that for emails and calls. I'll have a sheet ready for you.'

'Then what?'

'Your personal trainer at half three and, at five, you are meeting the Mayor over the new construction site in TriBeCa. Your driver will take you directly home from City Hall at five forty.'

He nodded. Going home: that was the part of the day he liked least. 'Anything else?'

'Well . . . you did mention you might speak to that young woman who called, about the beauty cream.'

'Yes. Cute. What was her name again?'

'Dina Kane.'

'See if you can squeeze in an extra phone call somewhere. I'll take her pitch. Ten minutes.'

'Oh.'

'What is it?'

'She's waiting outside, sir.'

Joel blinked. 'Did I say a meeting?'

'No. She says she would prefer to speak to you face to face. She understands you will only have a few minutes for her; says she'll wait. Do you want me to tell her to go away?'

He laughed; he liked a kid – of either sex – with balls. Mostly they were eager young Ivy League grads who'd watched *Wall Street* one too many times. Mostly they were men.

'She can go away and come back after lunch, if she wants. Or she can wait. It may be several hours.'

'Very good, sir.' Marian didn't argue the point.

'Bring me some coffee, please.'

He had few vices these days, but caffeine was one of them.

Dina waited. She came prepared; she had her notes, her print-outs, her projections, the case summary. And she had her phone. As the hours ticked by, she didn't idly leaf through magazines, or stare out of the vast Gaines Goldstein windows at Sixth Avenue below. She read up and studied, digging through the *Journal*, the *New York Times*, *Forbes*, *Fortune*, whatever was out there, following all the deals that Joel Gaines had ever done.

It was gripping. Dina got it immediately. There was a beautiful logic to the way he worked, mixed with a gambler's touch that made it artful. The private jet, the exclusive prep schools, the house in the Hamptons – all of these were less interesting to her; they were just the natural result of the brilliant mind at work in the office behind her.

She watched as men were shown in to the inner sanctum and returned, hours or minutes later, awe-struck and babbling amongst themselves. From Japanese businessmen to a journalist and photographer to some hard-looking, weather-beaten guys in lumberjack shirts and jeans. It wasn't clear precisely what he was doing, but from their reactions when they came out, he was doing it brilliantly.

It was exciting. It was thrilling. Another time, she might have been happy just to be in his presence. But not today. This wasn't just a courtesy call, nor was she a mere fan. She needed him. She needed this deal.

Finally, at almost noon, his secretary emerged: immaculate in pencil skirt, silk shirt and kitten heels; an elegant fifty-year-old blonde.

'Ms Kane – Mr Gaines can see you.'

She jumped to her feet, trying to calm her ragged breathing.

'I must warn you, this was meant to be a phone call. Mr Gaines has an absolute maximum of ten minutes. Try to make it less.'

Dina knew better than to sass the assistant. She meekly nodded her head. 'Yes, ma'am.'

The door opened into a cavernous office, exactly as she had expected. But that didn't make it any less impressive. The soft woollen carpet in eggshell grey led up to a wall of windows at one end, and stark white walls on the other three sides, hung with enormous canvases of modern art; she recognised a Basquiat, a huge Warhol print, two others she didn't know, but that still reeked of money. There was a large Wall Street ticker moving across one wall relentlessly, in an electronic banner.

Dina swallowed dryly. She was impressed, even a little aroused, despite herself. It was so in-your-face.

Gaines was sitting behind his desk, reading through some papers as she approached him. Dina took him in – the square, powerful shoulders, the muscled body under the well-cut suit. He wore a plain steel watch, nothing fancy. His square-jawed profile was striking and he had salt-and-pepper hair cut very close to the head.

'Thank you for seeing me, Mr Gaines.' She sat down, without being asked. There was a chair, and Dina didn't have time to waste with pleasantries.

'We were supposed to do this over the phone.' Gaines turned and looked at her, and Dina flushed with surprise.

He was sexy. The eyes were dark, fringed with black lashes so thick it looked like he was wearing mascara. He had a large nose and a cruel, arrogant set to his mouth, which matched his aura of power and the muscles of his body. She flashed to imagining him in a gym, lifting weights.

'Yes, sir.' She dragged herself back to the present. 'I thought I could get the point across better if I could see you.'

The dark eyes flickered up and down her body, and Dina felt desire licking at her.

He leaned back in his chair. 'Go ahead, kid. Pitch me.'

'I partnered with a man who ran a small beauty store – a chemist who hadn't worked in years. I love beauty.'

He inclined his head a fraction of an inch, without paying her a compliment.

'We were doing too well for the store, but he didn't want to expand. I persuaded him to develop a great day cream. I put up the money for lab costs, packaging: a loan against my apartment, in exchange for half the product. It's called Meadow and early orders are really good. Here.'

She passed over her fact sheets. 'It could be a blockbuster, if we had the right distribution. A new Crème de la Mer.'

Gaines looked over them. 'Congratulations. What do you need me for?'

'My partner is suing me – for ten million dollars. They're saying I stole half the cream from him. He wants to make other products in the line, without paying me. Glamour Store offered him a million bucks for a night cream.'

'Messy.'

Dina swallowed hard. 'I saw a lawyer and she says I can't fight it. Even though I can prove I funded it, he hired this big-shot firm and they can file so much stuff, I have no money to defend the suit. I spent all I had on funding Meadow.'

'Why is he doing this to you?'

She was ashamed to find tears prickling in the corners of her eyes, and fiercely blinked them back.

'Maybe I pushed him too hard. Hector just wanted a quiet life. Now he wants money first, then a quiet life.'

Gaines glanced at her, and then down at the papers again. It was a solid little bundle, presented by somebody who had judged him well. She had included not just the sales figures and her contract, but costs, projections and – more than that – press.

There was a small sheaf of articles and reviews, neatly clipped from beauty magazines and supplements. From her package, he got a sense of a wonder cream breaking into the market, a product with legs.

'My lawyer said somebody with money could fight this suit easily. But I don't have any.'

'What's your background?'

He pushed back in his chair. The girl was intriguing, and not just because she was beautiful. As a very rich man, he was around pretty girls all the time; the models swarmed at the nightclubs and the country clubs, hoping to pick up a financier, married or not.

She was elegantly dressed, wearing fitted black trousers and flats, and a dark red silk blouse. No jewellery; she didn't need it. Her face looked like it had been made up by a pro: gorgeous light rose blusher on the tops of her cheekbones, a translucent pink gloss on the lips, some sheer kind of foundation, eye shadow the pale brown of lightly done toast. When a girl like this spoke about beauty, young as she was, he got the sense of talking to an expert.

'I started out as a waitress. Then got into beauty retail, like I said.'

'No college?'

'There was no money. My mom was widowed early.'

He arched a brow. 'You don't think a sob story will have an effect on me?'

Dina flushed again, this time with anger. 'What sob story? I've done well.'

'Up to now.' He liked her spirit. Loved it. He was just playing with her now, enjoying himself. 'You can't fight this case.'

'No, sir. But, for you, it would be peanuts. They would wet themselves if they saw you coming.'

'That's probably true.' Gaines smiled. 'When it comes to lawyers, I have depth on the bench.'

'And a reputation.'

He pushed his chair back a little, examined her more closely. 'What reputation is that?'

She blushed. 'I'm sure you know that, Mr Gaines.'

'Very well.' The plain speaking amused him. Nobody ever talked to him like this. They were craven, flattering, obsequious. This girl hadn't got the memo. 'And knowing my reputation, why do you think I would be interested?'

'In the *Journal* it said that L'Audace was looking to expand its beauty presence, to add to its brands. You need a skincare line.'

L'Audace was a tired luxury goods house with a glittering past behind it that Gaines Goldstein had bought out two months ago.

'Meadow could be a big part of that revival. I will sell you my fifty per cent, and all my interest in future products and brands in the line. When they know you'll fight, they will probably cave themselves. You can buy out Hector's half, and the formula. And you'll have a great product. You see, Meadow actually works, because Hector is a talented chemist. It's what made our store good.'

He nodded. 'How does a waitress get a property she can borrow against?'

'My mom made me a small loan and I saved; I bought a studio, fixed it up, flipped it, did the same with another place.' She tossed her hair, a proud gesture. 'I did very well.'

'Excuse me. Sir?' Marion Harris was at the door, tutting impatiently. 'Your lunch reservation.'

'Coming.' He stood up, and the girl did too, dismissed. 'The idea has some merit; the figures need to back it up. I'll make some calls, get back to you.'

'Would you like my phone number?' Dina said.

'No.' He didn't look back at her as he strode towards the door. 'We can reach you if we want to.'

* * *

She spent a depressing afternoon trudging around the banks.

'We can't help you.'

'Far too complicated.'

'You have no assets. That's a piece of paper.'

Nothing she could say would persuade them. And the other venture capitalists she tried would barely talk to her; one of them gave her an appointment, three weeks away. By then she'd be a dinosaur.

Weary, discouraged, she headed back to her apartment. If this didn't work out, if she had to defend the suit, she might go bankrupt. *Jesus*, Dina thought. *Back to square one, back to nothing.* Tomorrow she would call a realtor, try to dump her apartment as soon as possible. Maybe, if she was lucky, she would get a few thousand to put in trust for Johnny.

And then what? She had no references, no proof of success. Would she waitress again? Hector would brand her a thief, when she caved; what beauty brand would want to work with her?

She went into the bedroom and lay down on the bed. Really, she should stand up, shower, change. But there was no energy; Dina just couldn't move.

This morning she thought she was really getting somewhere. But he hadn't called. It was a hopeless, stupid, extravagant play . . .

The phone rang at the side of her bed. 'Dina Kane.'

'Joel Gaines.'

She sat bolt upright, immediately. Her palm holding the receiver started to sweat.

'Yes, sir.'

'Here's the deal: I will buy you out for half a million dollars.'

She gasped in shock. 'My God.'

'I'm not doing you a favour; I'm taking a gamble. That will include all your interest, not just in this cream, but in anything developed for the Meadow brand, the line, the intellectual property, everything. I will accept all liability belonging to you.'

'I don't know what to say.'

'"Yes," is my suggestion,' he said.

'Yes. Sir. Thank you.'

'You aren't listening to me. By making this deal, you are putting yourself in Hector Green's position. I'm advancing you a relatively small amount of money. If the cream takes off, you will have sold a half share that could be worth tens of millions, maybe more, because you need money now. And don't try to come after me when that happens. There is no crying in baseball.'

'Yes, sir.' Dina couldn't stop the huge smile spreading across her face. He was so fair, straight with her. But not giving an inch. She loved it. 'It may be worth tens of millions to you, but it isn't worth that to me. I can't fight the suits.'

'Are you going to try to bargain?'

'I'm not in a position to bargain.'

'That's right. You're not,' he said, softly, and again, Dina felt that squirming lick of desire trawling across her belly. *Cut that out*, she ordered herself, thankful that she was on the end of a phone and he couldn't see any of her reactions.

'I do need the money fast, though.'

'They always do. You can meet me for coffee tomorrow morning at eight. I'll have papers for you to sign.'

'Meet for breakfast? OK. Yes, sir.'

'I said coffee. This is a half-million-dollar deal. You don't rate breakfast.'

Dina smiled. 'Of course not. Where should I come?'

'French Roast,' he said. 'Sixth and Twelfth. Don't be late.'

'Yes, sir. Thank you, Mr Gaines.'

'See you tomorrow, Dina Kane.'

The hooker was one of his favourites. An exotic mix of black and Hispanic, skin the colour of creamy coffee, she bounced up and down on his cock with a lazy smile and enthusiasm. She went by the nom-de-fuck of Coco, which was all right by Edward.

'Ah. Yeah.' He shifted around, watching those perfect, huge fake tits jiggle. 'Work it. Come on, show me.'

'Ohhh,' she groaned, theatrically. He scowled, hating it when they said anything. What Edward wanted was an anonymous screw. Quickly, he closed his eyes and thought of Dina Kane, that slim, sexy, younger body. He thought of the lawyers, and of breaking her. Mostly he thought of having her, desperate and penniless, coming back to him, humbly, and kneeling down to suck. He groaned, and came.

Coco slipped off him. '*Chérie*, that was wonderful.'

She affected some Creole shit. Not that he gave a damn. She was already heading to the shower. This was a classy joint, and her little apartment saw a lot of action. The two o'clock was already on the way.

He tugged on his pants, not bothering to wash. By the bed lay his little silver-topped vial with the tiny spoon for the coke. He helped himself to another small hit. He was just like an English gentleman of the eighteen hundreds with his bottle of snuff. Edward liked that image; it made him feel good.

As he buttoned his shirt, the chemical rush hit him. Yes, things were fine; things were better. His weak-ass father had bailed, so fuck him. Edward had no intention of working for a living. And, as for the army – that stuff was for suckers.

He didn't need therapy. He just needed to bury Dina Kane. And it was happening sooner than he'd ever hoped. Hector Green, that stupid, confused old man, had told him what he wanted to know.

'She did offer finance, though, Mr Johnson. She mortgaged her apartment . . .'

'How did she get one of those?'

A sugar daddy no doubt. Like his father. *Whore.*

'I don't know. We didn't talk much outside of business. I'm a private person. So is she.'

Not that private.

'OK. Thanks, Hector.'

It was especially delicious hiring lawyers that could dump all over Dina's stupid little discovery from a great height. Now they would be able to steal her little face cream – Jesus, a *face cream* – and whatever she'd borrowed against that apartment. The middle-class dream, climbing the property ladder . . . That would have to go.

The letters got sent, and it made him hard. There were drinks in a nightclub, quiet words with a discreet dealer, and then a visit to a hooker.

No more chasing teenage pussy, poor students or bridge-and-tunnel girls. He was going to select a classy wife, and fuck call girls on the side. The cocaine sparkled in his blood; Coco seemed like a great decision. Discreet. Easy to hide. He was smart; he was going to stick to professionals – whores with Blackberries and health certificates you could view.

But he was done now.

'See you soon, sugar,' she called as Edward headed out the door, ignoring her. He hadn't come for the conversation.

The car – with his mother's chauffeur – was parked outside. So what if it was nearly two in the morning? Time to earn his money. Edward felt like hitting a club, but there would be time for the big party later, once Dina was officially bankrupt. He expected the capitulation from her lawyers tomorrow, a letter begging Hector for mercy. Edward couldn't wait to show the girl who was really pulling the strings.

Edward was getting his shit together. First, he'd come out of the club and gone home. If Daddy wasn't going to be his meal ticket, Momma would have to. He *deserved* it. It was his *father*'s stupidity that let Dina take advantage. Edward had to drop out of college to preserve the family honour. They owed him. He was the victim here!

'Momma.' He marched into her bedroom and pulled back the

ornate drapes; sunlight streamed into the dusty room. 'Get up.'

'Oh, God,' she moaned. There were bottles everywhere – beside the bed, on the bedside cabinet – champagne and whiskey and liqueurs. She didn't seem particular, just anything left in the cellars, anything she would not have to go outside the house for. 'Leave me alone.'

The room stank of sweat, even a little vomit. Edward wanted to gag. He tugged the covers off the bed; his mother was lying there, fully clothed in the slacks she'd put on two days ago.

'Get into the shower.' He ferociously yanked her to her feet as she gagged and gasped. There was a master bathroom attached, with a wet room, all in marble, that his father had designed.

'No! Leave me alone!' Her hand reached for a whiskey bottle on the side, but Edward knocked it back, hard. His mother disgusted him, they all did.

'Get your clothes off, or I'll do it for you.' He flung a bathrobe at her.

Choking, she peeled off her stinking jumper and shirt. Edward turned his back, ignoring her, and walked into the shower, twisting the taps on full blast, lukewarm.

'Get in.'

She stumbled in, still wearing underwear, and Edward went outside and summoned a maid.

'In ten minutes, go into Mrs Johnson's room. You will throw away every bottle, strip the bed, remake it, and thoroughly disinfect and clean.'

'Yes, sir. Of course.'

'Tell Rafael to go through this house and remove everything alcoholic, including mouthwash.'

'Yes, sir.'

'And have the chauffeur get the car ready.'

He went to his mother's chest of drawers and pulled out a bra, a T-shirt, underwear, socks and a pair of lounge pants, and laid them on the embroidered French bench in the dressing room.

'Mother – get out.'

There was the soft sound of Penelope crying. Edward ignored it. He was driven with rage, pure white rage that felt so good for the soul. When she didn't move, he stepped into the shower and turned the dial all the way down to ice-cold.

She shrieked with misery and stepped out.

'Edward! Why are you doing this to me?'

He flung one of the huge Egyptian cotton bath sheets at her; was anything more repellent than the sight of his mother, shivering and half-naked?

'It's over, Momma.'

'What's over? You are acting crazy . . . I need a drink.'

'No drinks. That's all gone. I'm afraid I can't afford for you to fall apart. Go and put your clothes on, in the dressing room. I'm taking you to the doctor.'

She dry-retched. 'I feel sick.'

'You are sick. Your skin looks like day-old porridge, your eyes are bloodshot, your hair is matted. You're drinking yourself to death. I'm taking you to the doctor. If you refuse, I will go to a court and have you committed. I'll put you in Bellevue, Mother.'

Penelope limped out of his sight, the towel clutched pathetically around her. As she dressed, Edward called Dr Rathbone, their highly overpaid, but always available, family physician.

'Why are you doing this? I'm sick. I feel so ill. God, Edward, if you only knew how much it hurts . . .'

His mother stood before him, dressed, her wet hair still plastered against her head. How he acted now would be key to his future.

He pulled her close, kissed her on the head. 'Somebody has to look after you, Momma. Daddy's gone now. I'll be the one to help you.'

She sobbed.

Edward wrapped an Hermès silk scarf round her head and selected a fox fur coat from her closet. A pair of Versace sunglasses, a relic from their last vacation at the Four Seasons resort in Costa Rica, was lying in her jewellery case; he slipped them on, hiding her bloodshot eyes, and doused her with Aqua di Parma to conceal the reek of alcohol seeping from her pores, despite the merciful shower.

'Come along. I'll take you to the car.'

'I don't want to go . . . I don't want to be seen out.'

'Don't worry,' he said. 'Dr Rathbone is fantastically discreet.'

He was. He admitted Penelope to his private clinic, with three recovery suites, mostly for models and film stars after their facelifts.

'She will experience delirium tremens.'

Edward shuddered at the thought. His own mother, calling out about spiders crawling on her skin, hallucinating.

'I don't care. I want you to sedate her. Keep her as an inpatient for a week. Get her clean.'

'That's extremely costly. Is she in a position to pay the bill?'

Edward was not surprised at the lack of sensitivity. Bill paying first, compassion later: that was Manhattan society for you. 'You need to sign this,' he said. 'It's a statement that she is medically unfit, giving me power of attorney. My lawyers will have it ratified today, and then you'll be paid from the family trust.'

Rathbone scribbled immediately. Edward smirked; this stay was tens of thousands to the doc.

'After she's sober, she'll be fit again. You do understand that?'

Edward smiled. 'Of course, doctor.'

He wasn't stupid. He couldn't just shove his mother out of the way. She would need to be persuaded. She would need to *depend* on him.

Every day, he came to the clinic. He brought flowers, toiletries. He sat with his mother. As she shook and shuddered, he gripped her hand, spoke soothingly to her.

'Don't worry, Momma. You're here. You're safe.'

Edward made sure the lights were kept on, the walls were clean white – that there was nothing to promote hallucinations. When Penelope started to gibber and panic, he insisted on sedatives.

'She shouldn't have too many benzodiazepines. That could be a whole different problem.'

'I don't give a damn,' Edward replied. 'Put her under.'

And his mother looked at him with wild, grateful eyes as the nurse administered another white pill.

She came home two weeks later, shaken and nervous, but sober, and grateful to him.

'I can't believe it.' Penelope looked round at her house. It was transformed: all the mess had vanished, the doors and windows sparkling clean. The stench of sweat and failure and crisis had gone. Edward had arranged fresh flowers in every room and conducted a complete clean out of her wardrobe and shoe closet. The fridge was stocked with healthy foods. Get-well-soon cards from some of her friends were arrayed on the mantelpiece of the drawing room. The garden was weeded and tended, and all the domestic staff had been paid. 'It's wonderful. Oh, Edward, I never want to go back.'

'The tendency will never leave you, now. You do understand that? No alcohol, ever again.'

Penny nodded meekly.

'I've arranged a small dinner party tonight.'

Her face creased with anxiety. 'I couldn't.'

'You can. You must. I have a programme set up for you, Mother. We will face our friends – tell them the stress of the divorce made you sick. I have enrolled you, in a small way, in a few local charities. And you can attend the odd benefit. I'm carefully selecting those where no alcohol will be present. And I am putting together a programme of events: concerts, plays, some spa and therapy days. I don't see why you can't resume your position.'

Penelope's lip trembled. Now sober, she was hideously embarrassed. Shame at what she'd done crawled over her skin like hallucinatory bugs in the clinic's hellish detox room.

'Do you really think so?'

'Mother, there will be weekly visits to the hairdresser, to a terrific massage therapist, and some work with the Episcopalians.' This was the least religious church Edward had been able to find. 'It will give you a wonderful new lease of life. You do understand, though, that you are very fragile?'

'I feel fragile.' She pressed her fingers to her forehead, the nails stubbed and broken. 'Oh, Edward, I'm not sure I'm ready for any of it . . .'

'If you sit and brood, you will wind up back in that clinic. Is that what you want?'

She shuddered. 'No! God, no.'

'Then let me handle things. After tonight, we will need to have a little talk about finances.'

'Very well,' his mother said, distantly.

She was staring at herself in the mirror; her face was lined and wrinkled, her blond hair streaked with thick grey roots, her nails cracked. She was clean and neatly dressed, but the woman gazing back at her had aged a hundred years.

'Oh, Momma.' Edward took her hand. 'Come into the guest bathroom. There are some therapists waiting to welcome you home.'

'Therapists?'

'I've brought in a manicurist to do your hands and give you a pedicure, and Jason Quigley is making a house call to tint your hair. After that, Dr Westin is coming in.'

Penelope Johnson smiled a proper smile for the first time in weeks. Jason Quigley was her hair colourist. And Dr Westin was her very able dermatologist, from a few months ago, from another life.

'And then we have Emma Lucille, who will attend to your make-up after everybody else has finished. She's a freelancer, but comes highly recommended.'

'What do you know about beauty, Edward?'

'I did a little digging,' he said, modestly.

The dinner was a great success. Edward felt the stone lift a little off his chest. The days when he and his family were social pariahs were gone.

He had invited friends he knew would come: the lower echelons of his mother's social circle, the ones who would still be grateful for an invitation from Penelope Johnson, and two other divorcees. Next, he made sure that none of the eight or nine guests drank alcohol. Finally, he had included Itsy Moran, a second stringer from *Society* magazine's gossip pages, whom he dated briefly. She could be relied upon for a sympathetic write-up: 'The Return of the Johnsons'.

Penny swept into the room with something like confidence. Four hours in that bathroom had restored her to herself; her hair was back to a dark honey blond and swept up in an elegant chignon; her face had been smoothed with Botox, plumped with filler and then carefully made up, light and neutral for a woman in her fifties. Her fingers and toes were neatly trimmed and glistening with French polish, and she wore a pair of flat Louboutins and a plain satin evening dress in cornflower blue, with long sleeves to hide the bruises on her arms. Add in her large diamond-stud earrings, and Penny Johnson looked well, even elegant.

'Penny! How wonderful to see you,' Itsy gushed.

'Darling! You look perfect,' said Bobby Grantham.

'Kiss kiss,' his mother said, distributing air pecks, just as she used to. 'Shall we eat?'

When they all left – quite soon after nine thirty; without wine, guests had other things to do – Penny Johnson came over to

Edward and gripped his arm tightly. Her eyes glittered with tears, happy tears.

'Oh, my. That was . . . enjoyable,' she said, as though she had not expected anything to be enjoyable again.

'You see? You can do it.'

She was looking at herself in the ornate gold-rimmed mirror in their hallway, and smiling softly again. 'Oh, yes, Edward – thank you so much.'

He returned the smile, concealing his contempt and resentment. Up to him to fix his own parents – both of them.

'Just step into the parlour room here, Mother,' he said. 'I have some paperwork that needs signing.'

She followed him into a small office – once his father's, now redecorated to remove every trace of Shelby – and Edward pulled out the French armchair for her at the mahogany desk. The bank forms were there, pre-signed by him.

'What is this, darling?'

'Just sign it, Momma. It's a transfer of money, so that I can take care of the house and look after you. You aren't in a fit state to do it – not yet.'

Penelope looked at the papers, her eyes crunching. 'This looks like a million dollars . . .'

'Two million, for the year. That's what I need. Can you sign by the crosses?'

'But that's so much money . . .'

'We have ten in the bank, cash. Believe me, this covers basic expenses, allows me to care for you. I need to make decisions, Momma. Aren't you a little better tonight? It went well?'

She nodded, hesitating.

'Look, if you don't trust me, I'm happy to step away,' he said. 'You can sort everything out here on your own. I've devoted myself to you, Momma; I gave up college for you. This is the only way things work.'

The pen trembled.

'Very well. Of course, you mustn't feel forced. I'll leave,' Edward said.

'No – no. Stay, darling. You . . . you manage things so well.'

She signed, and Edward Johnson was finally a millionaire.

The next morning, he was in the offices of Shaman and Kebler, Attorneys-At-Law, with a retainer cheque for a hundred thousand dollars. First order of business – going after Dina Kane.

Chapter Nine

French Roast was one of her favourite coffee places. It was almost like he knew. She loved the rich scents of the flavoured beans and different syrups, the bohemian crowd that thronged through day and night, the way it sat on the very edge of the Village, across the border at Sixth Avenue, like a gateway.

But it wasn't the kind of place you'd expect to meet Joel Gaines. Nowhere fancy. Nothing to suit a billionaire.

Dina was there, waiting, by half past seven. She ordered a plain omelette, mostly to secure a table. She was too nervous to eat.

It was wrong to be turned on by this. It was a business deal. For him, barely worth noticing; for her, everything. She tried to think about Meadow, the cream, the potential. Hector Green was a good chemist. The product would work, would fit with what Gaines was trying to do . . .

It was no good. Her mind kept flashing back to him: the salt-and-pepper hair, the dark eyes, the air of complete confidence, complete power.

Goddamn, Dina thought. *I need a boyfriend.*

But how stupid and small that word seemed. Boyfriend. What? Some skinny youth with acne from a world she'd never entered? A student? *Edward Johnson*, or another rich boy just like him?

Gaines had blazed his own trail, conquered his own worlds.

Dina forced herself to dress down for this meeting. Gaines was not for her – obviously not. He was married, for a start. Two teenaged kids. Far too old for her. And he was her only hope in life, right now. This deal would save her ass.

She put on a uniform: a fitted grey woollen skirt from DKNY, cashmere tights in pewter, and gunmetal pumps, with a cream silk blouse and a crewneck sweater in oyster; a silver woollen scarf and a black military coat from Prada lay over the back of her chair, with her leather gloves. Her make-up was almost non-existent: a touch of powder, a little bronzer on the cheeks for health, concealer for her sleepless eyes. Neutral shadow and a clear gloss. As businesslike as she could be.

Dina was sipping her coffee – Irish Whiskey scent, the closest she ever got to alcohol – when he arrived. He was bang on time, walking purposefully through the doors. His greatcoat and dark suit did nothing to hide that body. When he spoke to the hostess, Dina could see the admiration in the girl's body language, and was instantly jealous.

She jumped to her feet and waved.

He saw her, and threaded his way through the tables. He was carrying a briefcase; she hadn't seen one of those on the street for years. In that briefcase was the key to her future. The dark eyes were fixed on her, and her heart started to thump. Fear, adrenaline. Something else, too, that she didn't want to think about.

'Ms Kane, good morning.'

'Mr Gaines.' She offered her hand, and he shook it, amused. 'Would you call me Dina?'

'Certainly.' He sat down and turned to the hovering waitress. 'Black cinnamon coffee. Grande. No sugar.'

'Yes, sir,' she said.

Gaines gestured to the omelette. 'I thought I told you we weren't eating.'

'You don't have to eat. I need the protein.'

He laughed. 'You have a lot of attitude for somebody who needs my help desperately.'

'Like you said, Mr Gaines, you're not doing me a favour. You're getting fifty per cent of a major beauty product for half a million dollars.'

Gaines looked the girl over, up and down. She was incredibly beautiful. The perfection of her make-up made her look better than a model: young, but put together. Underneath the bravado, he could see the nerves, and he liked her more for that. Her body, beneath the form-fitting clothes, was tempting – tight, lush, with plenty of curves, despite the slimness.

Jesus. Get a grip.

He thought of his wife, back home. They had quarrelled that morning – it was becoming too frequent, lately – an argument over her lack of desire to do much of anything: shop, arrange charity dinners. Susan was far more polished and groomed than Dina Kane; she worked on herself every day, from the Pilates classes to the private hairdresser. Nobody could rock an evening gown and a diamond collar like his carefully blonde wife. It all seemed OK, back when the boys were young.

'What's your problem? I have work to do – running our home.'

'Of course,' he replied, reaching for his work papers. He had been looking forward to seeing the kid this morning – the fighter.

'Really, Joel, what would be the point? I could study as a lawyer, and then we'd have five hundred million dollars *plus* another ninety thousand.' Susan laughed lightly. 'You have somebody home here; isn't that priceless?'

She picked up her tennis racket and blew him a kiss. Gaines tried to imagine having sex with her tonight. Susan never said no to him – part of the wifely code, so he gathered. But she came to his bed without enthusiasm these days, like it was just another chore, a workout.

Dina Kane did not remind him of his wife. Nor of the younger, sexier set that hung out in the Hamptons – on the tennis courts, in the country clubs – with their blond hair worn long. She wasn't a Park Avenue Princess. She reminded him of *him*. Back when he was poor. Back when it was fun . . .

'Here.' He reached for the briefcase, snapped it open. 'A letter, several forms . . .'

She took them, pulling a plastic pen from her purse.

'You can do better than that.' Gaines removed a pen from an inner pocket: Montblanc, pure gold. 'Sign your first deal; start as you mean to go on.'

Dina took it, delicately. The flamboyance of the gesture heated her. To hide it, she bowed her head, dark hair tumbling around her face as she signed.

'Done. Thank you.'

'One copy's for you.' Gaines pushed the papers towards her. 'And keep the pen.'

She started. 'I couldn't.'

'Do great things with it. Make more deals.' He stood up, before he looked too long at those green eyes. The schedule was busy today – like always. 'Call me again when you've made your first ten million.'

Dina's belly fluttered with desire. 'You joke with me, Mr Gaines.'

'Joel,' he said, standing up. 'And I never joke.'

She watched his back as he left the room.

Edward Johnson arrived punctually at his new office. Penelope had signed away part of the trust-fund management to him and he'd set up a shell company, EdJo Inc, listed as 'private wealth management'. Edward enjoyed printing up little cards that said *Director*, and leasing one smart room in a block off Columbus Circle.

He had no intention of actually doing any work. There were brokers, good ones, who handled the Johnson money, now his mother's money. This title gave him something to pretend to do. Screw Columbia. Screw Dina. Once she'd handed over Meadow, he was planning another little sit-down with Hector Green. It would be amusing to take a share in that product himself, run it and make a success of it. Women went crazy for beauty; it was a billion-dollar industry. He loved the idea of making money there – New York Fashion Week, fucking the models, front row at the shows, designers cosying up to him. *Far* more fun than some stuffy law office or Wall Street traders' shop.

For now, there was a boring, cheap secretary in her late forties – practically dead, but you don't shit where you eat – and a little desk with a view. He would make a few calls to some of the brokers to 'discuss investments'. More importantly, there would be lunches, dinners, cocktails . . . Ed Johnson had a list of every little fucker that abandoned him, all those Ivy League fair-weather friends. He had money, position again. And he would pursue some girl to marry – one with a lot of cash and no crazy ideas about business.

'Good morning, Mr Johnson,' said Faustina Kopek, his new assistant.

'Morning. Get me some coffee. Jamaican Blue Mountain with cream. And croissants. There's a Whole Foods downstairs.'

'OK.'

He preferred *Yes, sir*; they would have to work on that. 'First things first, put me through to Giles Shaman at Shaman and Kebler.'

'Right away.'

He closed the door so he wouldn't have to look at her pudgy ass, and right away the little red button lit up on his phone. Just like a real office. Edward smiled.

'Johnson,' he said, pompously.

'Edward. This is Giles. I'm afraid we have a little bit of a problem.'

Dina called her bank to make sure the money was there. Then she called Brad.

'I've got the money – for rehab. Can you help me get him there?'

'You're kidding?' Brad breathed out, a long, guttural sigh of relief. 'Did your mother change her mind?'

'I got it myself. It's a long story.'

'He's cut back some . . . just some. He still needs the help.'

Dina could hear the stress in his voice. 'I'll be right over.'

Johnny was dressed and out of bed; that was the good part about it. But Dina looked with horror at her brother's skinny, half-skeletal frame, the hollows under his eyes, his shaking hands. His hair was long, grown over the collar. No longer handsome, he looked years older than himself.

As soon as Dina walked in, he burst into tears.

'I can't stop it,' he sobbed. 'I'm out of control. Brad asked me to move out. He said he can't take it.'

Dina looked over at Brad, who stared at the floor. 'I'm sorry,' he said. 'It's too much. I wish I were stronger.'

Johnny wept, his frail shoulders shaking pathetically. Dina's heart creased with pity – for her brother, for Brad, for everybody.

'Johnny, you'll get better. I have a place for you. The best rehab in the state.'

'We can't afford it.'

'It's all taken care of. You just get strong – get better. I'll speak to the dean's office; get you a medical leave of absence. You can finish college next semester.'

'I can't go yet,' he pleaded. 'I need something. One hit. One last hit . . .'

'I've got a car waiting outside – to drive you.'

Johnny got to his feet, unsteadily. 'I don't have a case packed . . . No clothes; can't go . . .'

Brad moved back into the bedroom with a small red suitcase. 'All your stuff is in here. Go with your sister.'

Tears sprang to Johnny's eyes. 'You just want to get rid of me! I loved you.'

'But you loved that stuff more,' Brad said, his own voice cracking, and then he turned away. 'Dina . . . please go.'

She hefted up the case with one hand and her brother with the other, cradling his weight by draping one skinny arm around her shoulder. It felt as though the suitcase weighed more.

'Come on, Johnny.' She wanted to cry too, but somebody had to be strong. 'They're waiting for you. We'll get through this; we'll get through it all.'

'That can't be.'

Edward's heart was hammering a million miles an hour, like he'd done too much coke. He felt his face flush with blood, his ears buzzing. Perhaps he would faint. He gripped the desk in front of him.

'Mr Gaines' lawyers have been on the phone all morning. They can run this case till the end of time. We can't possibly fight them.'

'You have to.' His voice rose in a high-pitched squeal. 'You goddamned have to.'

'Actually, we don't. Dr Green is our client, not you.'

'I paid you bastards. A hundred thousand!'

'To represent Dr Green,' said Giles Shaman, smoothly. 'The proprieties were explained to you at the time. We have to give our client the best advice.'

'I'm the client!'

'Please calm yourself, Mr Johnson. There is nothing for it except to advise Dr Green to sell his share. The good news is he's content about that – even relieved. Mr Gaines has offered him two million dollars, to include all intellectual property, the trademark, the brand. He's going back to Austria, to retire.'

'I don't care where he's going. I don't care about him! He has to sue her!'

'You don't seem to understand. Dr Green can't sue Ms Kane. Her interest has been bought out by Gaines Goldstein. If he alleges she fraudulently claimed half of Meadow, it's Gaines Goldstein lawyers who will defend the case. And they could countersue. My advice was to settle. Dr Green didn't have any real appetite to litigate against Ms Kane in the first place.'

'Who gives a fuck what he wants?'

'I do. I'm his lawyer. I am, however, willing to give you some free advice, Mr Johnson.'

Edward heard the suppressed laughter, the mocking tone in his voice. Red rage surged up in him, a bilious taste in his mouth. He wanted to curse but found himself gasping for breath, unable to speak. He'd given these fuckers a *hundred grand* and they'd screwed him over. Just like that, man. Just like Dina Kane.

'I will take silence as consent. Very well, then: at present, nobody knows you were good enough to pay Dr Green's legal costs. He is heading back to Europe before questions can be asked. If I were you, Mr Johnson, I would want to keep very quiet about my role in this. Whatever your relationship with Dina Kane.'

'I don't care what they think,' Edward lied.

'Everybody cares what Joel Gaines thinks. He does not have a forgiving reputation. Now he's a player in this, speaking for myself, I would get the hell out of Dodge, so to speak.'

Edward felt sick. 'How much?'

'Excuse me?'

'How much did she get? For her share?'

'Not as much as Dr Green, but it came encumbered with a possible lawsuit.'

'Give me the number, not the fucking footnotes.'

'Half a million dollars, I believe. A fair price, but not a spectacular one.'

Half a million.

In a year, that whore had gone from coffee waitress to business-woman. She could pay back her loans, sell another apartment. In his world, here in Manhattan, a half mil only got you to first base. But Dina had made that base in record time. This would be a seed – seed money for something bigger, something better.

A nightmarish vision swam before him: Dina Kane, a big success, famous, rich. Maybe owning a better house than his mother's. Maybe even moving past him, in the fast lane. Laughing at him. *Ruining his life*.

It could happen now. She was playing, doing it deliberately to spite him.

Unless he did something to stop it.

Edward forced himself to be calm, to show control.

'Good advice. Thank you. It feels so unfair, to know that she cheated Dr Green, the way she blackmailed my father. He was gulled into taking less because of her.'

'Yes. Well.' The lawyer was discomfited. 'I can certainly understand that perspective, Mr Johnson.'

'Destroy all records of our correspondence, then. I will cease to pay your bills as of now. Dr Green should understand that.'

'His flight to Austria leaves next week. So this whole matter is at a rest.'

The hell it is.

'Goodbye, Mr Shaman.'

Edward Johnson hung up, put his head in his hands and thought of Dina Kane. His body shivered with pure hatred.

There was a knock on the door. His secretary entered with his coffee in a plain china mug.

'I'll just get your croissants,' she said. 'Shall I call anybody at the broker's?'

He looked at her with loathing. *Stupid bitch*. Like she couldn't see his stress. He didn't want coffee; he wanted pussy. Better, he wanted some girl to kneel and give head; no talking, no nothing. Most of all, he wanted a snort or a drink, but that's where the Kane slut had driven his mother.

Better to find a couple of hookers. Or a sex club, one of the fancier ones, with masks and screwed-up girls who liked to be beaten. He could get into that. Every blow would be for Dina, every thrust for Dina . . .

He was getting hard, feeling sick. He shook his head.

'Forget the croissants. I have an urgent investment meeting outside. I may not be back today. Cancel lunch.'

'OK, sure,' his assistant said, but Edward had already brushed past her to the door.

'Payment in advance. In full. That's the policy.'

'Of course,' Dina said. She was just so glad that they had space. Johnny had cried the whole drive up, mewled like a cat in the back of the hire car. Twice, the driver had had to pull over so Johnny could vomit.

'Sixty thousand for a month's stay. Special interventions may be more – any hospitalisations, operations. We don't take medical insurance, but we can give you a letter for reimbursement.'

Yeah, that's likely. Dina nodded in the quiet, plush lobby of the facility, built like a giant wooden lodge, a luxury ski chalet. The difference was the uniformed nurses, and the occasional shouts and cries from within, far away, like somebody being tortured down the hallway. Her dark head lifted nervously.

'Heroin withdrawal is very difficult. Methamphetamine is worse.'

'I understand.'

'Everybody is here voluntarily. The therapists' time is booked in advance – that's why we take payment in full.' The receptionist allowed a hint of a smile to show through. Gallows humour. 'Sometimes the money is the only thing that stops them walking out. You'd be surprised – even addicts don't want to blow tens of thousands.'

'It makes sense.'

'Your brother may well need additional treatment. Please sign here for the amount you are prepared to pay.'

Dina wrote down two hundred thousand. *Easy come, easy go,* she thought. Johnny was all the family she had in the world.

'Can I visit him?'

'We don't allow it during treatment, unless it's exceptional circumstances. Patients have to progress. Mr Kane may need hospitalisation, intravenous nutrition, physical therapy . . .'

She couldn't argue. Johnny was a skeleton.

'Just take care of him,' Dina said. She signed her name and left.

The next two weeks were amongst the busiest of her life.

After Johnny, there was little money left. She paid the taxes, set aside the cash for his treatment, and renovated her apartment the way she always wanted. The city clerks, the building board and the painters didn't know what had hit them.

'Which architectural firm are you with?' asked the clerk in the permit office, looking at Dina's beautifully printed plans.

'Kane and Kane,' she said, smiling.

'That's not the right paint colour. We ordered ecru, not eggshell.'

'Hang the door exactly on those hinges – you don't want to lose a millimetre of space.'

'Make sure the glass is treated against reflection – it lets far more light in.'

'Jesus, honey, you're a real hard case. The owner knew what she was doing hiring you.'

Dina smiled and said nothing.

Within a month, her plain, dull apartment was transformed. The kitchen wall was ripped out and the cramped living room combined into the space to form one large living area with a small, chic kitchen alcove. She compensated for the lack of space with luxury: a small counter-top, but Italian marble; a compact fridge-freezer, but SubZero; a microwave, high in the wall; a built-in Viking oven and small range. Every cupboard and shelf was maximised for space. The tiny den was sacrificed, and Dina created a huge single bedroom with a walk-in closet, beautifully laid out with shoe racks, shelves and dress hangers, mirrored walls and overhead lighting. In the loft-like living area, Dina mounted a huge flat-screen TV above her newly installed, remote-controlled gas fire, which produced dancing flames, just like the real thing. The small bathroom was a problem, but Dina ripped out the shower and created a medium-sized wet room, with a stone bench and a steam-free mirror, to make it look larger.

Then she called her realtor.

'You can't be finished already. If you want a higher price point, you need serious upgrades.'

'It's done. Come and see.'

'I can't be in for an assessment until Friday,' said Laurel Sloane.

'That's fine. I'll find another realtor.'

Sloane swallowed hard. This girl was unbelievable. 'You know, let me check my diary . . . something might have opened up earlier . . .'

'My window is two p.m. today.'

Laurel surrendered. 'Two p.m. That's fine. I appreciate your business, Ms Kane.'

When she walked into the apartment, hours later, the lie became the truth. Laurel Sloane was open-mouthed. She had never witnessed such a job, so fast. The cramped one-bedroom-plus-den standard unit was now a luxurious loft, packed with boys' toys, playing up its spectacular view.

'My God.' She didn't attempt to conceal her surprise. 'It's like a James Bond movie.'

The younger woman nodded, and Laurel took another look at her. She was quite something in her tight riding pants, knee-high flat boots and luxurious boyfriend sweater. The hair was twisted into a French plait and her make-up was delicately done in pinks and neutrals; you never saw a twenty-something so polished.

'This apartment is a reasonable size for two, but big for a one-bedroom. Plus, it's near the UN; you want to market it to a diplomat or a staffer. They have large budgets, and they want the best.'

'The best is Fifth Avenue.'

'Right, but now, for a lot less, they come here, get all the bells and whistles, and walk a block to work. No subway. It'll sell.'

It sure would. Laurel Sloane put aside her jealousy. This girl was a natural. She had zeroed in on the buyer perfectly. If she stuck with her, Dina Kane could make her tens of thousands, maybe more, in commissions. It was all about the deal.

'How much do you want for it?'

'One and a half million,' Dina Kane said.

That would mean it had doubled its value in six months.

Laurel didn't hesitate. 'Yes, ma'am. No problem.'

Dina was home, trying to relax. Until it sold, this was her place now. Johnny was in rehab. Hector had gone. The last of the workmen had departed. She had some money, not much, and things were expensive here.

I've been pushing myself too hard, she thought, pouring out a large glass of fresh pomegranate juice. *I need security. A home. I need to stop.*

Joel Gaines drifted into her mind. The way he looked her over, his dark eyes assessing her – so different from the boys, those immature, mocking youths her own age.

He's married. Get over it. Stop.

I need a more normal life, Dina thought. *A normal life, period. It's not like I've ever had one.*

Ellen – barely a mother. No father. No love. Her talent stifled. The teenage girl appealing to the Mafia don.

Her escape to the city. Working round the clock. Trying to change her life. And then Edward Johnson taking her virginity, her self-respect – mocking her like it was a game.

Shelby Johnson – hypocrite and letch. Her anger had been enough to get her into his bed. Anything to confront that rich, powerful, selfish family that she hated so much.

Hector Green – success, opportunity . . . then another man she'd trusted turning against her.

And nobody in her life – nobody since Edward. *No wonder you're getting a crush. A stupid, infantile crush. If you don't stop pushing yourself, you'll crack up . . .*

Dina tried to be logical. There must be guys out there, guys her own age, marriage material, guys who weren't Edward Johnson. She needed to date, find a nice guy, get married, have some kids. Make that real family her momma had denied her.

People do that, she thought. *They meet at college – or socially.*

Only Dina Kane had no social life.

Then there's the job . . .

The obvious thought occurred to her, out of the blue: it was time to give up on the dream of being some kind of mogul. If this apartment sold, she could be comfortable. Time to get an enjoyable job, one she'd be good at, but where she could leave work at five p.m., make friends, have a life. Have a chance to meet guys. Catch up on her sleep.

Slowly, as she sipped, Dina thought it through.

Hector hadn't sued – Joel Gaines changed all that. So all that really happened was she'd sold her half of Meadow. The companies who'd been buying it all knew her. Her reputation was good.

Dina loved beauty. But, right now, the only person that appreciated it was herself. She wanted to run a boutique, to run it successfully – but for somebody else, for a big salary. Maybe she'd have to work her way up, but Meadow's success should get her through the door. Meadow was her reference, her college degree. *The University of Gorgeous.*

Dina laughed to herself. Saks, Glamour, Bloomingdales . . . She'd go to work in one of these places, and she'd show the store what the beauty business was all about. And after the job, she'd pick up a lover. And stop thinking about Joel Gaines.

Definitely stop thinking about him . . .

The punching bag reeled from the force of the blow.

'Man!' Shamek Ahmed, his trainer, stumbled back a little. 'That's good. That's real good. Something got into you?'

Joel Gaines was stripped to the waist. Beads of sweat dewed the muscles of his back and legs. Outside the walls of his office, the sun was low in the sky as it rose.

New York City was just waking up. Gaines had been working for nearly an hour.

Shamek liked Joel better than most of his celebrity clients. They said he was a son of a bitch, and he didn't tolerate lateness. Or softness. But he worked himself harder than he worked the staff. By seven thirty a.m., this workout would be done and he would have showered and changed into one of those limey-cut suits and be kicking Wall Street ass.

'Nah.' Another flurry of blows – like the punchbag insulted his mother. 'Same old shit, different day.'

'I hear ya,' Shamek said. He didn't do *Yes, sir* and Gaines didn't ask him to. When you bellowed at guys all day long, deference didn't come natural.

For the last month, Joel Gaines had been coming to the city earlier. Working harder – much harder. There was a gym set up in one corner of this cavernous office, better than many professional places Shamek worked. And it wasn't just for show, either. Gaines went for it. This morning he had piled on the weights, grunting, pushing, hefting everything up; thirty minutes fast on the treadmill – six, seven miles an hour; a hundred push ups; working the barbells, now the bag. He was like a man ten, fifteen years younger. Or like somebody very angry, very frustrated.

None of Shamek's business. He admired the dorsal muscles in Gaines' back, knotting, releasing.

His timer buzzed. 'OK. You're done. Make that shower hot, and get some aspirin. You're going to be pretty sore.'

A dark smile. 'That's how we know we're still alive, right?'

'Right.' Shamek grinned. 'Stretch.'

'No time.'

'At least five minutes or I'm cancelling tomorrow's session.'

'Fuck you!' grunted Joel, but he started stretching.

Shamek slapped his client on the back. If only they were all that way . . . 'Well done, Joel.'

Bob Goldstein looked at the spreadsheets projected on the wall in front of them. 'This was really first rate.'

'Yes, sir.' Leo Tsardis, L'Audace's interim chairman, spoke up. He had the face of a drowning man who's just been thrown a lifejacket. 'Meadow is a lead product already. Our early production run is sold out. The new factory is going to ship fifty thousand units for spring. We have a team of chemists taking the formula and working on a range.'

'It's rebranded Meadow – Audace,' chimed in his colleague, Tamara Miller. She ran the company PR, and that haunted look was gone from her face. 'The industry loves it; they're saying it's an extraordinary acquisition. Really, the business pages are full of it.'

'Stores are taking everything we can ship. We estimate five million in sales in the first six months.'

Goldstein thumped the table. 'Anchor product. Bought for peanuts.'

'The initial marketer made good contacts. Very young kid: Dina Kane was her name. Knew how to sell. We had an easy time going in.'

'Maybe we should hire her,' Bob Goldstein said.

'No.' Gaines spoke up. 'Definitely not. She's far too young.'

Goldstein arched a brow. 'I remember when they said that about you.'

Gaines shrugged. Dina Kane had been on his mind far too much. Nothing he did could erase her image. Not sex with his wife, beautiful and mundane as she was. Not work. Not the way Meadow was flying off the shelves. Everything brought her back, reminded him of her. If she came to work for the company, he wouldn't be able to control himself. And Joel Gaines was always in control.

'She's not the corporate type. She got more money than she ever dreamed of with Meadow. Leave it at that.'

'Maybe she needs a job,' Tamara volunteered. 'It would be a great story.'

Gaines' fingers curled into a fist. 'Drop it.'

She dropped it.

'We need some more products to sell – maybe not another Meadow, but still higher quality. The brand was pimping itself out; it lost its reputation for high-end. Do you have any more tricks up your sleeve, Joel?'

'L'Audace is our major focus for the year,' Goldstein said. 'You guys concentrate on cutting costs, making Meadow, growing the line. Other products will be joining it.' He looked at his partner. 'Joel will make that happen. We want to have the company healthy for sale by the end of the year.'

'Sure. No problem,' Gaines said. 'Let's wrap this up. I'm seeing our bankers in forty minutes on the airline deal. Car's waiting.'

The limousine purred through the traffic.

Gaines glanced out of his tinted windows. He enjoyed these rides, the cavernous seats, the buttery leather, not having to think. It was a small vacation from the chaos of his day. His habit was to switch the cellphone off and stare at the traffic flowing silently past his soundproofed car.

It was hypnotic. Meditation.

Maybe he shouldn't have done that – stopped the girl from getting a job. She was a good kid; ballsy as hell, hard working,

inventive. And he'd spiked her just because he found it uncomfortable thinking about her. Because he, Gaines, feared a lack of
control.

He winced at the thought.

There were all kinds of good reasons to call Dina Kane. He
would find her a job – someplace else. That was the solution: get
her work, but not too near him. Salve his conscience.

And then, products . . . The chemist had ducked out, headed
back to Europe and a comfortable retirement. Gaines Goldstein
wasn't interested in developing new products itself – the company had no research labs. He wanted to buy other little brands,
ones like Meadow that worked out of the gate, that would make
L'Audace a cosmetics house. And then he could dump it.

At Gaines Goldstein level, you moved forward or stepped
aside. That was it.

Dina Kane knew where he could find the good stuff. Gaines
much preferred to work that way, rather than through inter-
mediaries.

Yeah. That was a perfect reason. In fact, he had to do it.

He pulled out his cellphone and turned it on.

Dina was running. The East River, to her left, was grey and cold,
but the sight of the water still soothed her. She was dressed warmly
– gloves, a hat – music pumping through her earphones; she would
never swap the street for the gym. There would have to be a
blizzard. You got the light here, the street, the people, skyscrapers,
traffic, streetcars: all Manhattan's variety, pace and power.

It drove Dina. It pushed her. She felt like she was going somewhere, seeing something. There was a point. That's what made it
so good.

Her music stopped. Incoming call. Her heart flipped in her
chest. She prayed it wasn't the rehab centre calling to say Johnny
was sick, or in hospital. Or worse.

'Hello?'

'Joel Gaines.'

She slowed to a halt, feeling the cool air on her face, calming the immediate blush. 'Mr Gaines. Yes, sir.'

'Joel.'

'OK.'

'You sound busy.'

'No! No, I'm just running. It's fine; I mean, I'd love to talk to you.' She winced, bit her lip. *I'd love to talk to you? Jesus.*

'I want some recommendations from you. The products you sourced at your little store. Do you still have access to a list?'

'Yes,' she said. 'You want to buy them?'

'Small producers.' Dina could almost hear the shrug at the end of the line. 'You told me you went into this because they worked. That's what I'm looking for. Will you send me the list?'

'Certainly, as soon as you send me two hundred thousand dollars.'

He laughed, and she could hear the shock. 'What?'

'Come on, Joel.' Dina paced, gripping the phone. 'You got a deal on Meadow. And now you want to save maybe six months of research by taking my list and making offers to European boutiques. If you say yes right away, I won't raise the price to two fifty.'

'My God,' he said. 'That's it. I give up.' There was a pause, then he added, 'Come to lunch. Come today. I'll cancel my appointment.'

'Where?'

'I'll book somewhere.'

'If you come to my apartment, I'll cook for you. I can also print you the full list, and you can hand me a cheque for the two hundred grand.'

'That's a deal, kid. One p.m. Give me your address.'

Dina returned home early. She was far too excited for anything else. Quickly, she peeled off her workout clothes, headed to the wet room, showered and washed her hair.

She towelled off frantically and selected an outfit: a simple, sleeveless woollen shift, scarlet red – bold, like she wanted to be with him – sheer Wolford hose and ballet flats. She was trying to look casual, when she felt anything but. Her make-up had to be perfect, in case he had second thoughts about buying her list. She dived into her old stock from the Green Apothecary, applying feather-light mousse foundation, putting bronze lipstick against olive-green shadow, a touch of ochre blush, high on the cheekbones, and then solid, Egyptian mascara, so her eyes popped like Cleopatra.

She applied fast – five minutes – then she set the table; thank God there was yesterday's chilli still in the fridge. Dina was no gourmet, but she'd learned to cook to save money – dishes that could last and be warmed through were a favourite. Chilli, a salad, sparkling water and she set the coffee grinds into her pot: done.

There was nothing fancy. She wasn't worried. Gaines wasn't that kind of guy.

Dina ran back into the dressing room and got out the hairdryer. It was super-pro; one of the Green Apothecary's clients, a girl who owned a salon, had lent it to her and it was ideal at a time like this, when she wanted to nuke herself.

She blasted the air, aiming the nozzle right at her English Mason Pearson brush . . .

The buzzer went.

Dina jumped out of her skin. Her hair was still damp and tousled against the chic little dress.

It buzzed again. She glanced at her watch. Twelve thirty. *Damn it.*

'Go away!' she called out. 'I have somebody coming round in half an hour.'

'You have somebody round now,' Gaines replied through the door.

She shuddered and hurried to open the door.

He was standing there in a light blue shirt and navy suit. Almost six foot, he loomed over her, the strong body looking even more developed than before. The dark eyes glittered with amusement.

Dina squirmed. 'Joel . . . I'm not . . . not ready.'

'You look ready to me. Can I come in?'

She surrendered. 'Yes. Of course.'

He stepped inside, glanced around her place. 'Stylish. Who's the designer?'

'Me. I buy tired apartments, put in a little cosmetic work . . .'

'I should have known.'

'It's on the market for one and a half, if you want a pied-à-terre,' she said boldly.

'I think you've taken quite enough of my money for now.'

He took her in: the sexy, nervous length of her; that stunning face and slender body framed by damp hair; the way she was looking at him – the challenge, the admiration. The desire. The obvious desire.

Susan never looked at him like that. Not anymore. Gaines didn't know that she ever had. There was fun once, mutual affection, friendship . . . But love? He wasn't so sure. And never passion. Susan was willing, welcoming, accommodating. When he was younger, with his eyes on the prize, achieving great things in business, it was more than enough. She made a great home, was an elegant hostess, a good mom. And that was marriage.

Passion was for the movies. Rich men's wives were a certain breed. Elegant, educated, active on their school boards, they played tennis in the Hamptons, remembered to send gifts on friends' birthdays; they remodelled their kitchens and maybe had some small job. What they did was a social enterprise, war on a thousand fronts that men didn't bother with.

Dina Kane was not that kind of girl.

And he was fascinated.

'What's for lunch?' he asked, to distract himself.

'Chilli and rice,' she said, still blushing.

'Really?' He smiled again. Nobody had served him a bowl of plain chilli in years. 'Goddamn, that sounds good.'

'Take a seat.'

He pulled up a chair at her sleek little dining table. His practised eye could see she had spent a few dollars well: a good omen for business.

Dina served them each a large steaming bowl of the meat and beans, with a little rice. After the workout that morning, he was starving.

'It's good.'

'Thank you.' She reached to pour him water, leaning over him. He breathed in the scent of her shampoo and bath soap.

Dina sat back down and lifted her fork. She ate, head bowed. She wouldn't look at him, almost like she couldn't look at him.

When he had finished, Joel said, 'That was excellent.' He stood and cleared his bowl away to the kitchen. 'You can always get a new career as a cook.'

'I don't think I'll ever be making morsels of salmon in a pomegranate coulis, or whatever they serve in the good restaurants these days.'

'Open a place on Wall Street that does chilli, steaks, lasagne. Most businessmen haven't had a proper meal in years. I could happily die without ever seeing *jus* on a menu ever again.'

Dina laughed. 'I'm better at what goes on people's faces than what goes into their mouths, Mr Gaines.'

'Joel.'

She blushed again. 'I know. I just find it difficult.'

'Why?'

'Because you're so . . .' Her voice trailed off. 'You know.'

'Enlighten me.'

'Powerful. Successful. A major figure.' Dina was now bright red, and she tried to cover it by jumping to her feet and clearing the table. 'You're a legend – as you know.'

'I do know. It's still enjoyable hearing you say it.'

Dina felt herself moisten with desire. He was so arrogant, so handsome, so cocky. And it was justified; who could say it wasn't?

'Do you have the list?'

'Yes. Of course.' She was relieved to be able to flee into her bedroom, to get the printout from her computer. It was thick – ten pages long. 'I've made entries in bold of the brands you should look at – small manufacturers; good sellers – I can send you some notes, too.'

'Excellent.' He took the sheaf of pages and flicked through it; a few companies there were already on his radar. 'You're quite right, of course. This will save us months of prep work.'

'Then you will give me the cheque?'

'You sound as though you doubt it.'

Dina shrugged. 'Two hundred grand for a computer printout.'

He looked at her. 'I made the deal. When I make deals, they happen: first rule of business.'

He snapped open his briefcase and handed her a neatly typed cheque. Dina looked at it, the figures swimming before her eyes. This was really happening, this, her life.

'Thank you, Mr— Joel.'

'You can't just bank it. How much is left of the half million?'

'Not much. There was this place. My brother needed rehab. Taxes.'

He nodded. 'You need a job.'

Dina's heart pounded. 'Can I work for you?'

'I'm not in the beauty business. This is just one of many for me.' His eyes swept over her. 'Besides, that might not be a good idea.'

'Why not?' she whispered.

'My turn to say, "you know".'

Dina's heart thudded in her chest. She thought she might gasp with longing. He'd acknowledged it, right there in her apartment – the electricity between them.

'I'm married,' he said.

'Of course.'

But he was still looking at her. Dina's knees trembled a little. She could not remember ever having wanted anything more than she wanted this guy.

'You need to work for somebody, however. I can mentor you a little. What do you want to do?'

'I'd like to be a director of beauty retail. One of the major stores. Something well-paid, where I can make an impact. Saks, Bloomingdale's . . .'

'How about Torch?'

Dina wrenched her eyes from Gaines' face and body. Torch was the veteran ladies' fashion emporium on the Upper West Side, with the Lady Liberty logo, packed into twelve floors of belle époque New York splendour. But the architecture of the venerable building was the sexiest thing about it. The store had a great past, but the future was kind of dusty. Big in the eighties, Torch had settled to become a sort of halfway house. It stocked everybody, but didn't get the hip collections. Saks and Bloomingdale's had all the luxe, Glamour was the ethical shopping destination of the liberal elite and Macy's, downtown, competed on mid-price and sheer space.

All Torch had going for it was that it was uptown, so it mopped up local shoppers who couldn't be bothered to get in a cab. And, living on past glory, its average customer was fifty plus. Big sellers were fur coats, shawls and a lot of jewelled sequin jackets.

Not Dina Kane's cup of tea. But a venerable New York name.

'If I had a free rein,' she said, carefully.

'It's perfect for you. Why would you want to go somewhere successful?'

Dina smiled.

'Very good. Bank your cheque. I know the old man that owns that store. He lives in California now, enjoying the sun. He'll take a recommendation from me.'

Dina didn't know what to say. Just like that, he could swoop in, swoop down and make her life better. The ease of it; the naked power on display.

'I . . . Thank you.'

'Thank me by proving how brilliant I am at sourcing staff.'

'Should I call them?'

'They'll call you.' He stood, picked up the briefcase. 'So, now we're done.'

'Joel, will I see you again?'

For a long, brutal second, he looked her over, wanting the girl, liking the girl, feeling her electricity, the desire, the lifeforce.

'Maybe one day.' The words he forced out, with supreme discipline, sounded like somebody else was saying them. 'After you get a boyfriend.'

'Then I'll get a boyfriend,' she said.

Gaines immediately wanted to kill him.

'Goodbye,' he said, and he walked out of her door before he said something he could never take back.

Chapter Ten

'Welcome to Torch.'

Regina Freeman was bored with her life, and it showed. African-American and passably elegant, she had reached fifty-one and the heights of high achievement in life: a big salary, director at a major store, a husband in tort law and two kids at college.

The fire of her early days was smothered in comfort: a nice two-bedroom in a tree-lined block just off Columbus; great health, dental and long-term care insurance; cruise vacations with the same people every year; visits to her folks in Jersey at Thanksgiving. You didn't rock the boat with your life like that. Not ever.

She ran Torch's day-to-day operations. Staff costs were low, volume was high; they carried just enough high-end clothes to remain a major store. Mostly, the matrons of the Upper West shopped here. The Morgan family owned it, and the business paid low rates and no rent. They could afford to coast, and that's exactly what they were doing. Regina's job was just to keep the bills paid.

'You come highly recommended,' she said.

She was wearing a neat little Ann Klein pantsuit with a pink cotton blouse and mules: safe, easy wear. The young girl before her was different. Startlingly well made-up, she was a beauty in chic green Prada with a Mulberry handbag and Kate Spade wedges. Her look said *fashion. Chic. New.* All the things Torch wasn't.

'Thank you, ma'am.'

Regina softened fractionally. She appreciated good manners; she hated how the youth of today usually stared at their iPhones and never looked at you.

'You have something to do with Meadow, by L'Audace? We stock that here.'

'I helped bring that to market. I sold it to Mr Gaines; I think he recommended me to Mr Morgan. I also ran a successful independent beauty store downtown.'

'Big retail is very different.'

'Yes, ma'am. I'm here to learn.'

'Quickly, I hope, since you're going to be directing our beauty sales. I must say, Ms Kane, I've never seen anybody as young as you hired for a major job like this.'

'I do understand, Mrs Freeman. Please, call me Dina. I'll do my best to show Mr Morgan it was a good hire.'

Regina wanted to ask the girl what she was getting paid, but restrained herself. It must have been into six figures, like her own salary. The kid was coming straight to management. One fluke with a face cream and she was jumping the queue. But Dina did seem different to most young kids. She had old eyes in that pretty face.

'Do you have what you need?' Regina asked.

'I'd like to spend today observing, and then tomorrow running through our sales sheets and the order book. And I'll come up with my recommendations next week.'

'Very good,' Regina said. 'So I'll see you around.'

She walked back to her office, up the marble staircase with its faded royal blue carpet, trying to figure out the puzzle. Ludo – it had to be him. Mr Peter Morgan's son was a New York playboy, top of the most-eligible list. He always had an eye for the pretty girls. Mostly they just scored jobs as eyebrow threaders or perfume spritzers, though. Not directors of beauty.

Well, Dina Kane was uncommonly attractive. But Ludo went through two girls a month – he would tire of the novelty soon.

She'd just be patient and let the girl hang herself with her own rope. No need to rock the boat. The retirement account in her IRA was looking exceptionally healthy right now. And everybody at Torch knew you didn't mess with Ludo Morgan.

Dina walked around the dull, boring store, and felt her heart thud with excitement.

Joel Gaines, you genius.

He was so right. This place was a disaster area, and she was thrilled at the thought of putting it right.

The shop floor was badly lit and crowded with stock. Bored shopgirls talked to each other all day, ignoring the customers. Items were marked at a discount everywhere – clothes piled on tables under red *SALE* signs. Brands were jumbled with haute couture designer items, as if the store was afraid of selling the goods.

Torch looked tired – old.

The beauty department was better – if you want to be average. The big cosmetics houses controlled their own displays. Torch carried most of them, so things were standard. There was almost nothing new. She smiled when she saw the small stand for Meadow, and the steady stream of customers it was attracting.

Dina looked at the assistants in their drab white coats with the square gold nametags. Some were talking to customers; most were staring into space. Beauty wasn't doing much business. This was an older crowd, who knew what they wanted. She watched women home in on Estée Lauder or Chanel, grab a product and take it to a counter.

Like a post office, she thought. *Like buying stamps.*

There was buying – no selling. No reason to be here and not down the street, except, at Torch, you could pick up lingerie down the hall, and a cushion on floor two.

In her head, Dina saw something completely different. Space. Light. Style. A building redesigned. Exclusive clothing. Classics mixing with hot new designers. The latest beauty hits. An event store. A destination. Teens, twenty-somethings, chic professionals in their thirties and forties. The older women, too – if they were hipsters, the ones that wore black and went to off-Broadway shows. And men – a small group, mixed in with the women. Hardcore luxury addicts.

It would be intense. Huge. It would own uptown.

And it would cost a lot of money.

'Do I have to?' Ludo Morgan sighed.

He had a fun afternoon planned: cigars at the Havana club with two of his friends; tennis; a phone call to his father; perhaps a trip to the helipad – there was a cottage in the Hamptons the broker wanted him to view.

'Your father wants you to see her, sir. Just to hear her first report. She came recommended by Joel Gaines.'

'Not interested in Gaines' cast-offs. Can't he find someplace else for his girlfriends to play?'

Eric Strom shook his head. The arrogance of the kid wasn't disappearing with age.

'Mr Gaines doesn't have girlfriends. She sold him a brand. Your father put her in as beauty director.'

Now he had Ludo's full attention. 'What? Beauty what?'

'Director. With a brief to revamp the cosmetics department.'

He coloured. 'I hire personnel.'

'Yes, sir, but your father put Ms Kane in direct.'

'What experience has she got?'

'None at this level.'

Ludo Morgan's annoyance increased. Why couldn't the old man enjoy retirement? It was his time now.

'This is a mistake. I'm going to fire her. Give her three months' salary and tell her it was some kind of miscommunication. I'll see her for that.'

Eric Strom smiled slightly. It wasn't often he got to put one over on the next generation of hyper-privileged kids, but he enjoyed it when it happened.

'No, sir. She actually filed her first report direct to your father, and he loved it. Thought it had potential. He wants you to see her to discuss how Torch can execute it.'

Ludo Morgan breathed in sharply. This girl was in her early twenties, according to the paper in front of him – and already going straight to the top, over his head.

This wasn't just an annoyance. It was a power play.

'Bring her to my office,' he said. 'Twenty minutes.'

Dina Kane was prepared.

She'd read up on her new boss, Ludo Morgan: twenty-eight years old; NYU and a business degree out in California. He looked set to succeed his father, who was taking that backseat out in the sun. He dated casually. One sister – married with two children – living in Paris, with no interest in the family store. Ludo managed Torch well enough to keep it in the black, but Dina sensed no commitment, no love of his grandfather's legacy.

That was OK. She just wanted to get on, make a change, prove herself to Joel Gaines . . . to the world. Prove herself to the *world*. Dina blushed a little bit. Gaines couldn't have been plainer in his rejection.

And she'd get over it. Any day now.

'This way,' Regina Freeman said. 'Mr Morgan has come in especially to see you.'

'That's great!'

'No, it isn't.' Regina patted her on the shoulder. The kid had talent, no doubt; Dina's paper had surprised her. And her ideas might actually work – somewhere fashion forward, like Sephora. At Torch – no chance. Dina Kane would have to learn to go along to get along, just like the rest of them. 'Good luck, honey.'

Dina knocked and entered the room.

She won't last a month, Regina thought.

The young man was sitting behind a hefty oak desk, with a small chair in front of it, designed to be uncomfortable – a contrast to the way Gaines did business. The office itself was like the rest of the store: wood panelling, faded European carpet, velvet-covered couch. There were filing cabinets up against one wall and a printer was perched on top of the one closest to the desk. It all felt fussy and cramped, despite the big pre-war windows.

He didn't look up as she entered; Dina saw he was scanning her report.

'What the hell did you think you were doing reporting direct to my father?'

'Mr Morgan hired me, sir.'

'Hired you as beauty director. I run this store. Once hired, everything goes to Regina first, then she decides whether or not to take it to me. Understand?'

Now he raised his head – and looked at her, with an involuntary jerk of surprise. Dina saw him registering, approving.

She was wearing tailored slacks and a blouse, with stacked wedge heels. Her hair was worn up in a modern bun with a chic Japanese chopstick driven through it, and her make-up was bronzed today, everything for a sun-kissed look – golden highlighters on the cheeks, copper on the lips, light browns and ochres on her eyes, with chestnut mascara – as though she would be heading to a yacht on the Mediterranean, any second.

She looked stunning. And Ludo Morgan was suitably stunned.

'Excuse me,' he said, as the moment became uncomfortable. 'I was taken aback. You look like a model.'

She blushed at the unexpected compliment. Morgan was wearing a good suit – relaxed, no tie – Armani. And at least he didn't play games.

He was handsome; smooth featured, with dark blond hair. Rather like he belonged on TV, or in a rock band. Matinée-idol looks and a dapper suit on top – she could see why a kid like this would be a playboy. The girls would lap it up.

'Thank you, Mr Morgan. Beauty is my expertise, so I take care of how I make myself up. If you're interacting with customers, the first thing they do is look at your own face. You wouldn't let a shabby tailor make you a suit, would you, sir?'

Ludo laughed aloud. 'Funny. No, I suppose I wouldn't.'

'I will definitely go to Regina next time with the work,' Dina said. 'But the store needs major changes, and I wanted Mr Morgan senior to see that . . . since he took a chance on hiring me.'

'These plans require an injection of cash.'

'Yes, sir. I know.'

'Too much cash. I'm not going to authorise it. This is too much of a punt. You're unproven, and for years our customer base has been much older. We need to cater to them.'

Dina chewed on her lip. 'But, Mr Morgan—'

'My father was taken by the report, but, at the end of the day, he isn't going to overrule me. Think again about how we can sell more cosmetics. No big upgrades. Bread and butter, that's what Torch is about.'

'I . . .' Dina swallowed – the young man's face was set. 'Yes, sir.'

'You can call me Ludo,' he said, genially. 'And, from now on, go only through me.'

She went home early, dispirited.

Damn it. This was life. Nobody had any vision; nobody took chances.

Except Joel Gaines.

Dina poured herself an apple juice and listened to her messages.

'Dina! This is Laurel Sloane. I've sold your apartment! Congratulations! A hundred thou over the asking price . . .'

'Dina Kane, this is Far Haven Fields. Can you call us about Johnny? He's been taken to hospital.'

She put the juice down on the table and called a car-rental company.

The facility was small, like a country hospital normally is, but well heeled and private. As Dina walked through the doors, she took note of the gleaming floors, soft lighting and fresh flowers in the waiting area.

Not cheap. But Johnny needed it.

There wasn't insurance to cover this. Half her gains from the apartment would go in his bills. *As long as I have my brother . . .*

'He's in here,' the nurse said, showing her to a private room. Dina didn't have the heart to ask if Johnny could go on a ward.

He lay on the bed, weak, hollowed out. He had bruised patches under his eyes, like he'd gone ten rounds with Mike Tyson.

'Baby sis!' he muttered, looking at her with a weak smile. 'Good to see you! Aren't you proud of me? I'm kicking it. It's gone.'

Dina patted his hands, gently. 'Sure, I'm proud of you, Johnny – so proud.' She blinked back tears.

'That's good.' He turned his head to the pillow and fell asleep.

'Ms Kane?' A doctor entered the room, tall and patrician. He nodded at her. 'Can I see you outside?'

Dina got up and followed the doctor into the corridor.

'There was a lot of methamphetamine – crack cocaine – in his system when you brought him in,' he told her. 'You don't recover from that. You almost certainly saved his life.'

Dina's heart thudded in her chest. 'Thank God. But why does he look like that? Wasn't he meant to recover, to put on weight?'

'Cold turkey is a rough process. Your brother's immune system is compromised. There has been vomiting, dehydration. He needs stabilisation with intravenous fluids, and then feeding. Possibly physical rehab as well. There has been some muscle wastage.'

'You make it sound like he was in a concentration camp.'

'Think of it as advanced anorexia. He has induced a kind of voluntary starvation.'

Dina felt faint. 'I hope I can afford all this.'

'I hope you can,' the physician said, blankly. 'Your brother needs the treatment. I suppose you could take him back to the city, and try a public hospital . . .'

'No.' Dina shook her head. 'I take care of my family.'

She thought of her careful renovation, and the ecstatic call from her broker. *Oh, well. Profit and loss – they were only numbers.* She would never be like her mother, hoarding what she owned. But, even so, now more than ever she needed the job. She needed Ludo Morgan.

Gaines looked at the email sitting on his computer.

It was only two sentences, but he must have read it a hundred times.

Hey Joel. Have started at Torch. Run into a problem. I could use some advice. Coffee?

'This has got to stop,' he said to himself.

Last night, making love to his wife, trying to ignore the faked lust on her face, trying to maintain an erection, he had closed his eyes and thought of Dina Kane.

'Wow,' Susan had said, afterwards. 'That was incredible. You must have really liked my dress.'

'Yeah.' He was lying on their silk sheets, panting. 'Great dress. You looked sexy.'

She went to the shower, humming, and he hated himself.

But the brilliant, feisty girl was still in his thoughts. Thank God for work – Gaines flung himself into it – but now this. It was like she had telepathy; she could read his goddamned thoughts.

He clicked reply on the message. Time to be firm. Tell the girl – no coffee, no advice, no meeting.

I'm uptown later, he wrote. *Come to Eightieth and Columbus at eleven – the café there.*

'Thank you for making the time.' Dina sat with a fresh-squeezed orange juice. 'It means a lot.'

'I was in the neighbourhood. What's up?'

She was dressed down today: tight blue jeans and a white shirt, with brown cowboy boots and her dark hair in a ponytail. Minimal make-up. She looked anxious, vulnerable and sexy as hell.

Gaines swallowed, hard.

'I know what the store needs. The owner seems willing, but not his son – who runs the place.'

'Remind me . . .'

'Ludo Morgan. Twenty-eight. Business degree from UCLA. He was polite enough.'

I bet he was, Gaines thought.

'But no money. He said I'm unproven—'

'Jesus.' She was so beautiful, sitting there, so hot. He couldn't have her, and he wanted her; maybe he was falling for her. Which was so much worse. Dina Kane would never be out of his system. Gaines felt trapped, old, out of control. And rage coursed through him. He spoke with anger. 'What? Do you need me to hold your hand? Prove yourself, then! Get a success – *his* way. After you do that, go for the major revamp. That or quit and start your own goddamned business.'

Her green eyes opened, shocked. 'Joel . . . I've offended you?'

He stared at her, furiously. 'Pointless! This is pointless. Treat him like you did me, like you want something out of him and you'll do what it takes to get it. The rest is noise.'

'I'm sorry. I didn't mean to waste your time. I just went to see my brother and—'

'We all have problems. Look. We're even. I'm married. Don't email me again. You're on your own.'

He stood up and walked out of the café.

Dina watched him go. The tears welled up and she covered herself by dabbing at her mouth with a napkin.

Why does it hurt so much? I hardly know him.

You're on your own. *So be it.*

As she walked back down to Torch, Dina tried to clear her head. Gaines was right; of course he was right. She was pursuing him. Why had she asked him for coffee? Why not stick to email? Or just figure it out . . . ?

I wanted to see him.

She'd seen him. And she'd got more than she bargained for.

Her apartment was in contract. She was going to have to hand over another two hundred thousand to Johnny's hospital. Time to grow up. If she wanted to be in business, she had to act like it.

'Come in,' Ludo said.

It was the girl, Dina. She was less made-up today, but just as pretty.

'Hi. I don't have long. Got a lunch date.'

Caroline was the daughter of one of his father's friends, and it would be their third time out together. She was blonde, stick thin, a social X-ray. She looked good on his arm, but had none of the curves of this one, none of the attitude. For a moment, Ludo imagined taking Dina out instead – working-class girl from nowhere; career woman on the make.

Don't be stupid. She works for you.

'I'm going to do a little revamp of our beauty department. Bring in some exclusive products. It doesn't need much money, just a few adverts. Would you be OK with that? I'd like a budget for samples.' She put a piece of paper on his desk, a modest enough sum.

'Fine. Go ahead.'

'I can make the ad buys?'

'Sure.'

'Thanks,' Dina said.

For the next month, Dina worked tirelessly. She negotiated with the cosmetics houses to reduce the size of their stands, limiting their range and increasing the stock of bestsellers. She imported several of her favourite products – the best performers – from the Green Apothecary, and hired some of the best make-up artists in the city. New mirrors and flattering lights were screwed in on every available surface, and the carpet in the beauty department was ripped up and replaced by light-stained woods.

The place started to look like a salon.

Dina called in the staff to talk to them. They assembled in the canteen, in their dull uniforms, looking mutinously at the much-younger girl who was disrupting all their lives.

'Ladies,' she said. 'You are being stifled. Believe me, I get it. Nobody wants to stand around all day, bored out of their minds.'

Slight nods.

'We have to do so much better. I know most of you dreamed of being in the fashion industry – maybe a spa therapist; maybe a beautician – today, we're going to make that happen. Torch is about to become a spa. You engage the customer, not pressing her; only offer your very best products for her. Then step back. When she's ready, encourage her. Always thank your customers, whether they buy or not. Don't be afraid to refer them to another company's products. We want to show women how beauty can transform their lives, their self-esteem. And, when you ladies step up, I'm going to go to Mr Morgan and get you all a ten per cent raise. Because sales will rise by twenty-five per cent. Understand?'

Bigger nods. Everybody understood ten per cent.

'This store is a dinosaur. Ladies, we're going to start our own little revolution. We're going to show them how it's done. We're going to show them what women really want. Are you with me?'

This time, Dina even got applause.

She stayed up nights, walking around the empty store, playing with lighting design, spacing. She designed poster advertisements, loyalty cards. And, finally, she pulled off her master list: bloggers – beauty mavens who sat on the internet – the ones with the cult following amongst editors at fashion magazines; the ones NYU students read on a daily basis.

Hi. I'm Dina Kane, who sold Meadow cream to L'Audace. Torch is relaunching its beauty division with brand new exclusives from Europe. These will only debut here at Torch. The launch will also feature major names, free gifts and a five-minute makeover for every customer next week. Come at lunch and leave looking like a goddess. Your man won't know what hit him. Torch – for the spark.

And finally it was ready.

The relaunch week started with a bang. Dina gave out her personal cell number, and the phone never stopped ringing.

'What's your job there?'

'Free makeovers for every customer? Every one?'

'What can you do in just five minutes?'

She was busy. Every time a blogger or a beauty writer turned up, Dina squired them round personally. She repeated the same spiel fifty times a day.

'Five minutes is plenty. New York girls don't have time to waste at work. Torch is the new beauty playground; we'll show you just what looks great on you.'

'It's toys for girls.'

No blogger left without gifts. And not just the standard samples. Dina boxed up full-size products – just two or three – ones that she thought would benefit the woman in question. No standard-issue press kit. Everything was tailored.

'Wow.' Kathy Rennet, the owner of BeautyBuyer.com, stared at herself in the mirror. The make-up artist had transformed her, with just two minutes on the clock and three products – a shiny gloss, a bronzer from Portugal and dark green Revlon mascara. 'That's incredible.'

'I love it.' Emily Jones wrote for *Marie Claire* and she was bombarded with junket invitations every day. But Dina's make-up girl had changed the look of her face with a soft powder foundation she would never have touched, rose on her cheekbones and thick black mascara that covered her short lashes. 'This is amazing.'

'Not all products are great for everyone. Torch believes in personalised beauty.' Dina gestured towards the Elizabeth Arden stand. 'Eight-hour cream? It's a classic, but it's not for you. Your skin would break out.'

'I've tried it. It does.'

'When women come to Torch, we will try to sell them what works. This isn't just a store; it's a retail beautician.'

'Love it,' the journalist said again, earnestly writing *retail beautician* on her little pad.

The reviews came out in the next few days. Dina watched at home, on her computer.

Torch has the Spark.

Try their free makeovers – the store has bussed in true experts. Not your normal push for products!

Dina Kane brings in finds – this is Aladdin's cave.

They know what works. Get on the subway!

But would it translate? She'd spent every last penny on the staff, the best makeovers, the goodie bags. All new customers had to do was give out their email address . . . Dina was going to capture a database: what they bought, how old they were. Targeted mail.

She felt as nervous as she'd been in her entire life. This had to work, or she was dead. Ludo Morgan would not give her another chance.

But she had placed her bets, and now she was all in.

Chapter Eleven

'Excuse me; excuse me.' Ludo struggled through the crowd. He couldn't believe it; only ten fifteen and the ground floor was packed. Women, girls, teenagers were shoving him aside, thrusting forwards. The route to his office was blocked. The staircase entrance was thronged with chicks.

He glanced upstairs; the store there looked the same as normal – a few scattered shoppers.

'Christ! What is this? Some kind of fire drill?'

'No, sir,' a shopgirl said. 'These are customers. It is kind of crazy.'

'Customers for what?'

'The beauty department. Miss Kane's promotion.'

Ludo looked at the women in disbelief. 'Is she handing out free Chanel lipsticks?'

This wasn't normal. This wasn't Torch. He was fearful Dina Kane had gone nuts 'No, sir. Just little samples, like normal. And the makeovers. Excuse me, they need some help.' And the woman vanished.

He fought his way through to the staircase, panting, and climbed up to the first-floor balcony for a second look.

Hell. It was true. The women looked a nest of termites, swarming over his beauty department. There was jostling, and big lines at the cash registers. He could see several of the new product stands totally empty, with *sold out* signs on them. Instead of standing around, his staff were right in there, talking to the women, showing them things. Girls were perched on stools, five or six of them, being made up. The hubbub reached right up across the store, to the other, empty floors.

Ludo Morgan went into his office and shut the door. Then he wrote a little email to his father.

'Dina.'

She jumped out of her skin.

It was quarter to nine, and the store had just closed. Dina Kane was wearing a red shift dress and an air of exhaustion.

'How long have you been here?'

'Since seven a.m.'

An hour before opening.

'It's been a long time since lunch,' Ludo said.

She smiled. 'I didn't eat lunch.'

'Lunch is for wimps?'

'Something like that.' She rolled her head on her neck, stretching the muscles. 'I need to eat now, though, I'm feeling a little dizzy.'

'Low blood sugar. Let's go to Chiang Mai Thai; it's not the best, but it is right next door.'

She just nodded, too tired to argue.

Ludo ordered champagne and Dina drank a glass. She needed the energy, needed to relax. Besides, it had gone well. No denying that.

She was too tired to look at the menu; she ordered a simple chicken curry and an iced tea. Anything. She was starving.

'That was excellent work, today. I admit it: I'm impressed.'

Simple praise. She glowed a little. 'Thanks. It won't be like that all week; that was first-day stuff, after the reviews. But we should get a steady stream. I'm ordering new products from Europe. It'll be a couple of days.'

'Dina, don't get too hung up on this. I don't see a future for Torch, not like you do. The highest and best use of the building isn't a creaky department store. I want to convert it into luxury apartments, then sell it.'

'Ahhh.' She lifted a brow. 'Now I see your plan. I couldn't understand why you didn't want to make money.'

'My father has a sentimental attachment.'

'It may not be as easy as all that, though. The building is zoned commercial. There are lots of fancy condo buildings round here, and not enough stores. And Torch is the only big department store north of Bergdorf's.'

He tilted his champagne flute towards her. 'At the moment, that is true. Our architects are having no joy with the building department. But permissions like this take years. You have to build relationships with politicians . . .'

'Bribes?'

'Campaign contributions.'

'Your father might not want to dismantle.'

'The family has a majority of the stock, it passes to me and my sister . . .' Ludo shrugged. 'Eventually he will see sense. Meanwhile, I work on City Hall. It's a medium-term project.'

Dina thought about this.

'You know, Ludo, you could have both.'

'What?' he said, draining his glass and pouring another. Goddamn, she was a pretty girl, hick or no hick. What if he could spruce her up? Get her cultured? If they were dating, maybe she wouldn't be so in his face. He was bored of Caroline already – just another Identikit blonde. None of them had one interesting thing to say. At least the girls out in Cali had big fake tits and a sense of fun, not like these society ball darlings whose personalities were ironed as flat as their flaxen hair.

'You could have both. I mean, if you turned Torch around.

You see, then you'd be known as a retailing genius, and the brand would be worth something.'

'The brand? We're a store.'

'Saks was a store. Now there are branches of Saks in malls across the country, and they have a website. Saks Fifth Avenue is the flagship, but they don't need it. With Torch, the uptown store isn't as well known. So you establish the brand, open new branches and head into online sales. And then your father lets you convert the building here, and he hasn't really lost anything. You cut down the apple tree and plant an orchard.'

'My God.' He stared at her. 'That's poetry, honey. Apples and orchards.'

'It's smart business.' She gave herself a second glass, too. What the hell? She deserved some relief from the endless tension, the workaholism. 'It's what I would do, if I owned Torch.'

Ludo raised a finger. 'You had a good day in the beauty department. *I* own Torch, don't forget.'

'It's your call.'

'See what happens this week. If sales stay strong, you can double the beauty department. Lose some of those accessory tables. We have too much old stock out.'

'You can say that again.'

He lifted a brow. 'Can you revamp the rest of the store? The same way?'

'Maybe, but I'd need a couple of years to study. Beauty is my passion; I don't know about table lamps and hosiery.'

'You can at least redesign the surrounds.'

'Yes. Of course. You need that desperately. The place looks like an abandoned theatre, all moth-eaten carpet and frayed velveteen. Ugh!'

'Done. Come to me tomorrow with a budget.'

She smiled, a broad, real smile that reached her eyes.

'You really are stunning,' Ludo said, idly. 'Who's the lucky boyfriend?'

'I haven't had time.'

'What, ever?' He was liking this more and more. There was something strange, something isolated about Dina Kane. She was rough clay and would be malleable.

'Of course I've had a boyfriend, just not one at the moment.'

So not a virgin, then. Pity.

'I think we should go out,' Ludo announced. 'Let's face it – you aren't going to have lots of time on your hands from now on. I'm in reasonably good shape; you know, a few careful drivers . . .' He smiled at his own joke.

'Am I fired if I say no?' Dina's eyes narrowed.

'Not at all. And you still get your budget.'

Her shoulders slumped a little, releasing tension. 'And you'd take me out? In public?'

'If we hide it, people will talk. They say you shouldn't date at work, but where the hell else can you meet people these days? Church? A nightclub? Please!'

Dina smiled back. He was a little smug, but not unpleasant, and at least he was asking her out, straight, with no blackmail. *Come on, sweetheart, Joel Gaines is taken. Are you going to be one of those desperate obsessives who pines over a guy for forty years then dies alone with her cats?*

Hell no. She wanted family. Some friends. To be normal, for once. And Ludo Morgan was a rich, goofy kind of normal. Maybe, with him, she could watch her troubled childhood disappear in the rear-view mirror. Along with Ellen, and Edward, and every other man who'd ever leered at her.

'OK,' she said. 'You can pick me up Friday night at eight. But first you have to ask your dad's permission. I need the job.'

'Sure.' He nodded.

Sweet. If she worked out, her job was going to be looking after him. But Ludo was happy with taking things one step at a time.

* * *

He got her into a cab, then went back into the store and rode the elevator to the penthouse floor, already the owner's apartment. It was the best thing about living in this city. Beverly Hills was sun-drenched, laid back, but Ludo liked to see the city and the park spread out around him through the pre-war windows on every side, like it all belonged to him.

One day it would. He wanted a life of ease and wealth, but also success – the heir who built his father's fortune up, greater than it was before. He wanted a pretty, sexy wife, well-behaved kids, the respect of his peers, the best of everything.

And the key to life was taking your opportunities.

He walked into his office, designed as a small library, with a flat-mount TV, speakers in the walls and the best gaming computer known to man. The monitor jumped to life and he sent his father an email.

> Beauty expansion going well. My programme will revamp the entire department and store. Dina Kane contributing a few ideas, too. A smart hire. I'd also like to date her, and she wanted your permission first. Seems like a sensible girl. A hard worker. I plan to expand our business once the brand is revitalised, to online and outlets. There will be a full year programme. Hope you're well, Dad. Love, Ludo.

That would hit the sweet spot: *Sensible. A few ideas. Hard worker.* His father hadn't taken to any of the women he'd got as far as introducing; found them dull and venal.

Dina would come up with her ideas, he would cherry pick and execute. Which meant he got the credit – the commander, not the sergeant major. She would be happy enough with her creative freedom, a big salary rise, bonus . . . As long as she didn't tread on his toes. Besides, once he picked up her rules, he could do it all himself. Dina would have other, more pleasant things to do by then: shopping – for herself; lounging by the pool; travelling with him. He wondered if she even had a passport. Probably never crossed the state line, unless it was to Jersey.

There was a whole world out there, and Ludo was prepared to show it to this girl.

As long as she understood the rules of the game. He was first; that wasn't even a question.

'Dina Morgan,' he said to himself.

It sounded good.

'Edward, you're sitting over there.'

Edward stared blankly at his mother. He had pulled out the chair at the top of the table, where he sat, where his father used to sit. It might be Momma's house, but he was head of the family now.

'No, Mother, this is my seat now, remember?'

He hoped it wasn't stress again. Wasn't any kind of crash. It wouldn't do for Penny Johnson to swap alcohol for pills, not when she was doing so well.

'Philippe is going to sit there.'

Edward almost laughed. 'What?'

Philippe Leclerc was his mother's boyfriend, if you could call it that. A Frenchman, a former violinist in the New York Symphony Orchestra, slim and dapper, if you liked pale grey suits. He was talented as a musician, but not first rank. Edward had no idea what he did for a living.

Philippe had been round far too often – laughing with Penelope in the dining room after dinner, playing bridge with her till all hours, taking her to the opera, the theatre, paying extravagant compliments. He gave enough bows and kisses on her hand for a Renaissance court.

'Yes,' said his mother, her eyes flashing unusually. 'I've asked Philippe to move in with me. So, while we're courting, I would prefer him at the head of the table. You do understand, darling?'

'Mother, I really think—'

'No, Edward.' His mother's voice was firm, even a little strident. 'I've been thinking hard, and you know I'll always be grateful to you, darling, but it's time I stepped back into life on my own. It's not healthy for you to be so *tied* to me. I know you'll be wanting your own place. You can move out now, because Philippe will take care of me.'

'Mother.' Edward saw the danger he was in. 'Philippe has no money – none at all.'

'Oh, I know that, dearest. But money isn't everything. He's a highly accomplished man.'

'He's a retired middle-chair violinist. Ten years ago he was accomplished. Now what does he do?'

'He lives simply,' his mother said. 'He's quite open about all that.'

'He's after your fortune.'

'Please don't be crass, Edward. You speak as though he couldn't be attracted to me on my own . . . His focus has been in music; not every man can be a banker.'

The doorbell rang.

'I know I can trust you not to make a scene,' Penelope Johnson said.

Edward reluctantly got up and moved to the side.

'Monsieur Philippe Leclerc,' the butler said.

Monsieur, my ass. He's about as French as a burger and fries. Probably born here.

Philippe entered the room, beaming, in his elegant suit, with a Louis Vuitton luggage set being received by the servants in the hall behind him.

'Penelope. *Chérie*. What a happy day.' He drew close and kissed her softly, on both cheeks. 'And the wonderful *Edouard*. *Salut*. I am so happy you could join us on this special evening.'

'I believe you're joining *us*, Mr Leclerc.'

Penny shot a look of daggers at him.

'*Bienvenue*,' Edward said.

'How charming! He speaks French. You have certainly raised a wonderful young man, Penelope. I look forward to getting to know you, Edward, as we live together now.'

'Isn't this wonderful!' Penny said. She looked eagerly at Edward. 'Aren't you two going to be such friends?'

'Ah! God! Not so rough! Angel! Angel!' shrieked the girl.

Edward looked down at her, splayed and tied over the table. Her buttocks were red – lacerated with the whip. *Angel* was her safe word.

He lashed her again. And again. The rage was thick in him. She was a hooker, undocumented; he could have her deported. His fury was all that counted. His fury at Dina, at his mother.

Strike.

Scream.

She was sobbing, begging. 'No more! No more! Please, I'll do anything. Anything …'

'You'll do anything, anyway,' he snarled, and hit her.

The girl moaned, then her head lolled as she fainted.

Edward Johnson unbuttoned his fly, and started to rape her.

The feeling subsided a bit, after that. It worked every time. But it always came back. He liked it, liked giving money-hungry sluts what they deserved. He would dress, drop a few hundred on the bed and leave.

Some men in the scene were dumb. They stuck with the same girls and the same places. They got caught – lawyers, police, lawsuits, names in the papers.

Edward bounced around – fake names, new clubs, paying only in cash. He went to motels, not the women's apartments. No cameras. They were hookers and they got money, enough for some quack to stitch them up.

Tonight, though, as he showered in his room in the hotel across the street, he already knew it wasn't enough. He wanted control, real control. Philippe Leclerc was sitting in his house, drinking his father's wine, fucking his mother, and all without a cent to his name.

The guy was dead meat. And he meant that literally.

'I think you should consider a prescription,' Dr Summers said.

Edward stared at him. 'What for? I'm not ill.'

'For anxiety. I'd like to put you on a course of Klonopin.'

Edward rolled his eyes. 'Please. Sedative pills? Do I look frightened?'

Yes, Dr Summers thought. *Very*.

'Edward, you have many issues to work through. They go back beyond your fling with the waitress, beyond the divorce. Your early behaviours with women . . . You have esteem issues, anger issues. This runs deeper than you know. I feel strongly that you need calm to begin the work.'

'I am calm, doctor. I'm just worried for my mother.'

'You're not sleeping, Edward. You're erratic.'

He sat on the couch, head bowed. 'OK, doctor, you can give me the prescription. Thank you.'

Always important to keep them happy. What the fuck did this guy know? Edward's mother insisted on this therapy, when she was the one who was insane.

Edward went to a pharmacy to fill the prescription. Who knew? It might come in useful. He wasn't sleeping, but then sleep was overrated. Besides, he had other ideas for those pills.

'Faustina?' His secretary was waiting in the little office space, sitting there, reading a magazine. 'What are you doing?'

'Oh, sorry, Edward; we haven't had any calls . . .'

She blinked; her boss hadn't darkened the door for days. Wasn't she supposed to sit here and be decorative?

'First of all, you call me *sir*. I'm the boss.'

'OK . . . sir.'

'Second of all, get me some real-estate brokers. I want to see apartments – between one and two million. And mortgage brokers, too.'

'Yes, sir.'

'Then get me a call sheet of all my mother's financial advisers. I want to check something.'

'Yes, sir.'

'And lastly, get Cabot Associates on the phone.'

The older woman blinked. What had got into Edward Johnson?

'Yes, sir,' she said, nervously.

This was a good job, where she mostly did nothing. She didn't want to lose it.

Edward went into his office and slammed the door, and Faustina picked up the phone. Better get dialling.

That shrink was right about one thing, Edward thought. He *was* angry. He was so angry, the rage was now cascading from his heart into a whirlpool of hate. His father. His friends. Dina Kane. His mother. He had *rescued* his mother, and now she treated him like this, moving him aside for some penniless Frenchman.

He hated her stupidity. He could hear them laughing on Park Avenue.

At first, Edward had been lazy . . . He'd only wanted the money and an easy life.

But now he wanted revenge. And it was going to require some work.

He thought about the girl, blubbering and moaning as he lashed her exposed buttocks, slammed into her unconscious, warm body. God, that felt good; the control felt good. It was a long time since Edward Johnson felt good.

He was going to take back what belonged to him – not his wastrel quitter of a father; not Philippe; not his treacherous mother, who valued a smooth tongue and a fake compliment over her own son – him. Edward. His mind drifted to his picture, his perfect-future picture. Edward Johnson on the lawn of his Hamptons beach house, kissing his wife goodbye as he headed off to a tennis tournament. He wore tennis whites and a Rolex. She was in cut slacks and a little cashmere sweater – a blonde in pearls. There was a dog and a maid. His friends were waiting for him. His company was back in the city. Everything was perfect. He was respected, admired . . .

Not like today.

They had forced him into this, forced him into the hookers, the drugs, the showdown with some French chancer. They'd taken away his position, everything he was. Time to put it back.

'Yes, Mr Johnson, of course I can show you some wonderful properties. Even in that lower price range, there are gems out there.'

Edward swallowed his annoyance. 'I want a perfect, single-bedroom apartment. With views.'

'What a pity you didn't come to us a week ago. I have a client who just sold her place overlooking the East River for one and a half. Real bachelor pad. She made a ton on it. She's that girl who founded the Meadow cream; you heard of her?'

He started. 'Dina Kane?'

'Oh, you know her?'

'I've just heard of the cream.'

'That's her. Great eye for real estate. She's buying someplace else. Anyway, we'll find you something.'

'I want to live on the West Side.' Close to his mother's house. 'Has the Kane property closed?'

'Not yet, but it is in contract.'

'I'd like to see it, just to take in her design ideas.'

'Sure. We can set that up for you.'

* * *

He ate a sandwich at his desk while the calls continued.

'I don't really know if I should discuss this with you, Mr Johnson.'

'Mr Traynor, you have to discuss it with me. My mother gave me power of attorney.'

'There have been changes just recently. Your family holding company, Johnson Columbus, has made moves to dispose of some of its stock and invest in properties.'

Edward sat bolt upright, although he already knew the answer to his next question.

'Properties? Where, exactly?'

'Paris.'

'Who authorised this?'

'Mrs Johnson did, last week. It's all quite proper. She came in with her fiancé, Monsieur Leclerc. Of course, you know he will be on the board of the company very shortly.'

Edward hesitated just a fraction. 'Yes, of course, I realise that. It's a family company, after all.'

When he hung up, he felt almost joyful. Good things were about to happen.

The last meeting of the afternoon came in at five p.m.

'Faustina, you can go home.'

'Yes, sir.'

Edward didn't want anybody listening in to this one.

Olivia Broadwell sat before him, rake thin, her hair mouse-brown and natural. She had clear skin and light eyes; no make-up of any kind. She sat there in her Burberry mackintosh, not bothering to take it off, like she had somewhere else to be, and Edward knew he'd found his salvation.

'What's the job?' she said.

'Dina Kane. I want to know everything about her. Where she lives; who she's fucking; what she earns; the content of her bank account; the car she drives; her friends – if she has any; family –

their addresses. Any vulnerabilities, business and personal. Medical conditions.'

'We work within the law,' she said, with a face that implied the opposite. 'We provide data. We never reveal to clients how we obtained that data.'

'I understand. I don't want the firm having any record of this transaction. Declare the income, but I prefer to pay cash.'

'Fine by us.' The rat-like girl smiled, flashing white teeth. Cabot operated on the very edge of the law. They weren't like any of the other white-collar spy firms. They were highly effective, very dirty. Not many lawsuits, either. Rumour was they had files on cops and judges in the city – files three inches thick.

Mostly, targets never knew they were investigated. He heard some bad bastards worked for Cabot. And that's exactly who he wanted to hire.

'How fast can you get me what I need?' Johnson said.

'Fee is three hundred k. Is she a cop? Military or intelligence?'

'She's a fucking beautician,' Johnson said, laughing. 'A girl.'

'Then you can get everything in a week's time. And I do mean everything.'

He smiled a rich, deep, smile, the warmth running through him like he'd just stepped into a hot tub.

'How would you like the money?' Edward asked. 'Hundred-dollar bills?'

He stopped off at a florist's before he went home. Roses and lilies: his mother's favourites.

'Oh, Mr Edward,' said one of the maids. 'She's waiting for you in the garden, sir.'

Penelope was indeed out there, wrapped in one of her silver fox coats – one that his father had given her. A fresh burst of pain wrapped itself around Edward's heart. Once his father and mother had been here together, and that vicious little bitch, Dina Kane, had destroyed them. Whatever happened now, it was Kane's fault.

'Oh, Edward! I'm so glad you came.'

He offered her the flowers, kissing her on both cheeks. The acrid scent of cheap aftershave hung about her. Edward's fingers curled into a fist.

'I've got some wonderful news, darling. Philippe proposed! He said he can't live without me.'

She turned to him and extended her left hand. On it, in the place of his father's giant emerald-cut diamond, was a small ruby, surrounded by seed pearls.

'It was his mother's. They love coloured stones in Europe . . . Oh, darling, I'm so happy. Philippe said he doesn't care about money; he just wants us to be together. We're going to honeymoon in Paris . . . Paris!'

'Mother . . . you hardly know Philippe. If he really loved you, he wouldn't ask you yet . . .'

'Edward, no.' She clutched the flowers, furiously. 'I've been dating Philippe quietly ever since I stopped drinking. You don't know everything about my life, darling. Now I must insist you don't spoil today for me, or I'll have to ask you to leave.'

Edward swallowed the bile in his throat. He was angry at himself for even trying. Didn't he know better?

'Of course. You understand it's my role to protect you, Mother. Philippe might be just the man for you.' He forced a smile. 'I do think Paris is a wonderful idea. You can get away for the spring . . .'

'Oh, yes. I can't wait to leave New York.' She clung to Edward's sleeve, almost desperately. 'And you'll give him a chance?'

He's had his chance.

'Absolutely, I will.'

'We're going to buy a place together, in fact. Philippe thinks it's a tremendous time to invest in Europe. You can trust bricks and mortar, whereas these stocks give us both a headache.'

'Paris has some wonderful properties.' Edward smiled. 'I can see you both on the left bank.'

'Darling, I'm so relieved you're going to be *reasonable*. He wants to see you, you know. He's waiting in the library . . .' She dropped her voice, conspiratorially. 'I think he's going to ask your permission. He wants to do everything the right way, just to please me.'

'Well, so he should, Momma. Don't worry, I'll give him my blessing.' He leaned in and kissed her on the cheek.

The servants had laid a fire in the library, the way his father used to do. It was maybe his single favourite thing about the house. A crackling log fire, old books: it gave the place that air of British refinement.

And now there was this bastard of a Frenchman standing in front of it, warming his ass. He saw Edward come in, and smiled warily.

'Edouard! I take it you've heard the happy news?'

'I have.' He frowned a little. Roll over too fast and the little weasel would get suspicious. 'Mother tells me you want my permission.'

'Her father is dead, so . . .' Philippe shrugged. 'This is the old-fashioned way, and if it would make your mother happy I ask.'

'Why don't we sit down?' Edward suggested.

Philippe settled into the old high-backed burgundy chair and Edward took the green leather armchair opposite it. The fire danced in the grate. How easy it would be to take up a poker and smash his head in, once, twice.

'You know, Philippe, I need to be sure you have Mother's interests at heart. It seems like a very early marriage, and she is a rich woman.'

'Of course, I will take no offence.' He smiled silkily. 'Your mother is of an age where she is not twenty-one anymore. After divorce, many women know what they want. I love her, and she needs a companion; it is not healthy for a young man such as you to remain in the house.'

'And a prenuptial agreement?'

His eyes widened innocently. 'Ah, we do not accept those. If one is not committed to marriage, why marry? Penelope seems very firm. She tells me, when she married your father she was a girl; now she is a woman. We will share what we have.'

'And you have . . . ?'

'My talent; my creativity. A lifetime of devotion. I can give Penelope guidance. Also, she wants to have a little fun, and this is my gift . . . The gift of laughter.'

Laughter, all the way to the bank.

He smiled warmly. 'She certainly deserves some laughter. Very good, you have my blessing, Philippe. Bring a smile back to my mother's face.'

Edward reached across and offered a handshake. The Frenchman's sweaty palm slipped into his, and he refrained from crushing it between his fingers.

The dinner was almost unendurable, but he endured it. It was good to see that Philippe liked to drink. Edward matched him, keeping his glass full, but taking only small sips, then calling for a different wine. But Philippe stopped at three glasses, looking sideways at his new fiancée, who stuck to water, gazing adoringly at him all the while.

'But it's so tremendous you get on so well,' Penelope exclaimed when they got to dessert. 'I couldn't be happier.' She pressed her fingers to her forehead. 'I may skip the coffee and petits fours, though; I have a headache.'

'Come on, Mother, you should go upstairs to rest. I'll send Philippe up soon, I promise.' Edward winked jovially at his stepfather-to-be. 'We'll just head to the drawing room for some conversation, a small brandy . . .'

Philippe perked up immediately. 'Well . . . if my *chérie* does not mind?'

'Oh, no! That sounds lovely. I will . . . I will be upstairs.' She pushed back her chair. Edward suspected a migraine, from the stress, which was fine by him. When those things came on, his mother could concentrate on nothing else.

'Philippe, come on through.' Edward nodded to the butler. 'Bring me some brandy – a special bottle from the cellar. Try the Hine & Co. champagne cognac – the 1934.'

'Very good, sir.'

'You know your wine,' Philippe said, admiringly. 'The 1934 is a masterpiece.'

Penelope walked slowly and painfully up the stairs, and Edward noted that Philippe did not so much as look back at her.

The drawing room was warm, the thick velvet drapes drawn against the cold. Edward poured himself a little brandy and swallowed and spluttered, pretending to have downed a great gulp. There was a fireplace here, too, and he passed Philippe a glass full of the amber liquid, enough of it to swim in. The warmth and the comfort was too much to resist.

'I must go to your mother,' the older man said, greedily eyeing the brandy. 'She will expect me.'

'No; I recognise the signs. She has a bad headache. She won't expect more than a kiss on the cheek. It's a special occasion; drink up.'

He took a deep sip. 'Fantastic. What a cognac. *Mon Dieu.*'

'We will have a better one served at the wedding. What do you think? A small affair, hosted here? Or something larger?'

'We want it done as soon as possible; we will head down to City Hall. Just on our own. Your mother doesn't want any fuss.'

And you don't want any delay, Edward thought.

'Oh, I agree, soon – but you must enjoy the moment. A few select friends. A society columnist, perhaps. Your entrée, Philippe, into major society. Come, you don't want to stand there in a dingy room with a strip light.' He packed scorn into his voice. 'We can have a judge marry you, here, in a couple of weeks. First, you can fly Mother to Paris, see the apartment you're buying together . . .'

'There would be press coverage?'

'Lots of it,' Edward promised.

'I *would* like to see the apartment.'

'Make sure you're choosing the right one. You and Mother need to spend your money wisely when you invest together. And she would like a break. Paris has some marvellous couturiers for a second marriage; an elegant brocade coat, perhaps. I can organise the wedding here. The Johnsons do things the right way; I'm sure the Leclercs do, as well.'

'Absolutely. Yes.' He took another deep drink of the brandy. 'This stuff is *merveilleux*. I must stop, though, Edouard, or I will have a terrible hangover tomorrow.'

'No, no.' Edward suppressed his excitement. It was all going so well; it was easy. 'Take five or six of these.' He pulled out of his pocket a bottle of baby aspirin. 'Drink some water, and you will be absolutely fine.'

'*Merci*.' Philippe chucked them down like candy, and Edward poured him a large glass of water from the jug on the table, ice cubes clinking delicately. Then he took the brandy away.

'It's settled then. I will tell Mother and make the arrangements: a society wedding in two weeks. Oh, and I will have moved out of the house by the time you return – I'm buying a place of my own.'

'Fantastic!' Philippe said. 'You will be very happy in your own place.'

'I'm sure I will. Goodnight, Philippe.'

Edward worked steadily, and it was a thrill. He contacted gossip writers; he booked a judge, set a date. Invitations went out in the post, just a few trusted friends, enough to make a wedding. His mother was ecstatic; he went to the house for dinner every other night.

Enough to get Philippe a little drunk, to pass him the aspirins, to settle into a pattern.

'Darling, this is so kind of you,' Penelope said. 'I don't feel up to organising a wedding, but you're taking care of us so well.'

'Momma, you and Philippe need a proper sendoff.'

She would sit with them nights when Edward organised the digestifs, watch him hand over the headache pills, make small talk about the apartment search. He called the family travel agent, booked first-class tickets for them to Charles de Gaulle, praised the nineteenth-century penthouse Philippe was buying on the Rive Gauche. He even invited some reliable friends of his mother's around, so they could gossip over his wedding plans together.

'What do you think of these?'

Philippe sat in his father's armchair, lording it over proceedings, nursing his vintage brandy. Matthew and Jane Elliott, and Lourdes and Spencer McCain, two of their old crowd of couples, had been dragooned in, reluctantly, but Edward had persuaded them.

'Edward – I did a lot of business with your father,' Matthew said. 'And this French guy . . . I gotta be honest with you . . . not our kind of thing.'

'Matt, Dad's gone. He's finding himself. Mom needs to see Jane. You know she's gotten over substance abuse. The wedding means a lot to her. Just show up once, please.'

Sigh. 'OK, son, since you insist.'

'I don't think your mother should marry this man,' Lourdes McCain told him. 'Please don't be angry at me, Edward.'

'It's not our decision, though – and she's dead set. Look, I just want her to be happy. You can help. One dinner.'

And they showed.

Edward took no chances. He booked the airline tickets and paid for them in full. He found a small apartment, right on Central Park West, a block from his mother's. It was overpriced and tiny, but that location always sold. To the world, he was totally involved with the wedding, backing it to the hilt.

There were no whores, no girls to hit, no S&M clubs. Edward had grown up. He was focused now. There would be time for all that later. The thought of Philippe, taking his mother's hand, changing her name, stealing his money, peacocking in his father's place . . . It was enough; it was everything.

As the time for the trip approached, he went over there more frequently, biding his time. Waiting for the opportunity.

And it came.

'I think it's another migraine,' Penelope said.

Edward exhaled, softly. He'd been getting worried. If she hadn't felt sick soon, he would have had to make her sick, which was a second layer to his plan. But the gods were smiling, not that there were any gods.

'You head upstairs. Philippe and I will put the world to rights,' Edward said. 'There's an excellent Calvados we want to work on.'

He enjoyed the evening, enjoyed it hugely. The excitement was almost unbearable. He filled Philippe's glass again and again. No water this time. Every trick he had, he employed to keep him drinking.

The guy was sloppy, revolting. He forgot who he was talking to. He laughed about the apartment, the joys of real money. He didn't want to work, and Penelope would help him concentrate on his art. Although, of course, he would be managing the family money now, since half of it would be his.

'Don't worry, Edouard – *ne t'inquiètes pas*; we won't forget you; there will be an allowance, or something . . .'

'Whatever. I'm not concerned about money. Your job is to make Mother happy. Here – one more shot; one for luck?'

'I shouldn't . . . I'm a little drunk.'

'A nightcap, then,' Edward said. 'You can sleep it off tomorrow. No need to get up early; you aren't some worker drone.'

'No – that's right.'

Edward lifted his own glass. 'To the good life.'

Philippe tittered. 'Why not? The good life. And I always make the ladies happy. They are so kind to me . . .'

Edward digested that . . . *the ladies*. Of course, this was how the fool had lived before: other, desperate women; gifts of money; a place to stay. He was a charmer, a sponger – essentially a hooker. And his mother had offered that ticket to the big time.

'Drink up, Philippe.' He gave him a shove on the back and Philippe stumbled and blinked. 'Best to take it all down. Your bride is waiting.'

He took the stem of the glass, laughed, and upended it. '*Sacré bleu*! It burns the throat. You will get your new papa in trouble . . .'

Edward swallowed, hard. *His new papa*. 'Here, take the aspirin. You want to take a few extra tonight, don't you think?'

'God, yes.'

He passed him eight little round pills, curled into the palm of his hand, and Philippe tossed them back, swallowing them.

'Great. Thank God for that.'

'Here, let me help you upstairs,' Edward said. He took Philippe's arm, draped it around his shoulder. 'Perhaps you should sleep in my old room tonight, so as not to disturb Mother.'

'Yesss . . .' Philippe was already slurring. 'Sure . . . No problem . . .'

Edward dragged him up, step by step. He figured he had at least five minutes. He waved cheerfully to the servants as they passed, and hoisted Philippe through the door of his own suite, placing him face down on the bed and slipping his shoes off.

Then took the small bottle of Klonopin pills from his jacket. He took off the lid and carefully formed Philippe's hand into a fist around the bottle, pressing his thumb and forefingers over the label, and twisting his other hand around the lid. Philippe was already drooling; Edward paid him no attention.

He put the open bottle of aspirins down on the bathroom sink. Then he turned off the light and closed the door, and, humming to himself, he left the house.

Chapter Twelve

Dina was in heaven.

Torch was humming. Every day the beauty department got a little bigger, expanded its floor space. Workmen mixed with the shoppers; there was yellow tape around the construction as she moved her territory forwards, and nobody seemed to mind.

New brands. Bigger stands. New products. More lights, mirrors and more blond wood.

She planned her days carefully: product selection, stock review, staff observations, new hirings, press releases – and at least three hours on the phone and email, working every girl in town.

The beauty bloggers were just the start.

Dina hit the editors, the beauty writers on magazines and the segment producers on local TV shows. She sent samples to personal shoppers for some of the biggest players in town. And she wrote all the press releases herself.

The result was a steady stream of good news. Once the blogs had moved on, Dina sent thank-you gifts. Torch's name was posted on internet forums. There was a snippet in the *Daily News*, two minutes on 'colours of spring' for NY1 at breakfast and then small items appeared in the magazines. Suddenly Torch was a hot ticket.

Ludo was thrilled, and Dina finally had a boss who was backing her all the way.

'These results are terrific,' he said, after the first month. 'I think you should take over the handbag space.'

'Move into sunglasses. They can go upstairs.'

'We don't need jewellery on the ground floor.'

With every expansion, her stock rose. And Dina loved it. Ludo treated her with respect, paid her compliments, came and talked to her team. He gave her carte blanche on hirings and backed her to the hilt. As the cash registers rang and the shoppers poured in, he asked her to come up to his office, every morning.

'You're doing wonders.'

'Thank you.' She smiled at him, confidently.

'I want to leverage the success for Torch. You're right. I'm going to make a series of announcements in the business press. My name should be on the end of all press releases – let them come from the MD.'

Dina's smile widened. 'That's great! Thank you, Ludo.'

'You can draft them, just send them up to me and my office will sign them off and put them out. Emails to bloggers you can do yourself. I'm thinking about a social-media campaign, too.'

'That would be incredible. We need to be all over Facebook, Twitter, Tumblr . . .'

'It's Torch, though – so your photo will be in there, along with the other department heads.'

Dina rolled her eyes a little; the other department heads seemed as wooden as planks to her. Whatever. The beauty department was making all the strides. Her team was hot, and the other store sectors wanted some of the magic they were creating. Dina understood reflected glory. Plus, at the moment they were jealous that the spotlight was on one person. Maybe she should share it around, soothe some wounded egos.

Looking on the bright side, if Ludo wanted all his senior people featured together, maybe they would bitch about her a little less.

'Sure. Why not?'

'I also want detailed notes on everything you're doing. We may replicate some of it elsewhere in the store.'

'Absolutely.'

'I'll speak to your hires when you bring them in, and eat lunch with the team captains.'

Dina had separated her staff into their areas of expertise: skincare; eyes and mascara; tan and body; cosmetics application; fragrance. She ripped up the old way of doing business, where you hired a dull girl who liked free samples and was willing to work for low pay. Dina recruited beauty students, fashion-school graduates, models who wanted some set hours, and placed them under well-paid pros who ran their departments: a consultant dermatologist, who'd quit her practice to fit work around raising her teenage boys, directed skincare; a renowned make-up artist, who wanted a steady job, was in charge of cosmetics; a former pro from Bobbi Brown was evaluating brushes; and two spray-tan salon perfectionists were running the bronzer area.

As well as classic brand booths, selling everything, Dina ran grouped walls of smaller products, the ones she could control. Indie eye shadows were together, racked by colour and type; lipsticks, fading from scarlet to clear gloss, tumbled down the colour chart like a computer screen. Women loved it when they came in for pale pink lips and found fifty glosses and sticks racked next to each other.

Even the part-timers were passionate. The old staffers had shaped up, or shipped out. Dina had transferred them elsewhere, if they couldn't cut it – to lighting, or cushions, or outerwear.

'Torch is for beauty. Torch is for babes,' Dina said, when the human-resources people questioned her. 'We want the cool kids, the enthusiasts, the elite. I don't carry passengers.'

They muttered, but she was untouchable. Dina Kane was backed by Ludo Morgan, and she always got her way.

The beauty division was shaping up so well. Dina was on a roll, and the money kept pouring in. Employees got spot bonuses

– a hundred here, five hundred there. If Dina saw or heard something good, she just passed out cash. Morale was through the roof, and the job applications rolled in.

And she was making money. Every month, Ludo increased her salary. There were perks – the free store card, the company car, parking included. She now drove an Audi, could afford to dress designer without having to wait for the good pieces to be marked down in price in the sales. Everyone was happy, and Dina Kane was happiest of all.

Except on the little matter of Joel Gaines.

She waited for the congratulatory call, the email. It didn't happen. Radio silence. Sometimes Dina would drift off, thinking about him. She would fantasise about him coming into the store, walking around, looking for her. And they would laugh, and he'd hug her, pat her on the head . . . When her thoughts drifted like this, Dina caught herself and tried to stop. *Screw him*, she thought, trying to pretend it didn't hurt her so much.

After all, things were good – even great. She had a dream job, was a big success. Even with Johnny's bills, there was enough money. Her apartment had sold and she'd moved to a new one on Eightieth Street, a block from Central Park, with a great view of the museum. Finally, it was something for herself. No more fixing and decorating – Dina Kane no longer had time. She was a retail mogul, a maestro, and busy from dawn to dusk. And she loved it.

There was something incredible about buying new. Her apartment had a breakfast terrace just outside the window, a spare room for when Johnny got out, a lovely kitchen – small, sure, but with Sub-Zero fridges and a Viking cooker; the flat-screen TV was already on the living room wall, and Dina's windows there looked out on to the tree-lined street and the Victorian townhouses opposite, giving a sense of the older, grander New York, of the Manhattan she'd arrived in.

Dina just supervised a little bit of design, using the crew

employed at Torch. She installed blond wood floors to open up the light, bought Danish furniture with sleek lines; the bedroom was a fantasy of oyster-white and the bathroom, which had both a European tub and a walk-in shower, followed a beach-slate palette. The pops of colour on the gunmetal couch were orange and bronze, and it looked modern Mediterranean, chic as hell. She invested in a gas fireplace to keep her warm all winter: realistic flames, and no mess with the flue. They worked while she was out, and she came home to endless luxury.

None of it was enough to make her forget Joel Gaines completely. But, if he had lost interest in her, others hadn't. Ludo Morgan was her boss, and he was also her boyfriend.

Dina liked how he kept it professional at work – backing her up, putting his name on everything, regular meetings. He'd kept his word: they were open about it; nothing was hidden.

That first Friday, Ludo showed up right on time. No flowers; no chauffeur. He took her for dinner at Jean Georges, one of the most expensive restaurants in midtown, and they lingered over a tasting menu for three hours.

The next week, they went to a play; Ludo procured tickets to the hottest show on Broadway, sold out for months in advance.

After that, he invited her to his palatial apartment, above the store, and they ordered Chinese takeout. He didn't pressure her to go to bed. Dina was wary, but happy.

Ludo would kiss her on the cheek in full view of the other staff, then go about his business. The staff – especially those outside the beauty department – resented it, gossiped and bitched. She knew that. But Dina believed her results were unarguable.

For the first time in her life, Dina Kane was part of a couple.

And she liked it. She liked the sense of respect, of fitting in. She liked the way people tilted their heads and smiled indulgently when Ludo kissed her on the cheek. She liked the way it felt when he opened a door for her, or flagged down a cab – like regular people did, people with lives. And, because she worked at

227

Torch, she could throw herself into the job round the clock and still see enough of her boyfriend.

Boyfriend. Boss. A taboo, but it worked.

'Good. So you'll see more of my stamp on your remodel, Dina,' Ludo said, bringing Dina back into his office, tearing her from her thoughts. He reached forward and clicked his mouse, closing the window on the computer, then pushed back from his desk, indicating the meeting was over. 'How are you fixed for Saturday?'

'I can't this Saturday,' she said.

Ludo frowned. 'Wait. What? You have a previous engagement?'

He made it sound ridiculous. And, she had to admit, she was wedded to the job.

'I'm going upstate to check on my brother. He's been making progress; they say he can be released soon.'

'Your brother. You're going to have to introduce me.'

'Sure, one day. I'd like to.'

He didn't mention her mother. Dina had already explained how little there was there. She sent money back each month, and never got a thank you for it. Often, she berated herself for still looking through the mail, as though that would ever change.

'Meantime, how about you go see your brother on Friday? I have plans for Saturday. Big plans.'

Dina laughed. 'Ludo, we work on Fridays.'

'You deserve an afternoon off. Take one. It's an order, if that helps.'

She smiled; as though he could order her about!

They were companionable together, friendly. She'd gone to bed with him, about five weeks in, once it seemed respectable and the right thing to do. She was nervous; the almost-virgin, the workaholic; boyfriend-free since Edward; no sex since bringing down his father. But that trauma was almost forgotten, and Ludo was tender and patient, and made sure she'd had a couple of glasses of champagne and, even though Dina felt little pleasure, it wasn't actually painful. She enjoyed his desire, his sweating, gasping lust, the way she saw herself through his eyes. The only time she sensed anything, was when she started to get excited, and then her thoughts drifted helplessly, inevitably, towards Joel Gaines; her eyes closed, she felt wet, open, as if she was lifting out of herself . . .

'Come on, baby. Oh, that's good; you're so good,' Ludo panted. She heard his voice, and the vision shattered. But she moaned and whimpered a little, and he came, and was done with her.

Maybe things would get better in time. When she got more used to him, and less shy. For now, it was enough to have a young man who treated her well, prized her, took her out.

But the whispers at work continued.

'She's caught herself a nice one.'

'Set her target the day she walked in here. The job's just for show.'

'Dina's smart; she got close; she'll be out of here in six months.'

'Lucky bitch.'

'This whole place will be hers one day. Did you hear about the palace he's got on the fucking roof? They say it's ten thousand square foot of space with a garden and a goddamned pool.'

'He can't even drive. Daddy got him a chauffeur.'

'Why does she bust her ass like that? All he wants is a respectable version of a model.'

'She's not *that* pretty. She must be on fire in bed.'

'No wonder he signs off on everything.'

'She isn't even the force, she's just the front woman, you know? Where did she go to college? He's got the MBA and she's just like this sexy brunette, fronting it, playing with make-up.'

'You've got to give it to her – she knows how to climb. She's from the middle of fucking nowhere, out in Westchester.'

Dina heard that stuff every day, out on the shop floor, as she moved about unobtrusively, amongst the crowds of women browsing and snatching. She tried not to resent it. They couldn't conceive of a girl who wanted to make money, not marry it. Ludo was great, handsome, good to her, but she tried not to think about it too much because she wasn't sure he was the one. He was a boyfriend, a good boyfriend, and Dina was trying to live a normal life. But marriage . . . ?

She shuddered a little. That was the sound of freedom gone and iron gates clanging shut.

Maybe other girls would jump at the chance, and they were surely welcome to go right ahead. Dina concentrated on her work. She was so sunk in Torch, she dreamed about it. That buzz when a beauty editor ran a feature, or they cleared yet another fifteen square foot for her playground, it was electric, inspiring. She lived on the adrenaline, and the humdrum love life was fine; Ludo was her friend, her boss.

And now that friend was asking for a favour.

'OK. I could do with a break.'

It was true, she felt exhausted. You couldn't mainline this stuff around the clock. It would be nice to focus on Johnny, not on the latest brand of cream eye shadow, or the new low-heat hair tongs she was bringing in to her beauty-tools section. 'So where are we going on Saturday?'

'Out to the beach,' Ludo said. 'I want you to meet my parents.'

Dina smiled tightly, hoping her nerves didn't show. 'Your parents! Wow. That's so great.'

'I thought you'd be pleased.' He smiled, and Dina tried to ignore the sinking feeling in her stomach.

Joel Gaines looked at his wife, reluctantly.

Susan had come bounding in from the beauty salon, wearing the hideously expensive 'casual' wear from Prabal Gurung's resort collection and Jimmy Choo ballet flats, and her hair was as big and bouncy as Farrah Fawcett's. She was done up to the nines, her eyes thick with mascara, artfully applied bronze shadow and chocolate liner, and her face was immaculately made up with some kind of airbrushed foundation and a high pink blusher. She looked like a model, an older model, perhaps, but still with that stylised perfection.

He hated it. All the women in the Hamptons did this, whenever a celebrity threw a party. It wasn't enough to have a fifteen-million-dollar beach house; you had to compete on the 'best trophy wife' circuit, like you were entering a prize dog at Crufts.

And he was as guilty as anybody. For years, Susan had worked the trophy-wife thing perfectly, and Joel had not complained. He'd bought her jewels, an emerald and South Sea pearl necklace, a canary diamond ring the size of an M&M, a platinum watch studded with rubies. Not so much to see her wear them, but as a vehicle for boasting about his wealth and power.

'How do you like it?'

Susan pirouetted. She was always happiest when she felt great about herself, when she was the star. They did less and less together these days.

'Stunning,' he lied.

Make-up should be subtle, present but not present, barely there, so you could see the woman. All the men that piled on this 'jewel eyes' crap were gay – the same men that designed the curves out of catwalk models and pushed 'menswear' trends on the girls every season.

Dina Kane, for example, had it down perfectly. Always groomed, but with a touch as light as gossamer . . .

No – *no*.

'What do you say we skip the party? I mean, altogether. Just go for a moonlit walk on the beach. We could make a bonfire, roast s'mores or something.'

Susan laughed. 'You're funny. We could do that every day. This is Roxana Felix's party, you know – the supermodel. *Everybody* will be there.'

'Right,' he sighed.

'Hey, honey, look at this magazine; I stole it from the salon. Though, with what I tipped them, they could buy a hundred of them.' She triumphantly plunked down a copy of *Vogue*. 'See this? A double-page spread on Torch. You know Torch, that fusty old store uptown? It's been turned around, like *completely*. All my girlfriends are shopping there, in the beauty department. This is an interview with Ludo Morgan; isn't he cute? You know the father, right?'

Joel nodded.

'Ludo is the heir and he's really transformed the place. He's everywhere these days! Interviews in *Vogue*, in the *New York Times* . . . Haven't you noticed? He's really the coming man.'

'Let me see that,' Gaines said. He looked at the spread, the young man with the bland features photographed artfully against the blond, well-lit beauty department. The article raved about the revamp, the coming shock to other departments, the soaring bottom line. Ludo Morgan was given all the credit.

'I heard they had a new beauty director – Dina Kane. She's had something to do with this?' he asked, casually.

Saying her name aloud was exciting. Gaines had tried, with minimal success, to forget her. Shouting at her, storming out of the café . . . His plan worked, if you wanted to call it that.

She was humiliated enough. She never called him again.

That was meant to be a signal for him to turn the page, move on, concentrate on Susan.

It wasn't happening. Daily, he struggled for mastery. Daily, he stopped himself making the call.

And she showed no mercy. Her brand was everywhere – growing, expanding, filling the business pages. At first, he saw her name on a daily basis in the press releases and announcements.

Then it changed – to the boss, Ludo Morgan.

Gaines reserved judgement. He made discreet inquiries; Dina had been promoted, given hiring privileges, perks, a bigger salary. Nobody was ripping her off, like they had done with Meadow. And yet, she was getting the cash, but no longer getting the credit.

'Who? Oh, yes, she works in the beauty department. All Ludo's staff are shown right here.'

Susan flipped the page and pointed to a small, inset picture. Dina was standing in the back row of a group of staffers, smiling and wearing a chic white shift dress that set off her tanned, toned body. No rocks necessary, and no panda eyes allowed.

Goddamn, she was pretty. A butterfly among the moths. But she was also an afterthought – just a director; one of many.

'You know, I knew that name was familiar,' Susan said, suddenly, and Gaines gave a guilty start. She couldn't know anything, could she? Impossible.

'From the store?'

'I'm not that much of a beauty geek; I don't memorise the *staff*,' Susan said contemptuously. 'No, she's a smart cookie, that one; she's actually dating him. I saw it on "Page Six". You know, the hot young couple. She's pretty and he has the brains and the money.'

Adrenaline flushed through Gaines' system. He felt something wholly unfamiliar: jealousy; rage. Ludo Morgan was unmarried and fifteen years younger than him, with money of his own. Not in Joel Gaines' league, but more than enough to offer Dina a life of endless luxury.

He tried to feel happy for his protégée. He failed.

'That's nice,' he said, eventually.

'Well, try and show some enthusiasm tonight, won't you?'

Gaines tore his eyes away from the tiny picture of Dina and looked up. 'What?'

'They're going to be there tonight – two of the star guests. His folks have a compound in Amagansett, and Ludo bought his own place in Sagaponack, just back from the beach on Daniels' Lane.'

He stared at her. 'What are you? A realtor?'

'I like to keep up with what goes on around here,' Susan said, smugly. 'You need to be up to date.'

'No kidding.' He passed a hand over his sweating forehead. 'And they are coming tonight?'

'Sure are. I can't wait to introduce you. I'm really into Torch.'

He stood up. 'That's great. I think I need to get some fresh air. I'll take the dogs out on the beach.'

Boxer and Clive bounded happily along the sand. Gaines knew a lot of rich men who envied their dogs: no therapists, no mergers, no taxes.

No women.

He walked here often when he needed to think. The scent of salt from the ocean, the breezes on a hot day: it lifted him, helped him to focus.

I won't go to the goddamned party. That would be easiest, but there would be fights for days, and it was also the coward's way out. Susan would pout, and wonder . . . He didn't need her to wonder . . .

Jesus. Wonder about what? There he went again, overthinking it. He hadn't done anything with Dina Kane. She was a cute piece of ass with a brain. Men were programmed to want pieces of ass. He hadn't even kissed her, let alone fucked her. He'd been dwelling on her, OK, Gaines admitted that. It was too embarrassing to discuss with his shrink, even. Just another rich guy's midlife crisis . . . She was young enough to be his daughter, if he'd started early.

Being near the water helped put things in perspective: the immensity of the ocean, crashing against the grey sand, soothing but relentless. Gaines could have any young piece of tail he wanted, either on a date, or ordered in from the most discreet escort services in the city, the ones where they tested the girls for diseases on a daily basis. He was a billionaire, and ass was available to him round the clock, if he was that way inclined.

He wasn't. Never had been.

He was also, he understood, very unhappy.

The moment he got up his courage and yelled at Dina Kane was meant to be a good one. He was supposed to have walked out of that café a free man, still the master of himself, still right with his conscience, like a junkie kicking the habit. And when she didn't email, didn't call, stopped dead, that was meant to be his victory.

Temptation was behind him. He was back with Susan, their long marriage getting longer.

Only, 'back with Susan' wasn't so great. Before Dina, he'd been so consumed with work he hadn't really cared. Now he did care. It bothered him that his wife seemed to endure sex, not enjoy it. It bothered him that she never talked about anything but their celebrity neighbours, like he gave a flying fuck, or how the kids were doing in college. Gaines loved his boys, but they were separate to his wife. When he arranged romance, like a quiet dinner, or a beach walk, she never talked about him, never asked about him. *How was your day?* was the extent of it.

He hated the spend-as-sport. Hated the panoply of servants disguised as teachers: personal trainer; personal tennis coach; personal shopper; personal stylist. Susan collected an army of redundant hangers-on, like their garden designer, and then spent hours in 'meetings' with them, making a life. He disdained the conspicuous dresses and the bold make-up; where was that chic, simple girl he married?

The boys were gone. Was this his life, for the rest of his life?

Gaines didn't know if he could take it. Why it suddenly mattered, the companion at home, he wasn't sure. Dina Kane was a witch, an enchantress; after just a few encounters, he was thinking about her all the damned time.

And now she was coming tonight. Very good. He would go.

He couldn't divorce Susan; they had been together too long. Marriage counselling, maybe; a heart to heart. He could talk to her, tell her what was missing. She'd given him two children, a lifetime of service. It wasn't good enough to trade her in for a younger model, like some scumbag who changed wives the way he changed cars . . .

That's what he told himself, anyway. That was what a priest or rabbi would say.

He wanted it to ring true. But all he felt was a horrible, sinking feeling. Maybe this was a midlife crisis. Older men were meant to buy a red sports car, right? Only he already had a red sports car. And a blue one. And a Humvee . . .

Gaines smiled grimly to himself. *Forget it.* It was a problem he had to think through, like any other. Forgetting Dina Kane hadn't worked, and running from her wouldn't help. What if this was a business issue? He should break it down like that, the way he was used to doing.

'Clive!' he called, because the golden Labrador was too far away along the beach, chasing the waves and barking. OK, so he was a little obsessed. Maybe yelling at her in the coffee shop wasn't the end of the story. He should talk to Dina again, get to know her, let her fall from whatever stupid pedestal he'd constructed. She had a boyfriend. It was good, he could see them together: two kids, the right age for each other. All's well that ends well, right? He recalled he'd once told her that they'd speak again when she got herself a lover.

He needed to process that. He was married, and she was taken. Nothing could be better than seeing her and the golden boy at the dumb celebrity party tonight. No doubt she'd love it just as much as Susan did, would fit right in to the deluxe soccer-mom crowd, and the scales would fall from his eyes. Perhaps he could see her how he was meant to, as an unusual girl, a comer, somebody he liked, mentored.

The dog came bounding up to him, and Boxer, his chocolate mutt, next to him. They were both good dogs. He liked this part of his life. It would be crazy to divorce, to give it all up.

But the thought was so tempting.

He turned for home. He wanted to have sex with Susan, but

knew already that she wouldn't go for it. Not a chance. Not with her hair all done and the airbrushed make-up so perfectly set. Sex would be his best shot of denuding himself of desire, so he didn't gawp over Dina like some drunken student. He didn't want to do it himself; that seemed sterile and hopeless when he was married and his wife was there.

Joel Gaines was just going to have to grin and bear it.

Dina looked at herself in the mirror and sighed.

'We absolutely have to go to this party?'

Ludo frowned slightly. 'Honey, please stop asking me that.'

She was exquisite, and he was enjoying being with her. Every month that passed was a testament to his good taste. First and foremost, she was gorgeous, and she was pliant when he wanted to have sex; but she just dressed with such style; her make-up was perfect – exactly like you'd expect.

And the workaholic stuff was fine with Ludo. It meant she never clung on to him, gave him whatever space he needed. Flying to Florida to watch baseball spring training? No problem. Gore-fest movie with the boys? She didn't care. Dining at a gentleman's club? Dina would be in the office. They did things when *he* wanted to do things. He led in this relationship, and that suited him perfectly.

Dina Kane had a lot of energy. Her six months at Torch had turned the store around, but he thought he could take it from here. She would need to be occupied. He could see her planning the most stylish wedding for years, then taking time out to raise great-looking kids.

Torch was his – literally. Ludo understood her passion, but she could channel it into home, kids, charity work. He'd been detaching her from the store without her realising, so ploughed in was she to everyday results. There was another 'Dina' installed in fashion now – he'd hired this cute young thing from *W* magazine – and picked up a former editor of *Wallpaper* to work some magic on home furnishings. There was a proper PR department in place, staffed full of hungry young kids who'd worked in the big agencies. Torch wasn't just beauty. He, Ludo, had a system, and he was motoring.

His father was ecstatic.

Dad and Mom had both liked Dina that week she flew out to their place in California. She'd stayed in a guest room, swum in the pool, helped his mother cook. They were pleased she worked at the store, and regarded her tales of stocktaking indulgently. His father had said something about Joel Gaines, and Dina flushed and replied that she deserved the job, on her own merits.

A little aggressive, that, but nothing to worry about.

His friends were jealous. And that was half the battle. Their air-headed models had no tits, no ass, and were hooked on drugs. Dina was curvaceous, and she was interesting to talk to, once she got off the subject of work.

'You know tonight's important to me. I want to show you off to everybody – our summer neighbours.'

'*Your* summer neighbours,' she said, but smiled.

'If you play your cards right, baby . . .'

'OK. I'll pack an overnight case.'

'No need; I had some of your stuff shipped to the house. Everything's there. You just pick the dress you're going to wear, and we'll take a helicopter in.'

'A helicopter!'

He kissed her on the cheek. 'This is how people live, Dina. You know, when time is more important than money.'

Her smile was a bit warmer now. 'I get that.'

'I don't feel like being stuck in gridlocked traffic for three hours. We'll head to midtown, for the heliport. So pack what you need in your purse.'

Dina blinked. She was wearing a sexy, figure-hugging Roland Mouret dress in structured green velvet, with folds and twists, and a simple single pearl on a golden chain at the hollow of her throat, like a drop of water. Her heels were cheaper – Jessica Simpson – but that was his girl; she mixed labels and high street with an irrepressible charm. The Simpson heels were ones she could walk in, she said, and they kept her going all night. The green velvet worked fine, and she carried a Prada clutch in khaki leather. It all looked effortless, and her dark hair piled on top of her head gave her the regal style of a Greek goddess.

'OK then, honey,' she said.

He liked the endearment; she rarely handed them out. It was kind of pleasing how little Dina Kane seemed to be after him and his money. She was ambitious and material in one way, always pushing for a bigger salary, or a bonus, or even stock options; quite surprising how hard she demanded that; he wasn't used to it in women employees. Ludo gave her a rise, a nice car, but fobbed her off on the stock. She was new to the company still, he said, and it wasn't right. Maybe at the year end . . .

But Dina was blind to the bonus sitting right opposite her. He laughed when he thought about it. A couple of hundred grand a year barely made you middle class in Manhattan, and he was offering her tens of millions. What was the problem? If she married him, she would have a penthouse, a beach house, resort vacations at the Four Seasons, and a car and driver, plus all the designers she could wear. Yet she showed little interest in commuting by helicopter or the fancy restaurants he took her to.

Other girls on the shop floor would kill for the opportunity. But Ludo Morgan liked Dina's brains. She brought class to the whole thing. And she was a challenge in a way he loved.

Growing up rich meant having girls fling themselves at you – in the nightclub, at the polo match, seniors in high school. Word went round, and the rich boys were prey. That made you resentful, made you distrust women. Maybe the best thing about Dina Kane was that she genuinely didn't care. That was the silver lining to this pushy, aggressive alpha female.

Ludo was wearing a bespoke tailored suit, paired with a crisp

Armani shirt – white with thin navy stripes – and shoes hand-crafted by John Lobb in England. He looked good, hair freshly cut: the new entrepreneur on the block, finally getting the recognition he deserved. Beauty was motoring, but only because he'd provided the funds and the vision to make it happen. Lots of companies had talented employees; Steve Jobs hadn't invented the iPod, but it was his company, so he led the way. Ludo had rearranged everything; the entire Torch building was now light wooden floors, mirrors, soft lighting. The old tables, piled with goods, had gone. A few designers showcased in each department. He'd brought furniture, fashion and accessories up to date as well. And the press was good – sales would catch up. A big spend, and a big return. This was what chief execs did.

In his pocket lay Dina Kane's next chapter. A small blue velvet box from Tiffany, containing a colossal ring: seven carats of internally flawless, round, brilliant diamond, flanked by two azure Thai sapphires, just to be different.

Ludo had it all planned out: their triumphant debut on the Hamptons scene; Dina as belle of the ball; himself as the coming man in retail. There were going to be actors there, directors, Roxana Felix herself and several hedge-fund billionaires. Susan Gaines, doyenne of the scene, and her husband, Joel . . . the guy who'd sent Dina over in the first place. He should shake his hand.

After some mingling, some compliments, a few glasses of champagne, he would walk Dina out to the beach and propose, right there on the seashore, under the stars. He had the exact spot in mind . . . The floodlights in front of Roxana's gates reached fifty foot. After all, Dina needed to be able to see the bling.

Then back inside – to receive congratulations, show off her rock. And then he'd have the chauffeur drive them a little way to their cottage. It was all laid out and ready: heated, warm, champagne on ice in a silver bucket on the kitchen island, a fire crackling in the grate in the living room, fresh silk sheets on the engagement bed. Dina Kane would fall asleep to the sound of the ocean in the distance, knowing that, in the morning, she would wake up as chatelaine of all Ludo owned. She could swim in the pool, eat a breakfast of strawberries and fresh-baked croissants, and then he'd broach the fact she was stepping down from Torch.

He needed a wife, not a rival, and it was time for her to break from all that stress. Besides, men in his position kept the family. The wives didn't work. Not ever.

'You're completely sure you have stuff at the house?' Dina said, now, breaking into his thoughts.

'Toothbrush, clean underwear, ten different outfits, sports gear . . .' Ludo ticked them off. 'Believe me, I have it all. Right down to your favourite perfume. Jo Malone, right? Pear and Freesia.'

Dina actually laughed. 'Wow! Very good. I'll just grab my coat, then.'

'Me too; I'm ready.' He stood up and walked to the door.

It was a crisp spring night, still cool. Summer would be here soon, and it was an excellent time for a drive.

Edward Johnson was enjoying himself behind the wheel.

Things were rolling his way. His mother, wracked with grief, had been packed off to a health farm in the Florida Keys, part of an exclusive resort, where she could have sun, water, a bunch of well-paid fakers to get her in touch with her spiritual self, and be guaranteed to meet absolutely nobody she knew.

It was a dry resort. Edward didn't want her diving back into the vodka bottle. After all, he loved her. He'd killed for her.

Once again, his mind drifted back to the delicious memories. The shrieking call at seven fifteen the next morning. His mother, hysterical. His careful call to the family doctor, to see 'if anything could be done'. The police interview; the way the detectives trampled through the house, his mother sobbing, Edward frantically trying to comfort her.

But it was all good. The prints on the pill bottle were perfect.

The alcohol and clonazepam in Philippe's blood had induced a coma, sleep apnoea; he'd just gone under, stopped breathing.

'It's such a goddamned tragedy. I had no idea he would mix them up. He was drunk . . . I didn't think he was that drunk,' Edward said, shaking his head. 'I blame myself.'

The detectives wanted to blame him, too, but he came up clean. All that wedding planning, the first-class tickets on his credit card. The staff, his mother's friends . . . so many witnesses to the bonhomie, to the habit of knocking back aspirin after a night on the sauce.

It was death by misadventure. Edward loved that. He read the coroner's report again and again. As he organised the simple and elegant funeral – Philippe, as a successful gigolo and con man, had no family and no real friends – Edward felt the most incredible surge of power. He hadn't fucked this up. The threat to his money, his dignity, was dead. Edward had killed him, and he'd got away with it, scot-free. The whole episode was gloriously pleasurable and, for a while, he went back to banging whores, not hitting them. It was like the monkey had been lifted off his back, and he was whole again.

'I'm finished,' Penelope sobbed at the crematorium. She buried her head into Edward's shoulder. 'Oh God! I can't bear it. All those women coming around. I can't take it; I don't want to see them.' She shuddered and started to hyperventilate. 'I'm panicking, Edward; I'm going to have a panic attack.'

'Here.' He pressed her hand and gave her a clonazepam. It was thrilling to medicate his mother with the same pills he'd used to kill her lover. 'Take this, quickly. Now breathe deep. It'll work soon – you know it will. Fill your lungs; hold your breath. Great, Mom. Exhale . . . Exhale . . .'

Her panics had returned. She was a mess; wholly dependent. It was a week's work to persuade her to give him full power of attorney. Edward drew up papers, lots of them. There were the ones giving him controlling shares in the family trust. The change of her will, to name him as the sole beneficiary. The irrevocable trust set up to place half her wealth in Edward's hands. His name was added to the deed on the family house. Penelope was in no condition to fight. She was desperately, pathetically grateful that Edward would take care of 'business things', as she put it. And he doled out what she needed: drugs and a flight out to someplace warm, where her days would be regimented and she wouldn't have to think.

Edward was happy to spend big money on it. He wanted Penelope out of his hair, and wanted to be able to show any court that he had done the best by his mother, in case they challenged things down the line.

Once her plane departed, he got to work. He let go of all the domestic staff, one by one. They had all seen too much, and he was the master of the house now. Some of them cried and wept, but Edward was implacable; there was severance, a hand-shake and he was done.

'I'm not my father, Ronald. I don't need a valet.'

'Mrs Johnson will be living very simply when she returns, Lia. She prefers to be alone.'

'We will be using a cleaning service.'

'But, Mr Edward, I keep house for you twenty years,' Consuela sobbed. 'Is all I know. My family . . .'

'I will give you an excellent reference.' Edward patted her hands. 'And four months' pay. We all have to move on. You can find another household; I'm sure of it.'

'But not like this. Oh, *por favor*, did you speak to Mrs Johnson, Mr Edward . . . ?'

'No, I didn't, and nor will you. We never did get your immigration status sorted, did we?' he asked, silkily. 'Four months is generous; you have plenty of time to find good employment elsewhere. And you will need my word for that.'

She got the message. 'Yes, sir. Thank you; *gracias* for the four months.'

'It's nothing,' Edward said, nobly, and of course it really wasn't.

Once they were gone, he hired the decorators. Every old piece of art was catalogued and sold. His parents' fussy French style was gutted from the house; simple, modern masculinity went in. There was to be nothing that reminded him of either one of them. The father who had destroyed them; the mother who had betrayed him: he didn't know whom he despised more. When Penelope returned, she would be living elsewhere, in a small, chic apartment more suitable for an older woman.

Like the one he had left.

Edward cleared house. The money from the art more than paid for the redecoration, and left two million dollars in the trust account. He put seven hundred grand aside for his mother's modest retirement, and kept the rest for himself. All of a sudden, his little office in midtown hummed with real activity. Now Edward was managing his own money, he suddenly cared – cared hugely.

The brokers were summoned. This time, they all came to him. Edward was treated to slides and presentations and talks on wealth management over coffee at the Four Seasons.

'I want the highest income,' he told them. 'Screw growth. This is my time to have fun.'

'Very good. Yes, sir.'

He started to dress well, to drink less. He made a few calls to those old school friends he hated so much, the ones that walked away after Dina Kane's stunt, and invited them round for dinner.

It was his house now. They came; money talks.

Edward circulated, careful of his image. No violence, no drugs, no loose women. He wanted to take a leaf from the book of poor, dead Philippe. Taking his mother's money was a piece of cake. Next, he wanted a wife that could cement things: an heiress with a fortune of her own.

Why work? That was for suckers.

A girl who was loaded would reset his personal clock. Once he had her married and pregnant, and tied up with an unbreakable prenup, it would be time to step back into the life he should always have led. The life he was leading before that bitch, Dina Kane, ruined everything.

You could blame *her* for Philippe; she split the family.

Blame her for beating those sluts; she drove him to it.

Blame her for his stupid, broken mother, and her stupid betrayal; Dina had put a wedge between them all.

Blame her for his father's pathetic attempt to grasp back his youth, to run from his past.

Edward was doing just fine. But he did not forgive, and he did not forget.

Philippe Leclerc found that out the hard way. Dina Kane was about to do so, as well. An eye for an eye, sugar.

Edward smiled, and put his foot on the gas.

Chapter Thirteen

'How do I look?' Susan asked.

She spun before him, and the hem of her dress flared out. It was a stately sheath in azure velvet, strapless, that flattered her ample bosom, lifted and firmed after breast-feeding the boys. Around her neck she wore a filigree necklace of white diamonds and platinum, shaped like a leaf, and he could see some sort of jewelled slippers peeking out from under her hem.

'You look great,' Gaines answered. It was certainly dramatic. He supposed, if she was going strong on the make-up, this was the way to complement it.

'Thank you, darling.' She came over, swishing as she walked, and kissed the air at the side of his cheek, so as not to disrupt her make-up.

'Let's go,' Gaines said. He didn't know if he was dreading this, or longing for it. Only that it had to be done.

Ludo held his hand out mutely, the wind from the chopper blades whipping round his coat and jacket. It was no use talking; the roar of the helicopter was too loud. Dina stepped out carefully, one hand on her head, steadying that up-do against the torrent of air; her coat lifted behind her like a cloak and her skirt moved deliciously up those legs. *Goddamn!* Those calves in old-fashioned silk stockings . . . the ladder to paradise, to those firm, milky thighs above them. He got a stir just looking at them.

He tugged her along, off the helipad and down the steps to where their chauffeur was waiting, hired for the night. It didn't pay to keep one in the Hamptons, but maybe in the future, once his shares in Torch were worth more, maybe double, he could upgrade the house . . . A bigger place, a proper estate, with a servant's quarters and a cook/driver to live in, year round. Everything on tap.

For now, though, he kept a Mercedes at the cottage, and this guy was from a decent service. He touched his cap and held open the door for them. As it shut behind him, he saw Dina fixing her hair, smoothing herself down; she was so pretty, so simple. He gave her a quick kiss on the cheek, and she squeezed his hand.

'You know the address.'

'Yes, sir,' the driver said. The limousine purred off into the darkness, the low lights of the Hamptons houses all around them, so different from Manhattan's endless neon towers. He was really looking forward to this.

'Who's going to be there . . . ? I mean, that we know?'

Ludo smiled. 'Not my parents. They went back to LA. I know a few people from the tennis club. There's Paul Turman and his wife, Mindy, and Luke Herlihy with Sophia, and I think my friend Emmett Lewis is coming along. Oh, and Joel and Susan Gaines; you've met Joel, haven't you? So that's at least one person you know yourself. Roxana Felix is a friend of my father's. As is her rock-star husband.' He looked over at her. 'What's wrong? You've gone all tense.'

Dina was sitting bolt upright, rigid, staring straight ahead. Underneath her perfect, light make-up, she had paled.

'Nothing,' she said. 'Nothing wrong.'

'What? You've fallen out with Gaines? Or you just feel overwhelmed? Come on, baby, you can eat all these people for breakfast back at the office. I know you can handle a social setting. They're our neighbours. And, besides, Joel Gaines is big business, major league. Much bigger even than my father. He could buy and sell us all a hundred times over.'

'I . . . I know that. It just might be a little awkward.'

'I can't afford for you to fall out with someone so powerful. His wife is a main mover in everything social round here. So be nice, OK?'

Dina swallowed hard. 'Fine. OK. I expect it'll be a big party.'

'It will, but I want to get us introduced. Anyway, didn't he call my dad about you? That's why you got hired.'

'Yes, I . . . he did. It was before we fell out.'

'Over what? He was making eyes at you or something?'

She blushed deeply. 'No! Of course not. I was just angry that he made so much money on Meadow – my cream. I only got half a million for it, you know. He . . . he ripped me off.'

That wasn't true, wasn't anything like true. But what could she say? She was so embarrassed at his casual joke. Making eyes . . . She had made them at Joel, and he'd told her to go jump in a lake. And now she had to see him again, here, tonight, with his wife.

Dina tried to collect herself. Come on, she would have to face him some time. Why not now? And see the woman he belonged to. And always would. She felt a moment of real thankfulness for Ludo, felt her ambivalence vanish; he was here beside her, her partner, boyfriend, whatever; she was with a man of her own, so she wouldn't look like some desperate bunny-boiling freak. Gratefully, she reached out and squeezed his arm. He wasn't muscular like Joel, but he was hers, he was there.

Perhaps she wanted too much, and this was real love. That sick, squirmy, sexual feeling she got with Joel couldn't be love; that was obsession . . . imagination. They hadn't ever even made love. Most couples weren't crazy about each other, right? They were fond of each other. Friends . . .

'Well, that's all forgotten now. Right? Promise me you'll be nice.' Joel squeezed her hand. 'This is a special night for me. I don't want anything to ruin it.'

'I'll be nice,' Dina managed. 'He probably won't even remember me.'

The mansion was incredible. Flaming torches were stacked across the wide sweep of the drive; lit candles, sunk into the lawn; the soaring modern architecture of the grand, thirty-million-dollar beach house was breathtaking. Dina clutched Ludo's arm as they fell in line with younger girls wearing Gucci, Prada, Prabal Gurung – all haute couture – and older women in St. John and fussy clouds of silk and taffeta.

The jewels all around her flashed and sparkled like strings of fairy lights. Dina had never seen such a concentration of wealth and power. Even as they waited to go in, party staff wearing chic light-green dresses or tailored suits hovered around them with flutes of vintage champagne, pink and white, and trays of hors d'oeuvres that looked meltingly delicious: tiny chunks of real honeycomb pierced with white Cheshire cheese, little paper flutes of home-made French fries, tiny quiches, little pear tartlets, caviar and chopped egg on whole-wheat blinis, and everything clever in between.

'Dina! This is Malcolm Bruce, the director . . .'

'Oh. Hi. I loved *Marianne* . . .'

'And you know Solomon Perry, the banker? And his wife, Sarah.'

'Hi.'

'And here's Jake Carter, the best tort litigator on the East Coast . . .'

One after another, Ludo hit her with them: actresses, models, hedge-fund guys, a defence contractor, an award-winning architect. These were the rich people and, she realised as she looked at the women, those pretty enough to hang out with them: the plus ones. You were either a wife with a string of pearls the size of gulls' eggs and a smug look of adoration for your husband, or a jittery model type, nervous and hoping to get lucky.

At least it kept her busy. Dina was shaking hands and smiling, and coming up with quick one-liners, fast enough to make her head spin. But that was good – she could see Ludo glowing – it was as if she were back on opening day at Torch, with all the beauty bloggers and the new customers pushing and shoving and trying to buy every product she could put out there.

And the girls, those eager girls who all looked at her, with Ludo on her arm, so enviously – it made her want to laugh – but they actually did a double take, and wanted to speak to her.

'Wait – Dina *Kane*?'

'You started Meadow cream, right?'

'You brought in the Dr Lowe stuff to Torch. I kill for that cleanser! It's the only place you can get it outside of London! Wow! I love you.'

'Don't actually kill for a cleanser,' Dina joked. 'But thank you.'

The redhead was beanpole tall and lean, with that clear Irish skin, a dusting of freckles, and Dina could see that she was flawless.

'In my line of work, it's the most vital thing there *is*,' the girl gushed. 'They make you up, like, *every* day. And it all has to come off. I can't *afford* a zit. You have the best stuff that works. Oh my God. Dina Kane.'

'I know, right?' asked a brunette, sidling up to her. 'I'm Erin Lanster. They made me up at Torch and, like, my boyfriend *proposed* that night at dinner.'

'I really don't think one thing happened because of the other, but I'm so glad you liked it . . .'

'Who did your make-up tonight?' asked a blonde. 'Can I get her number?'

'Uh, that was me.'

'Oh my God! Like, wow.'

Ludo laughed, delighted. He'd been in the middle of a crowd of girls like this, but never had their attention been focused on anything else. A crew of pretty chicks paying homage to his woman; he felt more secure than ever in his choice.

'Excuse us, ladies; I have to take Dina to meet our hostess.'

He extricated her and steered her into the centre of the vast room, with a huge fire blazing in a two-sided chimney. There was the sight of the sea, lit up from the enormous open windows, just in front of the stretch of private beach.

'Roxana? I'm Ludo Morgan.'

He introduced himself to a tall, stunning older woman with long, dark hair, wearing a gorgeous tailored evening pantsuit in silk, and teetering heels. Chandelier earrings hung from her lobes, and she looked as wild as a gypsy.

'Hey; good to see you. You've bought the cottage down the road?'

To her it was a cottage – he swallowed his annoyance.

'In Sagaponack. Yes.'

'Well, we look forward to having you around. You should say hi to my husband; he's upstairs playing guitar, I think. Lots of boys.' She laughed. 'Never stopped being a rock star, in his heart. And who's your girlfriend?'

'This is Dina Kane. She works for me at Torch, in the beauty department.'

'Hi,' Dina said, nervously. Roxana Felix was a legend – one of the great supermodels of the nineties. And she still looked incredible.

'I heard you're doing great things over there, Dina.'

'Thank you, ma'am.'

'Ma'am is my mother. Did you make yourself up tonight?'

Roxana was leaning closer, and Dina suddenly, desperately, wanted her to approve. She was a hell of an expert.

'Yes, I did. Do you like it?'

'I do. You have real talent. I've started to use Meadow, by the way.'

Dina flushed. 'How did you know that was me?'

'Oh, my friend told me. He was actually just talking about you. Let's see if I can find him.' She turned around. 'Susan! Joel! Come here.'

Dina gripped on to Ludo. She breathed hard; she felt dizzy.

'Come on, baby,' he whispered.

Desperately, she grabbed a flute of champagne from a passing waiter and tipped it back, downing half of it in a couple of seconds; the icy cold alcohol hit her tongue, bubbling and soothing, promising her a little courage by the time it had soaked into her bloodstream.

She looked good; she knew it. That was important to her. She had a man. She had a job, a career. Success. Time to hold her head up. Dina forced herself to calm her ragged breathing. *Do you want him to see?*

'Dina, Ludo, this is Susan Gaines.'

'Oh! Hiiii!' A tall, older, groomed blonde with talon-like nails painted scarlet and an artfully made-up face smiled at her from a pillar of blue velvet. Dina tried to take her in. She was beautiful, in a way, but plucked and painted to within an inch of her life; diamonds glittered around her throat like stars, and there was a massive ring on her left hand, the size of a marble. Her ears were studded with long, dangling columns – more diamonds – and there was a huge pearl and conch brooch at her ample bosom. Blonde, big-breasted, she said *rich* in every possible way. *Wife. Queen.* Dina felt ill; she swallowed a little more champagne.

'Hi to you. What a pleasure!' Ludo said. 'We've heard so much about you. Looking forward to getting to know you guys better. Dina owes your husband a favour, don't you, honey?'

'Oh, yes. Mr Gaines has been very good to me,' Dina said, weakly.

'Mr Gaines! Come on, you call him Joel, don't you? If you don't, you're going to start,' said Susan. 'Joel! Sugar! It's that couple I was talking to you about. We were discussing you guys *just* this afternoon,' she said, as Joel walked towards them, and Dina could not take her eyes off him.

Her heart thudded against her ribcage; she was dizzy. *Hold on. Keep it together*.

She couldn't let him see. He would laugh, thinking she still wasn't over him. Dina forced a bright smile on to her face with the utmost effort, and threaded her arm through Ludo's, bringing him closer to her.

'Hi,' Gaines said, offering his hand to Ludo.

'Good to meet you, sir,' Ludo said. There was something like awe in his voice, and Dina blushed to hear it. Gaines was the kind of man other men feared and envied, and it turned her on to see them scurry and scuttle about him. To have Ludo do it was an exquisite humiliation. 'My father knows you well, I believe.'

'For a long time.'

'And you sent us Dina. She's quite the worker.' Ludo smiled proudly. 'I should thank you for that, and a lot more, because I got a beautiful girlfriend out of the deal.'

Joel Gaines turned his dark eyes to Dina Kane, looking down at her; she couldn't read their expression. Nor could she move her gaze from his. She was utterly mesmerised. She felt her lack of jewels, of haute couture, of evening make-up. Simple had seemed chic; now she felt like some kind of shepherdess who had wandered into Versailles. Outclassed and out of place.

'Isn't it hard dating somebody that works for you? Office romances are notorious,' Susan Gaines said, conspiratorially. 'All the other girls will complain about how you got the job, Dina – and they'll be after your man. Although I'm sure you quite hold your own!'

'Oh, no. Dina's a great worker. She's really helped in my turnaround of the store,' Ludo said.

Dina wasn't listening. She was looking at Gaines, lost in his eyes like her body was crying out to him. Dimly, she became aware that Ludo was looking at her, and forced herself to break the spell, look at the floor.

'Yes, that's right,' she said, automatically.

'It's interesting that you put it like that, though,' Gaines said, lightly. 'I thought it was Dina, not you, who had turned the store around. I'm sure you wouldn't want to take credit for the way she blitzed your beauty department.'

It was a shock. She hadn't been expecting that, not any of it. Gaines was defending her; he was taking Ludo on. And he knew – he knew about her work. Not a word from him, not an email all these many months, but he still knew all about it, and this was firm praise.

'She submitted plans, sure. I ran with them. And I have been revamping all our other departments.' Ludo didn't bridle, he couldn't afford to, but he was furious. What did Gaines mean by it, at a social gathering? And was this his life, to have his woman upstage him in front of bankers, investors? His anger hardened – at Joel, even at Dina. This charade would be finished by the end of the night, he vowed it. The ring came with a price. 'Isn't that right, Dina?'

She was put on the spot.

'Is it, indeed?' asked Gaines, as if idly curious.

'I . . . Yes.' She could not fight with Ludo, not right now. She was with him, here, as his girlfriend. That meant loyalty, or go home. 'Many of the suggestions came from Ludo, and he's the one working the rest of the store . . .'

'And I'm in charge of social media, development and purchasing,' Ludo said, curtly. 'I run our press campaigns. Perhaps you saw me in *Vogue*?'

'I did! I did!' Susan squealed. 'I swear, that's what I was show-ing Joel, like, just today! It was amazing! You looked fantastic. You've done wonders; your father must be proud as hell, young man. And you, Dina, you have a *great* boss. I think Ludo's going out of his way to talk up her contribution, am I right, Dina? After all, there are a lot of staff who make up that beauty department. I've been there. The make-up artists are to die for. And the girls at the counter are all experts—'

'Yes, and Dina hand-picked them,' Joel said. 'But never mind; I hope the rest of your rebranding goes as well as the beauty department, Ludo. We shouldn't be all business tonight.'

'Hey, thanks,' Ludo said. 'In fact, I was hoping your wife might give me some tips for the summer, now I'm moving in.' He turned to Susan. 'Good restaurants, reliable pool cleaners, that kind of stuff. And perhaps we could all have dinner?'

Dear God, no. Dina groaned.

'Oh, yes! That would be perfect. We'd love to. And we'll get a few friends round to meet you.'

Ludo smiled, that was what he was hoping for.

Susan turned to Dina. 'Sweetie, can I steal him for a second? We have lots to discuss. Joel will look after you.'

Without waiting for an answer, she grabbed a willing Ludo by the elbow and led him over to one of Roxana Felix's cavernous leather couches.

Dina breathed in, a shuddering breath of excitement and fear. She clutched the stem of her champagne flute like it was a lifejacket.

'Oh, yes,' said Joel, softly. 'I'd love to look after you.'

She bridled. 'After you last saw me? You basically told me to drop dead. You implied I had a crush on you.'

'And you didn't?'

The casual, teasing power of his voice . . . She couldn't help it, her body responded immediately, her nipples tautening, her belly warming with blood.

'Don't talk to me that way. I'm with Ludo.'

'So I see.'

'And you're with Susan. Nice dress. Nice jewels.'

He lifted an eyebrow. 'You sound bitter.'

'I guess I just don't understand what you have in common, Joel. And I'm not bitter; I'm angry.' It was tumbling out of her now, and she couldn't stop it, didn't want to. 'You shouted at me; you dropped me. But you wanted me just as much. Perhaps I shouldn't have asked you to meet me, but we both know how you looked at me, Joel Gaines. It's goddamn *cruel* of you to lay it all on me.'

He stared down at her, and his eyes softened.

'Maybe so.'

Her heart leaped. 'So you did want me? You admit it?'

'I wouldn't put it in the past tense.' He glanced over at the couch, where his wife was holding court, and Ludo, like a little puppy, was sitting next to her, making notes in his phone. 'Let's step outside, into the garden. He'll find you. You can say you went for some air.'

Meekly, she followed him, her blood singing, the desire and excitement crackling across her skin like electricity. She had the feeling of being right on the edge with him, of saying things that could never be unsaid. But she didn't want to unsay them. She wanted to speak the truth, let it all out, tell him, plainly, how she felt, and then let the cards fall where they would. It would be a relief, a massive relief, not to have to pretend.

He took her outside, away from the spotlights, across a lawn with a few people on it, and into a garden with hedges; through the darkness, she could see roses and English topiary, lit with candles.

'Stop here.' She did, stumbling after him, her heels sinking into the grass. He stood close to her, really close, his huge, tall, strong body looming over her, in her space, and the eroticism hung about him so hard she could hardly breathe.

'There's something I have to do,' Gaines said, and he drew her in close, his arm around her waist, pulling her tight, and kissed her, full, deep. His strong arms folded around her, his tongue in her mouth, and she was wet, hot and open, moaning with a desire that he swallowed, his lips strong on hers, firm, exploring her, feeling her need, and the warmth of her body stretched all across him.

And then, finally, he let her go.

Dina wiped her hand across her mouth, panting.

'I had to taste you,' he said. 'I've been thinking about it, dreaming about it since we met. You have no idea how hard I've fought to get you out of my system. I wanted to be so foul to you, you'd never speak to me again.'

She sobbed. 'And it worked.'

'No. I couldn't stop thinking about you. I was obsessed. I couldn't even tell my shrink.' He chuckled, without mirth. 'And I haven't even slept with you.'

'Nor will you,' she said, wiping away tears. 'I won't be your piece on the side. Ludo is good to me.'

'You don't love him.'

'And you don't love your wife.'

He sighed. 'I deserved that. I guess I love her enough not to divorce her, after all these years, and two kids together.'

Dina froze; she couldn't disagree with the words, but the pain in her heart was acute, so strong she could hardly breathe.

'Then please do not torture me,' she said. 'Let me make a life.'

'I want to be in touch. I want to be your friend. We don't have to see each other, just talk on the telephone.'

'That's fine.' She wiped her eyes, trying to repair her face. They would have to go back inside. 'Ignoring you didn't work.'

'I get that. Same here. You know I want you; I want to make love to you. I want to turn you inside out. I think about it all the time. I hate to see you with Ludo Morgan.'

'He's a good man,' Dina said, flatly. 'What the hell difference does it make? It would be the same with anyone else.'

'You might be in love with somebody else.'

She shook her head. 'I'm in love with you, Joel. It's stupid and hopeless, but there it is. I know it now. I knew it when you kissed me. So I may as well date a friend. There's nothing better out there for me.'

'Oh, God,' he said. He crouched down, squatting, and put his hands over his head. 'Oh, God. This feels so wrong. I can't; I wish I could. My God. I just want to have you. Only that's not it. I want to talk to you the next day. And every day.'

'You can call me,' she said. 'It's probably unhealthy, but I don't care. If talking is all I can have, I'll take it.'

He stood. 'We must go back. You know, Ludo Morgan is ripping you off. Perhaps you've been too busy to see it.'

'He's backed me.'

'Backed you by signing his own name to every press release. Backed you by ripping off your ideas as his own. He does the interviews; he's the brand. Susan was crass, but that's how people will see you – as a better paid version of a make-up girl.'

Dina slowly turned the idea over in her mind. 'I really don't think—'

'Yes, you do. You just didn't want to admit it to yourself.'

'He gave me a pay rise, a company car. A budget—'

'That's cents on the dollar, baby. You're making the stock of his company soar. Come on, Dina. Don't let this guy screw you. At least not like that.'

'He's not that way. He really loves me, wants me to succeed.'

'So ask him to make you a partner. You deserve it; the company was treading water. You've opened up everything. You should have stock.'

She walked with him, back to the house, back to her life.

'And, Dina, you can do whatever you want, of course you can, but I think you're wrong. Don't make any big decisions while you're on the rebound. You . . . you can find the right man.'

'You really have no say in that, do you, Joel?'

He bowed his head, and they walked back into the house together. She left his side as fast as she could, and went to look for Ludo; he was still sitting there, like a puppy looking up at its mistress.

'Hey, Susan. So sweet of you to take Ludo under your wing! But he's really got to come back to me now, or I'm going on strike.' She flashed a bright smile at the older woman.

'Sure! I hope Joel took care of you.'

'He was the perfect host,' Dina said, lightly. 'Sweet of you both.'

'I'd better get back to him myself. But we're looking forward to seeing you both soon!'

Susan stood up; Ludo did the same and they exchanged air-kisses. Then she smiled benignly at Dina and wandered off into the crowd, looking for Joel. Dina pictured it: the clutching at his arm, the laughing, the rich patroness regaling him with stories of how she'd helped the eager young man. She wasn't looking forward to the rest of the party, not one little bit; socialising was too much.

'Hey! How was it?' Ludo was peppy, full of excitement. 'Please tell me you made friends? Susan was so great. They want to have a dinner party for us next month—'

'Oh, let's not go so fast. You've hardly settled into the house—'

'No time to waste. He can really help me, you know. Joel Gaines is an *incredible* person to know. I'm excited, Dina. Did you get on with him?' His eyes were wide and hopeful.

'I got on fine with him,' she said, dying a little inside.

'That's perfect! We'll be such a hit here. I can't wait. Come on outside, would you?'

She baulked. 'Not the garden – I really don't want to go out there . . .'

'No, Dina – the beach. The ocean. It's romantic, see?'

He gestured out front to the door, and the spotlights on the shore. 'I would really like you to come, OK?'

Dina nodded. 'OK. Sure.' She could hardly turn him down.

'And then maybe . . . maybe we could go home – to the cottage? I'm feeling a bit overwhelmed by all this.'

'Oh no, sweetheart. You're doing great. Believe me, you'll want to come back in after this.'

He held out his hand, and Dina took it. It was clammy with sweat. She followed him out of the packed crowd of beautiful people in their jewels and silks and bespoke suits, grateful at least to be outside, away from everyone, away from Susan Gaines – away from Joel Gaines.

'Come here, where we can see the sea.'

She dutifully followed. She was barely paying attention. Her mind was back in the garden, in Gaines' arms, in the insistent mastery of his kiss.

'Stop – that's enough.'

Dina jerked herself away from her thoughts and looked around. They were just at the edge of the light, and in front of them was the dark, quiet sand of the beach, with the immensity of the ocean crashing on the shore. It was lovely, and soothing, and she wished to God she were almost anywhere else.

'I have something to say.'

She looked at him. She could still hardly pay attention to him. Whatever it was, it could wait.

'Dina, we've been going out for a while now, and each month I feel I'm getting closer to you. You're so beautiful, and stylish, and stunning, and you make me feel great about myself. You're funny and you work so hard. *Too* hard. I'd like your work to be different, to be us, and our family.'

'Our family?' Dina repeated, blankly.

'Yes. The one we can start, any moment now. Once we get married.'

She gasped. For once, Ludo Morgan had taken her completely by surprise.

'You can't believe it, can you? But it's true. Dina, fairy tales do happen. We met by chance, and now, this.' He reached into his pocket and drew out the small Tiffany box; as she looked, transfixed with fear, Ludo flicked it open.

Proud. Smug. Looking up at her for acceptance.

'My God,' Dina whispered. The diamond was huge, the sapphires exquisite.

'Yes. It's true. I want to marry you,' Ludo said. 'What do you say, Dina Kane?'

She didn't hesitate.

'No.'

Chapter Fourteen

'You have a visitor, Mr Kane.'

The therapist put her head round Johnny's door. She wore those green slacks they all wore, with different T-shirts to make them look a little less medical. He hated how she never knocked; you lost your dignity fast in here.

But then he'd lost his dignity a long while ago, somewhere in all the pills and the bottles. Same as he'd lost Brad.

'Show her in.'

There was Dina – and he loved Dina – but Johnny Kane almost hated her, too. So she was spending all her money on him, and for what? To save his body, so he could go back to his shitty life? Without Brad? What the hell was the point?

He was better – maybe. He was bored and depressed, and the anxiety crept all over him, every day, like ants. No college – he was long since a dropout – no job prospects. Of course, Dina would find him something to do, or keep him, but he didn't want to hang round his little sister for the rest of his life, like a bad smell.

Maybe she was a half-sister. Jeez, they were so different, he wondered if his mother had been fucking around long before it became obvious. He was the product of the construction worker with the bottle of booze in his pants pocket, and Dina was the secret daughter of some high-powered mafia boss. Johnny smiled – that would totally fit.

'It's not your sister,' the therapist said. 'It's a man called Johnson. Edward Johnson. Do you want to see him?'

Johnny considered. He didn't know any Edward Johnsons, but he was bored out of his skull and there was nothing to drink or smoke up here.

'Sure,' he said.

The door opened wider and a handsome blond man, around Johnny's own age, thin and well dressed, stood there. He was gorgeous. Man, Johnny hadn't seen any hot guys for a lifetime.

'Come on in,' he said.

'How are you doing?' said the young man. 'I'm a friend of Brad's. I thought maybe you'd like to get out of here.'

Johnny Kane beamed with pleasure.

'Of Brad's?'

'Hey, don't get too excited. He left for Europe with his new boyfriend. But he did want to check up on you. He asked me if I would come see you when you got better, take you home and give you a little fun. He said you've been real short on fun, and you've got your life in front of you.'

'Why would he do that? If he left for Europe?'

The blond shrugged. 'He didn't want to see you himself, said it would be too emotional for both of you. But he did want to look out for you. Brad left a place you could stay in the city, and a list of a few guys to hang out with. At least till you get back on your feet.'

Johnny chewed his lip.

'If he did that for me, he must have feelings . . .'

'Johnny, please. He's rented a furnished place for you for two months – so you can find something. Thought maybe you'd want to organise your own life. It's paid for, but then it runs out. Up to you if you want to live with your sister instead . . .'

'I want Brad's phone number.'

'No can do. He made me promise not to. I think he's serious about this new guy – a Brit. They went to Paris together for a while and they're getting married in London.'

Johnny sank back against the pillows on his bed, despondent. 'Then what do I care?'

'There are other fish in the sea.'

'Like you?' he asked, idly. The boy was so smoothly good-looking; maybe he could be distracted from his broken heart.

'I'm straight.'

'Of course you are.' Johnny sighed deeply. 'And I bet you didn't even have the courtesy to bring me some cigarettes.'

'How wrong you are,' Edward said. He reached inside his jacket and drew out a pack of smokes, then fished into his pants for a lighter; it was solid gold, and monogrammed *EJ*.

Johnny stared. He licked his lips.

'A little smoke's hardly going to kill you. Face it: you aren't drinking anymore. Anyway, since you don't want to come out, I'll leave you here to wait for your sister. Doing well, isn't she? So busy these days . . .'

'Dina always does well.' Johnny stared at the cigarettes. 'You know, there's no smoking in here.'

'I know. They were for the car ride; kind of a celebration. If you checked yourself out . . .'

'Checked myself out?'

'It's not prison.'

'Doesn't Dina have to sign off on it?'

'Dude, I don't know. Is your sister your jailer? Maybe she had you committed? Because then I can't help you.'

He got up and put the cigarettes down on the table. 'Good to see you're in good health. Keep them, but you need to find your own matches.'

Johnny looked round at the little room that had been his oppressive prison for almost a year now, in between hospital visits and bouts in the little cell nobody talked about – the padded one where they sent you to kick.

'Screw it,' he said. 'I've really had enough. I'll come with you.'

* * *

Ludo shuddered with fury. He was having trouble believing it.

'No,' she said, just like that.

After that, she tried something softer: not ready, liked him as a partner, wasn't in love with him yet, not sure if it could be anything more. She even tried the line about friends. And then the one about colleagues.

'I'm so sorry. You know, maybe it's for the best, Ludo. I was getting kind of uncomfortable working for you and—'

'No, you weren't. You never had a problem.'

'I just – I liked dating.'

'Liked my money, our restaurants, is what you mean, isn't it?' he said, though he knew how dumb that was. She was turning down millions. 'I hired you; I backed you; I *made* you. I brought you here and you humiliate me like this?'

'Nobody knows. Nobody's out here but us.'

Thank God he hadn't told Susan. 'You'll regret this, Dina. You led me on.'

'Ludo, please. You don't want to marry somebody you don't love . . .'

'How do you know I don't love you? I had a *life* planned for us. You were going to make the best wedding, decorate our beach house. We'd have children. You were going to be the star at home, just like tonight, Dina.' He waved at the beach house, Roxana's glittering party. 'Why the hell not? Are you seeing somebody else?'

'I'm not seeing anybody.'

'Fucking somebody else, then?'

She looked at him, mute in the face of his anger.

'Ludo, I need more credit for my work. You shouldn't have told Susan Gaines that you revamped the store. It's mine. You really need to stop doing press like it's all yours.'

He pressed his fingers to his temples. The girl was insane, clinically insane. She was walking out on a vast fortune – and now arguing with him over her shitty six-figure job?

'Is that what this is about? Your job?'

'It matters to me.'

'You're nuts. I don't believe this. Jesus Christ!' He looked around, snapped the velvet ring box shut and shoved it back in his pocket. 'I think maybe you should just go home.'

'I don't know where the cottage is.'

Ludo stood up. 'I meant go to your home. I'm not interested in being around you.'

Dina almost laughed. 'Ludo, Manhattan is hours away. You brought me here; you have my stuff at your place. You will take me there for the night and you will take me back to Manhattan in the morning.'

'Or what?' he snarled.

'Or I go right back in there and I will make the most horrible scene. And the first person I talk to will be Roxana Felix when I ask her for a spare bedroom and if I can borrow pyjamas.'

He swallowed, hard. It was bitter. Back home, the house-keeper would be waiting with champagne. He had to call her, tell her to get the fuck out and put Dina's stuff in the smallest guest room.

'Fine,' he said. 'And tomorrow the chauffeur will drive you and your case all the way home. And you can start looking for another job. You're fired.'

Dina laughed. 'I will sue you.'

'You don't have the money and you don't have a case. Look at your contract: under a year, still. I can terminate you without cause at any time and pay you two months' salary. And, since you signed off all the documents listing my contribution to Torch, if you start claiming credit, the company will sue you.'

Dina blinked. 'Ludo – you can't do that.'

'I can. I will. It's done. Go wait at the front of the house while I call the driver.'

* * *

When she woke up in the morning, Dina Kane felt like she'd got drunk and had the world's worst hangover.

Her head was thumping. Her body ached from poor, stressed-out sleep. For a few moments, she was so groggy she didn't realise where she was.

Then the sound of the sea came faintly in at her window, the small single bed looking out over farmland to the water, and she remembered it all.

She pushed back the covers and sat up in bed. Surely Ludo wouldn't be this much of an asshole. He wouldn't fire her, just because she turned him down – she was the key to everything at Torch. It was her job, her life, her everything . . .

Dina shrieked. Ludo Morgan was standing in the doorway of her room, staring down at her.

'Get dressed,' he said, contemptuously. 'You're leaving in thirty minutes. Or you can walk home.'

She didn't cry. She showered quickly, hating to be naked in a house with him. And then she pulled on clothes as fast as she could from the half-packed case Ludo had dumped in her bedroom: panties, jeans, last night's bra and a T-shirt; screw style, anything that could cover her. Frantically, she closed the suitcase and hauled it downstairs, her dress and shoes from last night shoved inside. Ludo had brought her a pair of flip-flops, for the beach; that was what she would travel home in.

'Enjoy it,' he said, coldly, as she lugged the heavy case across his flagstone path, laid out over a manicured lawn. 'It's the last limousine ride you'll be getting for a while.'

It was a long drive home. Dina sat and thought for most of it. Who could she call? Her mother? What a joke. She had no one.

Maybe a couple of the girls on the shop floor? But she didn't want to put them through it. Ludo was their boss, too; they would be risking their jobs by talking with Dina. She felt ill, frantic that she'd been this stupid. Of course, he was right, the little asshole; her contract had a year's grace period, and they could fire her whenever they liked.

Dina had to go quietly, or Ludo Morgan could make her name mud. She thought of Gaines, of his kiss, of his advice. He was right – goddamn him – he'd seen in a moment what she'd blocked out for months.

And she could call him, if he wasn't in bed sleeping with his wife.

In the end, there was only one person she could talk to: Johnny. The thought of hearing his voice made her happy, made the tears she'd been suppressing well up and drift down her cheek. Somebody was there who loved her, who would not sell her out. Who wouldn't fire her. And who, any minute now, she would get to see again. He was coming home.

Tears trickling down her face, Dina dialled the number.

'Hi. Can you put me through to Johnny Kane's room?'

'One moment please.' Pause. 'Oh, Mr Kane isn't with us anymore, I'm afraid.'

'What? That's impossible. This is his sister, Dina. He hasn't been taken back to hospital?'

'No, ma'am. Mr Kane checked out yesterday, with his friend.'

She dabbed at her face. 'His friend?'

'Said he was a friend of Brad's, or something.'

She relaxed. 'And Johnny was fine to leave?'

'He seemed OK, but you know it is up to the patient. We can't compel them to complete treatment.'

'I've been paying his bills. You can send me the final accounts.'

'Yes, ma'am.'

Dina dried her tears. If Brad had sent somebody for Johnny, that was wonderful news. She thought they were all over, all finished. Nothing could welcome her brother back to the world better than Brad taking him back.

* * *

Edward looked around the flat, very satisfied with it. It was scummy, cheap – Red Hook in Brooklyn – and right around drug dealer central. It had been rented in cash for him by Olivia Broadwell, his private investigator, using a fake ID; the owner never saw or met him. The furniture was revolting, but they had cleaned it up, tidied it with throws and pillows and put clean, cheap sheets on the bed. The fridge was stocked with food, and there was a rack of wine – screw-top; easy to open. He had cigarettes, lighters and ashtrays, and cold beers in the fridge, along with soft drinks. Nothing too pushy or obvious.

Most importantly, there were the 'friends' sitting around: male hookers – gay and gorgeous. They made Edward's stomach turn; he hated perversion – scorned everybody not like him. He despised Johnny, that weak, detestable fag with the bitch sister. But he loved what these boys were going to do for him. Olivia's hires; she'd bought them to order: twenty-one through twenty-six, blonds, brunettes, a couple with muscles, mostly smooth-featured pretty guys. There were five of them, all well-paid and known for being discreet.

And following orders.

The orders right now were to show Johnny a *great* time, to party with him and to pretend they were friends with this guy, Brad – just maybe knew him casually – but to talk more about the scene. They'd been instructed not to be found out. Sex – yes; clubs – yes. And as many drugs and as much alcohol as they could take.

Olivia supplied the bonuses: ecstasy, pure coke, high-level heroin – mostly unadulterated. It was on them what they did with it.

'Hey, here he is!' one of them said, as Olivia opened the door. She was unrecognisable, dressed as a graduate student, Iona college sweatshirt, beanie on her head, coloured contact lenses. 'Hey, Johnny! Welcome back. My name's Mark.'

'And I'm Joaquin.'

'David.'

'Justus. How you doing?'

'I'm Karl; I don't really know Brad that well, but what the hell? Welcome home, dude.'

Johnny waved hi, and his eyes lit up. People – *guys*. He looked around at the low-rent apartment like it was paradise.

'All yours for two months,' Edward said, breezily. 'Paid upfront. OK, so, my job's done. There's one more thing, though – can you come into the bedroom a second?'

Johnny followed him in there, while the hookers laughed and catcalled.

'Those boys are incorrigible. Well, look. It's not much, but Brad wanted you to have a fresh start, not be so dependent on Dina while you think about a job. And remember, the rent's taken care of.' He handed Johnny a white envelope, fat with bills. 'There's ten grand in there, plus another two grand in twenties. Please don't contact Brad, though.' He put on a fake air of concern. 'Are you sure you'll be OK with alcohol in the house? We figured, for your friends, not you. And, anyway, you can drink Diet Coke, or moderate it or whatever.'

The sound of beer cans cracking open and young male laughter came from the other room.

'Of course, you can also tell them to pour it away, but it might be a pretty short party. Up to you.'

Johnny's eyes looked hunted. He heard the sound of the booze pouring, the boys having fun. 'I . . . I guess. Like, maybe it'll be OK. If they drink it all.'

'Sweet. And now I've got to split.'

Johnny nodded. 'Hey, thanks, man. When do I see you again?'

'You don't. Brad's farewell gift, you know? Better make a clean break of it. Have fun! I think those guys like the look of you. *Sayonara.*'

And Edward left with a wave, closing the door behind him.

He walked down the stairs as fast as he could, scarf pulled up over his face, woollen hat low on his eyes. There was no doubt now. He was happy to bank on Johnny Kane's weakness.

Nature was tough, and she was going to take her course.

His limousine was heading back to the townhouse when Olivia called.

'You wanted to be kept updated on Dina Kane.'

She never indulged in pleasantries.

'Obviously. Go.'

'She's been fired. Last night. Word went out at Torch today.'

Edward sat up. 'You're kidding me?'

'Not at all. The rumour is that Ludo Morgan, her boss, dumped her. They were dating, remember?'

'Of course I fucking remember.' The only way to get to that bitch had seemed to be through her brother. Morgan was serious about the girl, Olivia had reported; and he was richer than Edward or his father had ever been.

That marriage would have taken her out of his grasp – at least, financially.

'Well, there was a party in the Hamptons. Some sort of scene. We heard from staff at the beach house that she was flung out and fired. Sources at Torch confirmed it this morning.'

'Any press release?'

'All the press has been in Ludo Morgan's name. She's just been fired. Their plan seems to be to replace her and move on.'

Edward thought of Johnny. Was he drinking, right now? Smoking something? How long would it take? And she was at home, crying and wailing, dumped and fired. He felt his cock hardening. Revenge at long last.

'Get something in the gossip columns. Dumped. Scene at fancy party. Trying to pass off Ludo's work as her own. Pattern with the Meadow cream invented by an old man. No respectable guy should date her.'

Olivia paused. 'Maybe I can do something on Ludo and the Hamptons, but the other stuff is boring, at least to the press.'

'Just do what I say,' Edward repeated. 'Use your connections.'

'Very well.'

She hung up.

Edward almost laughed. What a pain in the ass, setting all this shit up, but it was going to be so worth it. The perfect one-two punch. In a moment, in a day, Dina Kane was going to be finished.

'There's nothing you can do.' The lawyer, Marie Costas, was a no-nonsense older woman, and she gave it to Dina straight.

'That can't be true.'

'Get another job.' Costas sighed. 'Look, Miss Kane, I'd be happy to represent you, but I'd just be stealing your money. You have no case. A trial period is just that. For the first year, they get to fire you, no cause needed.'

'Sexual discrimination, though?'

'You signed the contract; you dated freely; this was an open relationship. In court, I can't prove you were compelled to do anything.'

'But they promoted me – gave me five pay rises, all in a few months.'

'Creative differences? Maybe you argued about how to present the beauty department, it doesn't matter. That clause means get out of jail free. I'm an employment lawyer and I have to give you the facts.'

Dina's fist curled around the receiver. 'I saved his store.'

'It doesn't matter. I'm sorry.'

She let out a long, whistling sigh. Johnny was nowhere to be found, Ludo wouldn't even return her calls, and human resources was sending her stuff back to her apartment in a box.

'I suppose I will have to find another job,' she said, slowly. 'Wow. It's going to be hard, starting from scratch.'

'Dina, there's more bad news.'

'What else could there be?' she asked, bitterly.

'Your next job. It can't be in beauty, or style. At least, not for two years.'

Dina actually laughed. 'What? What's that? Beauty is all I know.'

'Your contract included a noncompetition clause. You can't go to work for any other department store, or any existing store in the United States that works in a "competing field", which they define as retail, beauty or fashion.'

She felt a cold wave of fear wash over her. 'You have to be kidding me, Marie. How can I support myself?'

'There are other industries. Maybe you could be a fashion journalist?'

'I make a good six figures.' Dina paused. 'That's insane. Can we challenge that in court?'

'We could, sure. You could make a case, it is too onerous. But it will be a long fight, and Torch has deep pockets. You couldn't start work unless you got a judgement in your favour. Nobody could hire you.'

The pain and disappointment started to mix with fear. She glanced around her new apartment, wondering how long she'd be able to afford it.

'My best advice is that you go see your ex-boyfriend and ask him to let you out of the clause. The firm could release you.'

Ludo Morgan was enjoying the day.

Maybe he'd been lucky. Dina Kane would have been a big mistake.

She wasn't from his world. Couldn't handle it. And all that pushy aggression was getting old fast. He wasn't interested in working hard all day, then coming back to a rival at night.

Dina had a lot of enemies. Lots of rivals. As word leaked out, women had been congratulating him all morning.

'Thank you, Mr Morgan – she was so bossy.'

'Oh, well done, sir. She was always trying to change your orders.'

'She made us work nights. Thank you.'

'Not my place, but I really don't think she was your type,' said the large-breasted blonde girl from mascara, fluttering professionally impressive lashes at him. 'You know – *so* ambitious.'

'Why, thank you – Tara.' He looked at her name badge.

'I'm sure many of the girls thought she was *very* lucky, but she didn't act that way.'

He smiled. He would bang the girl, since she was practically begging for it, but that was about all.

No more employees. No shopgirls. He would head back to the Hamptons and let Susan Gaines fix him up with somebody's daughter.

The calls came in to the office, too: reporters, bloggers, other executives.

'Was it wise to dismiss Dina Kane? She was one of the prime movers on Torch's relaunch, wasn't she?'

'We have a great team, which I head. She was one part of it, but it's time to move on. The company has other plans.'

'Mr Morgan, thanks for taking my call, we just heard the news this morning . . .'

'What news is that?' Ludo asked.

'About Dina Kane. Your beauty director.'

'Oh, Kane. Yes, well, there were a few differences of opinion. We have a terrific team implementing my changes. I'll be appointing a new head of social media soon, to reach out to you guys.'

'You don't really credit Dina—?'

'Lots of people did a lot of good work, and we wish her luck.'

'So your relationship wasn't a part of this?'

'We weren't a good fit, personally or professionally, but I enjoyed spending time with Dina, and hopefully she'll find the right person for her someday soon.'

'OK,' said the woman, tentatively. 'Uh . . . Thank you.'

He gave out the same line all morning, then stopped taking calls. No press release; best not to encourage the idea that she mattered.

Finally, after lunch, there came the call he was expecting.

'Do you want to take this?' his secretary, Eileen, asked. 'It's from Dina Kane.'

Ludo smiled broadly. The anger inside him, from last night, was still clear and bright, cold as a diamond. It was interesting how much he minded her rejection.

But, best of all, he was in a position to do something about it.

'Certainly. Shut the office door.'

'Yes, sir.'

He depressed the red button on his phone.

'Dina Kane.'

'Ludo. I need some help.'

He chuckled. 'Then you've come to the wrong place. I'm not interested in working with you, and your contract is rock solid.'

She paused, and he tried to imagine the turmoil crossing that beautiful face.

'I understand that, Ludo. I think you're making a terrible mistake. We were a good team, professionally.'

'You led me on – probably so you could rise at Torch. You may call that professional, I don't.'

She gasped. 'That's bullshit. You asked me out.'

'And you couldn't wait to say yes. Look, I'm not interested in your little games. I just thank whatever's up there that I avoided a horrible mistake.'

'You sound so bitter,' Dina said, after a pause.

'Bitter? No. You're a joke, and I'm annoyed at the time I've wasted. Now, do run along and play in the traffic. If you're looking for favours, you used up your share long ago, baby.'

'I don't want my job back. I accept you can't work with me. I just need you to release me from the noncompetition clause—'

'So you can go and work for a rival? Drive sales up at Bloomingdales? What, you think I'm dumb? Always under-estimating everybody else, that's you, Dina Kane.'

'Come on, Ludo! Beauty's all I know. Just because we broke up, you want to ruin my life?'

'Enough with the drama queen. Go get a job bagging groceries. I don't give a shit.'

'That clause is totally unfair. It's restrictive—'

'We paid you enough in bonuses to keep you for a couple of years.'

'Not in Manhattan.'

'So move back to Westchester, the suburbs, where you came from. If you don't like the clause, take us to court. Torch has *great* lawyers, Dina.'

She breathed in and out, hard, ragged. He wanted to laugh.

'I'll go to your father. He's the one that hired me.'

'Don't bother. Dad and I have already had this discussion. He's not interested in you working in beauty for anyone else.'

Ah, yes . . . his father. The one cloud over his day. His father had been pretty goddamned furious that he'd fired Dina.

'Ship her down to Los Angeles. We can open a second store; she can run it.'

'Dad! Christ! I can't work with her. She dumped me.'

'Girlfriends are two a penny, Ludo. She's done wonders with the goddamned store.'

'I've seen what she did. I can replicate it. Please don't worry. You can't have me humiliated like that, Dad.'

His father sighed. 'Next time, keep it in your pants. She was *useful*.'

Still, at least he'd agreed: no Dina anywhere else.

'Make sure she doesn't go to Saks. They're already eating our lunch; we don't need Dina Kane making things worse. Or opening a Manhattan branch of Harrods.'

'No, sir,' Ludo assured him. 'Not a chance.'

Now he was glad to be able to rub it in. 'My father specifically asked me to bind you to the noncompetition clause. You will learn that what you did last night has consequences. And your precious career is one of them.'

She spoke slowly, clearly. 'I had no idea you were such a bastard, Ludo, but I promise you – you and your company will live to regret this.'

He laughed. 'Sure, Dina.' He hung up.

Goddamn you, Johnny, Dina thought. *I don't need this right now – I just don't need this.*

She was fighting to keep her head up. The emails were flooding her inbox; there were dozens of Google Alerts on her name. Reporters were calling. There were instant blog pieces, some supportive, others mocking. A lot of jealousy out there. And Ludo, such an asshole; she felt small and stupid ever to have dated him, ever to have thought it was OK.

Yet, even as she cried and tried to control herself, she could not find her brother. Every time she hung up the phone, she looked for news. The rehab was no help.

'We can't give you any assistance, Ms Kane. Yes, we know you paid the bills. But you don't have a power of attorney. Mr Kane was free to leave with whoever he liked.'

'My brother wouldn't just leave me without word.'

'If you get a power of attorney, we can send you videotape of the man who picked him up. Although he wore a hat and scarf . . .'

'Goddamn it!' Dina sobbed. 'He was an addict. He's in danger.'

'Have you filed a missing-person's report?'

'It hasn't even been two days; he's an adult. The cops won't touch it yet.'

'Well, then,' said the receptionist.

'I just want to know the name of his visitor. Please. Just give me a name. They sign a book; how confidential can it be?'

'Miss, please, I've told you, I need some kind of release. You can't ask me to break the law. He warned me against giving out the name, the gentleman.'

Dina's hand gripped the phone. She was suddenly struck with a horrible thought.

'OK,' she said, faintly. 'I'll come back to you.'

Her mother wasn't answering her phone. Dina left four messages, then she called the police. A Sergeant Mukowski listened to her politely and told her he couldn't help her.

'Ma'am, he's not a child. He could be anywhere. Could be on vacation. This could be a boyfriend, from what you say.'

'But can't you at least look for him?'

'No, ma'am. He's not a missing person. Why don't you wait a few days?'

Maybe he's right, Dina thought, as she hung up the phone, yet again. Maybe they were all right. She was worrying for nothing.

But her heart told her different.

She lay on the bed. She wanted to call Joel Gaines, tell him her fears, tell him everything. But she didn't dare.

If Johnny had been kidnapped, the people who had him knew where to find her. But where was the call? Where was the ransom note?

Even as she agonised over her future, the thought – that bad idea in the back of her head – would not go away, would not shift.

It had been years – years. And she hadn't heard a word from him.

Edward Johnson.

Of course, she still had the address, the phone records, tucked away – everything she'd found out from his father, whilst mercilessly screwing him for revenge. She'd hoped that the rage within her would calm afterwards, but instead she'd felt like she was dying inside, a little, every day.

What she'd done had destroyed Shelby Johnson. And his son. She understood now that it also destroyed her.

Workaholism had redoubled. No real boyfriends. No trust; no hope. She had been fixated on the safe . . . until Joel Gaines came along and she was tempted again by another married man – for good this time.

Dina buried her face in her hands. She was a disaster, an emotional cripple. And now she was nothing at work, either.

But her brother was still out there, out there somewhere. Feeling sick, dizzy with fear, she dug out the old number and called it up.

'Johnson residence,' said a voice.

'I want to speak to Edward. Is he there?'

'Who's calling, please? I'll see if Mr Johnson is available.'

Dina felt that surge of hatred again, jolting through her heartbreak. Overprivileged, spoiled little brat; rich guy who'd done nothing to deserve it; pampered prince, laughing at her. Her remorse over his father, what she'd done, that dirty, arid, deceptive sex, almost vanished at the sound of the servant's voice. Jesus Christ! What fucking century were they living in? One where you could bang the help, laugh about it and just walk away.

'My name is Dina Kane. I think he'll remember me.'

'Hold a moment, please.'

She waited maybe thirty seconds, and every one of them, an eternity. He was there, playing with her, making her wait. The acid bubbled in her stomach.

'Dina!' said that familiar voice, too brightly, and she understood at once that he loathed her. 'What a pleasant surprise to hear from you again, and on such a worrying day for you! Or so a little bird tells me.'

'Edward –' she choked down the insults that sprang to her lips – 'do you know something about my brother?'

'Oh, Dina. I know *masses* about your brother. He was kind

enough to enlighten me, all the way back from the rehab facility. It's a long drive, when you're stuck with such a *boring* companion. I can't abide sob stories.'

She shuddered with horror. 'If you've done anything to him – I'll go straight to the police.'

'My dear girl, don't be foolish. I've done nothing to him. He checked out quite voluntarily. The staff will tell you that. He had a very slow time of it up there: no drink; no boyfriends. So, to celebrate his checking out, I gave him some champagne. He asked to be dropped off in Red Hook – quite a party zone, I believe. He was going to visit a few fellows.'

'You gave him alcohol? After all this time?' Her heart thumped wildly. 'Where is he, Edward? For God's sake, this is his life.'

'He's an adult with choices, Dina. There's nothing criminal in it.'

She whispered. 'Where is he? Is he dead?'

'How the hell should I know?'

She sobbed. 'You bastard! I'll call the police—'

'And accuse me of what? Offering him champagne? That's not a hanging offence, even in Manhattan. Think hard, Dina Kane. Do you really want the police to sit down with us? What I did isn't illegal. Blackmail is, however. Do you know what happened to my parents?'

'They are adults, too.'

'Right – isn't it marvellous? Everybody's an adult here! My mother was free to divorce my dad and slide into alcoholism; my father lost his position and became a hippie for the world to laugh at. My mother nearly died, too; forgive me if I don't give a flying fuck about your junkie fag of a brother. Except in so far as it makes us even.'

'I never killed anybody.'

'And nor did I, darling. Not that you can prove, anyway.' The sarcastic lightness of tone dropped away. 'It's on your brother. Or, if you prefer, it's on you. The same as your failure at work,

281

and your failure with your latest ex. See, that's the problem with whores like you: you just fuck around.'

Dina gasped. She hung up, shaking, trembling across her whole body. A wave of panic coursed through her, so strong her legs gave way, and she collapsed on to the couch.

When it passed, she had only one thought.

She picked up her cellphone and dialled Joel Gaines' number.

'Dina.' He answered immediately. 'Give me a second. I'll call you back.'

She waited, miserably, knowing that he was leaving his wife, leaving Susan, to take her call, heading out of their kitchen, or bedroom. Sneaking around.

It was low and dirty, reaching out for Joel, but she had no choice.

The phone rang two minutes later. 'It's me. I heard; I'm so sorry.'

'This is not about Torch. It's my brother, Johnny. He's in trouble and I need help.'

Gaines' voice changed immediately. 'What do you need?'

'He's an addict.'

'You told me his story. What happened?'

'An enemy of mine sprung him from rehab, gave him wine and dropped him in Red Hook. The way he was talking, I guess it was more than wine.' She sobbed. 'He won't tell me where Johnny is and, the way he was saying it, I think he's dead. He was close to death before we got him clean. It wouldn't take much.'

'Presumably Johnny's not answering calls?'

'Nothing. I've tried emails, calls, texts. My mother hasn't heard from him – doesn't seem to care. The police won't get involved, because he's an adult. He's all I've got, Joel.'

'Why would this . . . this enemy do this to you?'

Dina twisted like a butterfly under a pin. The shame of

admitting it to Joel Gaines . . . admitting any of it to Joel Gaines . . . Maybe he would never be hers, but she didn't want him to know. She didn't want to shatter whatever image he had of Dina Kane.

'His name is Edward Johnson.'

'Edward Johnson? The kid, the son of Shelby Johnson?'

'Yes. He's a psycho, Joel.'

'Why would he try to kill your brother?'

She sobbed. 'I . . . I . . . slept with his father, Shelby, to blackmail him.'

There was a long pause and, in that pause, Dina felt all her hopes and dreams sputter out, like a candle that had burned to the very end.

'I can find your brother.'

'Don't you want to hear what happened, Joel?'

His voice was cold. 'No, Dina. You were clear enough.'

She wept.

'Let me find out what happened to Johnny. It may not be tonight. Hold tight. When I know, I'll call you.'

'Joel, please—'

'I'll call you,' he repeated, and hung up.

Dina walked numbly into her bathroom and peeled off her clothes. With an incredible effort, she forced herself to throw them in the laundry basket and step into the shower.

She dried off mechanically and reached for her cotton pyjamas. The toothbrush in her hand was like a lead weight. Just keeping herself upright seemed more effort than she could bear.

Before bed, she reached into her medicine closet and brought out a small bottle of anti-anxiety pills: Valium. A doctor had recommended it once, and Dina had laughed at him. Weakness? That was for other people.

She wasn't laughing now. She took one, swallowing it with difficulty, gulping the water. And then she crawled into her exquisite antique sleigh bed, made up with crisp Irish linen, and lay down in it like she would never get up again.

Chapter Fifteen

Joel Gaines looked at the body bag.

He had put out the word, and taken the call about an hour ago. His anger at Dina – his disgust, his disappointment – it was wide and deep, but he wasn't going to refuse the plea about her brother.

She was desperate; he recognised that. And, if Johnny Kane was alive, Gaines was going to find him.

It didn't take too long for the answer to come back. Not the one he wanted. But he left his office immediately and met the cop at the scene.

The plastic body bag was unzipped, and there was the unmistakable face of Johnny Kane – bruised, skinny, pale in death, but otherwise matching the photo Dina emailed him. The wasted frame of a young man. He'd been a failure in this life, his potential unrealised, killed by a fatal weakness. Stemming from what? The tension of a bad childhood? It had made Dina – and broken her big brother.

Looking at the corpse, Gaines had no doubt that Edward Johnson did more than hand out wine. There were drugs in the system, the medical examiner said, lots of drugs: heroin, methamphetamine, coke. There was recent sexual activity. All of this, for a penniless ex-student with no money in the bank account, kept by his sister.

The apartment had been ghost rented. There were no signs of anything other than a party, and an OD. Nothing forcible; no murder.

He knew all this because he could hire investigators when he had to. And his law enforcement connections were rock solid. Gaines knew people in the police department, in the Mayor's office, throughout the city.

But Edward Johnson could not have tempted Johnny Kane without that huge void in his life. They were screwed up, both the brother and the sister.

He wondered about it – the dead father, the mother who was there in the most literal sense, but not really there for her kids.

'We'll need next of kin to ID the body,' the cop said.

He wanted to spare Dina that. 'No need; I knew Johnny Kane,' he lied. 'I can ID him for you.'

The guy pursed his mouth, but nodded. Everybody knew Mr Gaines: richest man in the city, but stand-up, nonetheless. His gifts to the Benevolent Fund sent hundreds of dead cops' kids to college, every year.

'Hey, no problem. That'd be great; thank you, sir.'

'Joel.'

The cop smiled. 'Joel.'

DOA was a shitty job, always, but you got used to it – so used to it in New York. This guy lightened the load. He would remember meeting Joel Gaines; he was some kind of big shot, man. The muscles were also impressive. The guy must bench like a maniac. He liked that; exercise was no respecter of wallets. Gaines obviously worked for it. Respect. He had no need to work out to get all the chicks fluttering; his bank account would be more than enough to do that.

'Over here, then.' He walked across and pulled the body bag open a little more. The corpse was pale, a little blood and drool dried on his cheek. His eyes had rolled up into his head. Classic OD.

'That's Johnny Kane,' Gaines said, without hesitation. He was glad Dina would never have to see it. 'Did the medical examiner sign off?'

'At the scene. Full autopsy tonight. Then the body can be released.' He hesitated. 'We really do need next of kin for that one.'

'I understand. Thank you, officer.'

Joel Gaines was not a praying man, but he sent a thought upwards – some kind of wish, intent, call it whatever you like – to whoever was out there, that somebody loved this boy now.

Dina. Her name shoved itself into his mind. *Dina loved him. Dina looked out for him.*

He didn't want to give her credit right now. Didn't want to think good thoughts. She was a low-life; what his wife said was true; what that schmuck Ludo Morgan said was true.

The shock of her words hit him like a fist.

I slept with his father, to blackmail him.

That was what all the jealous bastards said about Dina Kane, that she was a user, a gold-digger, that she latched on to rich men. Shelby Johnson – by her own admission. Who now could believe her story over Meadow? Maybe she took that old chemist guy, Dr Green, for a ride like the rest . . . Stole his idea. And then at Torch . . . she winds up, in two minutes, banging the owner's son.

A job she got via him.

And he was a very rich man, too.

Loser. Idiot. It's a pattern. You're meant to be good at patterns.

He was like some drunk asshole in a strip club, going, 'She likes me!' because the girl shakes her ass nearest to the dollar bills. What a fool! What an idiot! Of course, he was way too old for her. And to think he had gulled himself into believing . . .

Believing that she loved him.

The struggling, the wrestling, the way he'd become so

dissatisfied that the torpor of his marriage was suddenly smothering to him – none of it had any point, because Dina Kane – so beautiful, so smart and so strong – was a self-confessed predator.

There's no fool like an old fool. Wasn't that what they said?

He didn't know why he felt so angry. Hadn't he vowed that kiss was the end? He was staying true. He wasn't going to sleep with Dina, see Dina, anything. They could be friends; they could talk.

And, within one day – this.

What a difference twenty-four hours made. After the party, and the kiss, he had been utterly unable to sleep. He had no desire for Susan, not even enough for the mechanics of sex. He'd told her he was exhausted, and he'd lain down in bed, staring at the ceiling.

And, the next day, he was staring at his cellphone from the moment he walked out of the shower. Waiting for her to call. Willing her to call.

When he heard the news that she'd been fired, his heart leaped. How pathetic – to be pleased that she'd broken up with Ludo Morgan, and was free again. He wasn't free – would never be free – but he rejoiced all the same. And when she didn't call him for help on her business, did not seek his protection, didn't ask him to extend his arm, Joel Gaines was bitterly disappointed.

He recognised the illogic. The selfishness. The dog in the manger. But he wanted – how he wanted – to ride into battle for her and show her what real power meant.

She would be helplessly aroused by it, he knew it: money and power as a proxy for sex.

But Dina Kane did not call. And, as the minutes ticked by, he found himself falling ever more hopelessly in love with her. The bravery of it – the standing on her own two feet – not coming to him, not begging.

When she finally called, it was late, and he assumed she just wanted comfort.

But Dina asked for his power, after all. Wanted it for something he could not refuse. And the price was telling him the truth.

He would have loved to have had that day over again. He'd have given a million dollars, ten million dollars, not to have heard Dina Kane say those words to him.

Johnny Kane was dead. And, for a moment, Joel Gaines envied him. There was nothing true in this world, nothing beautiful.

As he walked away, towards the limousine, that aggravating voice in his head corrected him.

Her love for her brother, her care for her brother was true and beautiful.

Johnny Kane didn't fit Dina's pattern. He couldn't help her career, or give her money. He was a cost centre, without prestige or usefulness. But Dina had been devoted to him. Devoted enough to spend money, even when she hardly had any.

Joel was not looking forward to the stop he had to make.

She was waiting when he knocked on her door.

'Dina, it's me. Open up.'

In a second, the door was wrenched open. She looked worse than Joel had ever seen her. That beautiful face was grey and lifeless. Her eyes were red; her hair was unwashed, unbrushed. She looked like she hadn't eaten in a day. She was gaunt, listless. Not a scrap of make-up on her.

'Joel,' she said, and her whole body teetered and gave way. He reached forward, automatically, and caught her, under the arms. Her head lolled.

'Easy; easy there,' he said, alarmed. He kicked the door shut and guided her to a chair, forcing her to sit. She hadn't fainted, but her head was pressed in her hands. Clearly, it was a dizzy spell. 'When did you last eat?'

'I . . . I don't know.'

'You have to eat, drink. It's low blood sugar. Here.'

He opened her fridge. There was almost nothing in it – a half-empty milk carton, some eggs, some wilting lettuce. 'Jesus. You don't even have orange juice?'

'Joel, please. I can't think about food.'

He felt lost. What did people say about shock? Sweet things – that was right. This was where women looked after men, not the other way around. He filled her electric kettle and hunted in the cupboards till he found a box of teabags and the remnants of a packet of sugar. She stared into space as he fixed her a cup of boiling hot tea and put three sugars in it, stirring it and brewing it, no milk. He didn't trust the milk. She was falling apart, and he was about to help her on the way down.

'Here.' He blew on it a little, to cool it. 'Drink.'

'What did you find out?'

'We're not talking until you've drunk half of that.'

Joel waited. As angry as he was at her and his stupidity, and as much as he wished he'd never heard the name Dina Kane, he could not stand there and see her broken.

She took the mug from him and drank, numbly, not resisting. There was no fire in her anymore. It was nuts, but he felt his heart clenching with emotion. As pallid and dirty as she looked this evening, she was unutterably beautiful to him – vulnerable in a way he had never seen. He could not shake his feelings for her, no matter what he did.

After she had drained most of it, he took the mug from her, so that she wouldn't hurt herself if she dropped it, and knelt down in front of the chair. He took her hands.

'Dina, you will have to be brave. Johnny's dead. I'm so sorry. He died of an overdose, and it was very peaceful.' God knows if it was peaceful or not – he remembered the blood and the drool – but that was what he was going to tell her. 'I identified the body. There were no signs of violence, and it went down as an OD.'

Tears sprang into her eyes, and her thin frame shook with sobs. Great, wrenching, heaving sobs, shocking in their intensity, jolted her out of her numbness and lethargy. He stood there, helpless, with no way to comfort her. In the end, he reached for the kitchen towel and handed it to her so she could mop her face, but the tears continued.

Joel Gaines leaned in and folded his arms around her, wrapping her close, so close, holding her firmly, not letting her slump, until, in the end, her sobs ceased and she was breathing hard, shuddering against him.

'I will take care of everything,' he said. 'They will release the body to you or your mother. The police will inform her.'

'I'll call Mom,' Dina whispered.

'I can have the best funeral home in the city pick him up and arrange any kind of service you like.'

'Catholic.'

'Fine. I give half a million to the Cardinal's appeal every year.'

She looked up at him with the suggestion of a smile. 'But you're Jewish.'

Joel gripped on to that tiny flicker of amusement. 'Baby, I give half a million to everybody important in the city. You buy friends as well as karma.'

'Always at work, aren't you?'

'Aren't we,' he corrected her, but he was thrilled to see this stirring of life.

'I don't know how I'm going to tell Ellen.'

He noted the first name. There was so little there, between mother and daughter; it was sad.

'I'll stay with you. I'm not leaving you right now.'

Dina shook her head; more tears. 'You have to go . . . Your wife . . .'

'My wife can wait.' He pulled out his cellphone and tapped on it. 'I'm just texting her that I'm staying in the city. That's normal on a weeknight.'

She said nothing, and he could see her thoughts dragging back to her admission, and the breach between them.

'You don't owe me anything else, Joel.'

'I didn't owe you this,' he said. 'Go get in the shower. You look awful and you're starting to smell.'

Dina opened her eyes wider, actually shocked.

'We're past the sweet-nothings stage, Dina Kane. Get in the shower. Now.'

She stood up, weakly, and headed to her bathroom. He waited a few seconds, to hear the sound of the water running, then walked in after her.

Dina gasped.

'Chill out, I can't see a goddamn thing with all that steam against the glass.'

Actually, that was not true. He could see the shape of her body just fine; not everything, maybe, just the still-firm curve of that ass, the long hair hanging slick down her back. He bit his lip against the surge of desire and tried to focus. Her clothes were on the floor. He gathered them up and laid out a white waffle robe for her.

'I'm going to wash these. And put new clothes on your bed.'

She said nothing.

Gaines went into her kitchen and found the washing machine. God, she still lived so small, for a girl that could have been married to millions of dollars. This was middle-management stuff, and Dina's brain was way above that level; she was meant to be a superstar, a CEO, a revolutionary.

He flung the clothes in there, added a bag of soap, then went into her bedroom and stripped the sheets from the bed. Dina was a minimalist: just a fitted sheet, pillowcase and a duvet cover in white linen. It smelled bad – of sweat and despair. So he added them to the wash.

Then he charged back into the bathroom. The steam was really up now. Dina said nothing, no word of protest. He imagined she had not eaten all day, maybe longer. Opening her mirrored cabinet, he found shampoo, conditioner and a disposable razor. He opened the door to the stall.

'I'm not looking,' he lied, and extended his hand. 'Take these. All these. Use them. Clean up.'

She lifted them from him. 'OK.'

'When you're done, there's a towel outside this stall, and a robe. Clean your teeth. Then you can go into your bedroom and change.'

'You don't have to do all this.'

'Where do you keep your spare bedding?'

'What?'

'Just answer the question.'

'There's a chest at the foot of the bed.'

He left her then, and went and made the bed, something he had not done since he was a student. The washing machine became a dryer; he was rather proud that he was figuring this stuff out. Her clothes hung in the wardrobe and lay in her chest of drawers: exquisite things, but not many of them. He picked a pair of soft cashmere lounge pants, a bra, panties and a draped jersey T-shirt. It would not be such a disaster if she fell asleep on a couch dressed like that.

Then he called for delivery: Chinese – Manhattan's answer to everything. He got her beef lo mein, for protein and carbohydrates, and a helping of steamed vegetables, and the same for himself. Then he called his assistant.

'Marian, I want you to get a week's groceries for one person delivered, right now. Get the best of everything: Häagen-Dazs, fillet steak, fresh-squeezed orange juice, milk, fruit, smoked salmon, cereals – everything. Tea and coffee. When the guy arrives, have him ring the doorbell but leave it outside. I will unpack myself. Tip him in advance; I don't want to see him. And I want it here fast.'

'Right away, Mr Gaines.' She didn't ask questions. 'What is the address?'

He gave it to her.

'And what name?'

'My name,' Joel said, shortly, and hung up.

He could hear Dina stepping out of the shower. The temptation to go in there, to give her something else, just to see her naked, was overwhelming, but he fought it. Goddamn it; he hated to be here, but he didn't want to leave.

'Do your teeth, like I told you,' he said, loudly.

He heard the sink running as she obeyed him. Right now, she was washed, clean-shaven and doing her teeth: coming back to life because he had ordered it.

Gaines was torn. This was real emotion, not faked. He did not know what to think of her. There was pity, and fury, and jealousy, and disgust, and concern, and admiration, and desire.

No woman had ever made him feel like this. He wondered who was weaker – she or he?

He waited. In a few minutes, he heard her pad to the bedroom, and then she came out to meet him, dressed in the simple clothes, exactly as he'd laid out for her.

'More tea,' he said. 'There's a meal coming. I'm not leaving until you've eaten it. Don't argue with me; I am going to watch you eat.'

'Yes, Joel,' she said. She twisted her fingers, like she was trying to get up the courage to say something else.

'You should ring your mother.'

'Yes.' Dina's gaze broke away. 'Of course; I'll do that now.'

He moved away from her as she made the call. He could hear her voice rise, pleading, arguing with her mother. More tears. The doorbell rang for his Chinese; when he brought it back inside, she was done, and in tears again.

'Here. Sit. Eat,' he said, laying it out on the table before her and fetching them both water. He pushed forward the cartons, just handing her a fork.

She ate, mechanically at first, not appearing to taste anything. He wolfed his down – he was starving – and, after a few moments, Dina began to eat properly, too, and to sip at her water.

Gaines was relieved. She was not likely to kill herself, after all, not once she started to treat herself properly.

The doorbell rang again. Dina started, but he held out his hand. 'Don't worry about it. I'll get it in a second. It's a grocery delivery.'

'I didn't order any.'

'I did. I'm not having you use depression as an excuse not to eat. Your brother is dead, but you're not. And you need to go on.'

'For what?' she said. 'I don't have Johnny. I don't have a job.' She sobbed. 'I don't have you.'

Gaines rose, opened the door and brought the bags in. There were a lot of them – all gourmet. Cinnamon and vanilla coffee beans. Zabar's smoked salmon. Stoneground bread. Artisanal cheeses and honey. Sugar, milk and farm-fresh eggs. Bottles of squeezed orange juice, and an elegant fruit basket, nicely wrapped. It went on and on. Filet mignon steaks, packets of Cheerios, steel-cut oatmeal, Greek yoghurt, smoked almonds, Charbonnel et Walker chocolates.

He unpacked them as she stared. She was almost licking her lips, now, he saw; the taste of food had triggered her suppressed appetite.

'I'll fix us some ice cream,' he said, as he packed away the Twinings tea. 'You will be getting the call that your brother's body is ready, after the autopsy; I want you to let me know. You can text me. Will your mother want to arrange the funeral?'

Dina shook her head. 'Ellen – Mom – she was embarrassed of Johnny by the end. He was her pride and joy, her favourite, but when he came out as gay, she just withdrew. She said she accepted him, but she didn't. I don't think she visited him in the city even one time.'

'And she never switched her affections back to you?'

'She had a new man by then. Somebody who would overlook the past. My mom never really loved either of us. She just covered it a little better with Johnny. But she dropped him like a stone at the first sign of trouble.' Dina's face hardened, a burst of anger surging through the lethargy of her sadness. 'You know, maybe that was worst of all. At least I knew I wasn't loved by the time I left home. She tricked Johnny. She made him believe she cared. And when he needed her most, he found out she didn't. She just loved the idea of a son, not the son she got.' Dina shook her head. 'No, she won't take care of the arrangements; why should she? She'll expect me to do that.'

'Will she attend?'

'She'll come along – not because she gives a damn – to look respectable.'

'Very well.' Gaines paused, to take that in. Whatever sympathy he felt, he couldn't express; Dina would fall apart again. The best thing he could do for her was to take over the situation, lift the burden off her back. That part was easy, and he ploughed ahead. 'I will arrange the embalming and the funeral, in a couple of days. Do you have a preferred cemetery?'

Dina wiped her eyes. 'Somewhere green – in Westchester.'

'Done. Will you come to the funeral mass?'

'Of course I will.'

'Then you need to eat, sleep, exercise. Be there for your brother.'

She nodded. 'I'll try.'

He finished with the groceries, and put out two small bowls of vanilla ice cream. Watching her eat it was unbearably erotic. He needed to get the hell out of here.

'I should go,' he said, as she finished and stood up to clear the table. 'You'll call me when you hear?'

Dina nodded.

'OK then.' He stood to leave, and his legs were as heavy as iron. This felt wrong, walking out on her. But he had no more excuses to stay.

'Joel, I want to thank you – for trying to help Johnny, for finding him and . . . and giving him dignity. I don't think I could organise anything well right now.'

'It's fine, Dina.'

'And for helping me. For coming here and . . . all this.'

'We were friends.'

Tears sprang fresh to her eyes. 'Please don't say that. Don't say *were*. Say *are*.'

He twisted. 'Look, it's not the time to talk about it. If you're grateful to me, don't make me talk about it now. I want you better. I want you healthy and well.'

'You can't forgive me? Let me tell you the story – the whole story. Everything that happened.' Her voice cracked, and she looked at him, openly pleading, imploring him. 'Joel, I can take it if you don't love me and you don't want to be with me. But I can't bear it that you should think so ill of me. I know what I did was wrong. But you need to understand what happened, why it all happened. I beg you, Joel; I beg you.'

'Who gives a damn what I think? Just live your life, Dina; be well.'

'I give a damn. Right now it means everything to me.'

'Why?'

'Because I'm in love with you.' She shrugged. 'I just don't care anymore; I can't hide it anymore. Even though I know there's no point, I need you to like me – I need that at least.'

'I do like you.' *God help me.* 'I like you very much.'

'Then you'll let me talk to you? And, if you feel the same after that, I'll accept it. I won't bother you again.'

He nodded. 'OK, Dina Kane. Here's the deal: if I see you at your brother's funeral, and you look well, and strong, and put-together, we will go someplace quiet for coffee afterwards, and you can tell me everything. Enough?'

She breathed out – a long, ragged sigh of relief. 'Enough.'

He leaned forwards and, with incredible restraint, kissed her on the cheek. Then he let himself out of her apartment, closing the door behind him.

Chapter Sixteen

The funeral was two days later, on a warm day, in a beautiful church in Bronxville. Dina wore black. She stood with her mother and Ellen's new husband, Oliver. Joel Gaines was the only other mourner.

Nobody had been able to track Brad down. Gaines was struck by the smallness and loneliness of it all. Ellen Kane never put her arm round Dina; she cried a little, but her daughter seemed destroyed.

The priest was sensitive, and kept the mass short. Johnny's corpse was beautifully embalmed and dressed, giving him a serenity he never had in life. But Joel had ordered the casket closed; he wanted Dina's last memory of her brother to be of a warm, living body – a young man getting better.

Oliver, the stepfather, seemed disengaged. He patted his wife's back and shook Dina's hand. Gaines could not see him attempting to make conversation. What a lonely, sad little family they were.

He stood at the back. There were limousines waiting outside the church: one for the casket, one for the family and the priest, and a third for him. He had ensured everything would be done perfectly. There were white and yellow roses atop the casket, and beautiful displays in various colours, labelled with love from Dina, from Ellen, from Oliver, and from himself. As the priest finished the final words, Gaines slipped out of the church to double check everything was ready. He wanted it to be seamless.

Immediately, he saw it. Leaning up against the old brick walls, the extra floral arrangement – a heart – stuck out like a sore thumb. It was made up of garish red and orange carnations, ridiculously huge; clearly designed to be noticed.

Gaines quickly walked over and checked the label.

So glad to have met Johnny. Dina, you deserved him. Love and kisses, Edward Johnson.

His heart thudded. *She was right.*

His driver had come out of the limo and walked over to him. 'Everything OK, Mr Gaines? Some goons got here just a minute ago and brought this thing up. Took two of them to carry it.'

'Get rid of it, Carlos. Now.'

'Yes, sir.'

Gaines ripped off the label, and Carlos hefted the huge arrangement up and hauled it away, round the back of the church; he heard him stamping on it.

At that moment, the church doors opened and the pallbearers came out with the coffin; the priest followed, and the three family members walked behind. Dina lifted her head, looking for him; tears had streaked her face and make-up, but she smiled at him, gratefully.

Gaines crunched the card in his pocket as they climbed into the limousines. His driver came back; he was ex-Special Forces, like all Gaines' personal employees.

'It's in a trash can. Anything else?'

'No. Thanks. Just take me to the cemetery.'

They buried Johnny Kane with final honours in the best plot money could buy, under a spreading oak tree, in the quietest part of the grounds. Gaines had ordered a simple gravestone, with a cross, and the name and dates. Dina threw earth on to the coffin, and a white rose Gaines had made available for her. The priest said prayers, and then they all walked back, quietly, towards the cars.

'Thank you so much, Father,' Dina said, when they had come to a stop by the limousines.

'God bless you, my child.'

She turned to her mother. 'Momma, I'm not riding back with you and Oliver. Mr Gaines is taking me to the city.'

'Suit yourself, Dina. It was certainly a beautiful ceremony, Father.' Ellen presented one gloved hand, as though she wanted it kissed.

Dina walked with Gaines to his waiting car. He opened the door, and she slid in, on to the seat.

'Take us to the office,' Gaines said.

'Very good, sir,' Carlos replied.

Joel pressed a button, and a soundproof, bullet-proof security screen slid up between them and the driver. Now they were as good as alone.

Dina kissed him on the cheek. 'Joel, thank you so much. That was an incredible relief for me. Thank you for arranging it all. I am in your debt forever.'

He shrugged. 'Least I could do. I'm sorry.'

She leant back against the soft pewter leather of his limousine seats. 'I feel like I could sleep for days. Emotion – it's exhausting.' Her eyes moistened. 'My poor Johnny.'

'Maybe you should see somebody – a counsellor. Grief hits you in waves, that's what they say.'

She shook her head. 'I don't think there's any shortcut. I'll be mourning Johnny for the rest of my life. But I still have to live it out.'

Gaines looked her over. He was truly done now; the brother was buried, and he couldn't hide behind the Good Samaritan schtick any longer. She was still thin, but clearly had been eating healthily. Her hair was washed and she had simple make-up on. Dina was back from the dead.

Now he had to decide where he was, in her life. If anywhere.

'You're looking at me.' Dina stared back at him, boldly. 'I'm not the mess I was a couple of days ago. Thank you for that, too.'

He nodded.

'But we also had a deal. You told me that, if I kept it together, you'd at least give me the chance to explain.'

His voice was cold. 'Slept with a rich man to blackmail him? An older man? A man my age? I don't think there's an explanation in the world that can take that away.'

'Joel – you said you'd hear me out. Over coffee.'

'This car is completely private. He can't hear a thing. Tell me now, Dina, because I don't think I can take any more game playing. My life has been on hold for you – because of the past, pity, whatever reason – but I'm nobody's sucker, girl, not even yours. So, if you have something to say, tell me right fucking now.'

She was taken aback by his anger. All the care, all the comfort – she had got used to it. But now that he saw she was well – coping – he was turning that fire back on her.

Dina responded. It was good; it felt good to be challenged. Gaines was treating her like a person, not a patient. Sympathy and kindness weakened her; aggression, a fight, she knew how to rise to.

'When I was growing up, it was rough. My dad died early, and my mom . . . My mom didn't really care for me.'

He nodded, said nothing.

'At school, the boys would try to feel me up and kiss me and stuff, and the girls didn't really like me, so basically nobody hung out with me. Except Johnny. He was my only friend. He couldn't stand up to Mom, though; he was always weak. I don't blame him; it was his way.'

She swallowed. She wanted this to come out just right, just well enough to convince Joel Gaines that she was serious, not guilty, that she was still worth his love, his lust, his patronage – whatever was going; whatever tiny part of him could be hers.

'My mom started drinking when she got a little older. And men started to come around at night. Different men, in cars, from the Family.'

'The Family?'

'My dad worked a Mafia construction site. They provided for the widow; it's good for morale. Anyway, I knew these guys were using my mom, turning her into some sort of hooker. They were all married.'

I'm married. The unspoken fact hung in the air.

'What did you do?'

'Everybody knew the local Don, where he lived. I got a bus; I went to see him. At his gatehouse, his bodyguards felt me up when they patted me down. Really groped me – touched me. I was fifteen and they made me feel like meat.'

He digested that. 'And the *capo*?'

'He listened to me. After that, somebody came by the house and spoke to my mom. No men came by ever again, and she never drank another drop. I think he told her he would kill her. Anyway, she never gave me another affectionate word after that.' Dina smiled slightly. 'There hadn't been too many before. I mean, she almost hated me; maybe she did hate me. She thought I had ruined her life – no parties; no fun. Before I had even turned eighteen she was ready to throw me right out of the house.'

He could no longer keep up the cold shoulder. 'Goddamn. That's hard.'

'She gave everything to Johnny – paid for his Catholic schooling, his college. I had to go to public school; there was no money for me to go to college, although I had the grades. She wouldn't take a loan on the house or anything. Swore she needed it all. I had to threaten her, too, to give me some cash for a deposit on my first rental.'

'What did you say?'

'That I would go back to the Don. After that, she ponied up. I would have gone to thank Don Angelo personally, except his guards probably wouldn't have stopped at feeling my ass.'

'No. Probably not.'

'They have this fucked up code. Kids get immunity – mostly.'

'So then what?'

'I moved to the city. No college; high-school diploma; small pot of money. I worked round the clock, waitressing. I got very good at it, helped my diner out by bringing in new customers, but, you see, all the men mostly leered at me. They'd proposition me. They'd offer me money to fuck them. I never had a boyfriend at school. I was eighteen and I didn't know how to date.' She paused. 'I started hating men, I guess.'

'I'm sorry.'

'I flung myself into work – I wanted to, and I had to. This guy who runs a coffee chain gave me a break, made me a junior manager of a café. It was uptown, near Columbia. I always wanted to study there; even though I was running the books at the café, it wasn't college-level stuff. I'd serve coffee to kids my own age, just a little older, and it felt like I'd be serving them all my life. All these rich, preppy kids. And the boys were the worst. It was exactly the same as the diner, except they didn't just leer, they laughed at me – took bets on who would be first to bang me. This one bastard – he totally humiliated me, and I poured coffee on him.'

Gaines laughed. He was gripped. 'I bet you did.'

'And, just when I was feeling sick, this guy, Edward, came up to me. Only he'd given himself a fake name: Edward Fielding. He acted really disgusted and sympathetic. He treated me with respect.' She choked back tears. 'It was the first time any boy had treated me with respect. We dated, and eventually I went to bed with him. Then he ditched his cellphone number and his fake name, and he vanished – completely vanished. I gave my virginity to a guy who just screwed me and walked out.'

'What happened?'

'Nothing – until he turned up at the coffee shop, with his friends. You see, he wanted to prove to them he'd fucked me. I was a bet.'

Gaines was starting to understand.

'I laughed it off, told the boys Edward had been drunk – too drunk to get it up. He denied it, of course; they argued; we argued. I heard one of them say his name – Johnson. That made me see red and I threw coffee on all of them. The café fired me, right away. So, then I had no job, no money left, and some guy – the first guy I'd ever trusted – had used me like a tissue. It was so funny to him, Joel, so goddamned amusing. That's when I started looking him up, finding out how I could hurt him. He's an only child; Mommy is a society queen; Daddy is this banker who wants to be a politician and who's buying his seat. Edward Johnson hurt me with sex, and I wanted to hurt him back. I wanted to humiliate him, like he did me. When the father was ready to jump me, I took full advantage: I screwed him; I photographed him; I sent his wife the pictures. Maybe it was whorish. I sold myself – not for money, but revenge. You've got to understand, Edward had already made me feel like a whore. So what was the fucking difference?'

The bitterness and anger in her tone was thick with regret.

Gaines asked a question to which he didn't want to know the answer: 'Money, Dina? You were out of a job, so you asked them for money?'

She shook her head. 'God – not that kind of whore. I wanted to put Edward Johnson in my position, let him see how that other half lived.'

'You're saying you *didn't* demand any money?'

'Hell, no. I told Shelby to step down from the campaign, and

Edward was to drop out of college. Beyond that, I didn't give a damn. I just wanted to take from him that life that made him so smug, so entitled. So, it was blackmail, if you like, but not for money. For justice. As I saw it, back then.'

Gaines took a full breath in, like he could drain all the oxygen from the world.

'You know what happened to the Johnsons?' he asked.

She flushed. 'I didn't care. I know – I know how that sounds. But I didn't think about it more than that. Edward told me when I called him about Johnny.'

'Shelby Johnson dropped off the face of the earth. There was a divorce, and he went to "find himself" in Florida. The wife started to drink. She's in Florida now, too, in a rehab camp. The family were a laughing stock.'

'I understand that. I didn't think . . . I didn't care.'

'Dina, your beef was with Edward, but you destroyed his parents to get to him.'

She bowed her head. 'I blamed them, for raising him. I hated them all. Rich bastards. I know it was wrong, now. The mother never did anything to me. And I seduced the father. He was unfaithful, but I tempted him pretty hard, as hard as I knew how. I understand if you despise me for it.' She sobbed. 'I despise me.'

'It was wrong, but I can see why you did it.' Gaines leaned back, next to her, his shoulders relaxing against the car seat as he let out the long-held tension in his body. 'You didn't ask for them to fall apart like that, though you should have been more careful.'

'I wanted them to divorce. I was angry – so angry. Maybe Edward was unlucky. He was just the last and worst in a long line.'

'And you snapped.'

Dina sobbed.

'What you did to his parents is bad news, Dina. You should try and set that right.'

306

She raised her head and looked at him. 'How can I? It's over.'

'You can try. Use your ingenuity.'

Dina was startled out of her crying. She'd never even thought of that, not for a moment. Put it right? Could she? Was there anything she could do?

Joel Gaines sat next to her, the most surprising man she had ever met. *Put it right.* No therapist would ever say that. It would be, *explore your feelings* or *write a letter and burn it.*

'And Hector Green? And Ludo?'

'Hector happened just as I told you, Joel. I deserved half of that cream. It was my idea. His whole store was my idea – all the expansion of it. It was where I learned to run a beauty business, and I took that into Torch.' She shook her head. 'I don't know what happened to Hector, who got to him, or why he changed.'

'You didn't have a relationship with him? Sleep with him?'

She laughed aloud. '*Hector*? He was about ninety. No, and he never asked. He just got tired, and greedy. I was ready to take the Green Apothecary to the heights, but he just wanted a little money and then to be left alone. It's not always that way with men, the sexual thing. I just haven't been lucky.'

'And Ludo Morgan?'

'You weren't available.'

He looked at her.

'I'm serious. Hell, Joel, I'm tired, too. I feel like Hector Green, right now. I can't dance around things anymore. I had fallen in love, and it was a disaster; you brushed me off. I don't blame you – you were married. The worst you did was flirt with me a little. I packed more into it than was there. But you hit me hard; I can't lie. I needed something to get over you, something that wasn't just a job. My career path was a little erratic, shall we say. I had made money – from Meadow, from our deal. But also some from the Green Apothecary, and quite a lot from real estate. Maybe I wasn't the most normal girl in the world. But I wanted to take a break from all the pushing, all the struggle to be someone.' She put her hand up to her face and dashed away tears. 'A weak moment, maybe. I just wanted . . . to get a job, and then get a boyfriend. A normal boyfriend, who wasn't you.'

'Is Ludo Morgan normal?' Gaines looked at her. 'He was the boss. His daddy owns the company.'

Dina shrugged. 'Torch became very consuming.'

Joel grinned. 'A pattern, Dina. Did you notice that? Even when you say you won't push yourself, you can't help it.'

'You might have a point. Anyway, Ludo solved a major problem for me. He was at work. That was part of it. I didn't have to take time out. And, after Edward, I insisted he date me in public, and he had no problem with that. So I guessed it was OK.'

He looked at her. 'But it wasn't OK, was it?'

She shook her head. 'I liked him; I didn't love him. I thought maybe love would grow. But we didn't fit – romantically; in bed it was just like going through the motions. Maybe that's what sex is.'

Gaines shook his head. 'Not if you're doing it right.'

'Well, I'm hardly going to be anybody's test case. So . . . at the party, when I saw you and you warned me he was trying to steal my work . . . And you kissed me . . .'

'I'm sorry,' Gaines said. He wasn't.

'Right after that, he took me out to the beach and proposed.'

For the first time, Joel sat up straight. 'What?'

'He got out this huge diamond ring and asked me to marry him, and said I should quit my job and just be with him.'

There was a long pause.

'You turned him down?'

'Obviously. And, when I said no, he wanted me to walk back to Manhattan. It was only when I threatened to make a scene at the party that he decided to be more reasonable. He said I could stay in his spare room, and that I was fired. Next day, he airbrushed me from all the company literature. Not only that, but it turns out I had a non-competition clause in my contract. And he's enforcing it. I can't work for anybody else.'

'You didn't mention that.'

'Johnny was missing. I didn't care.' Dina breathed out. 'Thanks for letting me talk, Joel. Now you know the whole thing. Ugly or not, that's my life.'

Gaines said nothing for a few moments.

'I jumped to conclusions,' he said. 'I apologise, Dina. If you were some kind of gold-digger, you were offered the entire mine with Ludo. But you turned him down. Ambitious – yes; desperate – yes. Gold-digger? No.'

She smiled sadly. 'Funny thing is, until he fired me, I kind of felt bad for him. He said I led him on, and maybe I did. I just didn't realise how little I cared for him till that night.'

'And you can't settle?'

'Apparently not.'

Gaines looked out of the window. 'Midtown. We're coming up to my offices. I have to get to work; I've been away far too long.'

She lowered her head. 'I understand. Thanks again.'

'We have to talk some more. I need time to figure this all out. One thing I can say is that I don't think badly of you, Dina. You messed up, but you're amazing.' He pressed the button, and the window slid back. 'Carlos, I'm getting out here. Afterwards, take Ms Kane anywhere she wants to go, OK?'

'Yes, sir. Of course.'

Gaines opened the door; as he did so, he reached back and squeezed Dina's hand.

When she got home, Dina went straight to her bedroom. She peeled off her mourning clothes and changed into her running gear.

It was a warm, beautiful day outside, and she had nowhere to be. She started running; a couple of blocks west was Central Park and, two minutes inside the perimeter, it was like being in another world.

There was music in her headphones, but she paid no attention to the playlist. Her mind was on Joel Gaines, and his words, and how he'd held her hand. His forgiveness – could he forgive what she'd done to somebody else? – buoyed her, excited her. The depression was lifting, and it was spring, and there was a future.

She loved Joel. God, the relief of admitting that to herself – and to him! She loved him. She wanted to be with him, and nobody else but him. There would be no more Shelbys, no more Edwards or Ludos. Unless and until she fell out of love, Dina decided, she wasn't going to try and date anyone else.

With every step she pounded on the hard paths, every stride she ran under the canopy of trees, she felt lighter, better. Her heart would fix itself. Joel liked her; he'd kissed her. Even if he wasn't hers, that was something. She could try to be a better person, get some therapy, not see herself as the victim.

So she didn't like Susan Gaines – fine – but if Joel was happy in his marriage, Dina needed to back off. So she wouldn't marry; it wasn't the only thing in life, right?

What was the point of being into beauty, if you couldn't look at yourself in the mirror?

Her heart was racing, thumping. It felt good to run, to sweat, to be alive. This was her therapy, her confessional. Dina let her thoughts go, abandoned herself to the sheer joy of movement.

When she arrived back in her apartment, panting but content, everything seemed a lot clearer.

If she couldn't have Joel, it was time to focus on something else she loved.

Like business. And sticking it to Torch and Ludo Morgan.

And, as for Edward Johnson, she would figure that out later. He had as good as killed her Johnny. Did she deserve it? Johnny certainly didn't. But Dina had no thoughts of blood, of payback.

He hurt her. She hurt him. Johnny was dead. Where did that cycle end?

The most revenge she could have would be to succeed – to get rich, to live well, to make a mark – and not need a single man to do it.

Dina loved Joel. But she didn't want to *need* him, not anymore.

And she had the perfect idea for what to do next.

'I . . . It's certainly a very healthy balance sheet.'

The banker's name was Raul Benitez and he was fifty-eight years old. Not everybody got into his office. There were too many time-wasters out there. He made loans to small businesses on behalf of Luisitana Bank; they were a Brazilian outfit, trying to expand into North America, and they were minnows out here.

He was tasked with bread-and-butter banking: selling money to little guys who would repay it and spread the word. No giant financial punts, just a solid basis within the community.

Somewhere much, much higher up the tree, in Lima, his boss wanted to turn them into Santander. But they were starting here, at the bottom.

Benitez only saw business owners with a certain amount of assets, a plan and a proven track record. These were mostly men in their late thirties to mid fifties. He had lent to some female-owned shops, too: cafés, manicure salons, eyebrow places.

This girl was different. She was fifteen years younger than anybody else he had seen. She had no roots in the community; she wasn't Korean or Hispanic. She was beautiful, like a model, but disturbingly cold, and she had the strangest résumé he had ever seen.

But she had a plan. And she had some wealth – money in the bank, and a very nice apartment. And she was willing to risk it all.

'Torch is a very big name in retail right now.'

'Because of me,' Dina said.

He pushed his spectacles towards the end of his nose, raised bushy eyebrows. 'Is that a little bit of an exaggeration, perhaps, Señorita Kane?'

'No, it isn't. I revamped the beauty division. All their sales flow from that.'

'Then why were you fired?'

He saw people taking credit every day. She was less believable when she praised herself like this.

'Because the boss's son wanted to marry me, and I turned him down.'

Benitez looked at her.

She leaned towards him, over the desk.

'Does your wife shop at Torch, Señor Benitez?'

He nodded.

'I joined that store six months ago. Ask her when she started to shop there.'

'Very well.' He glanced down at her financial statement again. Everything was in place: all the bank statements, six months' expenses. 'You have very good security. For a million dollars, we will need to have a lien against the apartment.'

'I understand that. This is the way I want to launch. You only have that chance once.'

He licked dry lips. 'It would be by far the largest loan I have ever approved.'

'I picked your bank because you need a home run,' Dina told him. 'You are scraping by on these tiny loans. You need a star client, for the publicity. It could make you.'

'And a million-dollar loss could break us, too.'

'No chance of that. My apartment is worth much more to you.'

He sighed. 'I'll ask my wife. Somebody will call you this afternoon.'

'Very good.' She stood up and, somehow, in her silk blouse and modest skirt, she was more of a powerhouse than all the older, suited males he was used to. 'I'm in a hurry, Señor Benitez. I don't want to have to head down the road to Chase.'

Dina Kane let herself out of his office. But he had the feeling he would be seeing much more of her.

Benitez took his lunch out to the park. He liked it there, especially on these hot days Manhattan specialised in, which reminded him of home.

There was a great little place just by the Hudson, with a wide running track the joggers raced up and down all day long, and a green garden on one side, with a few fountains and benches. New York was very good at that, carving out green islands in the forest of glass and concrete. This was almost a sea garden, with hardy, silver-grey plants and grasses that could take the swell and spray from the great river, the blasting summer heat and the winter freeze and pounding winds.

There were a couple of benches he liked. He could think here. Nature found its way. And so did women, so did beauty.

As he wolfed his sandwich, he looked idly at the women racing down the track. Some were heavy, just starting out – good for them. Most of them, though, were in tight Lycra, neon sneakers, their hair caught back in ponytails. Now he took time to notice, almost all of them were made up – even to run.

It was huge, the market in America. Especially in this city. Manhattan was goddamned expensive. If you lived here, you had money – enough to buy all kinds of beauty products.

He called his wife. What the hell? She had been noticeably more attractive, less frumpy, since she'd started shopping at Torch.

'Cristina, it's me.'

'*Hola*, baby.'

'I have a strange question. When did you start going to that department store uptown? Do you remember?'

His wife paused. 'Maybe six months back. When that new girl

313

came in and revamped it. I heard from my girlfriends we should try it, and we all took a cab together.'

'That new girl?'

'Oh, there was this kid they hired. It was all over the blogs and magazines. Then you stopped hearing about her. Whatever; she did a marvellous job.'

'You have been looking wonderful lately. But then, you always did,' he lied.

In truth, Torch had transformed his wife; she'd got rid of the harsh blond hair dye, the layers of mascara and bright red cheeks. The new light stuff she wore on her face, the olives and brown shadows that picked out her eyes, and the gloss on her lips made her look years younger. She was wearing less and looking better, and he loved it. They were having more sex; it felt like they were closer than they'd been in years.

'Why do you ask, sweetie?'

'You won't believe it. The girl you were talking about – she was in my office this morning, asking for a loan.'

'Get out!' his wife said. 'Really?'

'She wants to start her own beauty store – with a website and big poster advertising.'

'Wonderful!' His wife seemed thrilled. 'Can't wait to go. You're approving the loan? Congratulations.'

'I haven't decided yet. It's a million dollars.'

'Oh, Raul. If you want to be the sucker who passes her up, go ahead. But, trust me on this – she knows just what she's doing.'

He leaned back against the bench. 'How can you be so sure? You've never even met her.'

Cristina laughed. 'No, honey, I *wear* her.'

He blew her a kiss and hung up. Then he crumpled up his sandwich wrapper with the meal half-finished.

Break time was over. He wanted to do this deal, before somebody else got the chance. Time to gamble.

* * *

Her phone rang at ten to three exactly.

'Yes?'

'Your loan is approved, Señorita Kane. When can you sign the paperwork? We can set a date next week.'

'I'll be back in your office in twenty minutes.'

The ink was dry before close of business; Dina Kane had a new corporate account, and a million dollars was winging its way to her.

She worked from home. No point hiring an office, and she would need every red cent of that money. Nothing was going to be wasted.

First, the store: it could be small, but it had to be beautiful – and right in the heart of town. Nothing else would do.

But it was easier said than done.

Dina tried everything conventional. She registered with all the commercial brokers, listened as they tried to sell her snake oil, but flagship sites were far too much, charging rents that would have eaten up her loan in two months.

'Well, you want the centre of town? That's what it costs,' said Roxie, a broker, standing in the middle of a small vacant space on Fifty-Third and Lex.

'This is the third business to shut here in two years. There just isn't the foot traffic. Won't the landlord consider a lower rent?' Dina pleaded.

'Honey, one tenant fails, another takes his place. This is Manhattan. He wants what he wants.' Roxie shrugged. 'Look, with your budget, I would suggest Harlem. Or Brooklyn. Or maybe something industrial, like off Tenth Avenue, or First—'

'I'm selling make-up,' Dina said.

'Sephora sells make-up – on Fifth Avenue. South of Saks.' Roxie sniffed. 'I wish you luck, honey, but you ain't Sephora.'

After two months wearing out her shoe leather, Dina was truly desperate. Nothing would happen without an anchor store.

Maybe the landlords were all correct; maybe she should go someplace cheaper. She travelled out to Brooklyn and looked at Cobble Hill and Prospect Park; she went to the outer streets in Manhattan, off the beaten track, looked at places in Chinatown, a former pawnshop near the jewellery district. Some of those spaces were bigger, cleaner, but they were also in Siberia, as far as she was concerned. And the ones in town were in the wrong area.

Yes, dammit – she wanted to be Sephora. But she didn't have any of the money, or the connections, or the corporate clout that it took.

Sometimes, after a full day's hunting for a retail space, Dina was so frustrated she felt like crying.

Maybe she should give it up. Perhaps online was the way to go.

But there were a billion online sites for make-up and skin care. Dina thought of the Green Apothecary, of Meadow, of turning Torch around. She was convinced in her bones that a store – a real place, a home – had to come first, and it had to be right there, in the news, where she wanted to be. This was the first time Dina had ever worked for herself, and she was a hell of a demanding boss.

It has to be big. It has to be perfect.

At night, she would fall asleep and dream of a flagship store, a landmark, a palace of light and digital displays. Nothing she could achieve – not yet; not for years. But, in the mornings, there was always another meeting with another realtor; another boarded-up shop in another scummy area, off the beaten track.

'You don't want much, do you, Ms Kane?'

Gunther Fassbaum was losing patience with Dina. He'd shown her ten stores already within her modest budget. At first, she seemed the real deal: an ambitious young comer with bank backing; an entrepreneur in a hurry. But he was starting to think she was just wasting his time.

'Centre-town premises, long lease, five to ten per cent rises, and you don't have much to start with in the first place. Maybe we're not the right agency for you.'

'But I can move fast.' Dina looked around the former boutique, another own-label clothes store on Lexington Avenue – too quiet, too old money. This place had been a vanity project; people saw Dina Kane Cosmetics the same way. 'And I don't need it to come with bells and whistles. I can fix up a scruffy place myself. I just want the right terms and the right location.'

'But you don't want to pay the right price.'

'It doesn't even have to be big. I'm not looking for a lot of square footage here, Mr Fassbaum. I'd take a small boutique in the right spot, any day.'

He stared. 'Miss, for you, the right spot is Times Square. I don't mean to be rude, but I've shown you some genuine bargains and you're still not satisfied.'

Dina's eyes widened. She took a step backwards.

'Are you OK?'

'I'm fine. Fine.' She tugged at her jacket. 'Look, bear with me, Mr Fassbaum. I appreciate you showing me this space. I . . . I'm going to do some more research and come right back to you. I hope that's all right.'

'It's quite all right,' Fassbaum said, to her departing back. Then he pulled out his Blackberry and erased Dina Kane from his contact list.

Goddamn time waster. He felt like an idiot.

Dina ran to the subway and got on the express to Times Square. She felt her heart beating, her pulse racing.

For you, the right spot is Times Square.

Of course it was. The centre of Manhattan: the neon skyscrapers, the moving advertisements, the giant billboards and stock tickers – the beating heart of the richest, most powerful, most *beautiful* city in the world. Was that nuts? Billboards here

317

cost two hundred thousand dollars a month, and that was just for the signage, before you spent one cent on electric screens. She could hardly afford market rent for a goddamn storefront.

And yet . . . And yet . . . Times Square: it was her home, it had to be, it just had to be. The train slid into the station and she rushed out, joining the throng of tourists and commuters, all that foot traffic, the most you could imagine. Here was the heart of everything, and of Dina Kane.

She walked around the square. It wasn't, of course – wasn't square. A sort of diamond-shaped space, everything that looked directly on to it counted: Paramount Pictures, Toys 'R' Us and ABC's flagship studio building. But Dina wasn't disheartened; she looked elsewhere – at the other subway stations, how people came here, where they travelled. Broadway was reserved for the fancy shows, but Seventh Avenue had a couple of diners . . . office buildings . . . and a subway station, right there. And, as Dina looked around, the answer was staring her in the face.

If 'staring' was the right word. Perhaps 'poking' was more accurate. There, right in front of her, was a silhouette of a bare-breasted woman with cartoonishly erect nipples. It was just a little store frontage, all black, with a faded red carpet and a sign, calling it a *Gentleman's Establishment*, inviting her to come downstairs.

Dina watched that entrance for twenty minutes straight. Not a single customer. This was an eyesore – a remnant from Times Square's sleazy past. It had to be rent controlled, and there was no doubt in her mind that the city would love to lose it.

She picked up the phone and called Fassbaum.

'What do you want?'

'I think I might have found somewhere. On Seventh Avenue. A strip club.'

'Why would the tenant want to give his business up?'

That was what she didn't know just yet, but she was determined to find a reason. 'Maybe I can make him a better offer. Can you run the address and see who rents the space?'

There was a heavy sigh. 'I'm busy.'

'Just for doing a few searches, I'll buy you a coffee and give you two thousand dollars in cash. Not the firm's commission – just your cash.'

There was a pause. 'I'll come back to you.'

Within ten minutes, her phone rang again. 'Find another strip club. This one's a non-starter.'

'Why? Who's got it?'

A beat. 'Some people from Westchester.'

'Westchester?' Dina repeated. Why would suburban hicks want a strip joint in Times Square?

And then it dawned on her. 'What kind of people? Italian people?'

'Do your own research. And keep your goddamned coffee.'

Dina hung up, ecstatic. She knew exactly who Fassbaum meant. What a blast from the past! She hailed a cab, heading home to do just that – work on her computer; do her research. She would need it for the presentation she would make tomorrow.

At nine a.m. precisely the next morning, Dina put her laptop in its carry case, headed out of her building and walked towards the nearest subway. She would go to Grand Central and work on the way. There was no time to waste. This company needed to launch within the month.

And that meant taking risks.

Chapter Seventeen

'There is a girl at the gatehouse, Don Angelo, asking for admittance.'

The mafioso looked up at his valet. This kind of thing was unusual, these days. His wife and children had long since been moved to a mansion outside of Bronxville, where they enjoyed the local schools and suburban life. He wanted to head into the city, but there was too much business in Westchester. Leaders who took their eyes off the ball wound up ousted, and that usually meant dead.

It wasn't machine-gun drive-bys outside steak houses anymore, either. Law enforcement was far too good for that. When somebody got whacked, it was far more subtle, more terrifying. Bad medicine. A heart attack. Yachting accident. The boys were getting smart.

Angelo had plans, and was executing them. As much of the junk stuff as possible, he was selling off, dumping, losing. Discipline was necessary amongst the soldiers; made men knew to keep their mouths shut, even amongst themselves. He was experimenting with online gambling, where the big money was made. The older, bloodthirsty types were pensioned off – buy them waterfront condos in Florida, mansions in La Jolla, even estates in Tuscany, in the old country – divide and rule.

Things were changing, and he liked it that way.

But there were privileges he wanted to keep. Business-men were afraid of him, afraid to say no. That mattered. He'd wiped guys out, didn't give a fuck about that. And girls never refused him, either. They opened their legs the way developers opened their wallets.

But he called for them, not the other way round. He didn't like pieces of ass turning up without appointments. They whined for favours, money, help. Some of the girls dared to think they could have a relationship. He wasn't like other men, though; they were warned off, and it usually only took one go. A friend paid them a visit, had a word. After that, the girl kept her mouth shut.

He enjoyed that – the basics – power, pussy, the fear he inspired in other men. Even while he legitimised, he kept all those things good and close. Besides, the boys expected it of a Don. They were all taking chances; that was the life.

'Which one?'

'None of the regular girls. Says you've seen her before. A beauty, though.' Tony kissed his fingers. 'Maybe twenty-four; a great-looking lay. She says she wants to do business. We can find some business for her . . .'

'Name?'

'Diana something. Diana Kane. Something like that.'

Don Angelo shook his head a little. 'That name rings a bell. Send her into the office.'

'You want company?'

'I think I can handle a twenty-four-year-old, Tony.'

'OK, boss.' His consigliere made a face. The killers came younger these days, and never like you'd expect. What if the girl had a needle? A pill? Angelo was his responsibility; anything happened to him, Tony was in trouble. And he had a wife and two daughters at home – they needed their dad – and the *famiglia* was unforgiving when it came to a *capo*. Which this urbane son of a bitch still was.

He pressed a button on the phone. 'Send her to the house. She can be shown to the office.'

They waited. A minute later, the girl arrived. Tony smacked his lips again. *Hell, what a great ass on that chick. A beauty – real classy.* He would put her rate at thousands an hour; a girl for high rollers on Wall Street. She was wearing demure clothes, which made her even sexier: a knee-length sweaterdress in cream cashmere and light brown flats. Her legs were bare, tanned, and her hair was twisted on top of her head in a bun. She had green eyes, and she carried a cute chestnut leather bag and, incongruously, a laptop in a case.

The computer would have run through the scanner. They put one in last year – same standard as you had in courthouses and public schools. Don Angelo took no chances.

'Do I know you?' Angelo said.

He lifted a finger, and Tony reluctantly took himself out of the room. He would hover outside, and that was OK. Angelo didn't think the girl was here to fuck, although he toyed with the idea of making her do just that. She certainly was gorgeous.

But not a hooker. You could go as high-end as you liked – and the fresh-faced girls always came the most expensive – there was always some desperation behind that pretty smile, some stress from alcohol and drugs and self-loathing. There was none of that in this girl's features. She wasn't in the life. And that made him more curious.

'You saw me once before, Don Angelo. Do you remember?'

'I see lots of people.' But then he did remember, and he started with surprise. 'Wait – you're the daughter . . . That guy on one of my crews.'

'Paul Kane. Yes.'

'You had a problem with your mother. I fixed it.'

'Yes, sir, you did. Thank you, Don Angelo.'

He liked that, liked it a lot. It was sexy, hearing the girl call him *sir*, the submission laced into it. He started to feel aroused.

She should be careful what she was playing with. She was older now, fair game.

'I know the men that knew my father were grateful you respected one of your own,' Dina said, like she could read his mind.

Boom! The start of a hard-on shrivelled right up again. Angelo almost laughed, she was playing the game so well.

'Nicely done.'

'Excuse me, sir?'

'You understand me. Don't waste my time, pretty girl, I'm a lot busier than you are.'

She smiled, ducking her head in acknowledgement, and he almost liked her for it. His was a pretty segregated society; he didn't have women friends, didn't mix with them outside of church and parties. This was something new, and he was kind of enjoying it.

'I would like to do some business with you, Don Angelo. Just something small.'

He pushed back his chair. His office was wood-panelled, filled with old leather-bound books he'd never read and Roman antiques his wife liked to shop for. The computer and phones were the only concessions to modernity. There were none to femininity.

'You have no business with me, girl. You understand, you are lucky to be Paul Kane's daughter. You're alone and you're tempting. Try not to be so stupid. Clearly, you're not Italian.'

Now Dina laughed. 'No. Irish. My father never got made, never got close. Anyway, don't be so sure about what business I do or don't have, Don Angelo. Things changed for me after I came to see you.'

'Unless you won the lottery, honey, they didn't change enough.'

'I moved to the city, launched a face cream, sold my share for half a million dollars. I bought and sold a few apartments. I ran the beauty department at a big department store.' Don Angelo settled back in his chair; she now had his full attention. 'They fired me after six months, even though I turned their shitty store around, because I refused the owner's son when he proposed marriage.'

'Why did you do that?'

'Didn't love him.'

Angelo chuckled. 'How old fashioned! Go on.'

'There's a noncompetition clause in my contract, so I can't take another job in the industry. Instead, I'm starting my own business. I'll be great at it; it's what I know.'

'And you've come back to me for funds.'

'No, sir. I've got the money.'

Dina Kane had surprised him for the third time that day.

'You don't want money?'

'You have a strip club operating out of a dark half-store in Times Square, just north of the main drag, and right by the Seventh Avenue subway.'

'It's a gentleman's club. It's legal, honey.'

'It might be legal, Don Angelo, but it's attracting attention. Women are starting to picket it. There's a city councillor trying to make a case out of it: flagship city icon, that kind of thing. You don't want a politician on the make crawling over your business, talking to the IRS.'

She had a point. This was simmering in the background; nothing much had happened lately, but it was a problem. He was looking to get out of strip joints altogether. They were too sleazy, too obvious. Money these days was in garbage collection, and construction, still.

'And you want the space?'

'I can't afford to pay market. But how about you lease it to me for six months? Three hundred thousand, with an option to buy the space after that – mid-point between our two appraisals. Reasonable appraisals.'

'Three hundred thousand? Don't be a comedian, honey. This is Times Square real estate. I can sell that lease to anyone.'

'Yes, but it's a small, ground-level piece of Times Square – mostly basement. Yes, you can sell, but it will take you another six months to find a kosher buyer, and they'll do inspections and all that crap. Lease it to me, and I will have the painters in there tomorrow. It's done, and your headache is taken care of.'

'You're too far under market.'

'Three hundred thousand for three months, then. By that time, I'll know if it's working. Beauty is a fast business, Don Angelo. You hit or you don't.' She laughed. 'No pun intended.'

He grinned, openly. She'd done it; she had won him over. She wanted the space – a prime-location dump – and she would take it without questions.

It didn't occur to him to challenge whether or not she had the cash. She obviously did; there was just that confidence about her.

'I want it all upfront,' he said.

Dina sighed. That was a huge chunk of her capital. 'Very well – if you agree to the right-to-purchase clause. I can make money out of this space; but, the thing is, Don Angelo, you can't. It's just too visible – which is why I want it.'

'How much money did you raise, kid?'

She hesitated. If she told him, would he ask for more?

'A million dollars.'

Screw it. You didn't lie to the Mafia. Not ever. No disrespect.

He lifted an eyebrow. 'No shit? Maybe you are Italian, after all.'

'I can email you a rent-to-buy agreement tonight, Don Angelo, and wire the money to any account you want.'

'Hold your horses,' he said, slowly. This girl was interesting, very interesting. She was a comer, and he was now taking inventory of her perfect make-up, her chic dress. She came from a shit-hole in Westchester and had made it, or close to, within a couple of years. *I can make money out of this space.* Yeah, he bet she could – many millions. And he wanted some. 'I'll give you the purchase clause, at your own appraisal price. But I want in. Five per cent.'

Dina Kane sat bolt upright. 'No deal.'

'What? You're saying no deal?'

'I won't give you five per cent. I won't give you any per cent.'

Angelo frowned. 'Don't fuck with me. You will give me what I tell you to give me. Be glad I don't make it ten.'

'I'm serious. This company is clean. I want to buy something from you at a fair price. My offer is speed, no questions. I don't want you looking down my neck for the next twenty years.'

'This isn't the old days. You've been watching too many films. Nobody's going to come round demanding protection money every month. I want in to a legitimate business. And I have the store you need.'

Dina shook her head. 'Sir, you don't understand. I wouldn't partner with you. I wouldn't partner with *anybody*. Dina Kane is my name, my company. Nobody touches it.'

'And you're willing to give up Times Square?'

She pulled her shoulders back. 'If I have to.'

Angelo relaxed against the soft leather of his chair again. 'Aren't you afraid of me?'

'No. You don't go after people on a whim. Besides, I don't have much to lose. No family. No husband.' Dina shrugged. 'This is what I want, my way or not at all.'

He shook his head. 'You're in the wrong business, kid. You should come and work for me. No – don't say anything – it was a joke. You can email me the contract.'

She breathed out. 'Thank you, Don Angelo. I won't forget it.'

He didn't laugh at this, as he would have from some other kid. Dina Kane might be Governor some day.

She got up to leave. 'You know, last time I came to see you, the goons in your gatehouse made me spread my legs and they patted me down, felt me up.'

His face was expressionless. 'They do that again this time?'

'I told them that, if they touched me, I would make sure you killed them.'

Angelo smiled. 'You should have been a man.'

Dina rode the train home, full of hope. Her computer was on her lap, and she tapped away on it, oblivious of the angry stares of other passengers trying to enjoy their magazines.

She was working.

She knew a handful of good lawyers already – guys she'd worked with at Torch – and one of them was now drawing up a simple rent-to-buy contract, which would be with her in an hour.

She was writing down her products – the stock she would carry in order to give the perfect combination of space, luxury and choice. Not too much choice. Big names might not work with her. That was OK. Dina Kane, Inc. would supply a new vision in cosmetics: incredible beauty that worked. Stuff you couldn't get anyplace else.

The transformation of that space would be a piece of cake. She wouldn't replicate Torch – they might sue. Besides, the bar was filthy and gloomy, with no natural light. She had a vision, and four apartments had taught her how to realise it.

On her screen, the vision started to take shape: golds, creams, clear lighting; staff in chic uniforms of fitted shift dresses or dark suits. Dina Kane would be a one-stop shop, with everything in it irresistible. She would cherry pick the best products, lay them all out, offer more free samples than anyone else and source the most gorgeous accessories. There would be a small men's grooming department, themed to remind customers of James Bond: photos of muscled men in Savile Row suits, Floris aftershave, real badger-hair shaving brushes and solid gold cuff-links. Goddamn, it was exciting. She wanted the place to scream *luxury*; and, more than that, *vacation*. To buy a lip gloss at Dina Kane would be like stepping into another world. There would be beautiful shopping bags and pale green and gold ribbon for women's purchases, thick gunmetal for the guys . . .

The billboard: she would buy the space, design it herself. The cheapest agency in town could put it together – Dina would control the image. She knew exactly when to put it up, when to launch, how to sell.

Electricity crackled through her veins. By the time she stepped out of the train at Grand Central, she was almost running, her cellphone fixed to her ear.

The space was ready for her by lunchtime the next day. Angelo could move fast, too. All of the strippers had left; the cheap, wine-stained tables and chairs had been cleared away; the scummy patrons had gone. Signs were still up in the window: a sad Martini glass in neon light tubing, with a nude girl's silhouette poking up from it, her breasts like olives on a cocktail stick.

That was OK. That was fine. Dina breathed deeply, taking in the scent of old beer, desperation, sweat and darkness. It was heady perfume. This scumminess was the reason she'd pulled off the deal.

'You know . . . it is what it is.' The caretaker was a jaded old guy, who had seen tenants come and go. 'The girls perform and the men pay.'

Bare electric bulbs revealed the squalor: peeling paint, mould in the ceiling corners, ripped up linoleum on the floor. There was a dirty glass booth where girls had squirmed and humiliated themselves for drunk men at two in the afternoon. Behind a faded red velvet curtain, fringed with red tassels, was a hideous enclave of glitz: wide red banquettes, cushioned to hold two people; fake plastic marble on the floor; low-light electric torches on the walls. Dina shoved from her mind the humiliations that must have happened here, the dirt and the sex and the hatred and the sale of flesh.

She looked, and, as the caretaker coughed his embarrassment behind her, a warm smile broke across Dina's face.

'I love it,' she said. 'It's perfect.'

'Lady, you're crazy,' he said.

'My guys will be in tomorrow. And so will I.'

The old man shrugged. She wanted this shit-hole, she could surely have it.

Dina worked. She set her alarm for five a.m. and went running, pounding along the streets of Manhattan while it was still dark. There were others with her, of course – the bankers, the lawyers – all those high-powered men and women who needed to start early. Dina loved it, the excitement of the city that never sleeps crackling under her feet.

She wasn't even tired. She was full of adrenaline.

The music pumped in her headphones, but she was paying no attention. Already, her mind was running on Dina Kane, Inc. The name was registered, the company incorporated, she had a blank website – it made it seem real. There was a bank account and she could hire staff, source products, get deep into it.

Within a month, she wanted to have something to show Joel Gaines. Not to ask for his help – never again – just to show him.

And it needed to be under the radar – a surprise – so Ludo Morgan, Edward Johnson, none of those bastards could come after her.

The first person she had to call was Piotr Ilyich. His crew knew her, had renovated her last three apartments. They were cheap, hard working and preferred cash. Besides, they liked a client who paid up and gave directions.

She never wasted Piotr's time on materials or finishes. Dina always knew exactly what she wanted.

The run was over. She headed back inside, showered, dressed and blow-dried her hair. A simple sweater dress, flats and her best make-up – Dina was a walking billboard.

She called Piotr. It was half six now; he would be up.

'Dina!'

'It's your favourite client.'

'I would say it's a bit early, but it's you. Moved house again?'

'Better than that. It's an office, mostly underground, needs a full gut job, an architect and a plumber.'

He sighed. 'I would – for you – but we are about to start a job uptown. An old lady's penthouse, on Eightieth Street. Big money.'

'Put her off. Say you need another permit. This is only going to take you a month, and there's two hundred thousand in it. Small space; tricky.'

He whistled. 'Two hundred thousand?'

'To include an architect – three days' work. I know what I want; he can draw up plans for it.'

'And where is this amazing office you intend to waste so much cash on?'

'Times Square. It won't be a waste; it's the start of my empire.'

He laughed. 'I think I believe you.'

'You know a good architect? He has to be good.'

Two hours later, they were at the site. Piotr came with Arek, the chief of his workmen, and a young woman, skinny with lanky, mousy hair, thick glasses and sallow skin. She was in her early thirties; older than Dina and, judging by the clothes, poorer.

'Hi. I'm Dina.' She looked at the girl. 'You work for Arek?'

'Natalya,' the woman said, shaking hands. She looked over at Piotr.

'Natalya is our architect.'

Dina bridled.

'She fled from Russia, where she worked at one of the top

331

firms. She was a star designer; helped with Naberezhnaya Tower in Moscow.'

'Why did you leave?'

'Husband,' the woman said.

'Natalya has little English. Her former husband is well connected to one of the oligarch families. He beat her and, when she left, she did not want to stay there. Now she has come here as a student.'

'She's legal?'

'She came on a nanny visa. Works all hours for a rich family on the Upper West Side. They treat her like a slave, but at least she has a sponsor. Four children and a house to clean. She cleans like maid, cooks like servant, but she has an advanced degree, a good career.'

'How is she here?'

'The family is on vacation. They don't want to pay for the extra air ticket. She's good, understands structure.'

Dina looked carefully from man to woman. 'What is in this for you, Piotr?'

'Natalya is my second cousin's daughter.' He shrugged. 'In Russia, we take family very seriously.'

'Translate,' Dina said. 'If she does this well, I will help her. No more housekeeping.'

Piotr spoke quickly to Natalya, and her eyes lit up.

'I want the office waterproofed. The whole place must be wired for internet and LED throughout. Spots in the ceiling and walls. Backlighting. Bulbs must be natural daylight, and we want climate control. Solid glass steps here. I want light wells drilled in from the ceiling, to bring natural light into the space, maybe tunnelled from the walls. The look is to be that of an urban garden. Air-hanging plants, ferns, a small rockery – greenery everywhere. In the back, I want a perpetual fountain, and tiny, luminescent fish swimming in a rock pool. There will be mirrors on every shelf, lit with smaller daylight bulbs, so that girls can make up.'

Piotr was talking as fast as he could. Natalya nodded.

'Every surface will be light, so that the space seems more open: glass, blond wood, cream and caramel marble, with specks of greenery and warm sandy pebbles. When a woman walks out of the chaos of Times Square – even in winter – I want this to be warm, moist, calming, soothing. She breathes out; she relaxes.'

'*Da*.' Natalya looked around, and Dina could tell her eyes were cataloguing the dimensions.

'Make sure the design is expandable. There's a Hooter's restaurant right above us; I'm going to want to buy that too.'

Piotr shook his head. 'You steal our strip clubs; now Hooter's too? Typical woman.'

Dina ignored him. 'Here are the materials I want. I brought samples – left over from my own apartments.'

She unzipped the heavy canvas bag she'd brought with her and laid out samples – chips of golden brown marble, blond Swedish wood, a hunk of sparkling, tempered glass, some mirrors, white limestone . . .

Natalya looked up at her. Her dull skin was already luminous; her face was bright with excitement. She nodded eagerly and spoke in a peal of Russian, words tumbling out of her.

'She says she understand very well, your vision. It will look beautiful. She says you bring California to New York – water and desert. She want you to know most important is electrics and water. Then light wells. She will give you drawings. We can make it.'

Dina smiled slightly, and the older girl nodded eagerly and clasped her hand.

'She says you very alike. You will see what Russia can do. She already create in extreme environment. You make this extreme beauty.'

'Extreme beauty,' Dina said, softly, rolling the words on her tongue. '*Extreme beauty*. I love it.'

'I do not understand,' Piotr said.

'Pay her. She will need your men to start today; she can tell them what to do as she draws. I don't have a minute to lose. The plumbers and electricians should be here right away.'

'Very good.' He had learned not to argue.

'And, Piotr, one other thing. I will give you extra money; hire a tutor for Natalya. Have him here, round the clock. I want her to learn English. We can work together.'

He spoke to the young woman, and she nodded, again, harder.

'I am intelligent. I learn English,' she said. 'Learn fast. Make building.'

'She's exactly what I need. Tell her I will be talking to an immigration lawyer. And I want her to have the basic drawings for the conversion ready in one month.'

Natalya reached out and grabbed Dina's hand. 'Boss,' she said. 'Boss.'

The days went by, dementedly. Dina sunk herself into it. There was the website, which she needed to be better, cooler, than anything else on the web. She hired some kids from NYU, and showed them her brilliant ideas.

'First, it needs to be easy to pay.'

They all sat there, in a cramped little room in the Times Square space, trying to block out the sound of the drilling and hammers.

'What was this place?' Damian Black, web guru, had thick glasses, skinny jeans and Converse trainers. He didn't see a lot of sun, but the dense, narrow darkness they were plunged into was something else.

'A strip club. This was the cloakroom,' Dina Kane said, matter of factly.

'I see.' They were sitting round a long, narrow table, made completely of Perspex, with laptops and a huge router plugged into the wall. 'What's it going to be next?'

The alcove was barely four paces wide, and the table took up most of it. Plunging, slippery black stairs led down to the hole where the men were working.

'You can't even fit customers in here. It's a useless space.'

Dina smiled tightly. 'Nothing's useless. This will be a giant wall of high-res screens, projecting our slogan and showing clips of ordinary women, their faces being made over with the products we stock. You won't see the hands of the make-up artist, just beauty appearing on the skin. Different women – all ages, all races – and, beside them, popping up in bubbles, some of the products we use.'

There was a moment's silence.

'Goddamn,' Damian said. 'That's fucking cool.'

'There will be men in there, too – groomed, shaved – looking sharp, like James Bond. We have a male section.'

'What's the slogan?'

Damian's partner was Cliff Green. He was just as brilliant, maybe a little more of a businessman. And this girl had his antenna up.

'Dina Kane – Extreme Beauty.'

He exhaled. 'I fucking love it.'

'It's perfect for New York,' Damian said.

'And building my site is going to get you guys where you want to go, believe me. I don't have the cash to go hiring the blue-chip firms, those tired old bastards with fancy offices. My architect is a Russian refugee. My first store is a basement strip club. You guys are students. But, together, we are going to build an empire.'

It could have sounded hokey, in the tiny dark room with the drills and the plastic table, but the young men were drinking in her every word.

'Everybody on this team is making their name. You're about to debut the smoothest site since Net-A-Porter. Since Sephora. You got it?'

'Shit. We're taking notes.'

'So –' Dina rose up and started to wave her hands, like she was literally building castles in the air – 'this website is the business. The store is going to be amazing – and there will be more stores, bigger stores – but the website is where we make our money. Chanel doesn't make money through ten-thousand-dollar suit jackets; it makes money through No. 5 sold in every airport concession in America.'

'Right.'

'So let's start with the basics: it's so easy to pay. Customers can use PayPal. They only need to log in once, then they stay logged in for six months. Credit cards are automatically retained, unless the opt-out box is selected. Password – six characters – anything you like. Understand?'

They nodded furiously.

'Next, Extreme Beauty is immersive. First, you organise the products by type. I'll give you the categories. Next, as soon as something pops up, I want videos of its application – just like the fashion sites show women walking in the clothes – consumers want it. We will have ten-second before-and-afters.'

'Yeah. Cool.'

'With every product, we add in partners. "Goes great with . . ." and two other things pop up. I will give you the list. There's also, "Best suited to . . ." and categories: blondes, African-Americans, oily skin, whatever.'

The boys were typing now, barely looking up from their screens.

'We want women to linger on this site – to play on it. Every image can be tacked to Pinterest – they all link back to us.'

'Great.'

'Search. You can search for product category, by your hair colour and type, by your skin colour and type, by new products, by most wanted, and the last category I'm doing is "Toys for Girls". That's like our personal recommendations. There will also be Extreme Style, the men's section, and gifts – stuff that works for everybody.'

'OK. OK. This is going to be a big site – lot of real estate; lot of usage.'

'I have the money. Animation must be smooth. Recommend- ations must fade in. I want you to think of this as the hottest make-up site you ever saw.'

'My girlfriend is going to freak,' Damian said.

'Dude, shut up. You don't have a girlfriend.'

'I will after this.' And he grinned.

'You can sign up and, after you spend a certain level, you become a VIP and get discounts, makeover vouchers and free samples.'

'OK.'

'There needs to be a community section. It'll be moderated; girls can send in photos of themselves using the products, offer their endorsements and suggestions. No reviews, though; I don't need spammers marking the stuff down. Everything on Dina Kane is going to be perfect – if it's properly used. Do you get it? Are you with me?'

They nodded furiously.

'This is more than a place to buy cosmetics. It's full of videos, bubbles, games, makeovers, enchantment. It's Aladdin's cave. It's immersive. You know, Net-A-Porter built a billion-dollar business selling purses that cost a thousand bucks. There are a lot more women out there who can buy a top-line lipstick at thirty dollars. You know why Net-A-Porter works? Because it's not work. They show the product on a woman. They video the product on a woman. You search by size and colour and they tell you what goes with it. Rich women are busy; they love it; it's like a personal shopper on their computer. Understand?'

They nodded. She could sell ice to Eskimos, and the two gamer freaks were suddenly all about the cult of mascara.

'So, you guys start. Send me links to the alpha pages. Use dummy items and prices.'

'Absolutely,' Damian said. 'Yes, Ms Kane.'

Dina smiled at that. She liked it.

The site was coming; the store was coming. The last piece of the puzzle was the billboard, but Dina wanted to wait on that. Everything would be exquisite, the way she'd wanted it for Torch – no, more gorgeous, better. She was doing things her own way, not limited by Ludo or other departments or anything else.

But it started and ended with quality. Perfection.

Dina would only sell the best. That meant cherry-picking from a range, just like the big stores did from the fashion collections. It meant limiting big, powerful companies, who wanted you to take their whole stock, including the stinkers. She had to curate it, do the customers' work.

Painstakingly, in between trips to the building site, conversations with Natalya in her halting English and meetings with the kids ploughing through her site, Dina Kane sunk herself into the world of beauty.

She tried to remember that wonder she'd first had with Hector at the Green Apothecary, when she was just a customer and everything he had was fusty and dust-covered and imported – but it *worked*.

As Dina toured stores, pored over make-up websites and underground beauty blogs, and scoured the magazines, she tried to forget everything she knew. In jeans and a T-shirt, she was just another girl with a pretty face. She went for free makeovers – everywhere except Torch; sat on little stools in Nordstrom and Bloomingdales, trying samples; took some days to spa at Bliss and Elizabeth Arden; wandered around Sephora and the boutiques in the West Village; she even studied the drugstore shelves.

What did women want? So much choice; so little time. It was all in the thrill of discovering a new wonder product, the thing you had to have – BB cream; Meadow; Great Lash mascara; Eight Hour cream; Chanel No. 5 – the blockbusters and their funky new cousins: Bobbi Brown's shimmer bricks; Urban Decay's nails . . .

Dina studied the executives swooping on the premier lines,

the younger women lingering, like kids in a candy store, trying several items, shopping as leisure. She listened to the chatter from the shopgirls making her up, followed the gossip on the websites. Everybody was looking for that new big thing. Minimalists, who wanted a small bag of reliable cosmetics; maximalists, fashionistas who loved to experiment; girls in the middle, who were just impulse buyers, influenced by the full-page ads in the women's magazines that week – there were so many types of girl, and Dina wanted to cater to them all, to own them all. Dina Kane was going to be different; taking herself back to that lover of beauty, that young girl . . . this was key.

The guys at the building site asked if she'd stopped working when she turned up with her shopping bags tied with pink ribbons, her face fresh from a makeover.

'I never stop working,' Dina said, and headed back out to the stores.

She tried to recall her first trip to Saks, her first muslin face cloth and Eve Lom cleanser, her first Bobbi Brown bronzer, the tight, bright Beauty Flash Balm by Clarins, Issima's Midnight Secret when she hadn't slept through the night. It was more than vanity; it was exciting – a thrill – to use her own face as a canvas, to be the artist. This was luxury she could afford.

Beauty was your best self. Beauty was armour; it was a weapon; it was a sign of great taste, grooming, elegance. Even a waitress could save up for that special Touche Éclat radiance and concealer. And then there was the joy of the drugstore find that beat all the boutiques – her Maybelline Great Lash mascara, which stayed on all night, didn't smudge, didn't run, beat her weary tears.

She was selling excitement. She was selling confidence. She was selling art. And everything for sale at Dina Kane had to be *great*. Just so goddamn good that a girl knew that *anything* she bought in the store, on the site, was quality. No fail.

She was asking American women to trust her taste. She was saying that this was important to women, and she could help.

Chapter Eighteen

She worked hard enough that every waking moment was spent sunk in Dina Kane. The visits to corporate headquarters were the worst.

'I'm sorry, Ms Kane, our brand has a stocking policy. It's the same for every store.'

'We like your ideas but we can hardly make an exception for a tiny premises in Manhattan.'

'If you take the primer, you have to take our Fashionista Mascara range. You can't just select.'

Dina sat in the offices of yet another cosmetics house and argued with a head of sales – fifty-five years old, with steel-grey hair and make-up free.

'Mrs Zagar, I assure you that being stocked at Dina Kane will be a mark of quality for every brand that works with us. Your best products will receive global attention. Their sales will shoot into a new stratosphere.'

'That's very nice, but they are bestsellers for a reason.'

'I don't want all your bestsellers. Some of them are no good.'

'Excuse me?' the older woman said.

Dina shrugged. 'Your Absolute Riches tinted moisturiser is chalky and your Forever Lips range dries hard on the mouth, leaving cracks. These are heavily supported by marketing, Mrs Zagar. The company didn't put any marketing behind the primer, and it sold by word of mouth. Appearance on the Dina Kane roster will *be* word of mouth.'

'Please, Ms Kane. I agreed to see you because we liked your work with Meadow. We hoped to offer you a job.'

'I have a noncompetition clause.'

'Well then I can't see what else we can do together.'

'I want you to license me to sell six products. I guarantee you that in one year those six products will make up a third of your revenue. You will be able to increase production, and drop from the manufacturing process those items not making you money.'

The girl's zeal was so all consuming that Mrs Zagar actually paused for a minute. On her computer screen, she tapped quietly, pulling up a list of the company's best and worst sellers. The marketing spend was beside each one. She noted that the primer had had hardly any.

Dina knew her stuff. Well, it was to be expected, with her background at Torch, learning from Ludo Morgan, who now had such a great reputation.

'What do you think are our worst sellers?'

She kicked herself for asking, for showing interest. Who cared what the girl thought? That was market confidential information she couldn't possibly have access to.

'Easy. Your Fashionista Mascaras, for one.'

Hannah Zagar jumped, but recollected herself. 'You guessed that because I told you it was part of the deal.'

'No, ma'am. I guessed that because the formulation is clumpy and the brush smudges. The colours are far too bright. Other worst sellers are your lip stains – again, the pigments are too bright. Your tinted moisturisers are being remaindered every-where because they're overpriced and chalky, and you're behind on the BB cream revolution. Your self-tanner comes out orange. Your whipped foundation is jar-packed; it oxidises right away when exposed to the air, and that means it goes too brown in about two weeks. Plus, your Tempting Trios in eye colour aren't tempting, because nobody goes for pops of colour on the lids – you're not selling T-shirts.'

Hannah Zagar glanced at her screen. The girl had called every one correctly.

'And the bestsellers?'

'Primer. Bronzers. Your cream peach blushes are translucent and unique on the market. If I might make a suggestion, you should rebrand them, and sell them as a double cheek and lip gloss. They can be dabbed on the lips, and last longer than regular gloss. Bronze cheek powders that work on eyes too are nothing new, but blusher for the lips is a good one.'

Hannah sat up, and looked at Dina very carefully.

'How did you come by this information? Have you had access to our servers?'

'No, ma'am. I just know make-up; I really know it.'

The head of sales chewed on her lip. Their company needed a break. Dina Kane was more correct than she knew; they had more misses than hits, and even clever advertising was not getting their products out of stores. They had good buy-in, but complaints from the boutiques that their lines were sitting on the shelves.

She had long argued they should cut the fat and just sell what worked. Now this young woman had penetrated deep to the heart of it, in a single meeting.

'How can you make the claim that being on your site will sell our products that way?'

'Because I only work with the best. Women will know they can trust Dina Kane for their cosmetics. It's the same way I got a reputation for Meadow – the same way I turned around Torch – only now there's nobody else holding me back.'

'And if I say no?'

'I still won't stock your other products. I'd rather sell fifty brilliant cosmetics than four hundred mediocre ones.'

Hannah Zagar considered it. 'I don't know, Ms Kane. It's

taking a great risk – even though I have found you very impressive.'

Dina said, impulsively, 'I can prove it to you, Mrs Zagar. I'll make you over, using nothing but Dina Kane, Inc. stock.'

She started. 'What? I'm not interested personally, Ms Kane. My younger days ended some time ago.'

'Allow me to try. Just as an experiment. You can wipe it off immediately afterwards.'

'You are joking.'

'Not at all. Women have to see it to believe it – cosmetics houses, too.'

Hannah Zagar resisted the impulse to steal a look at her reflection in the glass walls of the meeting room. She always dressed neatly, but she was in her early fifties. That was all there was to it – age was age. Right?

She laughed. 'I tell you what, Ms Kane. Come back here after lunch with a bag of your products. If you can turn me into a glamour girl, we'll take a chance on your store and your site. But don't hold your breath.'

Kane was cocky, confident, but a little too presumptuous. Hannah Zagar didn't mind that – she had been ambitious too, when she was younger. She would teach the girl not to overreach, and give her a valuable business lesson.

Her good deed for the day.

'How long is this going to take?'

Hannah's chair was away from the mirror. They had set up in a little-used bathroom on the top floor – she hardly wanted to make a spectacle of herself – which had a large window, as Dina had asked for natural light. She had returned with a disappointingly small make-up bag, the primer was the only product of theirs. Any fantasies Hannah was secretly harbouring about being transformed evaporated, but, then again, she had agreed to go through with this farce.

'I'll only need a few minutes. May I shape your eyebrows? It stings slightly, but it will look very good on you. I'll be using Perfection Tweezers, which we'll be stocking.'

Hannah sighed. 'OK. But get on with it. Really, I must get back to work. This was a mistake.'

Dina said nothing; she leaned in over the older woman with the tweezers, plucking and shaping. She moved very quickly, and Hannah waited, although she winced once or twice. There was no chatter. In a few moments, Dina was wiping something soft across her brows. She added a touch of primer, and then dusted some eye shadow lightly over the lids – one, two strokes of the brush, different shades. Dina worked across her whole face: eyes, cheeks, lips. Then, after just a few minutes, she stood back.

'That's it,' she said.

'That's it?' Kane had barely spent eight minutes on her face. 'You think this will make a difference?'

'Dina Kane stocks only the world's best products. Take a look for yourself, Mrs Zagar.'

The younger woman watched her expectantly, and Hannah reluctantly turned her chair around to face the bathroom mirror.

She gasped.

The face staring back at her was unrecognisable. Not younger – just better, so much better. Her skin was smoother, and the foundation on top of the primer gave her an elegant, even glow. Her pale cheeks had a light shimmer of bronzer on them, which brought out her high cheekbones; her eyebrows, thick and beetling, were lifted into elegant arches that widened her whole look. Her eyes, pale blue, suddenly popped in her face, with light brown shadow on the lids and a little chestnut on the creases. The shadows under her eyes had vanished, making her look lively and alert. She was wearing lip gloss – an attractive, natural peach – and it wasn't bleeding into the lines around her mouth, which was why she had given up wearing it. As she stared,

Hannah now remembered Dina dabbing powder there, and primer, and then two coats of gloss.

She breathed in, stunned. Taking in this version of herself.

'Primer – your primer – is very helpful on the mature face, but you still don't need much, just the right foundation, bronzer, powder and gloss. I would add mascara at night.'

'My husband won't believe it.' She wished the day was over already, so she could rush home and surprise him. 'I . . . It's incredible.'

'You could look even better if you dyed your hair to cover the grey and got a chic cut. I can recommend you a great salon for your type.'

'Really? Could you?' Hannah stopped herself – she was sounding like a teenager. But Dina Kane had transformed her, literally transformed her, in minutes.

'Of course. Can I have the primer? And my selection?'

'Ms Kane,' Hannah Zagar said, unable to look away from her reflection, 'you can have anything you want.'

Joel Gaines sat in his office, staring into space.

Below him was the great expanse of Manhattan. This view had always inspired him: the city, pulsing with life and money. Power ran through its crosswalks. This was where the great deals were done, where American fortunes were made. This was where he'd changed his life.

He had crushed the opposition. And when things at home were stressful, or boring, or frustrating, it didn't matter; he could come to the office.

Glass walls, installed custom by his architect, had been designed to mercilessly intimidate the guy on the other side of the desk. And for his own pleasure. He wanted to be looking down on it all, like a bird of prey in his eyrie – literally, at the pinnacle.

But today, he didn't see the view. He was just staring into nothingness.

Dina Kane. He could not forget her. Get over her. Get past her. She was the most remarkable, the bravest chick he'd ever met.

That scene in the cab, where she'd made her peace, said her goodbyes – it was too much emotion, too heavy for him. But still, he'd been expecting a call. A text. Something.

Dina Kane had vanished off the face of the earth. Nothing. It was like she'd never come into his life at all.

He worked and went home. The boys were at college. The younger one had come home that weekend, played some tennis. His wife swam and went to the beauty salon, attended a house party, threw a lunch for their friends. Gaines had sat around, unable even to socialise. When he looked at Susan, all dressed up, wearing her jewels and heavy make-up, talking to him about couples therapy and working on himself, he felt a suffocating depression.

But that was commitment, that was marriage. Why couldn't he deal with it?

His phone rang.

'Yes?'

'Sir, I wanted to remind you: you have therapy with Dr Fallon in fifteen minutes.'

Therapy. He was usually never late. It decompressed him, helped him relax, but he could not speak of Dina, and it seemed pointless right now, so pointless – talking about his life, instead of doing something about it.

'Cancel it.'

'Yes, sir.'

'Cancel all my meetings. I'm going home.'

There was a pause at the end of the line. 'But, sir, you have a partnership meeting on L'Audace. You have Goldman coming in on the Durant deal – their senior VP. And you're expected in the Mayor's box at the opera tonight, for the opening of *Der Rosenkavalier*. You accepted that invitation months ago . . .'

'Doesn't matter. I'm going home.'

347

'Are you sick, Mr Gaines?'

'I'm not sick. I hope you're not deaf.'

'No, sir. Very good, sir. I'll cancel your meetings.'

He walked to the executive elevator, the one that went directly down to the lobby, and below, to the garage. The shaft was designed for exactly that reason: so Gaines could get in and out, if he chose, without seeing another living soul. It was pure Master-of-the-Universe stuff, and today he was glad of it. He just had no desire at all to see his secretary's curious face right now, like he was a crossword puzzle she had to crack.

It was funny, he thought, as the elevator car whisked him down, down into the floodlit open space of their senior executive garage, that the one person he wanted to talk to about this was Dina Kane. But he couldn't talk to her.

Not yet.

Not till it was done.

'I think you should know about this, Mr Johnson.'

Edward sighed. He had just finished smoking a joint, a deep, mellow feeling was stealing over him, and he really didn't want any hassle from Lena just now. Bills, unfinished accounts: it was all from the past.

His mother was due back up from Florida tomorrow. He had persuaded her that staying in the townhouse – *his* townhouse – would be wrong. It was, after all, the site of her addictions. She would occupy his old apartment. In the end, he was going to persuade her to move out of state permanently.

There was no way he would allow her back to take what was his. His parents screwed things up; it was Edward's time now.

The stock portfolio was doing well, under the manager he had hired. He had a plan: to marry, and then sell either her house or his and buy a beachfront place in the Hamptons. That would rent out for a million a year, and there was his income for life. Edward had decided that work was – well – too much like work.

Women were the cause of all his problems; women could solve them. A rich spouse. It was one of the oldest transactions: his name for her cash.

He was already having some success. Back in the social circle, invited to all the parties, Edward Johnson was no longer a pariah. Crazy father? Drunken mother? So what? He had the house, and did you ever *see* such a perfect gem? There was private money. He was a trust fund, baby. He was a catch for some lucky girl.

Most of the best set wouldn't date him – the pretty blondes with the long limbs and white teeth, swinging their tennis rackets and setting their cap at the hedge-fund guys, the investment bankers. But that still left a lot of rich pickings. The ugly chicks, the girls who were overweight with the dull skin and disappointed eyes, they were there for the plucking. They were the nervous ones, the aggressively political girls – camouflaging the pain of not being wanted with activism and ideology.

Edward was careful. It wouldn't do to leave a trail of broken hearts. So he threw parties and dinners, and invited a good selection of the richest wallflowers from Wall Street – ugly chicks with great financial résumés. He was sociable, he didn't hit on them, taking his time to scope them out.

His plan now was to date just one, maybe two, if that didn't work out. He would be remiss if he didn't get some chick to the altar in three dating partners.

First, he had to ensure they really were solvent. Not just pretend rich, like him. Was there a solid trust fund in the girl's own name? Were her parents the kind of crazy liberals that left their money to foundations? Did she have her own house, income, stock portfolio? Were the parents achingly rich? Were there brothers and sisters? Who had she dated before?

It took time, and it was work Edward didn't want to contract out. If the slightest whisper got back to any of them, he was ruined. He investigated public records and gossip columns, chatted to friends about his own investments, drew them out . . .

Some wine, cigars for the men, moving on to a private smoking club where the scent of cigars, money and fine cognac all mingled together. By the end of a month of socialising, he had three women picked out, and had already dined with two of them alone.

The room came back into focus and he remembered Lena was in front of him, one of the only staff he had retained in the house: the cook. You couldn't get rid of a brilliant cook that worked cheaply. Edward liked his food, and there was something so *colonial* about having servants.

'Yes? What?'

He was filled with foreboding. What had she seen? What would she say to his mother? Perhaps he'd been stupid, keeping her around.

'It's on the computer.'

He stared at the older woman. 'I'm not going to the computer. What is it?'

'Well, sir, it's on one of the blogs. As Mrs Johnson is coming back . . . You wouldn't want her upset . . . I think there may be some publicity tomorrow about a *certain person*. Perhaps if you can get her to delay her return just one more week, it might be better.'

'A certain person? Is my father returning?'

'Oh. No, sir. Nothing like that.' Lena twisted her hands. 'It's just, you know, that awful young woman. Dina Kane.'

The shock hit Edward like a physical punch to the chest. 'What? What did you say?'

'Dina Kane, sir, if you remember.'

He remembered. 'But she was fired. Ruined. She can't work again. What are they saying on the fucking computer?'

Lena winced. 'Sir, please . . .'

Edward bit his lip. Rage was simmering, he could feel it, that old rage he thought had gone, it was just lying in his blood, waiting for a spark to ignite it. He felt dizzy, sick, like his careful world was shattering – shattering *again* – just as he was putting it back together.

'Tell me,' he hissed.

'That she's opening a store.'

'For Torch?' Had that jerk off, Ludo Morgan, taken her back?

'No, sir. Her own store, they say. And a website. It's happening tomorrow. All quite secret, but the blogs are leaking now.'

Edward Johnson stared. 'Lena, you read the beauty blogs?'

His cook was a mature woman, but she was slender and dark haired, somewhat elegant. He supposed he had never looked at her as a person before.

'I . . . Sometimes. Yes, sir. Sometimes.'

He took in her dress. It was dark and well cut, and her hair had a short, fashionable shape to it.

'And I read up on the news when that girl was fired, sir, and you were very pleased.'

'I hardly noticed,' snapped Edward.

'Oh. I'm sorry, sir. I suppose I thought you might. Never mind – my mistake.'

She made to move away. Edward forced down the bile, the impulse to grab her and shake her by the shoulders.

'Lena, wait! If you think it might upset Momma, I should like to know the details. I'll go and sit in the study. Can you email the piece to me?'

'Yes, sir. Of course. Can I go?'

He waved his hand and dismissed her. 'Yes. And I'll eat out tonight.'

'Very good, Mr Edward.'

The last thing he wanted right now was chatter with this woman: discussing Dina Kane . . . giving something away . . .

She scuttled off, and he forced himself to wait, to pour a large whiskey from the decanter into a cut-crystal glass, so that he was not rushing off to his office. He didn't want to give Lena clues.

This was important; he didn't yet know why, but it was important to him.

Dina Kane was off limits.

He sipped the whiskey, neat, feeling the alcohol burn against his tongue and his lips. He allowed the tang of it to slow his anger, make him stay there, to work through the spurt of rage. Agonisingly slowly, he drank one finger of the golden-brown spirit and it relaxed him a little.

Then, finally, he headed off to his study.

The computer was there before him. His email box was blinking with the link from Lena.

Edward clicked on it, sucking in his breath, and read.

Big launch tomorrow. Dina Kane vanished from the scene when she got fired by Torch – but now she's back in a big way. Dina has been doing more than just counting her savings in the piggy bank. She's opening an exclusive new boutique in Times Square, selling top-rated beauty finds. Dina Kane, Inc. is aiming to be the new Sephora, but Dina has added a new twist: the walls of her ultra-chic basement getaway sport scrolling videos of real women being made over by the products on sale. It's hypnotic – as is the underground oasis Kane and her architects have built. You won't believe how the tiny space, formerly a strip club, transports you to an underground jungle, serene with waterfalls, white woods and natural lights. But every inch is beautifully used, with fewer products on shelves than normal, yet each one a standout. Kane has found some of the best freelance make-up artists in the city, and samples are available with larger purchases. Her base range is high-end. We predict a riot – and that's before we even consider her stunning website.

The preview, which bloggers were shown, of DinaKane.com got most of us very excited! Expect a wider range of first-class beauty finds, brushes and accessories, and – more than that – a masterclass in Kane's natural look on every page. Just like a designer fashion site, she breaks new ground for make-up by including video tutorials with every item. That's right – see your Bobbi Brown Brick in Pink Quartz applied to the face, or an African-American model experimenting live with IMAN's BB Crème! DinaKane.com is too cute. And it suggests other 'pieces' you might want to go with your purchases . . . An Urban Decay eye shadow palette matches beautifully with a Chanel bronzer; do you need a Shu Uemura brow pencil with those Kevyn Aucoin brushes?

I don't like hype, here on Unfashionista, but I think we may just be seeing the next big name in beauty – and, in the next days and months, we'll find out!

Edward read the review twice, three times. There were pictures of some kind of spa with make-up in it, a hanging garden, a waterfall, bright daylight flooding a basement. It looked architectural, stunning, inviting – deeply rich.

Toys for girls – wealthy girls. He wanted to kill her. How the hell . . . ? How had this happened? With what money? It had barely been more than a few months. How did she get up this fucking fast? *Times Square*? His head was spinning. How had she found the stock? Wasn't there a clause? A fucking clause that stopped her working?

Dina Kane was supposed to be falling apart in a corner somewhere. He'd intended to finish the job, get her addicted, get her fucked up, just like her worthless brother, after he was done at home. Managing his mother and picking a girl – those were his priorities. Settling the money, the finance, the easy way.

Once he had a rock-solid prenup and title to the new wife's assets, Edward planned to go looking for Dina. The dead brother was meant to be a warm up.

He had to think. But the rage was rising inside him, rising into a frenzy. Impotent and enraged, Edward thumped at his desk.

The phone rang.

'Yes?' he barked.

'Edward? Oh, it's Janet . . . Is this a bad time?'

'Janet? Jesus! I'm busy!' One of his girlfriends. He tensed with annoyance.

'Oh. Oh, OK; I'm sorry to have bothered you.'

This was Janet – *his* Janet; if he worked hard enough, she was his ticket to comfort and fortune. What the hell was wrong with him?

'No, Janet, wait. Wait . . .' Panicking, he tried to force some calm into his voice. 'It's a fine time to talk, don't worry—'

'It's OK. I didn't expect to be shouted at.' Janet was teary down the phone, reproachful, exactly what he hated in women. 'We've only been out once, I mean . . .'

'Yes – absolutely. I didn't mean to snap; I'm sorry. Can I take you out tonight to apologise?'

There was a pause. 'I'm busy tonight.'

'Tomorrow night?' He kicked himself under the desk, now he was chasing, sounding desperate.

'I have a date with Peter Lucas tomorrow night. We can talk some other time – *maybe*,' she said, and hung up.

'Goddamn it!' Edward shrieked. He slammed down the phone and buried his head in his hands.

Peter Lucas was his rival; a poor but sleekly handsome young guy on a full scholarship to Columbia, he was invited to parties as a guest, getting a taste for the high life. He specialised in the rich, ugly chicks, although he dated around, not settling on any one of them. Edward knew he was after Janet, but hadn't worried. At least Edward had a good name, had his own townhouse, a presence on the Upper West Side. Lucas was some pretty schmuck from Brooklyn.

But he was soft-spoken. *Greedy, not pathological.*

Pathological. Edward had wondered – every now and then – in the days after he'd found out that Johnny Kane OD'd . . . But so fucking what? *If I'm pathological, Dina Kane made me so.*

He would watch the launch tomorrow. He didn't kid himself that it would fall flat.

Dina Kane was his disease. And Edward Johnson needed it cured.

Their home in the Hamptons was truly magnificent. He had spent many happy days here. And Susan had built up the estate, planning the garden, the tennis courts, looking after their boys and the dogs. Perhaps they were detached, but they had been a team.

The sprawling mansion reached out, through its Italian front garden with four interlinked saltwater pools, down to a stretch of private beach, one of the largest in Sagaponack. He would sit here with his phone and make calls, with the ocean crashing before him, feeling calmer, feeling the intensity of triumph at his success: a wife and children who would never want for anything; being able to afford any toy he chose – even his own jet, although he only kept a modest Gulfstream V.

Joel drove to the house. He didn't park the Lexus in the garage; he left it right in front of the front door, which was open slightly. Maria, his housekeeper, was dusting along the marble staircase.

'Where is she?' he said.

'Out in the garden, señor. I think she just finish tennis.'

'Very good. I need to talk to her privately. Tell the staff to give us some space, OK?'

Maria lifted a brow. 'Yes, Mr Gaines.'

She knew better than to ask her boss what he was doing. When Gaines spoke like that, nobody questioned him.

He waited there a little, as she scurried away, listening to the sound of workers quietly moving to the back wing of the house. And then he walked outside.

Susan was bending over some rose bushes with her secateurs. She always liked clipping fresh roses from the garden; they grew all kinds, a riot of colour, across the spectrum, with flowering from May to August. Picking flowers was as close as she ever really got to getting involved, but it helped her to believe she had a green thumb. And, indeed, she had a good eye, telling the gardener what to plant, the cook what to make and the housekeepers how they should store Joel's things. She ran a tight ship at home and, as a chief of staff, he had no complaints; as a mom, she was fine.

It was just their marriage that was dead. As he breathed in, feeling the weight of pain across his chest, of what he was about to do, Joel Gaines suddenly understood that he had been aching for years. It wasn't just the sex, as routine and dull as that was, scratching an itch; it was the lack of adventure, of passion – for him, for life. They never argued politics. They never talked late into the night, not unless it was about the kids. He had friends, business deals, his sons: that was his life. Plus this lovely, comfortable home, which had become a prison.

'Susan,' he said.

She stood up straight, surprised. 'Honey! I wasn't expecting you till tonight. What happened? The office close early or something? Look –' she thrust a bouquet at him: pale green and cream roses – 'I thought these for your study. You like them?'

God almighty, but this hurts. He took the roses, laid them down on the grass.

'Susan, I have something to say to you. It's important. Can we sit down somewhere? Go inside?'

She blinked at his tone. 'What? Why? Are you sick?'

'I'm not sick. But we need to talk. Can you come into the study with me?'

Looking anxious, she followed him indoors, into his downstairs study. It had a window looking out on to the garden, but it was small and private, and he could close the door.

'Joel, you're scaring me.'

'Please sit, Susan.'

She did, on the burgundy love seat, and he faced her on the

hard English oak chair he used at his desk, turning it to look directly at her.

'We've lost our money?' Her face was grey with anxiety. 'Something at work? Oh, God, Joel, you're not into some kind of Bernie Madoff thing, or anything . . . ?'

'No. Nothing like that. Susan, there is no good way to say this, so I'll just come out with it. I want a divorce.'

She slumped. 'What? What did you say?'

'I want a divorce. I'm in love with someone else, and our marriage has been miserable for years now. We've been living separate lives – emotionally, at least.'

Tears sprang to her eyes, and that made Joel feel awful, sick. The powerful weapon of tears. He didn't love Susan; he couldn't spend the rest of his life with her. But having to hurt her was dreadful.

'What are you talking about? We're not *miserable*. We have two kids. We have a lovely life!'

'Our boys are grown, Susan. Yes, the *life* is lovely –' he gestured around the garden, warm in the sun, at the roses and the sea beyond – 'but *you're* not in love with me anymore. Are you?'

'I am!' she protested.

'You're not, Susan. You don't want me in bed; you don't ask me to come home and spend time with you. We live very beautifully, but we live separate lives. I work; you do . . . your thing – socially and otherwise.' He could hardly say, *Shopping, yoga, Pilates, visiting the salon.*

Her tearful face was hardening now – to anger. 'You said you're in love with someone else. You *cheated* on me? The mother of your children? How could you do that?'

Gaines didn't deny it. 'I'm sorry.'

There had been no sex, but there was intent. Flirtation. Bonding. Love, even. Could he say he hadn't cheated on her?

'What is her name?' Susan hissed. 'Tell me that bitch's name!'

He swallowed. 'Dina Kane.'

There was no point in hiding it; she would know soon enough.

Susan blinked. 'What? Dina Kane? That girl Ludo Morgan dumped? *The girl at the party?*'

'Yes. It was after that night that I fell in love with her.'

Susan looked around wildly. 'But, Joel . . . you can't do this. *We're* married. You made *vows* to me. We have kids. I've always been honest and faithful . . . and you're leaving me?' She was frowning with rage but not crying anymore; her face was red; she was screeching. 'It's just a mid-life crisis! You're an old man to her, an old man with money. Don't you get it? She's playing you for a fool. You can't throw away our *family* for this!'

'Susan –' he wanted to take her hand, to calm her down, but didn't dare – 'please. Dina didn't ask me to do this. She doesn't even know I'm doing it. I haven't spoken to her for weeks.'

'Don't defend that slut to me!'

'I want you to understand this is about us . . . first. For years now, we haven't had a real marriage. You reject me in bed.'

'Lies! I never turn you down.'

'And you never ask me, either. It was always a duty to you, Susan. Do you realise, in all these years together, you never once came to me and asked me to take you to bed?'

She flushed. 'I'm not built that way. It's up to you to lead . . .'

'Men want to be desired, just like women do. Susan, you don't ask me to come back home here unless there's an event, or a party. You never come down to Manhattan to spend time with me in the season.'

Susan Gaines bit her lip. 'But you never said you wanted it!'

'I need you to take the initiative, not simply act like a secretary that runs the Hamptons house. Look, we have wonderful children together, Susan, but once they were grown, you just weren't interested in me. I always thought you were a great mom. But I want a wife, a partner . . . More than this.'

'Well, you never complained to me.'

He winced; that was true.

'If you were unhappy, why didn't you say anything? What are you going to tell our children? *My* children?'

Joel sighed, long and deep. 'Yes. You're right. I should have said something. But I didn't know how much I missed being loved until I found a girl who really did love me.'

'Bullshit! You're going to throw away twenty years together for a gold-digger?'

'Susan, look me in the eyes. Are you in love with me? Do you love me?'

For a few seconds, he held his breath. If she said yes, she loved him, he couldn't really go through with it. Not yet. Not after twenty years. There would have to be counselling, and trying again, and what his sons deserved. He was afraid, fearful she would say yes. He loved Dina Kane, and he had finally done this, and now he wanted to pursue her, openly, and desperately. But if Susan said she loved him . . .

The moment hung in the air, and time seemed to slow down, to freeze.

Susan lifted her head and stared at him. There was a long, long pause, and then she crumpled, folding on the couch.

Joel felt the wave of relief crash over him, merciful obliteration.

'You think you'll get away with this?' She was flushed with anger now. 'Humiliating me like this, with some slut?'

'Dina's not a slut.'

'This is *my* house. She's never setting foot in here. I've been married to you for twenty years; don't think you're just going to give my home to her!'

'Be reasonable, Susan. We can work all that stuff out.'

But she was lost in her rage now, and nothing he said could change it.

'I want the money, you goddamned bastard! You owe me.'

'You'll get half of everything, Susan.' That much was easy. 'Including this house. I'm not going to cheat you.'

'You should give me more than half. You should give me all of it.'

He shook his head. 'The lawyers will do their thing. But I wanted you to know that you will get half of everything. I'm sorry, Susan.'

'I hate you!' she shrieked. 'Get out of my goddamned house!'

And Joel Gaines got up, left the study and walked out of the house, and out of his old life.

A day later, Joel Gaines was sitting on a weather-beaten green bench in JFK park in Cambridge, Massachusetts, gazing out at the river and trying not to look at the mutinous face of his son.

'So that's it, Dad? You can't be persuaded?'

'I'm sorry, Noah. We fell out of love. It happens.'

'When it happens, you guys are meant to work on it. Twenty years – that should mean something.'

'It does. I just . . . I can't be unhappy for the rest of my life, Noah. I'm sorry.'

'And you think this girl really loves you? You're a very rich man.'

'I know. She's different.'

'Family is supposed to be forever,' his son said. 'I don't want to meet her. I don't want to know.'

Joel breathed in. 'Noah, I love you and your brother very much. I always will. But you can't sentence me to a life of misery. You're an adult now, making your own decisions. I can't say if it'll work out between me and Dina, but I can say that, when I asked your mom if she loved me, she didn't say yes.'

'Have you spoken to Seth?'

'This morning.' His older son had shouted at him, railed, called him a moron; it was preferable to this quiet disappointment. 'He was mad, too. I'm sorry.'

'Not sorry enough.'

Joel squared his shoulders. 'Noah, I'm not yet fifty. You can't seriously think I owe it to my adult kids to continue in a loveless marriage.'

His son kicked at the gravel on the path, his head bowed.

'Maybe it's not loveless, Dad. Maybe she was hurt and that's why she didn't say it. It might be you needed to work things out.'

'That would just prolong the pain.' He blew out air, like he was lifting a heavy weight. 'I'll always be your father, and I'll always love you.'

There was a silence, a heavy beat that hit him in the gut like a fist.

'We love you too, Dad. But we have to be there for Mom right now.'

Noah reached across and gave him an awkward hug. Joel patted his son on the back, running his hands up and down his spine as he'd done when Noah was a baby.

'That's fine, buddy. You do everything you have to. I'm still going to be around.'

And he breathed out because, in the end, after this was all done, and the anger was spent, when Susan had her settlement and maybe another man, Joel believed it would be OK.

It was done; it was over.

He was in the car, driving mindlessly, glad of the monotony, back to the city, trying to let the task clear his mind. The pain was real, but so was the relief; those iron chains, the ones that had locked him down for the last ten years, were shattered, broken. He was a free man.

There was no question of what he would do next: go to his apartment; dump the car; call his business partner; call a lawyer. That was the housekeeping taken care of.

And then . . . Joel Gaines was going to find Dina Kane, wherever the hell she was, and tell her he loved her, and take her to bed. That was the only certain thing in his life, and the one thing he was holding on to.

Chapter Nineteen

Dina sat with Natalya in the bar of the Victrix. It was late. She never usually drank, but tonight they had a bottle of champagne between them: Cristal, the house brand of Manhattan's most luxurious hotel. They were drinking from cut-glass flutes, and she was finally relaxing.

It was over. Win or lose, she couldn't do any more. The money was mostly spent; there was just enough left for a month's expenses. She had a handful of staff: make-up artists she trusted; girls who could stand at a register and also socialise; there were the geeks running the website, and, now the store was built in record time, there was Natalya – a friend.

They had seen each other daily for weeks as the underground club transformed from sweat-soaked strip joint to an architectural jewel. Even the city inspectors had been impressed. Dina had spent real money on an immigration lawyer, and got Natalya into the system as an applicant for a professional visa; she quit nannying for the family that treated her like a slave. Piotr was right: she was a star. She jumped at Dina's vision for the space, working and reworking everything, directing plumbing, engineering, everything perfectly. And something else: she was as hard a worker as Dina was, herself. Each night, she left at eight p.m. for a night class in English and, when Dina visited the site, if Natalya was alone, she found her plugged into her earbuds, talking to herself aloud, doing English on her phone, teaching herself around the clock.

By the third week, she was arguing with the suppliers – in broken English. By the fourth, she was talking haltingly to Dina. Natalya applied herself not just a few nights a week, but day in, day out. She plunged into the language like Dina flung herself at the business. And now her English was passable.

Dina admired it. She loved Natalya's work ethic and the clear way that she understood and executed Dina's own creative vision. The space was light-filled, just as Dina dreamed, temperate and warm, with water cascading down the rock sculpture, daylight pouring in and the beauty products mounted on the shelves like jewels. The limited space was maximised with light and mirrors, and everything said *luxury* and *simplicity*. In addition to her clear architectural skills – bringing that sense of space, light and peace to a small underground room – Natalya had a flair for design, interpreting what Dina wanted to do and sourcing the exact pieces that could make it happen; she took her time, but the perfect modern stools showed up, the right blond woods, the clean, pale-grey tiles, mirrors to reflect the piped-in sunshine . . .

The space was transformed. First, the cleanup, then the wires, the plumbing, the light-well and the glass. Next, the interior element: neutral colours, recessed lighting, the LED displays, a waterfall and bright, open shelving for customer space and comfort, designed so nobody would have to jostle to see the stock.

There were stools, brush bars, testers and pots of wipes. There were alcoves for the make-up artists to work on clients. The web address of the store was everywhere, scrolled on the walls, on the sides of shelving, on their newly printed stiff paper bags with the pale green and gold ribbon. And the men's corner was a gorgeous contrast in slate greys and black marble, with dark green leather and old-fashioned grooming products; a Manhattan

Wall Street shark could come in here and pick up solid gold cufflinks, some Floris aftershave, or Hermès Eau d'Orange Verte shower gel, and feel himself well groomed in the capitals of Europe – feel himself a gentleman. Natalya had down-lit the old world into the new, so that they melded beautifully together. And Dina's web designers, kid geeks that they were, loved it, too; they took photographs, blogged it and styled it right into the site; DinaKane.com carried through that seamless look.

Another bonus: Natalya was good with money. Dina found that out early on, when she heard her screeching at the contractors in Russian.

'I talk them budget,' she haltingly explained. 'I tell, they not pay at end if spend too much now. Waste wood if not planks cut right.'

Dina looked at the floor, and saw what she meant – the wide Swedish blond planks were not fitting right at the end of the room.

'Waste money,' Natalya said, frowning. 'Stupid fault.'

Dina laughed.

'What wrong?'

'Sorry – no – you're absolutely right. It's just the English.'

'Working on that,' Natalya said.

'I know. It's fantastic. I'll leave you to it.'

As they progressed, Natalya brought her budget breakdowns, every day, on a spreadsheet – everything from wages to MetroCard expenses. She listened avidly as Dina outlined her vision for the store, for new stock, for the uniforms of the staff.

'Plain beige dresses. Short sleeves; fitted waist; knee length. Any designer they like, prêt-à-porter, and we pay. Dina Kane says chic, not straightjacket.'

'I like this. Everything must say *style*.'

'Creams, golds, beige, neutral: that's the design of the wrapping paper, the tissue, the ribbons and the gift boxes. Kane Men is dark grey and burnt gold.'

'Also very good.' Natalya nodded. 'Russian men like very much, the oligarchs who want London style. Your taste very beautiful.'

'Do you have a boyfriend?'

Natalya's shoulders hunched up defensively. 'No time; I work here all day, English all night, and everyone here is married. Or maybe stupid.'

Dina laughed. 'Piotr's friends, you mean?'

Natalya shrugged. 'It's the community. When you want to be ambitious, you cannot take off time for – what you say? – Frivolous . . . Messing round.'

'You need a private life, otherwise you'll burn out.' Dina looked round the store; the last of the workmen was heading out. 'Mikhail, it's OK – I'll lock up.'

'Fine, miss.' He nodded his head, just glad to be getting back home.

Dina walked up the stairs and shut the door from the inside. Now they could not be disturbed. 'Natalya, do you have five minutes?'

The older girl immediately hunched. 'Why? What is wrong?'

She's used to being attacked, Dina thought. *She thinks I'm going to pack her up and ship her back to the spoiled kids and the slave-driving parents. Or stiff her on her wages with an immigration threat.*

'Nothing. Nothing at all. Your work is incredible. I would just like to practise on you.'

'Practise?' Natalya shook her head. 'I do not understand.'

'The make-up booths; the styling – would you consider being a guinea pig for this process? I'd like to make you up, and maybe also do your hair. And dress you. No charge,' she said, hastily. 'All on the company.'

Natalya winced. 'You must need me do this?'

'No, not at all. Not a job requirement. You don't have to, not in any way.' Dina ventured a smile. 'I just think . . . you might enjoy it.'

'Enjoy it,' said Natalya, as if this were a foreign concept. 'You think?'

'I do. And I was hoping that, when we are through here, you might consider working for me. Not as an architect. I'd like you to help me run the company. If –' she corrected herself – '*when* we get new stores, bigger ones, you can design them, but mostly I just want your business input. I have plans – across America, and then into Europe. Why not?'

Natalya gasped with pleasure.

When her face lights up like that, Dina thought, *she can be truly beautiful.* She understood better than she could speak, and the hope in her eyes was something to see.

'Yes. Wonderful. Thank you.' She struggled for the right words. 'I very alike you. Not so imagination, but working hard. And your business good one. I understand American women; they love all this things.'

'Well . . . if you want to be number two at Dina Kane,' Dina said, slowly, 'maybe you really do need to let me at you, after all. My first management hire has to be well made up, beautifully dressed. They will take photographs when we launch.'

Natalya considered this. 'Yes, OK. I understand this.' Then she frowned. 'But now is time for my English class.'

'Fine. Tomorrow, no architecture. Meet me at Daniel Gibbons, the hairdresser. Here's the address. See you there at nine.'

Daniel didn't open his doors till half ten, but he loved Dina, and she knew he would fit her in. Besides, once she explained, he'd see that this was going to be fun.

The next morning, she met a nervous Natalya at the salon.

'You just lie back,' Dina said. 'Daniel will do all the work.'

Natalya's Russian face tightened; the shutters in her eyes came down. 'Fine,' she said.

Dina fed her magazines, but her face was impassive. Daniel washed, and cut, and shaped her hair, exactly as Dina told him;

her style was legendary, and he was happy to be the instrument in her hands.

'Shape it into a flame. It's fine and thin, so it should hold that shape. Cut the edges diagonally across the face, and end it just below the collarbone. And I want it lightened. Highlights, till she's a good caramel blonde, with just a couple of truly fair streaks, OK? Not framing the face – scattered, not symmetrical. This has to be an easy cut she can just blow-dry and go. Are you with me?'

'That's going to look fabulous. Leave it with me.'

After they were done, Dina didn't let Natalya look in the mirror. She put her in a cab and took her straight to Saks.

'You're a size four.'

'How do you know?'

'I can tell. Come with me.'

They visited DKNY, Hervé Léger, Prada and Ralph Lauren. Then she crossed the street to Uniqlo and picked up jeans and puffer jackets in a rainbow of colours, with soft cashmere sweaters. Lastly, at Columbus Circle, they stopped at Cole Haan, and Dina took out her credit card.

'You're a seven. You need more shoes, but this will do for summer – heels, courts and flats. I love these, they have the same air cushioning they put in the Nike shoes.'

'I don't understand.'

'You will.' The girls were laden down with shopping bags. Dina hailed a cab for her apartment. 'Just come with me.'

Once there, she pulled out a fitted dress in red, some hose and a pair of platform pumps, and sent Natalya into the spare bedroom to change.

'Yes. Wonderful,' Dina said when she reappeared. The red dress woke her up, clinging beautifully to the slim curves of her body, and the pumps made her look model thin. There was no bag, but Dina figured she could pick up one of those tomorrow. She caught Natalya glancing around, trying to see a mirror. 'Not yet. The reveal is the whole fun of it.'

The older girl looked doubtful.

'Just sit on the chair. We're nearly done, and then I'll get you a cab back to Brooklyn, OK? And you can take the afternoon off.'

Natalya sighed. 'Yes, Dina, OK. You not be too long.'

It was quick work. She applied BB cream, two shades mixed together, and highlighted Natalya's slim cheekbones with a dusting of Bobbi Brown's Pink Quartz Brick in gold and rose. There was no point going heavy; Natalya was a dark blonde with a fair skin, and natural would always suit her. Dina used the most basic cosmetics: light brown eye shadow from Mac, a single coat of lash-separating Maybelline mascara – drug-store cheap – and a Revlon glittering lip gloss in clear, to give a wet look to her lips.

'OK. Stand. Come to the mirror,' she said, taking the girl into her own bedroom, to the full-length French antique that stood there by the bed. 'This is how you should look.'

Natalya stared at the mirror, as if spellbound. She reached her hands up to her new hair and touched it, gingerly. Then she smoothed down the dress and turned. She walked closer, examining her face.

Then she said something in Russian. And then she burst into tears.

That was the start of their friendship. Natalya became even more confident, stronger. She looked wonderful, and the men on the crew propositioned her, but she said no. Each day, she attended work in a casual, chic outfit, fitted to her body, and experimented with make-up the way Dina instructed her to.

Within a month, she had a boyfriend: a doctor. He was from Texas, working paediatric oncology at Mount Sinai.

'How did you meet?'

'At the theatre. I go for my English. He had the next seat. His friend is not coming; she gets called into hospital. I was wearing the red dress,' Natalya said, happily. 'He asked me out the next day. And so I like him, very much.'

'That's great.'

'It's you, Dina. It's this.' She gestured at herself. 'Maybe I'm not so beautiful, like you, but I feel beautiful – for me. It gives me confidence to know I can look this way.'

Dina grinned. 'Great. That's exactly what we're going for.'

'Confidence makes me happy. And he tells me all the time I am beautiful, but not just this, also brave and clever. He loves my story.' She giggled, and it was strange to hear that light laughter from Natalya. 'He even likes the accent. Isn't that crazy?'

'Not crazy. I'm glad for you.'

'I can't know if we are to get married yet.' She smiled. 'But I like being with him, getting to understand him.'

Dina hugged her. 'Oh, seriously, that's perfect, Natalya. Take it slow. I'm thrilled for you.'

But there was an ache under the words, because Dina didn't have anyone, couldn't have anyone. The mad work of setting this company up was slowing, her days were slowing, and now, when she wanted it least, Dina was thinking about Joel Gaines once again.

There would not be anyone else. And when Natalya talked about her doctor, Jesse, it sent the old longing rushing back through Dina's veins.

She hadn't called him, hadn't been weak. But he hadn't called her, either.

There was nothing, just silence. No emails, no texts. It was as if none of it had happened, or as if it had happened to someone else, long ago. In another life.

She dreaded the days after the launch. When things settled down, and she had time and space to herself, and Dina Kane, Inc. was growing, but more slowly, then how would she stop thinking about Joel? How would she manage to get a grip on herself?

But, for now, she just hugged her new friend.

* * *

Tonight, she was glad to be with Natalya. It had been a very long day. At nine p.m., her deputy forced her to put away her cellphone and stop talking to the beauty bloggers and fashion PRs and editor types who were all due in Times Square at nine a.m. tomorrow; their little space would be full to overflowing. Dina had to parcel out invitations, and that made it better. She now had a b-list of smaller bloggers and magazines, due in an hour later, at ten.

'Starting small is unfortunate. But you made it into a virtue,' Natalya said.

Her English was almost perfect now. The two girls chinked glasses.

'I think it'll go well.' Dina shrugged. 'Scrub that. I know it will.'

'Your cash on hand is very low. Your apartment is the security?'

'I'm not worried,' Dina replied. She took a long, cool drink of the champagne, playing with it, letting the bubbles crackle around her mouth. 'Dina Kane, Inc. is going to work. We will double our financing within the month.'

Natalya shook her blond head, admiringly. She was wearing a chic little brown dress and comfortable ballet flats in burnt orange: perfect for the coming days of fall, for New York's warm September. Style was something she was learning, along with her English; she felt accomplished, beautiful – reborn, almost. Dina believed in her, and she was starting to believe in herself again.

Every day, she thanked God for her cousin Piotr, who had brought her to this woman.

'How can you have such certainty?'

'The products are good. The design is good.' Dina drank a little more. 'I'm good. We've worked the insider beauty press relentlessly. It's a story because of Ludo and Torch, and the products and the store back it up.'

371

'They ran a server test on the website. Do you really think you're going to get all those hits?'

Dina nodded. 'We have to be ready. If we crash on day one, it will be a disaster.' She thought for a second of Edward Johnson. 'And there could be a cyber attack, who knows?'

'You've spent so much on that website.'

'It matters more than the stores. That's beauty now, Natalya – global. Somebody could log in in Auckland and get our stuff. We will ship it to Reykjavik. Every girl has a dream; we want to inspire them. Even those who can't afford it: we want them on that site, playing our videos –' her eyes lit up – 'learning how beauty works, the canvas of the face.'

'But if they can't afford it—'

'Maybe one day they will grow up and be able to. Or suddenly get a better job. We want them to sink into beauty with Dina Kane.' She drank a little more, feeling a sudden rush of pleasure, of triumph. Her dream was here – and she had made it, against all odds, against everything. The launch, the money – it seemed like an afterthought. This was her dream for other women, and it was coming true.

'I understand.'

'Beauty was my escape. I want it to be their escape, too.'

Natalya drained her glass. 'You will be very successful with it, Dina. And I can't wait to work with you.' She glanced at her watch. 'I should go; Jesse's shift is ending. I'd like to be back for him.'

'Of course.' The girls hugged. 'See you tomorrow,' Dina said. 'Be there at eight?'

'Seven thirty,' Natalya promised her.

She knew she should probably get up and leave, too. But Dina didn't want to move, not just yet. She was tired, happy, enjoying her champagne.

'Have a great night.' She kissed Natalya goodbye, and tipped the glass to her mouth, savouring it. And then she took out her phone. Maybe there were some bloggers she could call, some last minute work she could do . . . just while she finished one more flute of the ice-cold, glittering froth of a wine.

There were no messages on her phone. But there was a text.

From Joel Gaines.

Where are you? We need to talk.

Dina breathed in, hard. Her hand gripped the side of the bar; her head swayed. Carefully, she steadied herself so the others around her – the couples, the businessmen standing around in knots, socialising – wouldn't see it.

She paused, then tapped out a reply.

I can't bear it, Joel. Please. It's a big day for me tomorrow.

His reply came through almost immediately.

Ten minutes, that's all. Where are you?

Dina took her glass and swallowed a large gulp of the champagne, tossing it quickly down her throat, letting it burn.

She shivered. What if she said no? She would be off her game, thinking about him, obsessing, on one of the most important days of her life. If Joel was here, she had to deal with him. Talk to him now. Get it out of the way.

Tomorrow she needed to concentrate.

He could come to her. She was on Central Park South, right in the heart of Manhattan. Not her apartment, where her bedroom was. Where she might do something stupid.

I just said goodnight to my friend. I was leaving, but I'm in the bar of the Victrix. Call me, or I can wait for you for fifteen minutes.

There was a pause. Dina held her breath, wishing it didn't matter so much. But it did. She was in suspended animation, staring at the screen.

My garage is a block away. I'll be with you in five minutes, Dina. Don't leave.

She texted back OK and sat there, sipping slowly. Time passed like treacle. She could not think, could not concentrate, could not act her age. When Joel appeared, would she have any dignity?

Frenzied work had distracted her, but they were close now, almost at the end. She had nothing to hide behind. And her feelings for Joel were beating at her resistance, relentless as the tides.

She was past dignity, maybe. One text from him and her body was on fire. Joel Gaines had only kissed her once. If he wanted more tonight, Dina had no idea how the hell she was going to turn him down.

And then, there he was, walking in through the door from the lobby, paying no attention to the wait staff talking to him. He was moving fast, the hugeness of that body, the spread of his chest, the power of it, striding towards her in his suit, like nothing could stop him; purposeful, intent.

Dina was immediately wet and aroused, absolutely responsive to him. Her body crackled with adrenaline, as though she'd been shocked.

'Joel,' she whispered.

She could hardly speak. Joel was right in front of her. His body was close to hers, in her space again. Towering over her. Looking down on her. She trembled; she couldn't say a word.

'Dina –' he grabbed her hand, fiercely – 'I love you. I've loved you for a year, maybe more. I want you. I cannot stop thinking about you. You're stronger than everything. I have to be with you. That's it. I have to be.'

Tears sprang to her eyes. 'But you're married.'

'I asked Susan for a divorce. It's done. I left the house. I told the boys. They're grown, and I want to be with you.' He clutched her hands. 'As soon as the papers come through, we can get married. Yes? Tell me yes.'

The tears brimmed over, running down her cheeks. She swayed where she sat, and Gaines put out an arm to support her. 'Yes,' she whispered. 'Yes. Why?'

'Because I couldn't take the rest of my life thinking about you, and not seeing you. Wanting you, and not having you. Because

I never met a woman like you. Because you are the girl I should have married first. I don't want a roommate; I want a lover, a friend, a challenge. I want you, and none other. You understand?'

She nodded. 'Yes.' Her face was in her hands, sobbing.

'Let's go home.'

'I have to get the check . . .'

Joel gestured to the barman. 'Put this on my account.'

'Yes, sir, Mr Gaines.'

The small display of power thrilled Dina. She couldn't help herself. Her body shuddered at his touch as he slipped her off the stool. The rest of her champagne lay on the counter, but she already felt drunk, almost high.

'Where shall we go?' she asked, as they stood at the coat check, and Gaines slipped his hands around her waist, her shoulders, touching her everywhere as he put the garment on her. 'Your place or mine?'

'Yours,' Gaines replied, immediately.

His apartment would need to be cleaned out, all of Susan's things returned: the framed photos of them together, the detritus of a failed marriage. Dina's neat, ambitious little place was perfect; she had won it on her own, succeeded on her own. It was small, beautiful, an up-and-comer's apartment. Everything he'd wanted to be, once, a long while ago. Everything he admired in her.

'Fine.' She kissed him, melted into him.

He felt himself stiffen, harden. He had to get her into a taxi. 'Dina. Not here. Let's go.'

Edward knew he was drunk. But that was fine, because he had cut it with cocaine – lots of cocaine. It made you see things clearer. He felt big now, confident; he could do exactly as he liked. And mostly what he wanted was to deal with Dina Kane.

Once. For all. Forever.

He'd sent Lena home, and the night housekeeper. And then he'd looked, and read, and drank, and pulled it all close into him. Dina Kane, Inc., the new wave, the next big thing, was launching tomorrow. Times Square. Tickets like gold dust.

Once he got good and drunk, it seemed he had to cut it. That was what the coke was for. It had been a while, but Edward still kept his stash. And, tonight, he needed to use it.

The bad feelings left him; he woke up, became powerful and strong again. Dina Kane, a ten-minute diversion, had derailed his whole life. He saw that clearly now. And, even as he was getting back on track, the bitch was returning from the grave to fucking haunt him.

It was time to be done. To get it over with.

He barely registered what he was doing as he walked upstairs to the bathroom cabinet and took out the Klonopin and the plastic gloves – little cheap plastic gloves, the kind that came with a packet of hair dye. He found a small bottle of whiskey and a long, sharp knife. He had a gun, too, but that was messy, that led to all kinds of annoying things, like splatter patterns on the wall; the FBI worked things out that way. Edward was smarter than them; he had seen the TV shows, all the cop series. He was no fool.

He'd killed Philippe, and Johnny Kane – or helped them on their way, at least. Both the assholes had got drunk themselves, taken pills themselves. So Philippe didn't know what he was doing, but Johnny did – fool; weak little fool.

Both of them, far too trusting. He knew that Dina Kane wouldn't be making that mistake. He'd have to be careful with her.

There was a key – that was the thing. Olivia had provided him with a copy – no questions asked. He could let himself into her new apartment, wait for her, jump her. One hand over the mouth, force the pills down her throat, pour the alcohol in after it. Maybe he'd leave her in the bath, knife in her own hand – her prints on it. She would slit her own wrists. He giggled; that was a neat trick to do when unconscious, but Edward would be happy to lend a little assistance before she was fully passed out. Olivia told him the apartment building had a security guard and cameras in the lobby, but they were turned off at night; they were just for show.

Why hadn't he done it before? It seemed crazy now. Stupid fears about getting caught. He wouldn't *be* caught. When Edward Johnson took care of them, they stayed down. No questions after Johnny, none after Philippe. Why would some bitch from Westchester be any different?

He snorted more coke, got a cap and muffler and a large coat, and walked out in to the night. It was only twelve blocks to Dina's apartment. He entered the front door purposefully, grunting at the guard and walking straight ahead. The man was reading a magazine, not paying attention. There were corridors and an elevator bank. She was on floor sixteen and, with the drug pumping through his veins, Edward Johnson rode up to the right floor.

Adrenaline mixed with the coke. What if she was there? In? And by the door? She was a hermit, that bitch, a fucking hermit; she hated men; never saw anybody. She was probably there, working, waiting . . . He'd have to move fast, jump on her. That was OK. That was fine. Edward didn't want to think it through. He took out his key, opened the door, entered the apartment and shut it behind him.

He listened. He didn't call out – didn't want the neighbours to hear anything.

It was silent. Silent as the grave; silent as her grave. He giggled. Funny. There was nobody here.

Just to make sure, he walked through the place, checked it out. Empty.

There was a large wardrobe in the bedroom. That's where he would go. He had more coke, of course; it was with him in a silver vial. And he could afford to swallow a little of the whiskey.

He had a celebratory swig and a snort. Then he opened the wardrobe door, climbed inside, and sat down comfortably on its base. Using his phone for a light, he put on the gloves, opened the pillbox and laid the knife next to it.

Everything was ready.

Dina felt like her hands didn't work. She couldn't find her keys; she was opening the bag, fumbling, kissing. Joel's hands were on her, possessively, running up her legs, her thighs, under her skirt, cupping her ass. She was wet, helplessly aroused.

'God – help me. I can't . . . I can't . . .'

He took one hand away from stroking her through the thin, damp cotton of her panties, found her key, unlocked the door and shoved her through it.

It closed, heavy, behind them.

'My bedroom's this way,' Dina said.

He was already lifting her shirt over her head, popping the bra undone with practised ease, feeling her full breasts that tumbled out into his hands, her nipples painfully erect. She was so hot for him, he could feel the blood rushing into her belly, her womb literally heating under his hands.

'Fuck the bedroom.' Gaines thrust her on to the floor, ripping the clothes from her, tearing the skirt down, the panties off. 'You aren't getting that far.'

Dina moaned. He tore off his clothes, too, impatiently, buttons ripping, his tie yanked from his neck. He kicked his shoes off, kissing at her neck, her face, raking his teeth and lips across her throat. She split her legs, wide, willing, desperate to feel him inside her. There was nothing but desire now, pure lust – not love, not friendship – just his power, his might, the strength of his body moving over her.

'Joel!' she gasped. 'Oh, God! Please. Please.'

Inside the wardrobe, Edward Johnson thought fast.

There were two people in this apartment. And one of them was a man. They were fucking, so they were naked.

He had a knife.

But the man seemed sober. And, underneath the glittering bravado of the coke and booze, Edward was a coward.

His body was skinny, even lanky. Any halfway decent guy could take him. That was the problem. And the voice outside sounded familiar.

Joel Gaines.

Fucking shit scared, Edward started to shudder. Gaines, the goddamned *billionaire*. Gaines, who was built like an army tank, who pumped weights like a Marine drill sergeant on a good day.

He ran through scenarios in his mind. Lurching out, drunk, high, with his little knife. It had seemed big when he was planning on slashing Dina's wrists while she was passed out in the bath. Now it was a fucking penknife. He would stab at Gaines, maybe hurt him. Then the big man would grab his wrist, break his arm. That was the thing with women: they were so soft, so weak. All those TV shows with karate-kicking female detectives – Edward laughed at them. Even a puny man could grab a woman, subdue her, wrestle her to the ground. It was muscle mass; it was power.

But against Gaines? No. Gaines would fight, and Dina would scream, and get to a phone.

He was trapped. He had to do something. If he left the wardrobe, they would hear him, probably. They were distracted, but they would notice someone trying to get out the door. There was a fire escape, if he could open the windows . . .

Terrified, Edward peeled off the thin plastic gloves and stuffed them in his underpants. The ludicrous smallness of this hit him. He wept with self-pity in the closet. The clonazepam was in its bottle. Maybe he could get to a window, drop that outside . . . For now, he hid it in an inner jacket pocket. The whiskey . . . It wasn't a crime to have whiskey. The knife . . . Jesus, the knife.

He grabbed a cardigan and used it to scrub the knife clean, then, holding it in the fabric, he opened the door as slowly as he could and tossed it under the wardrobe, all the way to the back of the wall.

It was no good. If he stayed here, she'd find him in the morning. He had to get out. He needed to get out . . .

She felt him against her – hard, urgent, forcing her legs apart still wider. Dina groaned with pleasure; she felt dizzy, almost unable to hold herself back. She was gasping every time he touched her, no matter how light, how soft . . .

Gaines pulled back. Dina felt the air on her skin, the rush of it where his body had been.

'What?' she whimpered, and not with desire. 'What is it?'

He sprang back from her, naked, crouching. His body was incredible – strong, knotted with muscles. Even in her dismay, Dina was stunned by it.

'Cover yourself. Get a phone. There's someone here. In the apartment.'

At that moment, there came a cry from the bedroom – a weak, mewling cry, sobbing, pathetic.

Dina gasped in horror and grabbed her dress, tugging it over her head.

'Who's in there?' Gaines barked. He lifted his trousers with one hand and slipped them on. 'Answer me or we call the police. And I'm coming to get you. I have a gun.'

Dina looked wildly at him but he shook his head.

'Don't shoot!' It was a shriek. 'Don't shoot, please! It's me – Edward Johnson. I'm unarmed. Don't kill me!'

'Don't you fucking move,' Gaines said.

He gestured, and Dina, hot, flushed, scrambled to pull on underwear, cover herself properly. Then she moved towards the bedroom door, but Gaines was ahead of her, his body covering hers, protecting her.

He lifted one leg and kicked the door open. A perfect, strong extension. The wood splintered and shattered in the middle.

Edward Johnson was sitting there on the bed, hunched, sobbing, tears and mucus streaming down his face. He was swaying, and there was a stench of alcohol, and powder was scattered around him.

'How the fuck did you get in here?' Gaines demanded. 'Get down on the fucking floor. Spread your legs and arms. *Now.*'

Meekly, Johnson obeyed. He looked so weak, flopping to his knees, then his belly, prostrating himself before Gaines and Dina.

Joel ran his hands quickly and efficiently across his body, pulling out the vial of meds. 'Clonazepam. You stink of booze. Where is it?'

Johnson said nothing. Joel kicked him, hard, between the legs. There was a whooshing sound as he sucked in his breath and then a high-pitched gasp of agony.

'Jesus! Jesus ...'

'He wants nothing to do with you. Where is it?'

'In the closet . . . I have nothing . . .'

Gaines placed one foot on Johnson's neck. Dina was staring, stunned, but he ignored her. He took inventory of the wardrobe; there was a bottle of whiskey, opened, a little drunk. Johnson had been on it for hours before this bottle, clearly. There was powder on his lip.

'What else did you bring?'

'What? What do you mean? Don't hurt me! I came here to confront Dina!'

'You came here to kill Dina,' Gaines said. His foot moved down on Johnson's neck. 'Like you killed her brother. What else, fucker?'

'Nothing else . . . I swear!'

'If I ask the question again, you're dead. You think anybody is going to give a shit that I defended a woman from a home invasion?' Gaines pressed harder, half-choking Johnson. 'Confession time, Edward. Right now.'

'Ugh – knife . . .'

Dina was shaking with fear and shock.

'Where's the goddamned knife, Edward?'

'Under the closet.'

Gaines looked at Dina. 'Check it, sweetheart. I don't want to move off him.'

Dina dropped to the floor. Gaines pressed harder. 'Close your eyes. Don't even look at her.'

'There it is. Oh my God, Joel.' She reached underneath and pulled it out, showing it to him.

He lifted Johnson up by the back of his neck and threw him on the bed.

'You are a pathetic, worthless junkie.' He reached out and grabbed Edward's hair, tilting his head backwards. 'Look at that: coke on your lip. You killed Johnny Kane with it, and now you've started killing yourself. Tell me how you got in here.'

'I had a key,' Edward said, weeping with fear. 'Somebody made it – someone in the underworld. I don't have their contact anymore. If I look too hard for them, they'll pop me.'

Dina moaned. He had a key. If she hadn't been with Joel, she'd have been dead.

'It's you,' he said, suddenly, wiping his eyes and hissing at her. 'You bitch – it's all you! The way I am. You split my family. You made my mother sick. My father – you might as well have killed him.'

'Bullshit, Edward!' Gaines said. 'You don't give a fuck about anybody except yourself. When did you last call your father?'

'I . . . We don't speak.'

'And your mother? You're not the only one that can do research. You packed her off to Florida and all of a sudden she signs the family trust over to you, am I right? You own the townhouse now?'

'How do you—?'

'I know. I watched you. I watched Dina.'

'She blackmailed my father; she's a whore. You know that? She's a goddamned whore. Fucked me for my money—'

Gaines punched him in the face. Dina squealed, and Edward spat out teeth, blood, and crumpled on the bed.

'She's more than you'll ever be.'

'Joel . . . Joel, he's nothing. He's over.' Dina clutched on to him. 'I'm sorry for what I did to your parents, Edward. I was so angry.'

'Say it to them, if you want. He doesn't care about either of them. He's a fucking psychopath.'

Dina moaned. 'I don't care. Let him go; let him go.'

Joel held her hands. 'If you do that, what woman does he kill next? This one is dangerous, Dina. Your brother? You? God knows who else! He broke into this apartment. We need to call the police.'

She gripped him. 'I can't think. My – my company launches tomorrow.'

'Let's hope they serve good coffee,' Gaines said. 'We're going to be up late tonight.'

Edward sat there, rocking on the bed, twisting his fingers. 'You can't do that – call the police – I'll tell them you hit me. I'll tell everybody what you did to my father. You're a whore, Dina Kane; I still have the pictures. Try running your precious business when that comes out.'

Dina held on to Joel and looked at Edward, the malicious, seething wreck of him, and then looked at the knife, shining, sharp, free of blood.

'Joel's right. Do your worst. We don't care. We need you off the streets – before you hurt anyone else.'

She held up her phone. 'Nine-one-one? Yes, I need the police. I'm in my apartment with a man who just tried to kill me. And I'm pretty sure he killed my brother, too.'

* * *

It was past midnight when they finally got back home – his place – Dina couldn't face her own. She walked past the pictures, and Gaines apologised, but she held up one hand.

'Stop. I don't care. That was the past.'

He took her face in his hands and kissed her, again and again, and she felt the warmth returning, like he was blowing on embers, fanning them back into flame. The heat that she thought was gone came back to her; she pressed herself against him.

'No.' Joel bent down and kissed her on the mouth. 'He's been arrested. He tried to kill you. It's not the time, baby.'

She moaned. 'Joel – I've waited so long.'

'We both have. But tomorrow you launch your business. You need to sleep, wake up and do that. I'll still be here. The first time we make love has to be when you're calm, rested, when you've thought it through. Not right after somebody tries to murder you.'

Dina laughed. 'Sweet talker.'

'If you want me when you wake up, I won't put up a fight.'

She kissed him back. The exhaustion, the nervousness was coming back to her. 'OK, OK. But I want to sleep next to you.'

'Deal.' Gaines bent down and scooped her up in his arms and carried her into the bedroom; she nestled against him, and he felt her slump. After he'd laid her down on the bed, within minutes, she was asleep, like a child after a long journey.

He watched her sleeping face for a few seconds, then placed a throw across her body and lay down next to her, closing his eyes, comforted by the quiet sounds of her breathing.

The early morning light was streaming into the room, the red sun of dawn. Dina woke, glanced around, realised where she was – who she was with.

And what was going to happen today. Everything. All of it.

Joel first.

She slipped the throw off her, careful not to wake him, and stripped nude. Then she padded into his wet room and turned on the shower, cleaning herself. She wasted no time; within a minute, she was rough-dried, back in his bed, slipping under the covers this time, pressing herself against him.

His eyes flicked open.

'That's a hell of a wake-up call.'

'I love you,' Dina said. 'I still want you.'

Gaines ran his hands firmly over her whole body. Feeling her calves, her breasts. Cupping her ass.

'Ohhh . . .'

He pulled the covers back; she was there, under him, naked. This was the first time he had ever seen her body clearly. Goddamn, but she was beautiful.

He knelt across her, stripping his own clothes off, piece by piece. And, as he slid his fingers from her breasts to her knees, Dina gasped with longing.

'Patience is a virtue,' he said, and teased her lightly with one finger, just grazing her, back and forth, as his other hand grasped her hands, holding them over her head. She was wet, so wet, and her belly was literally hot, warm with blood under him. She bucked and lifted herself to him. She was beside herself with longing, and he wanted to laugh with the triumph and love of it.

'Oh my God!' Dina gasped. 'Oh Joel! Please . . .'

And his knee nudged her legs apart, and he took her, swiftly, hard, his mouth on hers, kissing her, bearing down on her, and her body dissolved in a wave of bliss, so intense and wonderful that it blew everything away.

Chapter Twenty

A buzz rippled through the crowd.

Dina Kane certainly knew how to make an entrance.

There was a portion of the street roped off with ribbon – a precious thirty-minute easement granted by the city, delighted to have another strip club removed from Times Square. And the space was completely full.

The Dina Kane, Inc. blog had been up for a week – promising samples, makeovers and all kinds of goodies to the first hundred customers. She had more than two hundred women milling around the avenue now, annoying commuters, spilling on to the street.

Among the crowd were tens of New York beauty bloggers – and not just the big ones, the giants from Makeup Alley and the rest. Dina had sent personal invites to all her favourites, the underground anarchist beauty sites, the one that focused solely on the over-sixty-fives, the gay beauty blog, the Urdu-only site for Asian skin . . . She had spent those months as a shopper delving deep into the bones of Manhattan's beauty addicts, and the result was a heady mix of eclecticism, ethnic beauty, impoverished students and Social Registry housewives from the East Side.

Every few minutes, her staff – the best make-up artists she'd poached from Torch, the sales consultants Natalya had signed off on – emerged from the gleaming entrance to the Dina Kane store, handing out free goodies: a lip balm from Scotland, a new mascara from California, fragrance samples from a tiny house in Austria. The journalists from the women's magazines, roped off separately, watched and scribbled. There was a palpable sense of excitement.

And it wasn't just them. Three camera crews were pointed at her tiny storefront: all local TV, but clearly Dina Kane was getting a name for herself, was worth watching. An ageing reporter in Versace, a doyenne of the gossip columns, hung around too, gawping at the commotion for a single shop, unable to report on the embarrassment he had predicted for Ludo Morgan's ex-girlfriend.

They were expecting a limousine, a big black monster, or a Lincoln Town Car at the very least.

But suddenly there was a light ringing of a bell – a bicycle bell – and Dina Kane had arrived. The custom-painted green and gold bike contrasted with her stunning outfit; she wore some beige leggings, rammed into chestnut high-heeled boots, a fitted cream silk shirt and a simple gold bracelet. As the flashbulbs popped and snapped, Dina Kane took off her helmet – letting her dark hair fall loosely down her back.

The photographers purred. The women breathed out. She was beautiful. She was stunning. Her young face was made up, lightly, nothing too heavy: a sheer mousse foundation, golden eye shadow, bronzer on her cheekbones, clear lip gloss and a separating mascara that made her eyes pop. Her teeth were white as she smiled, and she looked healthy, attractive, young and confident.

'Dina! Where's the limo?' a journalist shouted.

There was a mike stand set up on the pavement in front of her, and Dina Kane approached it, laughing, her helmet under one arm.

'No car. This is New York! We bike. We love fitness – it's the best blusher you can't buy.'

All the women laughed. The flashbulbs popped once more.

'Ladies and gentlemen, if you'll just look over there – Dina Kane, Inc. has come to Times Square.'

She pointed and, above them, to the right, a huge rectangle thirty storeys high suddenly blazed into light.

DINA KANE, it said. *BEAUTY.*

The company logo and website address flashed up, and then a smooth morph of a slender forty-five-year-old's face, with make-up being applied, becoming groomed, beautiful. It was replaced by a plus-sized teenager, an African-American mom cradling a baby, and a blonde twenty-six-year-old – all with the Dina Kane message scrolling behind them.

There were *oohs* and *aahs*, and when Dina was satisfied they had gazed, transfixed, long enough, she spoke into the mike again.

'And now, I'm so happy to say that Dina Kane, Inc. is open for business. All women are beautiful – we hope to help show that to the world. Thank you – and enjoy yourselves.'

She lifted a hand, and the glass doors slid open; the wall at the top of the stairs played makeovers, and women stumbled in from the street, rushing down into the gorgeously appointed space.

Dina handed her bike to an assistant.

'Ms Kane, they're ready for you,' Natalya said, walking up to her.

She was beaming with pride. The store looked incredible, the crowd was wonderful, and the neon billboard at the heart of Times Square – a third of the budget, just on that, and they could only have it for a week – meant it was major league. 'The press want to talk to you – about Ludo Morgan, you understand, as well as the store and the site. They want to discuss Torch and Joel Gaines. And there was some arrest this morning . . . ?'

Dina turned around and smiled at the little knot of journalists, looking directly into the TV cameras.

'Of course,' she said. 'And I'll happily make a statement. For now, though, we have Dina Kane customers waiting. Excuse me, OK? I need to go and serve them.'

And she disappeared down the wide stairs into the brightly lit underground oasis of beauty that was to be Dina Kane's new home, shaking hands, calling out greetings.

Natalya looked down after her boss and saw the women mob her as she walked into the store, applauding, pressing round her with compliments, already holding up face creams, asking questions. Behind her, the press pack was following; they were pursuing her down those stairs like she was a celebrity already.

She felt a frisson of excitement. It was only a store, but it was a damned good one. Casually she flicked open her cellphone and pressed the icon for the Dina Kane, Inc. app – it took her directly to the online store, which opened for business the moment the retail one did.

Already, she could see a few golden *sold out* banners.

Something was starting, right now. The result of one girl betting on herself, completely. And Natalya had a feeling it was going to be big – very big.

She breathed in deeply, and followed her boss down into the store.

Epilogue

The launch was a complete success.

Within forty minutes, shoppers had cleared the stock from the showroom, and within an hour they'd taken all their reserves. Natalya had runners out to their suppliers for more; and the press had to wait, and watch Dina Kane do business.

It was quite something. They reported the success, live, like financial reporters counting down to the closing bell.

And Dina did not disappoint. As soon as she'd shaken hands with the last customer, she walked up the stairs and back out to Times Square, where the cameras had been set up for filming.

Joel Gaines came down from his office. He watched discreetly from across the square. There was a scrum of media there now, and Dina faced the cameras head on.

'Good morning,' she said. 'Thank you all for coming to cover the opening of our store. I'm sorry I couldn't get to your questions earlier, but, as you can see, we've been a little busy.' There was a ripple of laughter from the hacks; Gaines shook his head, admiringly. She had them eating out of the palm of her hand. 'Let me pre-empt some of your questions. I'll try to be as frank as possible.' Now they were rolling their eyes; nobody did frank, not in Manhattan, not where money was at stake. But Dina Kane stood tall and unafraid, and she kept talking. The effect was mesmerising.

'Edward Johnson has been arrested for trying to kill me,' she said. 'There's going to be a trial, and I can't prejudice it.'

'Is it true you slept with his father?'

'Yes, it is true.'

There was a gasp of surprise from the press pack. She *admitted* it?

'I did so for revenge. Although it was years ago, I still regret that very much. I would like to apologise to Mr Johnson, and his wife, and his family.'

'Revenge for what? What did he do to you?'

'So you slept with father and son?'

'Look this way, Dina! Over here!'

'What else can you tell us?'

'Absolutely nothing whatsoever.' She smiled brightly. 'The legal process will take its course. I'm sorry I can't go any further.'

There was a clicking of bulbs and a whirring as cameras were trained towards her, boom mikes shoved in her direction.

'Why were you fired from Torch, Dina?'

'You'll have to ask Ludo Morgan that.'

'The company says there's a non-compete clause in your contract – that you can't work for anyone else. They're going to sue Dina Kane, Inc.'

'How typically male,' Dina said.

That provoked shocked laughter from the women there – journalists and style editors.

'Let them try. The suit will be baseless. I'm not working for Dina Kane. I own Dina Kane.' She flashed another strong, brilliant smile. 'By all means, let Torch try to compete.'

'But Ludo Morgan has so much power in retail! Torch have all the financial muscle!'

Dina lifted her head and looked around. Gaines stiffened; she had seen him, standing back there, gazing out at her. She winked at him, and his heart turned over with pleasure and love. To be at the start of this journey with her . . . And their journey – their journey together . . .

'They do have a lot of muscle.' Dina gestured towards the bright doors of Dina Kane, the electronic makeovers dancing, a little crowd outside as fresh boxes of stock were being carted hurriedly down the stairs. 'But I've never worried too much about brawn. I'm going to put my faith in beauty.'

And she raised one manicured hand to the press pack, and walked across Times Square, towards her first store, and her new life.

Acknowledgements

No book is a solo project, and I have been fortunate to be edited by Imogen Taylor and to have the endlessly patient Michael Sissons as my agent. Fiona Petheram, Robert Caskie and Isabel Evans have all shepherded me at PFD; I also want to thank Jateen Patel. At Headline, Emily Furniss in publicity and Emma Holtz have been working on the team and I am grateful to everybody who put *Beauty* together in record time with an amazing cover.

And finally, thanks to you for reading it – ultimately all stories are a collaboration between the writer and the reader. Dina's adventures happen in your head, and that's the true beauty of this novel.